Chuckerman Makes a Movie

Chuckerman Makes a Movie

A Novel

FRANCIE ARENSON DICKMAN

SHE WRITES PRESS

Published October 9, 2018
Printed in the United States of America
Print ISBN: 978-1-63152-485-1
E-ISBN: 978-1-63152-486-8
Library of Congress Control Number: 2018935991

For information, address:
She Writes Press
1563 Solano Ave #546
Berkeley, CA 94707

Interior design by Tabitha Lahr

She Writes Press is a division of SparkPoint Studio, LLC.

This is a work of fiction. Names, characters, places, and incidents either are the product of the author's imagination or are used fictitiously. Any resemblance to actual persons, living or dead, is entirely coincidental.

FOR MY FAMILY, and in loving memory of
my grandparents, and everyone else's,
who are watching down on us
from card tables in heaven.

CHAPTER 1:

The Ride to the Bottom

ᴡ

My official arrival at rock bottom occurred on May 7, 2002, the day of the annual Slip Melman Birthday Ride—something I invented five years earlier to honor my grandfather. On Slip's seventieth birthday, back in 1977, my father gave him a cutting-edge, fourth-generation, two-door, yellow Cadillac Coup de Ville. The yellow Caddy was the crème de la crème of cars, and Slip drove it until he could no longer drive.

The surrender of his license occurred around 1992, the same year I dropped out of medical school. I was floundering, so he loaned the car to me. When he died a few years later, he left it to me, along with a pile of illegally acquired cash. I've been driving it since then. And every year, on Slip's birthday, my niece, my nephew, and I bring a cake to the car, and I retell the Story of the Cadillac so we never forget who we are and from where we came. It's our tradition. Our personal Passover. But traditions, I suppose, are made to be broken, and it seemed my sister Marcy was looking to bring ours to an end.

The threats began as soon as I pulled up in front of her bakery last Sunday to collect Estie and Ryan. As usual, the bakery was bustling. On Sunday mornings, folks—mostly women from the various and sundry walks of Marcy's life—fill the bakery because Marcy offers the "Melman Special," a discount on the donuts of the day. After 9/11, Marcy said it was our duty to build community. "And if I can do it with discounted pastry, I will," she declared to anyone who would listen.

Apparently it was working, since when I honked that morning, the kids came running from a store teeming with women. Marcy, with apron on and hairnet in place, followed with the birthday cake. After handing me the cake, she told me, as always, to be careful and to not buy them any more presents.

Then the derailing began. Marcy turned her skinny neck toward the backseat and winked—a disturbing, mouth-opening, eye-scrunching gesture. The kids gave maniacal winks back at her. A cop could have positively identified them as her children on the winks alone.

"Subtle," I said.

"Enjoy the cake," Marcy answered. Then she slammed the door and ran back to the bakery.

"What was that all about?" I asked, looking into the rearview mirror.

"What?" Estie said. She glared at Ryan.

Ryan shrugged.

"I'm not going anywhere 'til someone spills it. I saw the winking. I wasn't born yesterday."

They both stared straight ahead, trying not to laugh.

I threw the car into park and pulled out my wallet. I waved a dollar in the air. Everyone in the Melman family except Marcy is genetically programmed to respond to money.

Ryan and Estie looked at each other and then at me.

"We're good," Estie said.

I pulled out a five. They again looked at each other.

"Each?" Ryan asked.

"Whatever it takes," I told him.

"Done," he said.

Two fives floated into the backseat, and the news flowed forward that I was too old for the Ride.

"We don't think you're too old," Ryan clarified. "Mom does."

"Why am I too old?" I shouldn't have asked. I didn't want an answer.

"You're thirty-five," Estie said as she folded her five-spot and tucked it into the light blue purse she started carrying this year.

"So what?" I answered.

"If you don't wake up and smell the coffee, you're going to die alone," Ryan explained.

"There you go again, listening to your mother. You know, you're not supposed to listen to her. We are all young enough for the Ride. Ten is young. Thirteen is young. Thirty-five is young."

"Thirty-five's not that young," Ryan said.

"It's kind of young," Estie qualified. "It's probably young enough for the Ride, but not young enough to be dating your clients. Share's only seven years older than me, and you still babysit for me."

She had a point. I'd never really thought about age. I generally don't dwell on an issue long enough to experience an emotional reaction to it. I do feel fear; fear is my friend. Though fear is an instinct more than an emotion. Nonetheless, I must admit, I felt afraid of Ryan's smelling-the-coffee comment. Not afraid that I was going to fail to smell the coffee and die alone, but that my niece and nephew were buying my sister's dubious opinion of me. Or, worse, that they'd formed dubious opinions of their uncle on their own. Was Uncle Davy, marketing and fragrance genius, cool and rich brander extraordinaire, somehow letting them down? This, I did not want to do. I was, after all, the family historian—the keeper of the Cadillac.

Ryan came to my defense. "It doesn't matter how old Share is, because Mom says Share isn't even a real person anyways. She's manufactured by you. She says Emily Kaplinsky would have been perfect for you, but you wouldn't have given her the time of day."

"When did she say this?" I asked, turning around to face them. Ryan was now on the floor, his five dollars plastered in embarrassment over his eyes, but Estie scooted toward me and, with her hands on the back of my seat and her chin resting on her hands, began to talk.

Before I showed up at the bakery, she explained, Marcy's friends had asked where she and Ryan were headed at ten o'clock on a Sunday morning with a car-shaped cake. Ryan said they were going to celebrate their great-grandfather's birthday in their uncle's Cadillac, which was really their great-grandfather's but now belonged to their uncle. When Ryan explained that we do this every year, my sister raised her brows and said to the women, "Don't ask." Then she added, "He's stuck in the seventies."

Estie claimed she came to my defense with, "No he's not. He's dating Share. How can he be stuck in the seventies if he's dating a pop star?"

Marcy, according to Estie, came back with, "She's not a pop star. You can't be a star if you only have one song. And he's not dating her anymore, thank God. Talk about hitting rock bottom."

Apparently, the remark about smelling the coffee also came out in this general time frame.

"But don't worry," Estie reassured me now, "no one was listening. Most of them were still asking questions about Share, like if Mom's ever met her and if she's ever going to release another song."

Ryan crawled back onto his seat to join the recounting. "But Laurel was listening, and she told Mom you should take her class."

"Who is Laurel?" I opened the cake box and swiped a bit of the frosting. Yellow, to match the car.

"You know, Mom's friend Laurel from yoga?" Ryan asked.

I shook my head no. He rolled down the window of the car and pointed to someone through the window of the bakery. "She's right there. You can see her legs. She's wearing cowboy boots."

"Who wears cowboy boots with shorts?" I asked.

"Laurel," Estie answered. She, too, was now licking yellow frosting from her finger.

"Dad calls her The Mormon Rodeo," Ryan said.

"She's some sort of movie writer, and she teaches a movie writing class," Estie chimed in, "and when Mom said she had no idea how to make you get a grip on reality, Laurel said that you should take her class."

I told my niece and nephew that their uncle has a perfectly fine grip on reality.

"You might want to take the class anyway," Ryan said. "Laurel said it's usually full of single girls. And she said she'd let you take it for free, to pay Mom back for all the free food."

"So you are in," Estie said. "Whether you like it or not."

"That's what the wink was about," Ryan said.

"It starts after Memorial Day, and you need to come with an idea for a movie." Estie grinned.

At this point, the car door opened and I found myself presented with Marcy's Knead Some Dough apron.

"Why aren't you going anywhere?" she asked. She looked at our yellow fingers, then reached down and slammed the cake-box closed. Seeing the frosting licked from one of her creations is her pet peeve. Her one and only peeve, she claims, in effort to distinguish herself from me and my other sister, Rachel—we have thousands.

"We're going. Right, David?" Ryan asked. He sounded as panicked as I felt at the notion that the Ride would not go on.

"Yep. Leaving right now. Don't worry, Sis, I'll be back in time for the writing class." I gave her an exaggerated wink.

Marcy poked her head toward the backseat. "What happened to keeping your mouths shut?"

Ryan waved his five-dollar bill in the air. Estie patted her purse.

"I told you not to give them anything."

"You told me not to buy them presents. I just bought myself some interesting information."

Marcy rolled her eyes and rested a knee on the passenger seat. "Don't knock the class until you try it."

I flipped my baseball cap around on my head. "You seriously think I've hit rock bottom?"

She shrugged. "I think you need a life based in reality."

"'Cause I'll be honest," I said, "if I ever thought you'd bottomed out, I'd offer up more than a writing class to save you."

"Let's hope it doesn't ever come to that."

"If it does, will you get us a dog?" Ryan asked.

"Maybe you should get a dog instead of taking a writing class," Estie said.

Marcy backed herself out of the car and said there would be no dogs.

"The Melmans don't do dogs," I said, which was true. We can barely find compassion for each other, let alone for animals.

"Then the writing class it is," Estie said. "What are you going to write about?"

"He's supposed to write about himself," Marcy said. "Laurel says that's the best way of getting to the bottom of things."

"I thought I was already at the bottom of things."

"You know what I mean." She sighed and adjusted her hairnet. The elastic at the bottom of it had imprinted against her forehead, further detracting from her already low credibility. Marcy is not known, at least in the Melman family, for her logical reasoning skills. Nonetheless, she continued to counsel me.

"You obviously have a blockage of some sort—a hang-up or insecurity that is keeping you from becoming a fully realized adult. I don't totally understand it. I'm a baker, not a shrink. But Laurel is deep, and she recommends writing. She says a person should always start with his worst fear. Laurel is—"

"The Mormon Rodeo, I know," I said. "You get a lot of information for five bucks."

"Well, Laurel suggested that you write about your worst fear."

"This is my worst fear. That my sister, in full baking regalia, will, right here on University Place, interrupt the Birthday Ride to tell her kind and supportive brother—the same brother who just bought her a minivan for her birthday—that he is leading an unproductive life. That is my worst fear."

"I never said you were unproductive," Marcy said. "I know you're successful. But who wants to drive a minivan in New York City?"

"The same person who drives this Caddy," Estie said.

"Well then, I would very much like to see the day you buy a minivan for your own family and not for mine," Marcy said.

"We *are* his family," Ryan said, looking up at Marcy. Nothing is better than having a guy on your team. He threw his torso into the front seat and said to me, "And I think your greatest fear should be losing your sense of smell, because if you did, your perfume business would go under and then you wouldn't be able to buy a minivan for anyone."

"That's not bad," I said. I pulled my baseball hat off my head and put it on his. A sign of camaraderie. "If I was ever going to write a movie, that's the route I'd take. Comedy."

Marcy said she thought I could do better. Estie said we should go for the Ride now and think of an idea later.

"I agree," Marcy said. "I'm going to tell Laurel that you are on board." She squeezed my shoulder before slamming the door shut.

"So you're actually going to do it?" Ryan asked.

I grabbed my hat and returned it to my head. "I didn't say that." I also didn't say I wouldn't do it. Could it be that I felt the slightest-ever gravitational pull toward the class? At the time, I assumed the draw was the promise of girls. That I might be seeking something more didn't cross my mind.

"Of course he's doing it," Marcy hollered through the window. "You are about to take a journey. Onward and upward!" she yelled as she backed herself toward the bakery door. "This is so exciting!" she screamed as she disappeared behind the door.

Had there been a billboard, it would have appeared just then: "Welcome to Rock Bottom. We hope you enjoy your stay."

CHAPTER 2:

What Do You Know?

"You'll know her when you see her." My brother-in-law Broc's words looped in my mind as I carted myself to Room 702 of the Tisch School on Broadway and wedged myself into a chair—the tiny kind that attaches to the desk, like at Baskin-Robbins on Columbus. I glanced at the syllabus on my desk. Sixteen lessons lined up one after the other, starting with today's, entitled, *June 11: What Do You Know?*

Not much about film writing, that was a given. But I did know how to dish out a name, and I was anxious to analyze whether my brother-in-law had chosen the right name for Laurel. In fact, I realized as the gentleman next to me introduced himself as Don and the woman next to him as his wife, Helene, my dread of this first day was trumped by curiosity.

The Mormon Rodeo? I had to meet her.

I figured she had to be big—not fat, but large, strong like a bull, curvy, perhaps, and buxom, the stock of rough-and-tumble Utah pioneers. And, of course, Mormon. Most novices of the naming game go purely according to the superficial. Take Broc, for example. He's forty-five and still going by his fraternity nickname. (At Colgate, where he met Marcy, he was tall and wiry, with a mess of dark blond, curly hair, like a stalk of broccoli. He's since lost his hair but he's still saddled with the name and my sister.)

My point being, if a name is going to help a person emerge into his or her true artistic self, as I tell my clients, and stand the test of time, as I tell their agents, it has to hit on aspects beyond those that meet the naked eye.

That said, seeing the person you are assessing never hurts, and thus far, I'd yet to lay eyes on the Mormon Rodeo. I'd yet to lay eyes on much, actually, as the shades in the room were drawn and the lights were out. There was enough light from the hallway for me to find an open desk and realize a dearth of the as-promised cute girls—at least in my area, where the average age was sixty-five. I could also see, crouched beneath a television stand at the front of the room, her back to the group, the silhouette of a woman.

Moments later, from her knees and above the whine of a tape machine and the chatter of the class, the silhouette announced, "Thank you all for being here." She paused to play with buttons and click a remote. Clearly, she was having technical difficulty. But her voice, so raspy I would have liked to have offered her a lozenge, did not convey it.

"Despite outdated technology," she said, "I assure you that you are about to embark on the most progressive film writing class around. I like to start off a new session with an inspirational montage." She went on to explain that she'd pieced together clips of movies that have shaped American dramatic film and which she hoped would help to shape our own scripts. "My selections reflect my opinion," she clarified as the machine started to make noise and the screen came to life. "I apologize upfront if I've left out anybody's favorites."

Apology accepted, I thought, as I had a hunch that my own chart-toppers, *The Big Lebowski* and *Caddy Shack*, were not going to make the cut. And they didn't. But others' apparently did. Within seconds my classmates were oohing and nodding with approval over clips I didn't recognize. I did suspect the Jews in stripes being loaded in black-and-white by Germans onto cattle cars was from *Schindler's List*—which, much to my mother's shame, I refused to see.

I've never been a huge fan of death. Or of movies, for that matter. Due to a fear of the dark, I never sat through an entire movie until I was ten. I'm still not a big fan of the dark, although I was doing okay—not great—in that dim classroom.

My anxiety eased somewhat when I started to see familiar scenes. *The Godfather. The Graduate. Midnight Cowboy. Terms of Endearment,* my mother's second favorite behind *Schindler's List,* was also featured. The montage took us all the way to present day—*Memento*—and by the time we got there, I'd settled in for the show. I might even say I was enjoying myself when suddenly, without warning, without a conclusion or credits, the montage ended, the lights popped on, and there she stood, front and center, the Mormon Rodeo.

"Welcome to Drama for the First-Time Film Writer," she said. She was applauding. "I'm excited to have you all, and I promise that if you commit yourselves to me and open yourselves to my process, you will leave at the end with a script in hand."

As she began her welcome speech, my eyes went to her boots, the same dirty-brown shit-kickers I'd seen through the window of Marcy's bakery. I'd assumed the Rodeo nickname had something to do with her footwear. Perhaps the association stopped there, because I was at a loss after the shoes. She was tall and thin, not big and buxom. Although her breasts were nice. And they were real. Most of my clients' boobs, they didn't budge. A bus could whack Share broadside, and her breasts would not so much as jostle. But the Mormon Rodeo's bounced beneath her T-shirt as she now paced the front of the room—as did her hair, which was wild and curly, with a considerable layer of frizz outlining her head. Her face seemed nice enough, from what I could see beneath the hair. She didn't seem to know from makeup or accessories, other than a thin gold necklace. She was jeans and T-shirt. Au natural. I might have gone so far as to label her granola, had I not had my new classmates to compare her against. They—primarily the faction in the front rows—took crunchy to new levels. A ring in every nose, a sandal on every foot. Against the backdrop of my peers, this teacher was a conventional beauty.

But would I, I asked myself as she promised to teach us the nuts and bolts of the craft, like to, you know, get her in the proverbial saddle?

On looks alone, probably not. Clearly, I assumed from his choice of names, Broc had come to a different conclusion.

When I tuned back in, the Mormon Rodeo had moved to the front of the room, her hands in prayer position. "To write stories that are real and true is to take an unpredictable journey," she was saying. "We must be prepared to go deep, to entrust ourselves to the organic nature of the process, to throw away our outlines if our characters go a different way." She moved her hands into her back pockets and again began to pace the front of the room, her hips moving in a motion-of-the-ocean sort of way, matching the measure of her speech.

"We will start by getting to know each other. I want you to think of this class as your home, a supportive place in which we all feel safe to share our work and bare our souls." Her body turned back to the front of the room, her hands came back to prayer. "If that sounds good to everyone, let's begin."

The plan did not sound good to me. Had I not been jammed into my chair like a piece of dental floss, I would have bolted. I did not soul bare.

Neither, apparently, did my neighbor Don, who, I would soon learn, was from Long Island and a member of the seniors couples club that had settled itself around me. He snorted and whispered something that prompted Helene, his wife, to turn her back to him and the woman behind him, his sister Susan, to give his chair a shove. This activity occurred as the Mormon Rodeo set forth the ground rules for our introductions and sweat began to conveyor down my sleeves. We were to say our names, share where we were from, explain our movie concept, and reveal an interesting fact about ourselves.

"I'll go first," she said.

"Well, I'm certainly not going first," whispered Don.

His fellow couples club members chuckled, but those in the front row, the group going for their master's degrees, turned around and snarled. The first lesson wasn't yet underway, the first introduction not even made, and already, a rift. I felt like telling the Mormon Rodeo to save her breath. We could play getting to know you 'til kingdom come, and we were still going to be a house divided. The goody two-shoes versus the nogoodnickas, a word coined by my Grandma Estelle to define a lesser form of scoundrel and most of the members of my family.

The Mormon Rodeo turned out to be Laurel Rene Sorenson, a thirty-three-year-old native of Manti, Utah—which, she said, was south of Salt Lake City and home to the annual, two-week-long Mormon Miracle Pageant. She'd been living in New York for fifteen years and teaching for ten, and was now writing a movie about a Mormon father of nine who commits suicide in order to provide his family with insurance money after he loses his cattle fortune in a pyramid scheme involving dietary supplements.

"Oh my," said Helene, whose high voice did not jibe with her significant height. "What a terrible tragedy. I hope it's not autobiographical."

Laurel smiled at Helene as she gathered her hair into a sizable mass and clipped it to the top of her of head. The rearrangement made an immediate improvement, as I'd suspected. Out of habit, I'd been making a mental list of how I'd go about transforming Laurel Sorenson if she ever stepped into my office asking for a makeover and an eponymous fragrance. Tinkering with her hair—smoothing her frizz and possibly highlighting the blond—topped the list. I wasn't yet sure what to do about the boots.

"Helene, you hit the issue of the day on the head. Is my story true?" She turned her gaze on the rest of the class and asked, "What is truth when it comes to writing? Are we talking about actual truth? The essence of truth?" Her voice and arms went higher with each question, like a preacher with laryngitis. "We could discuss it for days," she said. "But for now, let's be patient."

"What about your interesting fact?" Don reminded her.

"Right," she said. She pulled the charm on her necklace back and forth while she thought. "Here you go: I am Mormon by birth but I'm taking Jewish conversion classes."

As a vigorous reaction to this news rippled through the couples club, I made a note to tell Broc that the Mormon Rodeo might not be Mormon, and Laurel called on her first candidate.

Rhonda was an Asian woman who wore a red bandana around her forehead and was writing about a girl who drops out of college to help her parents run the family store. Rhonda was followed by Judd, who explained that he was writing a movie about teenagers who sneak into the Central Park Zoo after hours and find all the animals dead. "It's going to kick off with this totally vile scene," he said, tucking a piece of hair behind his ear. "Working title is *Vile Bodies*."

As I wondered whether he was working from a place of actual truth, Laurel commented that the title seemed appropriate, given his description. I thought she might have said "ironic," as Judd's own body was covered only in a yellowed undershirt, jean shorts, and the aforementioned Birkenstocks, and nothing is more vile than sandals on guys.

The introductions revealed a real mishmash of folks. A conglomeration of undershirts, attitudes, NYU undergrads the same age as Share, senior citizens far older, two women in burkas, and finally one asshole in an Armani suit. Me.

I stood out of habit. "My name is David Melman."

"You don't need to stand." This was Candy, who'd introduced herself right after Judd and whose sweet name, I could tell already, was an oxymoron.

I dropped back to my seat, embarrassed and still apparently susceptible to being bossed around by girls, the effect of growing up with older sisters.

"I usually stand when I present to clients," I explained to my new friends in the couples club. Then I told the class that I'd be writing about a perfume maker named Mort Chuckerman who loses his sense of smell.

My concept was met with silence, and finally broken by the clomp of cowboy boots as they headed down the center aisle. I held my breath as the Mormon Rodeo came at me. She paused when she reached my desk and nodded slowly to herself as she sized me up, as if for the first time appreciating the magnitude of the mess she'd volunteered to take on. Then, as the class stared and I loosened my tie for more oxygen, she smiled.

"So you are Marcy's brother?"

I heard Don ask his wife, "Who's Marcy?" as I exhaled and forced myself to look up at her.

"For better or worse, I am."

She tucked a clump of fallen frizz behind her ear. "It's a pleasure to meet you." She held out a hand, and I quickly wiped mine on my pants and held it to hers.

Firm shake, soft hand. Part Rodeo. Part not.

"It sounds like you're writing a real tearjerker." She winked.

Was she flirting with me? Flirting was familiar ground. I regrouped. "You never know, Miss Sorenson, I might have Mort Chuckerman commit suicide at the end." I winked back.

Laurel shook her head up and down and played with the charm on her necklace, which I could now see was a Jewish star. "Touché," she said.

I wondered how far along she was in the conversion process, and if she wanted my professional help, because the last thing she looked like was a Jew.

She smiled, all Utah-friendly. "You are right, Mr. Melman. You never know what might happen. I should withhold judgment."

"As hard as that may be," added Candy, the bully.

Laurel came to my defense by telling Candy to withhold the commentary. Then she ordered me to issue my interesting fact.

"I'm not sure I have one. I have a lot of facts, I'm just not sure any of them rise to the level of interesting. The rest of the class set the bar pretty high." I was speaking in earnest. Don had survived prostate cancer; Susan, his sister, was recently widowed; and Candy had just revealed, naturally, that she'd donated a kidney to her dying brother, only to have him die anyway. How could I compete with that?

"I find that hard to believe," Laurel said. "You think about it. I'll get back to you."

Forty-five minutes later, we came to the end. Laurel turned to the blackboard, apparently having forgotten my missing fact.

"All of your topic ideas," she said with a knock on the blackboard. "Take a good look."

People did as told: eyes went to the board. As they did, Laurel grabbed an eraser and with a few swoops of her arm, did away with our entire collection of intended works.

Her tush shook as she erased. I couldn't help but notice. Don did too. He elbowed me as Laurel said, "Kiss your concepts goodbye," and the class gasped.

"She's got one hell of an ass," Don whispered.

Helene kicked his seat again, while the recently widowed Susan tapped my shoulder and asked, "Are you single?"

I nodded yes. Was she hitting on me? She was old enough to be Share's grandmother.

"You're adorable," she said.

"Thanks," I said. I wondered if Marcy would be happy if I came home with Susan.

Don leaned toward me. "You should go after the teacher."

"She's not my type," I whispered. "Besides, she's converting to Judaism. She must be engaged. Why else would you convert?"

"He has a good point," Helene told Don.

"Maybe the conversion has something to do with the suicide," Susan suggested.

Helene pointed out that she wasn't wearing a ring.

I said I hadn't noticed.

Susan told me she had a single daughter in the city, Betsy. "I have a good feeling about you. You should take her out." She wrote Betsy's number on a corner of her syllabus, ripped off the corner, and handed it to me.

Because I was passing notes, I didn't hear the portion of the lecture during which Laurel informed us that instead of writing a script based on our movie ideas, we were to write about our interesting facts.

"New writers tend to start with stories they think they want to tell, but those aren't the stories asking to be told." She grabbed a syllabus from Judd's desk and read, "Lesson 1: Familiarity v. Discovery: What Does It Mean to Write What You Know?"

I had no idea what she was talking about. In my experience, stories don't ask to be told. People just tell them.

"Let's take the couples club, for example." Laurel nodded toward the group. "You want to write a movie about a cruise ship that runs aground in the Greek Isles?"

The club, all five of them, nodded and smiled.

"My guess is that your own cruise ship ran aground in the Greek Isles."

"Just like the Titanic. Except our boat didn't go down," Don said, and the rest of the club laughed.

Laurel rested herself against the empty desk next to Helene. "And you plan to recount the episode."

The nodding and smiling continued.

Then came the Mormon Rodeo's knife. "Rule number one: writing what you know does not mean recounting an experience. You folks could probably tell us the tale of your trip in five minutes. We'd all have a good laugh and that would be that."

"It's one hell of a story," said Don.

"I don't doubt that it is," said Laurel, "but the purpose of writing is not to simply inform but to discover something about yourself or life in general, and you can't discover when you just retell facts.

"Likewise," she rasped, "you cannot *discover* when you write about characters or situations to which you have no connection or know nothing about."

Medical school was less confusing, I was thinking, when I heard my name.

"David. Tell me a little bit about your idea. Mort Chuckerman, the perfume guy. Why are you interested in writing about him? What is your personal connection?"

I held back that Mort Chuckerman was the name I gave my medical school cadaver. Although, as far as interesting facts go, I could have gone toe-to-ugly-toe with Judd if I'd offered up my obsession with that cadaver, an obsession that's likely connected to my dropping out altogether.

"Mort and I both market fragrances for a living," I said.

"Okay." She nodded and hopped on her desk. "Anything beyond

what you do for a living? Is he married? Where does he live? How old is he?"

"I haven't ironed out the details," I admitted.

Candy groaned. Laurel nodded again and told the class that my idea was a perfect example of writing about what you don't know.

"Discovery lies in a middle ground between what we know and what we don't. When we stick only to the familiar, we don't give ourselves a chance to discover. On the other hand, when we have no personal connection to the story we are creating, we cannot reach a higher truth about our lives, ourselves, our predicaments. Face it, that's the reason we write: to discover, to be enlightened."

Her suggestion to us was to build stories out of the bits and pieces of ourselves and our experiences that we found interesting. "Infuse your characters with what you know," she said, "and put them in unfamiliar situations that force them to act or confront or decide. What happens to Mort Chuckerman after he can't work in perfumes anymore and is forced into a new job?" She didn't look at me for an answer, thankfully. I didn't have one. "That," she said, "might allow for some discovery."

I spent the rest of the lecture stewing on what would happen to Mort. He would probably retire, I decided, not being able to imagine Mort as anything younger than a cadaver. He'd move to Miami, or at least winter there, like my grandparents did. Unfortunately, due to his sensory loss, he wouldn't be able to appreciate the salty air. But he would be able to get out, take walks, play cards. Maybe he'd make a lady friend. I thought of Susan.

A wave of protest interrupted my thought. Laurel had written our new assignment on the blackboard: "Take your interesting fact and incorporate it into your movie."

Candy was talking. "What if our movie idea and our interesting fact are one and the same?"

Now *I* groaned.

Her film, she said, was going to explore the reality of living when a piece of you (metaphorically, her brother; literally, her kidney) was already dead and buried.

"Consider yourself lucky," Laurel said to her.

Follow-up questions came in a deluge. Do we need to use the interesting fact we told in class or can we choose another? Can we combine the interesting fact with another interesting fact? What about format?

Laurel said to do whatever we needed to open the floodgates and to not worry about format.

Then came the money question, the one I'd been planning to ask privately in the after-class office hours advertised on the blackboard: "What if you have no interesting fact about yourself?" Don asked, slapping my shoulder.

"You get to pack up and go home," I said.

Again, the Mormon Rodeo came my way. One hand on hip. The other on her necklace. "I happen to have it on good word that you drive a 1977 Cadillac."

I nodded, realizing immediately where she was headed and that I'd been outsmarted by Marcy. A first.

Laurel explained to the class that the Cadillac had once belonged to my grandfather, I inherited it, I still drove it, and every year I celebrated my grandfather's birthday in the car with my niece and nephew. She finished by saying, "I want a show of hands. Does anyone think that fact about Mr. Melman is interesting?"

Only a few nods issued from the front of the room, but the men of the couples club came to life. Don reminisced about his '79 Caddy while I fumed, more angry with Marcy for getting me into this mess than with the Mormon Rodeo, who seemed to be earning her name. No matter how hard I bucked, she would not be thrown.

"As I suspected," Laurel said, nodding along with the most enthusiastic of them and smiling at me. "And I agree." She put a hand on my shoulder. "Write about the Cadillac."

"I already know everything there is to know about the Cadillac," I said. "You said we're not supposed to write what we know."

"Factually, I'm sure you know everything there is to know about that car. But why do you still drive it? Is it symbolic? What would make you get rid of it? That's where your story is, David. Make your car a character. I guarantee you'll end up with a movie."

CHAPTER 3:

The First Scene

M arcy's bakery, like Marcy, is hard to take seriously. Two of
the walls are painted bright pink and two are bright yellow.
Estie and my sister Rachel's oldest child, Julia, chose the
colors when Marcy first opened her doors seven years ago, back in
1995. Estie and Julia were both five at the time. Slip, who was also
at the grand opening, was near ninety. He'd flown in from Chicago
with my parents and Rachel and her family for the event. This was
the last trip he'd take—I think he knew it would be.

Slip brought with him the frame that held the first dollar he'd
made when he'd opened the Jackson Street Smoke Shop in 1943. I
knew the thin black frame. We all did. It had hung on the wall next
to his bed in Florida. Now, for Marcy, he'd removed the dollar.
"Put in your own goddamn dollar," he said with a wink. "Hang it
up for good luck."

Marcy did hang the frame. No dollar. Instead, she put a photo
taken that day of Slip with his arms around Estie and Julia. Every
time I look at that photo, the whole day comes back.

Having pretty much funded the bakery, my grandfather was
elected to "christen" (his word) the register. I remember him saying

to my nieces, his first customers, "How can I help you two lovely-looking ladies?"

Estie and Julia held up chocolate donuts and the quarters I had given them.

Slip held out a shaky hand. The coins landed in his palm, and then Marcy's hand grabbed them away.

"What the hell are you doing?" Slip said.

"You can't charge family," Marcy said.

"They're buying, ain't they?"

"Family eats for free at Knead Some Dough," Marcy declared.

"Your own family ain't gonna be eating at all if you keep up that policy," Slip replied as vehemently as his last bits of energy would allow. "You can't be soft and survive in this world."

He died of heart failure five months after his visit to New York. Meanwhile, Marcy ignored him, and here she is, nearly a decade later, with the photo still hanging and her business as alive and as well as can be expected for someone who gives free food to family and friends.

I usually avoid the bakery on Sunday mornings, when it's packed with women and babies and strollers and the toy corner is crammed with small bodies. The routine is for Ryan and Estie to run out to my car. But this week, the Sunday after my first class, I left my morning basketball game early to allow myself time to find a parking spot near the bakery large enough for the Cadillac. I opened the door to Knead Some Dough just a sliver, careful not to set off the bell.

Marcy jumped when she saw me. "What are you doing here so early?"

It was 8:05 a.m., according to the giant donut clock my mother made for Marcy a few years ago. The clock hovers behind the register like a chocolate UFO with colored sprinkles and white hands, dwarfing my grandfather's photo, which hangs below.

Marcy was on her knees, loading mini coffee cakes into a bottom shelf. In order to cut down on the financial bleed caused by giving merchandise away for free, she makes the freebies in miniature. Today, so far, she'd stocked mini jelly donuts, mini lemon meringue pies, and mini long johns, which she calls short johns. She looked at me through the glass of the Sunday Special pastry case.

I bent down to her level and waved my papers. "I've come to share my masterpiece."

She had no idea what I was talking about. She scrunched her tiny nose, which, along with a slight deafness in one ear, she inherited from my mother, and pressed it farther into the case, presumably for a better look.

I pressed the title page against the glass. "My script," I said. "I went to the film writing class Tuesday night, as ordered."

Marcy stood up and smiled. "That's great." She pulled off her gloves and reached for my script. "I forgot about that. Why are you giving this to me?"

"As proof of my attendance and my enlightenment." I directed her to the title, *Slip and His Caddy*, by David R. Melman, and explained how I'd gotten conned into writing about my car instead of Mort Chuckerman. "But I did it," I said. "I wrote a whole scene, and I learned a few things, like don't write what you know and don't write what you don't know."

"I'm not sure what that leaves," Marcy said.

"Me neither, but at least I'm no longer at rock bottom. I'm hovering a level above." I gave my script a pat and helped myself to a mini meringue.

"Maybe an inch above," she said, moving the tray of pastries out of my reach.

"I hope an inch is good enough for you, because I'm not going back to the class."

"Then I was too generous with the inch." Marcy flipped through the first few pages. "And I think you're being a bit generous by calling this a script. This looks nothing like a script."

"Since when are you such an expert?"

"There's no dialogue, David. There are no scene headings, either."

"Well, your friend Laurel told us we weren't supposed to worry about format. We were just supposed to write our story."

The bells over the door rang, and I jumped. The two teenage girls who help Marcy serve and clean on Sundays came into the store, and my niece and nephew raced out from the back room, summoned by the bells.

"What are you doing here?" Estie said as Ryan slapped me on the back.

They helped themselves to mini Boston creams as my sister explained that I had come early to share my homework.

Ryan grabbed the pages off the counter.

"It's the beginning of your uncle's movie," Marcy said.

Estie, looking at the pages over Ryan's shoulder, said, "It doesn't look like a script."

I scowled. "It's just the first assignment, woman."

"And apparently the last." Marcy took my script from Ryan and fanned the pages. "There's not much here. I don't think six-plus pages can constitute enlightenment."

"Quality, not quantity," I said.

"How come it's the last?" Ryan asked.

"Because your mother proved her point," I told him. "I could stand to broaden my horizons. Consider them broadened. I'm a new man. Unfortunately, I have the same old job, which I need to focus on so I can pay the bills. You don't need to be enlightened to know that this script is never going to pay the bills."

Estie took the papers from Marcy. "Let's read it and see."

"It's the story of the car," Marcy told her. "You've heard it a million times; you don't need to hear it again." She put her gloves back on. She also handed a pair to Ryan and told him to put the Boston creams in place.

"I'll read it to everyone," Estie offered.

Marcy told her to have at it.

I told her absolutely not.

"Then why did you bring it here?"

"Definitely not for a public reading."

Estie seated herself at one of Marcy's tables. "We are hardly public." She patted the chair next to her, an invitation for me to sit, and dove in.

"*Slip and His Caddy*, by David R. Melman. Act One, Scene One, Take One."

Marcy interrupted her. "I don't think the writer is in charge of the takes."

"So this is how it's going to be?" I demanded. "We're still on the cover page and the nitpicking has already begun."

"I'm just saying," Marcy said.

Estie, with a clearing of her throat, continued with more authority. "Stage directions. The camera opens on Slip's brand-new, yellow Cadillac as the year 1977 flashes at the bottom of the screen. The car is shiny and sharp. The hood is perfectly polished, the Cadillac emblem on the front stands perfectly straight, the white roof is perfectly white, the silver-spoked hubcaps (an upgrade) capture the sparkle of the sun."

Ryan held up his hand. "Don't you think that's a lot of stuff about the car?"

"The movie is about the car," I said and motioned for Estie to continue reading.

"The camera will pull back to reveal the car in a parking structure. The wall in front of the Cadillac is pale pink cinderblock with squares cut out intermittently to create a decorative, airy feel. 'The Hustle,' by the late, great Van McCoy, begins to play."

Estie put down the script. "'The Hustle?'"

"You know," Marcy said. She began to whistle the chorus and do the line dance. "Do the Hustle!" she called out.

Estie told her to stop, she was embarrassing herself.

"The song is reflective of an era," Marcy explained. "And it reminds me of my yellow satin disco jacket."

"It's full of motion," I explained. "Suggestive of a journey on its way."

Marcy told me I was already a real Martin Scorsese, and Estie told her to stop talking.

"If we could continue on the journey," she said. She sounded annoyed, and it dawned on me that this was her debut, too. Both of my nieces—Estie and Rachel's daughter, Julia—have the acting bug, and now Estie was working every role in my movie.

She started to read again. At the same time, the bells rang again, announcing the arrival of the first customer. As Marcy paused to greet the woman and her boys, I headed for the footstool Marcy keeps on the floor behind the register. After signaling my new whereabouts to Estie, I sat down, safely out of view from any customers who might enter the bakery.

"The camera expands upward from the edge of the parking garage and windows begin to appear," Estie read, her voice expanding with the camera, projecting through the bakery. "Row upon row. Windows, windows, windows. Until a huge white apartment building comes into focus. Thirty-five stories high and a football field long. As the building becomes clear, the Narrator starts to speak." She cleared her throat, apparently to shift into the part of the narrator. "This is where my story takes place," she said, trying to sound like a man. "Even though I haven't been to Imperial Towers Building One Hundred for over twenty years, even though the residents who'd occupied the little units at the time are gone, the Buildings, all eight of them, survive. They are still going strong, like my memories of those days."

Without a pause, she shifted back to her own voice. "Opening credits hit the screen as all eight buildings, four facing four, with a palm tree-lined drive down the middle, come into view. Enormous parking structures hang off the back of each building. The structures are topped with enormous pool decks. The Intracoastal surrounds this entire concrete housing project."

"Your grandparents lived in a housing project?" one of the teenage helpers asked Marcy.

"All of the grandparents lived in buildings like that," the woman with the boys answered. "Florida was filled with them."

At this point, a conversation splintered off about where this woman's grandparents lived relative to ours. Estie was put on hold, and I leaned back against the cabinet that stored bags, first aid supplies, and other miscellaneous junk. I closed my eyes as I awaited the return to my story, and I wondered whether the image on screen of Imperial Towers Building 100, a block off Collins Avenue in Miami Beach, would convey to my movie-going audience, as well as the one assembling in the bakery, the building's significance.

For us kids, it was the only vacation destination we knew. Our trips were a given, a constant, part of the rhythm of the year—yet never taken for granted, because we all understood, as young as we were, that our grandparents were old. Indeed, death, or at least a heart attack or two, was part of every visit. Rarely an evening went by without the paramedics rushing into the card room or an apartment to resuscitate. It was such a regular scene that unless the grandparent being carried out on a stretcher was yours (or unless you, like me, had a fear of sirens), the process barely interrupted the ordinary flow of evening lobby activity.

For our parents—especially those, like my mother, who were residing with in-laws—the trips were perfunctory. At best, two weeks of so-so weather, deli food, and cigarettes. At worst—well, at the time we didn't consider a worst. It was what it was.

Now I know that our annual visits were special. Especially the Christmas break of 1977. *If it wasn't,* I thought as the bell to the bakery rang a few more times and Estie's voice carried my audience into the living room of Apartment 1812, *why would anyone bother making a movie about it?*

"Davy," Estie screamed. "Davy!"

I almost jumped to my feet—and then I realized that she wasn't calling me, she was just reading the part of my mother. I'll have to make a note in the script that the yelling is not intended to be guttural, as my mother wasn't mad. Yelling was just the most commonly used method of communication at Imperial Towers Building 100. Maybe because so many people were always talking at once, or because most of them were hard of hearing. It clearly had nothing to do with proximity, because we were all stuffed together like little meatballs.

I assume our closeness will become clear the moment the camera comes into my grandparent's one-bedroom convertible apartment. During our stay, the bedroom belonged to my grandparents. The rest of us lived in the convertible portion, which was just a room (small, even by New York standards) separated into areas by furniture type rather than by doors.

I had been sitting that night on my pullout bed organizing quarters and baseball cards when I heard my mother call my name. I immediately knew what she was after. I knew the same way a parent can distinguish his baby's cries. This was a cigarette yell.

I stuck my head through the partition to see my mother sitting on her pullout bed in my father's ratty blue bathrobe, her hair wrapped tight like a tourniquet in a towel to control the effects of the humidity on her thick curls. In the beige towel, my mother's head reminded me of a giant monogrammed seashell—*EMS* for Estelle and Slip Melman, my grandparents.

Estie was doing a fine job in the role of my mother. "Davy," she said, imitating my mother's I-have-a-favor voice, "do you think you could be so sweet as to run down to the machine and bring me some cigs? I'll give you a quarter for yourself so you can play a game of pinball afterward."

"Thanks, Mom," I heard myself saying.

"But bring me the cigs before you go to the game room."

"Okay, Mom."

I remember grabbing the coins in my fist and sliding the extra quarter into a side pocket of my painter's pants. I had no intention of going to the game room. But my mother didn't need to know this.

My two older sisters spent their evenings in the game room (which was really the building's multi-purpose room, converted for the holidays into a holding pen). I knew they didn't want me in there any more than I wanted to go in and watch them flirt with the boys. They were eleven and thirteen, so the flirting was in its infancy, and it made me sick. Besides, I had bigger plans for myself that evening, if I could ever make it out of the apartment.

As I headed to the door, Grandma Estelle grabbed me around my waist and rumpled my hair. "He's got the most beautiful hair I've ever seen. Like Raggedy Andy," she said to my mother as she flipped solitaire cards onto the dining room table.

Unlike my mother, she was dressed like she was hosting a party—which in a way, she was.

At this point, I directed in my script, the full dining room area is supposed to come into view, including, at the far end of the table, a woman sitting with her head tipped back and mouth open and a man—my father, Allen—standing over her with his gloved fingers in her mouth. The woman was Gloria from 14, one of my father's regular dental patients. Although the audience will never guess by looking at her contorted position and the cane next to her chair, she was also one of the dancers in the annual Imperial Towers Building 100 Vaudeville Review. My grandmother, a professionally trained dancer, wore the dual hats of choreographer and star of the show, which took place every year on New Year's Eve. The show was a source of excitement and pride for everyone, but no one more so than Grandma Estelle.

Frieda from 9 was also in the apartment; she practiced the routine while my father treated Gloria.

Estie was now channeling Gloria, who never let the presence of my father's hands in her mouth deter her from speaking. "Raggedy Andy has red hair. Davy looks nothin' like Raggedy Andy. Davy ain't got freckles or overalls, neither."

Ryan, now playing the role of my father, answered, "Save the gabbing 'til the cement dries, please."

The bakery audience laughed. My niece and nephew always laugh at the many uses of the convertible portion of the apartment, our personal multi-purpose room, but I explain that this activity was business as usual for the Melman family. Many residents of Imperial Towers 100 used my father as their dentist back home in Chicago, and as a perk, he offered them free services during our two-week stay in Florida. My father called it the Melman Special.

My mother was not a fan of this complimentary dental program. It limited her time out at night. Not that she had many places to go, but while many families spent their evenings at dinner and a movie, our outings covered dinner only. Then we headed home for the Melman Special.

My sisters didn't mind. They loved the game room. I didn't mind. I hated the movies. My grandfather didn't believe in doing work for free, but he didn't complain because he had the card room. Day or night, there was no place that Slip would have rather been than in the Men's Card Room. In this regard, we were exactly the same.

My grandmother wasn't bothered by the routine, either. The pride and power that came with wearing the title of Mother of

Dr. Allen Melman far surpassed the inconvenience of finishing dinner by six thirty on weeknights. By six forty-five, friends and acquaintances of my grandparents were waiting in line around the dining room table.

"It's good for business," she'd tell my father as she put out a tray heaped with Salerno Butter Cookies and Lorna Doones. Estelle had a sweet tooth the size of my grandfather's Cadillac. We all knew who the tray was for.

At this point, with Estie announcing the introduction of another of my grandma's friends, Ida from 27, into Apartment 1812, Marcy's friends began to pile into the bakery en masse. Estie paused every time the bell rang. The women, too, paused as they tried to make sense of what was going on.

From where I sat, I could see their heads. With every ding of the bell, I checked to make sure that the Mormon Rodeo's head had not been added to the mix. I had anticipated the possibility of running into her this morning but dismissed it as remote since I figured I'd be gone by the time the yogis arrived. I decided that if she showed up, I'd crawl into the back room and sneak out the emergency door. How embarrassing to be caught premiering one's work after a single lesson. Although I have to say, the bakery audience seemed to be entertained. Whether they were being enlightened (as was the goal, according to the Mormon Rodeo), was another story.

"Davy, whatcha doing up here with all the old hags? Shouldn't you be playing downstairs?" Estie was really hamming up the part of Ida from 27, giving her speech a very slow cadence and a heavy New York accent.

Ida didn't have a New York accent; she was from Chicago. She did, however, have arthritis. Her knuckles were gnarled and her fingers bent in inhuman directions. That night, when she put a hand under my chin and lifted my head, I had to force a smile and look away from the knuckles.

"Leave him be," my grandma told her. "He's getting Paula cigarettes and then he's going downstairs."

Ida's face lit up and she began to rummage through her purse.

"Be a sport, David dear. Whatever you're getting for Paula, get a pack for me too. Save me the hassle in the morning."

"Paula smokes Marlboros," my grandma offered.

"Marlboro Lights," my mother corrected.

"A cig's a cig," Ida answered as she pulled a pile of change from her bag.

"I agree, Ida," my father interjected. "One rots your teeth same as the next."

Ida put a hand on a hip. "Dr. Melman, not only am I sixty-eight years old, but thanks to you, I've got access to free dental services. Rotten teeth don't scare me." She looked up at me. "What is it? Fifty cents?"

Again, a hullaballoo in the bakery broke Estie's rhythm. Some of the women—the smokers, perhaps—felt the need to remark on how cheap cigarettes were back then, which gave more recent arrivals an opening to ask when this story took place.

"Whenever it was," someone said, "they didn't even realize that cigarettes caused cancer."

"It was 1977," I heard Marcy say.

The rest of the reading continued like this, at a snail's pace, as Marcy's friends interrupted every other line to comment. I wanted to stand up and order them all to be quiet, to stop squabbling over details and listen or else they would miss my favorite part of the scene: the part where Gladys Greenberg makes her entrance.

Truthfully, at the time, I didn't notice it happening because I was still fixated on Ida from 27's misshapen fingers as they headed in my direction with her coins.

But then Gladys Greenberg spoke. "I don't know why we're paying all that money for those cockamamie pinball machines if the kids ain't using them."

My head whipped around to see her standing on the border of the kitchenette and the dining room, staring down at me.

Up to this point (and this should really be in the script), I'd never had a personal exchange with Gladys Greenberg, but I was aware of who she was. The Poncho Lady. Everywhere she went, she draped herself in a poncho. To the pool, she wore ponchos that matched her bathing suits. Now, apparently to woo free dental services from my father, she wore a black-and-gold poncho with a blue-and-red rhinestone pin on the collar. The pin said CUBS.

Gladys Greenberg was the president of the Imperial Towers 100 Condo Association and sister to a man named Big Sid, whom the audience will meet soon enough. At this point, all moviegoers need to know was that my grandfather and Big Sid were archenemies from way back when. As a result, Estelle and Gladys Greenberg were also enemies, and Estelle expressed her loyalty to Slip by repeatedly refusing to allow Gladys Greenberg a spot in her Vaudeville kick-line, which everyone knew Gladys Greenberg coveted as much as her presidency.

Ordinarily, I would have bolted from the apartment the second Ida's coins hit my hand, as I was anxious to get on with my evening. But the appearance of Gladys Greenberg was an unexpected event, and it drew me in.

I wondered if it was drawing in the bakery crowd, too. Although I wouldn't admit this to anyone, a part of me was enthralled by my bakery audience. I've always been the silent observer, the guy behind the brands and the stars, the idea man. Who knew I'd be susceptible to the pull of the crowd? But as it happened, I was, and at that moment, as golden-ponchoed Gladys Greenberg crossed into the dining room, dumped her purse (black-and-gold, to match the poncho) onto the table, threw "how-do-you-dos" around the room, and took a cookie, I decided that I'd continue the class.

Maybe my creative well could dig up more than names for pop stars and perfumes. I began to envision my relatives on the big screen. My mother in the role of her mother (my Grandma B, who had yet to make her appearance in the movie). Estie as Marcy. *How ironic*, I thought, as Estie threw herself into the part of Gladys Greenberg, *that the guy who hated movies as a kid would one day have one of his own.*

Who would play the part of Gladys Greenberg? Hers were obnoxious shoes to fill. Everything about Gladys Greenberg was oversized. Her body, her opinion of herself, her mouth—and so, too, it seemed, her dental implants. She explained this to my father as

Ida from 27 took a seat, my grandmother stared down at her cards, Frieda from 9 kicked up her performance a notch, my mother looked at my father, and I backed up toward my mother.

Gladys Greenberg started in with, "Dr. Melman, dear, could you be a doll and take a peek in my mouth? My upper implants are making it nearly impossible for me to eat."

"You seem to be doing fine with the cookie," Ida commented, pointing as best she could one of her bent fingers at a butter cookie.

My grandma's shoulders shook with repressed laughter. She shot me a wink, collected herself, and in her official receptionist capacity, interjected, "I'm sorry, Gladys. Dr. Melman only sees existing patients while he's on vacation."

"I *am* existing," Gladys Greenberg responded. "I don't think anyone would argue with that." She chuckled at her joke and eyed her reflection in the mirrors.

Now my father got involved. I knew he hated her too. But my father was a master peacekeeper, as the son of Slip would have to be. So, much to my grandma's chagrin, he handled the situation with diplomacy.

"That is the policy, Mrs. Greenberg. However"—he paused as my grandmother groaned—"if you are willing to wait, I will see if I have time for you after I get done with Mrs. Pine and Mrs. Bliss. I am almost done with Mrs. Pine."

Gloria from 14 (aka Mrs. Pine) spoke up. "No need to rush, Allen. I've got all the time in the world. Maybe you'd even like to drill a bit, for fun." She raised her head and, through the mirrors, gave Gladys Greenberg a look of disgust.

"Well, I'm certainly going to take a while," Ida from 27 (aka Mrs. Bliss) said. "My pain is getting worse by the minute."

Gladys Greenberg was not deterred. "I'll take my chances," she said as she sat herself down next to my grandmother. "I'll wait."

And wait she did. She took another cookie, too, while my grandmother rolled her eyes.

My mother smiled at me. "You better skeedaddle," she said. "It's getting late, and if I didn't need a few cigarette puffs before, I sure need them now."

My mother waved me on as Gladys Greenberg's head gave a disapproving shake.

"You know," she said to my mother, "I'd be more careful if I was you. It's against code to smoke in bed."

Then my mother: "It only looks like a bed. It's really a couch."

Laughter came from my grandma and Ida from 27 as Gladys Greenberg fired back, "Do what you want. But you're asking for trouble."

"Enough," my father declared. "If I can't work in peace, I'm not working at all."

While my father gave a cautionary point of his pick, I went to the door.

My grandma called after me, "Davy, when you come back, why don't you use your quarter to buy your way into a gin game with me? We'll see if you can beat me."

"Maybe," I told her, as if I'd seriously consider the offer. I did not want to draw suspicions or hurt my grandma's feelings. She'd taught me how to play the game—the basics, at least. She viewed my victories as a testament to her teaching abilities. But the truth was, I'd picked up the finer points of the game from sitting with Slip in the Men's Card Room—which was, in my mind, the most exciting place if not in Miami Beach, then certainly in Imperial Towers Building 100. It was a place of lawlessness. Of thick wads of cash. Of cigars and smoke. Of language I wasn't supposed to hear. No one under the age of eighteen was allowed in the Men's Card Room. But since Slip was the tsar of the card room—and everything else, actually—an exception was made for me.

My mind was way ahead of my movie. While Estie was still wrapping up the dialogue between my mother and Gladys Greenberg about smoking in bed, I had in my head already run down to get the cigarettes and tossed them into the apartment. I was well on my way to the card room when I heard applause. Apparently, Estie had finished the reading.

I held my breath and cocked my head as far back as possible to get a better view of faces and reactions on the other side of the counter. I figured if people looked pleased, I might stand up.

"Is that the end?" someone asked.

"Just of this scene," Estie said.

"Well, fabulous job," said a woman whose baby hung around her neck in one of those slings. "Did you write that? That's very good for someone your age."

"But not so great for a thirty-five-year-old man," Ryan said.

Marcy told him to be quiet. "My brother wrote it," she said.

"Yeah," Ryan said, and nodded in my direction. "He's down there."

The crowd peered over the register and a fuss broke out. Some women apologized for not realizing that the writer was present. Others said they enjoyed the reading. One woman asked me if readings were going to become a weekly thing.

"I don't think so," Marcy said, motioning for me to stand up. "My brother has no plans to continue his writing." She paused to give me a formal introduction. I stood up and waved. They waved back. The bakery was more crowded than I'd imagined. I whispered to Marcy that I'd premiered to an SRO crowd. She rolled her eyes.

A cute woman—the type I'd been hoping to find in the writing class—asked if I was the brother who created Share. The women came closer to the register, Estie came around to work it, and I fielded questions. Most of them about Share. How did I meet her? What was she like? Was she going to release any more than the one song?

"You're, like, famous here," Estie whispered.

"No, Share is, like, famous here," I said.

Finally, the woman with the baby in the sling asked, "Why aren't you going to continue writing?"

"He's not really a writer," Ryan answered for me. "My mom made him do it."

Marcy told Ryan to mind his own business, and then she explained to her friends, "The story's not that simple."

"Well, it's too bad," said a skinny woman wearing a black sweatshirt over black, flare-out exercise pants. Based on the pants, I assumed she'd been to yoga that morning, and as she spoke, I wondered whether the Mormon Rodeo had been too, and if she was now on her way to the bakery. "I want to know the real reason the Poncho

Lady comes to the apartment," she said. "I have a feeling she wanted something besides getting her teeth fixed."

"Of course she did," Marcy said.

"How do you know?" the woman asked.

"It's a true story," Marcy explained. "However," she added, looking my way, "you got some of it wrong."

"You weren't there that night. You have no idea what happened."

"Basic facts, David. Gloria from 14 had the bent knuckles, not Ida from 27. Grandma set out Salernos, not Lorna Doones. And Slip hated the Melman Special. He never thought Dad should give services away for free."

I told her she was wrong on all accounts. "But," I said, "you want the story told your way, take the class."

"Funny, David." Marcy explained to her skinny friend, whom she introduced to me as Claire, that I was taking Laurel's class.

"I adore Laurel," Claire said. "So do her students, from what I understand."

Ignoring her, I told Marcy that if she took the class, she'd learn that a writer doesn't need to be accurate on everything. "In fact, writers aren't supposed to be," I said. "You can ask your friend Laurel when she gets here."

"She's not coming today," Claire offered.

"Of course not," I said to Marcy. "She probably didn't want to have to tell you how sorry she was that she let your brother into the class."

"No, she's in LA," Claire said as Marcy headed to the back of the store for more pastries.

I followed Marcy. "Is LA where her fiancé lives?"

"Her agent. She doesn't have a fiancé." Marcy opened a refrigerator and began to pull out sheets of additional miniatures. She motioned for me to hold out my arms.

"Then why is she converting to Judaism?" I asked as she loaded pastry sheets across my body.

She stuck her face back into the fridge. "How do you know she's converting?"

"She told us. It was her interesting fact."

Marcy's head came out of the refrigerator, along with another tray of sweets. "Interesting," she said. "What was your interesting fact?"

"I didn't have one. Why is she converting?"

"Why do you care? And why are you just standing there with my stuff?"

"I'll deliver as soon as you answer the question."

"I actually don't know the answer." She began to stack more minis onto the trays I was holding. "But I would like to know why you're so interested."

"I'm not interested. I'm curious." I moved my trays away from her and pushed into the door that led to the bakery. "You really have no idea?"

"Not really. I know she's taking conversion classes, but she doesn't discuss it much, other than to ask questions here and there about holidays. She's never explained, and I've never asked. Some things are personal."

"Then she might have a fiancé."

She shook her head. "Nope. She dates. As it so happens, she left me a message about you after your class."

I let the door swing shut as I recommitted myself and my trays to the back room for a minute. "Really?" Not wanting to come across like I cared, I said, "I never would have pegged me as her type. I'm way too conventional. You should have seen the crew in that class. They all came straight off a commune. Except for the—"

"The makeup of Laurel's student body is irrelevant to her taste, since she is there to teach the students, not to date them. But she said you seemed funny"—she started pushing me back toward the door—"and interesting."

"There's no way she said I seemed interesting," I said. "I didn't have a fact."

Marcy winked at me. Eyes scrunched, mouth open.

"You're just trying to get me to go back to class, aren't you?"

Marcy shrugged. "Maybe, maybe not. Is it working?"

"Maybe, maybe not," I said. I'd rather have her believe that I was driven back to class by the prospect of a date with Laurel than by my new romance with pleasing an audience. I could never give my sister the satisfaction of thinking that her original idea was a good one.

"But don't mess with me," I said, rocking the trays of pastries on my arms, humming a few beats of "The Hustle." "I am, thanks to you, the one writing our story, and I could do a lot worse than just describe your yellow satin disco jacket."

I imitated my sister's dance moves of 1977 and hustled my way through the door to the front of the bakery, saying over my shoulder, "Exit Davy."

CHAPTER 4:

The Catalyst Scene

～ⁿ／

The Mormon Rodeo blew into the classroom the following Tuesday as if the plane from Los Angeles had opened upon its approach into LaGuardia and dumped her like excess fuel. Her hair was going every which way. Her pants—these long, white linen things—were as wrinkled as Ida from 27. Her messenger bag, the same beat-up brown purse from which she'd produced the syllabi the previous week, hung open around her body. She yanked it over her head, tossed it on the desk in front of the room, and, without a pause to adjust any aspect of herself, asked for a show of assignments.

"Who did the homework?" she asked. "Raise your papers high."

I raised mine only semi-high because I don't do group participation, but most hands headed to the sky. Laurel gave a quick nod of approval and appointed Rhonda, the Asian woman with the bandana, to collect them.

She continued to dig through her bag as Rhonda collected our papers and Don kicked my foot. I looked at him.

"I see you're slumming it now like the rest of us," he said, nodding in the direction of my shoes.

Yes, I'd dressed down this week, in a T-shirt, shorts, and basketball shoes. I hadn't thought anyone would notice.

"Just adjusting to the hot temps," I said.

The entire couples club was staring at me. They did everything—wrote, traveled, and even opined—collectively.

"You're trying to fit in," said the widow, Don's sister, Susan. "How adorable."

"Must mean you're here to stay," Don said.

"When I come in sandals and tattoos, you'll know I'm here to stay," I said.

"I think it's a good sign," Don said. "Helene said you wouldn't be back. She thought the teacher scared you away. Mel said you were put off by the front row up there." He nodded toward Judd and Candy.

"I don't scare that easy," I told them—realizing, as I spoke, that I was telling a lie.

"Great," Don said. Then he turned to the rest of the club members. "Pay up."

Wallets and billfolds emerged and five-spots floated in Don's direction.

"What are you doing?" I asked.

Don explained that they'd taken bets as to whether I'd be back. "I was the only one who had faith in you, kid."

"Are you joking?" I spoke to Don but my eyes were on Laurel, who was almost done constructing a sizable figure eight with the dominoes she'd produced from her satchel. Side conversations died down. I decided ours better as well.

Laurel gestured toward her dominos. "Everyone familiar with these?"

Some folks responded with, "Yes," others with, "They're dominos," and Don with, "If you want to know the truth, I also bet a hundred dollars that you'll end up in bed with the teacher."

Before I could respond to either Laurel or Don, Susan tapped me on the back. "I bet you'd end up with my daughter."

As Don commented that Susan had made a sucker's bet, Laurel commented that her figure eight was almost perfect. "Pretty to look at, right?" she said.

Most of the class nodded.

"But is the display fun to watch?" Her gaze landed on the front row. "Judd, you have a good view, right here in the front. Would you enjoy sitting here with a bag of popcorn and watching the figure eight or would you get bored?"

Judd sat up in his desk and tucked a piece of hair behind his ear. "Bored?"

"Are you asking me or telling me?" The Mormon Rodeo had an edge that I didn't recall from last week. Something about her also looked different, though I couldn't say what.

Judd slumped back down. "Telling, I guess. But I didn't want to offend you."

"No offense taken. Boring is bad. But I have a plan to fix that."

Laurel walked toward the back of the room. Her pants were so long, I couldn't see her feet. She pointed to the stack of fives on Don's desk. "Put that money in your wallet and come up here. You are going to be my assistant." She held out a hand, which Don accepted happily as he squeezed himself out of his kiddy desk and was led to the front of the room.

"On the count of three," Laurel said, "you are going to make this interesting to watch."

Don looked confused. He was a big guy, I saw, as he stood next to Laurel.

Laurel, who was tall in her own right, looked straight up to talk to him. "Push a domino," she ordered.

Don raised his bushy brows and smiled. "Which one would you like me to push, Ms. Sorenson?"

Laurel ignored his flirtation and shrugged.

Now Don seemed nervous. "Are they all supposed to fall?"

"I don't know. Let's watch and see."

Laurel counted to three. Don looked to his group to see which one to push. Laurel told him to rely on his own instinct. He took a deep breath, exhaled, and poked a tile at the top of one of the loops, sending the dominos reeling, clinking, one after the other, all the way around one circle and most of the way around the other.

Laurel patted his back. "Good work."

Don gave a little bow and a thumbs-up to the couples club.

"Give me the first tile," Laurel ordered. "The one you pushed."

Don reached down for the domino and handed it to her.

"Ladies and gentlemen, this is the catalyst," she said, holding the domino above her head. "The one that caused the rest to topple." She went on to explain, as Don ambled back to his seat, that every movie has a catalyst event that sets the rest of the story into motion. "When everything is lined up neat like the figure eight, you've got no story, nothing to watch. You need something to happen, something to trigger a series of events. A movie is a study in causation. One thing leads to another. As the writer, you need to know what that one thing is. What is your first domino?"

She told us to take out pen and paper, we were going to spend the next twenty minutes fleshing out our catalyst scenes—which, she told us, we should write next.

I nodded my head to show that I was with the program. I didn't have paper, but I did have a next scene. After my bakery reading, I'd planned out the Card Room Scene in my head. It was going to start off, I'd decided, the same way Laurel started off the domino exercise, and the same way I start that part of the story when I tell it to Estie and Ryan: with a count of three. On three, we all scream, "Baby Face Davy!" as this was the greeting I got every time the double doors to the Men's Card Room pushed open and I appeared inside.

I found the attention embarrassing, but I liked the name; it sounded cool. Baby Face Davy was a gangster name. It was tough— the only tough part about me. The name was reserved for Florida only, although Slip used it until the day he died. And now it is enjoying a bit of a revival, thanks to Estie and Ryan, who think it's hilarious.

"Are you in?" Don whispered to me as Helene ripped pages from her spiral notebook and handed them to Don with directions to share some with me.

"In on what?"

"The bet of the century. Fifty bucks from me and anyone else who thinks you'll manage to take her out by the next class." He waved the paper in my face.

I reached for it. "On a date?"

Don lifted the paper above his head. "On whatever you want to call it. None of us here are concerned with semantics, sonny. We just want to live vicariously."

While I contemplated the proposal and its improbability, the Mormon Rodeo declared that we should be ready to write. "I assume you were all smart enough to bring paper. This is a writing class, after all."

I grabbed the paper from Don. My acceptance of his wager was apparently implied by my actions because as I took the paper, Don gave me an "Atta boy."

I began to write in big letters on the top of the page, creating the illusion of productivity as the Mormon Rodeo walked by my desk. *In the card room, I will be greeted by my grandfather's friends—about four tables' worth of guys.*

"What if our next scene is already written?" Candy asked, interrupting the quiet, as the Mormon Rodeo nodded in approval at my sentence.

"The catalyst event determines what your story is truly about," Laurel said. "So even if your next scene exists, you best make sure it has a catalyst in it. Make sure it's clear to you, your character, and your audience."

I had no idea what my story was truly about, but I did have a catalyst. *I* was the catalyst. I kept my head down and began to doodle. Sketching is a skill of mine. I inherited it from my dad, just like Marcy inherited my mother's bad ear and Rachel got Slip's nerves of steel. My fortes are drawings of perfume bottles on whiteboards and sketches of women on cocktail napkins. The perfume bottles, naturally, are an outgrowth of my profession. The women are part of my dating routine, as I've discovered that guys who can draw are almost as desirable as guys who can play the guitar. I wasn't great at drawing card rooms though. So far, I'd sketched a table with four men around it, Slip and friends.

Slip knew everyone in the card room. Most he'd known from childhood, from the West Side of Chicago. Where the West Side was, I wasn't sure (certainly not the Upper West Side, I'm always sure to clarify for Estie and Ryan), but Slip often talked about his days hanging around those streets. His scene sounded rowdy and volatile, like the Men's Card Room itself.

"Ante up," he barked when he saw me. He slapped the empty chair next to him. "Need some dough?"

"No thanks." I plunked myself into the chair and set my mother's quarter on my grandfather's card table. I gave a quiet hello to the other men around the table and waited for their game to end—the same way I now glanced around the classroom waiting for the writing session to end. Everyone was working. Even the couples club members had rotated their desks to face each other and were now talking and laughing as Susan took down ideas. I heard the clock tick and Laurel's dominos clink as she gathered them back into her bag. Every so often, I caught Judd crumpling paper and dropping it to the side of his desk. His flick, *Vile Bodies*, was apparently missing a catalyst.

I suppose I'll use the down time in the movie as a chance for the audience to take in the card room. The dark maroon and silver wallpaper. The two poker tables and ten or so heavy wooden card tables with maroon leather chairs. The Lucite bowls of peanuts on the tables with shells littering them and the maroon carpeting. The ashtrays. The cards. And, of course, the men. As for the room's signature stench—humidity mixed with cigars mixed with the stale sweat of people who've been sitting for hours on end—I'm not sure. I could bottle it, but capturing the smell on screen is beyond my expertise. Perhaps a fog machine will do the trick.

I sketched the scene, adding myself to Slip's table, holding his cigar while he shuffled cards. There's nothing like the sound of a perfect riffle shuffle, when the cards arch down and then up like a bridge, creating that breeze as they stagger into a pile. If done fast and right, it's mesmerizing. Hypnotic.

Less hypnotic was the sound of the old men's raspy breathing and coughing. I could also hear conversations going on at other tables, which all had slowed when I'd entered but were picking up again now that the men had forgotten about my presence. Above all was the voice of my grandfather, explaining his hand to me and

commenting on others' moves and the strategies of the game—
tonight, gin.

"Show me my next move," Slip whispered, his arm around me.

I pointed and whispered back to him.

He winked and bopped me on the head, indicating that I'd
gotten it right. Gin didn't take long to play, and so before I knew it,
I was in a game.

A tap on the blackboard interrupted my artwork. The Mormon Rodeo stood in front of the board with a book open in her
arms. "Food for thought while you write," she said. Since I wasn't
writing, I watched as she explained that the book was *Screenplay*,
by Syd Field, some screenwriting bigwig. As she went on about
using catalysts to draw your character into the storyline and throw
his life out of balance, I began to sketch her next to my card room.
I decked her out in cowboy boots and a cowboy hat, hair radiating
from beneath the hat like electrical current. I stuck a tiny Jewish
star between two enormous breasts on long, stick-figure legs, and
then, for her face, gave her an oversized smile, with sparkling teeth
and freckles.

As I compared my drawing to the real thing, she said, "According to Syd, this scene should be one of the most exciting scenes in
the movie." She told us to keep Syd in mind as we wrote.

I had another Sid in mind as I sketched, and thanks to him,
excitement in the card room was about to reach an all-time high.

"Hey Slippy, you teaching your kid the rules of the game?"

I knew the voice. It belonged to Big Sid. Everyone knew Big
Sid. He was just like his sister, Gladys Greenberg, but without the
ponchos. Large in stature, hence the creative nickname, but otherwise diminutive—your classic bully. Big Sid was one of the few
men in the building without a wife or an apartment stocked with
kids on vacation. One would have thought this personal freedom
would have made him less agitated than most. I remember the
adults used to say this and laugh.

My grandfather barely reacted to Big Sid's remark. A courtesy
chuckle would be the directive in the movie script. Then he puffed
his cigar and offered me one. I declined, my father's disgust for

cigarettes already ingrained in my head. Plus, I had to concentrate on my hand, which was terrible, a mumble-jumble of cards.

"So you've got the whole family gambling now?" I could see Big Sid's bald head sticking up above the crowd a couple of tables over.

"Why don't you keep to your own cards, Sidney," my grandfather replied. He didn't look up from his own when he spoke.

"Is he as good as you, Slippy?" Big Sid laughed. "Hey Davy boy, does the apple fall far from the tree?"

Laughter filled the card room. Before this, I hadn't realized that everyone was listening. I supposed the back and forth had drawn in everyone.

I looked at my grandfather and whispered, "Do I need to answer?"

He shook his head and answered for me. "Nope, Sid. He ain't as good as me. But he's better than you." The men liked my grandfather's response. The laughter for Slip beat out the laughter for Big Sid.

"Doesn't take much to be better than Sidney," said the man sitting next to Big Sid.

Sidney shot him an elbow while another guy wearing a green cap added, "Well isn't that the God darn truth. Only a fool could blow three hundred bucks against Morry Pine."

Morry Pine (Gloria from 14's husband) was my grandfather's closest friend and a hustler on the shuffleboard courts. He was also sitting at my grandfather's table. He now explained to the room that earlier in the day, he had duped Big Sid by claiming that his hand-eye coordination was shot due to a recent stroke.

A riotous moment followed as the men got a load of Sidney's loss. I prayed that the distraction would put an end to the conversation with my grandfather.

"No wonder you're in such a fine mood," someone said.

"Shut the hell up, will you?" Big Sid growled.

People did, and for a while all was quiet.

Perhaps the evening would have remained so. The fight never would have happened. Our strongest memory would be of some other silly episode. My grandfather's Cadillac never would have come to be sitting in my garage and my movie still would be about nothing more than Mort Chuckerman, the Perfume Guy—if only

I hadn't lost my hand and announced defeat so loudly as to catch the ear of Big Sid.

My loss was the catalyst, the ground zero moment. My reaction started the chain, which was, as Laurel explained it, the definition of a catalyst. How does one convey the significance of such a subtle action to an audience? Maybe ominous music will sound. Maybe a subtitle reading "catalyst event" will appear at the bottom of the screen as the actor who plays me tosses his cards on the table and says, with sour grapes, "I'm out."

My grandfather will muss my hair.

The guys at the table will wink and tell me, "Nice play, Davy Baby." The game will go on, as it did that night while I pouted, watched, and wondered to whom my precious quarter would go.

"What's this I hear?" Big Sid's voice rang out. "Did Slippy's boy lose?"

I turned my head in his direction. He was looking back at me, smirking and chomping on peanuts.

"Don't worry, sonny. Your grandpa will give you more money to lose. Your grandpa's a real pro at losing money."

I turned to Slip. "I don't want any more money to play again," I whispered. I knew he would give it to me. Not because Big Sid told him to but because, as I've mentioned, Slip was generous with his money. "Need some dough?" was his second favorite phrase after, "You goddamn motherfucker."

My grandfather pushed a quarter from his pile toward me. "Play again."

I pushed it back and shook my head. "No."

"Don't let no punk like that bother you," he said to me, nodding in Big Sid's direction. "Nothing but a bag of wind, talking to hear himself talk." He gathered up everyone's money and doled it out to the winner.

I watched as Jack Glassman, a man who also lived on the eighteenth floor, set his bills and my quarter in his pile next to him. Even though I'd played dozens of times and mostly lost, the pang of seeing my money in someone else's hands made me sick to my stomach. My grandfather knew this and to make me feel better, he always left a fresh quarter on the table beside my bed after I went to sleep. He never told me what to do with it, but Slip was a gambler. He'd never tell me to save it like my dad did.

"You know, kid"—it was Big Sid again—"your grandfather loves to help other people lose their money. Don't you, Slippy?"

Finally, my grandfather looked in Big Sid's direction. "What are you trying to do here, Sidney? If you're still picking at bones, pick 'em with me. You hear? Leave my grandson out of it." Slip's voice was cool, but I could detect (and the camera will show) the powerful wrinkles around his eyes and forehead tightening—a quiet preparation for battle.

I was less subtle with my emotions, and the audience will understand this as they watch the color drain from my face and my body shrink into my seat.

My grandfather, too, noticed my reaction. "Go get yourself a Coke," he said, nodding toward the door. "Bring me one, too."

As the cards began to shuffle again, I headed to the pop machine, which was just outside the card room next to the cigarette machine from which I'd acquired the Marlboros. A Coke cost twenty cents, but if you stuck your arm up high enough into the bottom of the machine, you could yank down bottles for free. The audience will watch as I do this, so they, like me, will miss the remarks that flew back and forth between Big Sid and Slip during that time. Whatever they were, they ignited my grandfather enough that he put down his cards and his cigar and walked over to Big Sid's table.

According to Jack Glassman, Big Sid had spouted off about the amount of money my grandfather had lost on bad bets at the track, but my grandfather hadn't retorted. Only when Big Sid suggested that my grandfather was behind Morry Pine's fix on the shuffle-board court did my grandfather make a move.

"He sat like a gent, unflappable until the last straw," Jack Glassman would report later that evening to my father. (However, Jack's credibility would be called into question due to his friend-ship with my grandfather and his hearing aids. "He's biased and deaf," would be the word at the pool the next day. "What kind of witness is that?")

Fortunately for the sake of my career as a film writer, I witnessed the next part of the night, and I myself will direct it in the movie. Why waste time putting the incident on paper? It is so emblazoned in my head that not a word, nuance of expression, or piece of choreography is one bit diminished today.

My grandfather's back will be facing me as I return with our Cokes. His head will not turn toward the double doors as it usually did when I entered. His salmon-colored sweater will press against the corner of the table where Big Sid sits. A couple of guys will call out for my grandfather to come back to his seat. Slip will wave them off and instead take a step closer to Big Sid so that his profile becomes visible to me. I will watch him pull off his glasses and put them down on the card table. (I remember that night being awed at how foreign he looked without the glasses. He never took them off. He was blind without them. Hell, he was blind with them.)

"If you got something to say about me, why don't you say it to my face?" Slip directed two fingers towards his eyeballs.

Big Sid stood up, all six feet four inches of him.

My instincts told me to run; I sensed what was going to happen. Almost every story about Slip involved physical force and victory. He'd once decked a garbage man who'd tried to rob my grandmother. He'd also beat up a landlord, a cop, and Big Sid. About fifty years earlier, Big Sid had cheated my grandfather out of money, and in return, Slip had socked him. Knocked him backwards down a flight of stairs in the three-flat they both lived in, right in front of Big Sid's girl and the neighbors.

"I'm not sayin' nothing that's not new to anyone." Big Sid had a gruff voice. He smirked as he spoke. "You are whatcha are, Slip. A bum's a bum." In his hand he dangled a cigarette—a Marlboro, same as my mother's. "Having your kid sit next to you doesn't make you anything different."

Slip's bony elbow poked into the sleeve of his sweater as his arm cocked back. He moved an inch closer to him. "You're asking for trouble," he warned. His voice still gave no sign of fear.

Big Sid didn't budge; his body loomed over Slip, his grin remained. "Is that so?"

With arms and mind unsteady, I put down the Cokes on an empty table and considered the role of the ten-year-old grandson in this scenario. Should I interfere, try to break it up, save the day— perhaps a life? That's what my father would do. Should I run? After all, I wasn't even supposed to be in the card room, which seemed to be exponentially filling with smoke as the men put down their cards, picked up their cigars, and watched. Talk about excitement. To the men, this was *Rocky* brought to life.

My grandfather put a hand on Big Sid's chest and gave a shove with his fingertips. "You've always been slow to learn, haven't you?"

Big Sid didn't budge. "Go ahead," he teased and took a drag of his cigarette. "You so tough? Hit me." With the fingers that held his cigarette, he pointed between his eyes. "I dare you."

In the script, there'll be a beat (movie lingo for a pause, according to the SCREENPLAY DEFINITIONS poster beneath the clock) between each of those last three words, to indicate how Big Sid spoke them.

Slip knew boxing. He learned at the Association House, the Boys & Girls Club of the West Side. The Association House introduced him to boxing, dancing, and my grandmother, the three of which got him through life. Compared to me, someone with nothing to show for an Ivy League education but pop stars and perfume, Slip clearly got the better deal—because *Bam! Whack! Right in the kisser! Smack in the puss!*

I drew these words in bubbles, like comic book superhero exclamations coming from the mouths of the men in the card room, as these were the words they used to describe Slip's punches to every last resident of Imperial Towers 100. And it was an accurate accounting, especially when accompanied by the arm swings demonstrating the left- and right-handed jabs, then a slip, and finally the left-handed hook that sent Big Sid thudding to the floor.

My grandfather's hands moved so fast that I didn't see three distinct punches. I only heard a series of grunts, one per pop, followed by, "Take that, you stupid motherfucker."

"What's the best way to film a fight scene?" The question popped out of my mouth as impulsively as Slip's punches. I didn't pause to raise my hand or even to locate the teacher in the room.

The Mormon Rodeo, who was sitting at her desk reading papers, looked around the room, unsure of who had asked the question. I put my pen in the air. She looked surprised to see me attached to it.

"What kind of fight do you have in mind?"

"A fistfight between two old men," I said.

She smiled. "That's quite the catalyst."

"It's not the catalyst," I told her. "The catalyst caused their fight."

She nodded and explained that fight scenes usually film best with several slow-motion cameras because they let you capture the punches and reactions from different angles. Although she seemed to know what she was talking about, I decided that in order to capture my recollection, the director should do the opposite: speed up the sequence to a total blur, slowing down only when Big Sid staggers back against his chair, moans in pain, and then collapses face first onto the carpeting not far from where his cigarette landed.

Because the fall of his massive body was gradual, a giant Redwood going down amid a forest of shrubs, I don't think we'll need to use a stunt double for the scene. However, we will need a fight choreographer to block body positions, punches, and the movement of Big Sid's head in reaction to each blow. We'll also need a special effects guy to make whatever they use in the biz for blood spurt from Big Sid's nose after the second slug, and a sound effects guy to match the spurt with the crack of breaking bone and the fall with a dull *whump*. The sound of the melee that ensues will be produced by men themselves, for as soon as Big Sid fell, the men charged to the front of the room.

A few dropped to the ground to tend to Big Sid. Arnold Camper, a podiatrist, took charge. "You alright, Sidney?" he screamed, leaning over Big Sid's body and throwing a handkerchief on his nose. "Sidney, can you hear me?"

"Move the hell away from me."

"He's alright!" Arnold announced back to the crowd.

No one seemed concerned. The majority of the men congregated around Slip, who had sidestepped Big Sid to squash out the cigarette burning into the carpet and now leaned casually against the wall, examining his hands.

In the movie, the men will pat him on the back and crack out remarks like, "You scrappy son-of-a-bitch" and "What you been putting in your Cream of Wheat, Melman?"

I was the only one in the room that didn't react. I simply stared, eyes wide, adrenaline gushing. I had no idea what to do.

Arnold the podiatrist did. "Call the paramedics," he ordered. "He's got to get to the hospital."

At the same time, Jack Glassman shoved his way to the center of the rumpus and gave my grandfather's arm a tug. "Slippy, let's get you the hell out of here."

It was as if he was speaking to me. My feet reacted instantaneously, carrying me out of the card room so fast that I forgot my Coke bottle, let alone logic. My first worry after I left was whether I should have stayed to tend to Slip—to stick by him, as my father was always reminding us was our duty to each other. As I dashed to the game room to track down my sisters, I decided that the fight was my fault. If I hadn't cared so much about losing and hadn't announced my loss so loudly, Big Sid never would have started up with my grandfather, and my grandfather would have not gotten himself into trouble.

"Sometimes," Laurel said, still at her desk, "putting your finger on the first domino is easy. A killer shark attacks a young woman on the eve of a holiday beach weekend. A tornado sweeps down in Kansas and carries a young girl to Oz. A guy who makes perfume loses his sense of smell." She sent an eyeball roll in my direction. "But often, such a determination is less obvious, like pinning down the moment when one's identity becomes threatened or the exact moment a relationship begins."

At the mention of a relationship beginning, Don gave a cough and elbowed me.

"External events are easier to spot than the ones that occur internally. External events, many times, are done with special effects. Internal events, which are usually driven by character rather than action, are harder to write. They require a writer who is in touch with his or her character's emotions. Think drama versus action flick."

Up until she said this, I'd been confident that my upset over the loss of my quarter was my movie's catalyst event. But I also felt sure that I was writing an action flick because of the fights and other crazy stuff that made this story fun to tell to my niece and nephew.

I raised my hand. "Do action flicks ever have internal catalyst events?"

"Not usually, but don't get too bogged down in semantics," Laurel said.

"What if," I said, looking at my sketch of Big Sid sprawled on the floor, his giant nose cracked in two, "you have an external event that occurs in reaction to an internal event? A chicken or the egg situation. Then which is the catalyst?"

The Mormon Rodeo put down her pen, stood up, and came around to the front of her desk. She leaned back against it, exposing her shoes for the first time: a worn out pair of Keds. "A complicated, thoughtful question," she said as I looked at my caricature and considered switching its shoes from cowboy boots to sneakers. "And from Mort Chuckerman of all people." She smiled. Her teeth; it was her teeth that looked different. They were whiter.

"I was wondering the same thing," Candy announced, as if trying to hijack my show of intelligence.

"Unfortunately," Laurel said, "I can't give either of you an answer, because there is none. Where a story starts depends on the story the writer wants to tell." Then she said, sensing my disappointment, "Why don't you see me after class? I can take a look at what you've written and try to help you make sense of it."

"Thanks," I said, staring at my paper. "I'll see. I'm not sure how much you'd be able to help."

"I've been writing for a long time. I'm pretty good at helping my students identify their stories."

"You don't need to be a writer to identify this one," Don assured her. "It's animated." He chuckled as he grabbed my paper and held it out to her.

In seemingly slow motion, the Mormon Rodeo glided her invisible Keds over to my desk and took the paper from Don, who put his hand on my wrist and told me to relax and thank him later.

If I could have run out the classroom like I had the card room, I would have. But I couldn't free myself that easily from the desk, from Don, or from Laurel, who now placed a hand on my shoulder as she studied my scene, including her caricature.

"Yes, Mr. Melman," she said, her eyes playing over the paper and coming to rest on her portrait. "Why don't you plan on seeing me after class."

I shrank down in my desk and started to apologize.

"Marcy didn't tell me you could draw," she added as she dropped the paper back on my desk. Then she paused, bent down so her eyes met mine, and with a smile, whispered, "I love what you've done with my breasts."

CHAPTER 5:

3 Woos and 3 Scenes

"**C**all it what you want, but this is a date," I said to the Mormon Rodeo as she sat next to me at the 3 Woos, the Chinese take-out place across the street from class.

How I ended up there was a chaotic unfolding of events, a falling of dominoes over which I had seemingly little control. Here's what I recall. The class ended. Judd stuck around to ask about Aristotle and how to force the plot of *Vile Bodies* into a three-act structure. Laurel said something about focusing on the integrity of a story and not the plot, then shooed him out the door and me down the stairs with a, "Hurry up, I'm starving." I chased after her, too scared to ask where we were going.

"You like Chinese?" Laurel asked as she hustled me to the corner.

I shrugged and said, "Not really. It's greasy."

She smiled. "I thought Jews liked Chinese food."

I considered whether she was being flirtatious or anti-Semitic. "Is this what you learned in your conversion class?"

"How'd you know I was converting?" she asked.

"You told us in class, remember? Your interesting fact."

"Oh, right." The light changed, and she charged across Broadway, her bag bouncing against her hip, the bottoms of her white pants dragging on the street, collecting soot.

She didn't flirt with me, but she didn't hold back either, and in the few blocks between the stoplight and the 3 Woos, she revealed personal information at a rate that only a woman can. She was feeling scattered, she said, because she'd just decided to move to LA—not for a fiancé, she said when I asked, but to write for a TV show, some new cable program about men in the ad world. "Like me," I said, and suggested I could be her muse. She said she wasn't sure she was going, the offer just came up, she had barely told anyone yet, she wasn't sure why she was even telling me, but if she took the job she'd be gone by October, and that probably wasn't enough time for me to become her muse. If I wanted to help her at all, I could pray to God that her current movie project, the one about the Mormon father who commits suicide, gets optioned, because if she could sell it, like she'd done with one other script, she'd have enough money to stay in New York, which she'd like to do.

This was the reason she was taking conversion classes, to fortify her script. Obviously a Jew was in her film, although she wouldn't specify what type. She also wouldn't specify whether she preferred me to pray to the Mormon God or the Jewish one about her movie project. She said that we were together to talk about my movie, not hers. I told her, as I struggled to keep pace with both her legs and her mouth, that I knew nothing about selling scripts, but I would suggest changing the plot to not involve suicide. And if that didn't do the trick, I said, I could lend her some cash if it would tide her over, give her more time to stay in New York.

Who knows why I offered that. Probably because I like to play the part of Slip, to be a sport when I can. Laurel looked back at me with a scrunched face, like I'd just offered to sell her crystal meth, and told me she didn't need handouts, especially from a stranger. I told her to consider the money a loan from her friend Marcy's brother.

"Thanks but no thanks," she said as we approached the 3 Woos, marked by a neon sign with most of the W burnt out so that it appeared to be the 3 oos. "I'll be fine."

"At least let me buy you an egg roll," I said as I pulled open the door and held it for her.

She stared at me and scrunched her face again as she walked through, as if questioning my sanity. "You're holding the door?"

"Did conversion class teach you that Jews don't hold doors?" I asked, following her inside.

"My experience in life has taught me that men in general don't hold doors. I'm not used to chivalry."

"I call it common courtesy," I said.

She told me that I was very into semantics.

I told her I preferred to call it marketing.

As I spoke, the Mormon Rodeo said hello to an Asian woman behind the counter, who smiled. "New student?" she said.

By virtue of simply being inside, we were at the front of the line.

"New session, new student," Laurel said, and then she ordered the egg roll. "This is Janet," she said as she rifled through her bag, past a nail file, the dominos, and God only knows what else, presumably looking for cash.

I pulled a ten out of my wallet and tossed it on the counter. "Hi," I said to Janet.

"Name on the order?" she asked.

While I wondered why she needed a name when we were the only people ordering, the Mormon Rodeo answered. "Put it under Mort Chuckerman," she said, still scrounging through her bag. She pulled out a five and slapped it on the counter. "You aren't paying. They are my egg rolls."

"I'm afraid that technically they are Mort Chuckerman's egg rolls." I pushed the bill back at her and winked. "Consider this your first official date with Mort."

"This isn't a date, it's a meeting," she said.

Which is when I said, "Call it what you want, this is a date." Then I added, "Mort Chuckerman just bought you egg rolls. I can't wait to see where the relationship goes from here. Too bad you're leaving in October."

"Suddenly Los Angeles doesn't seem too bad," she said, walking over to the 3 Woos' three stools. She plunked herself on one and her messenger bag on another. "Listen, if you're trying to impress your cronies in the back of the classroom, call it a date. Knock yourself out."

"You heard that conversation?" I asked. I tried to hide my embarrassment by pretending to not be embarrassed.

"Heard? Your friends don't talk, they scream."

"They're old. That's just what happens when you get old," I told her. "Read my movie. It'll teach you a thing or two about old people. Especially old Jews. Actually, you might be better off reading my script than taking that conversion class if you want to learn about Jews."

"Shouldn't you write the script before you start recommending it for reading?" She motioned toward my folder. "Speaking of your script, give me your sketch."

As I pulled out my drawing, Janet announced that Chuckerman's order was ready. I grabbed the plate from her without leaving my stool. Three egg rolls—hot as the dickens, as my grandma would have said, and as thick as trees—served up on a flimsy plastic plate, which I set on the counter. The Mormon Rodeo put an egg roll on napkins in front of each of us and ripped the third in half, presumably for us to share. She filled the plate with an ocean of sweet sauce, and ordered me to "dig in."

I declined and watched instead as she tore into her egg roll like the boys from *Lord of the Flies*. I was mesmerized. Most of the women—or girls, I should probably call them—I've dated over the past ten years have only ordered dinner. They haven't eaten it. They'd never touch an egg roll. And they'd never talk with their mouths full. But the Mormon Rodeo did.

"Let's get to work," she said. She fished a pen from her bag. With it, she wrote on the top of the sketch I drew in class. SCENE 2: EVENING. INTERIOR CARD ROOM OF DAVID'S GRANDPARENTS' APARTMENT BUILDING. She narrated as she wrote. As a result, Janet, who hadn't left her post, could hear.

"Is that his movie?" Janet asked. She shook her head. "Usually the students come in with full scripts for Miss Laurel. You're the first with just one piece of paper."

I looked at the Mormon Rodeo. "Full scripts? Really?"

She admitted that most of her students were repeat offenders.

"Groupies," Janet interjected. "Everyone loves Miss Laurel."

"Like Judd?" I said to Laurel, who was now dabbing the corners of her mouth with a napkin, suddenly as dignified as the Queen of England. "What go-round is he on?"

"Only his second," Laurel said. She laughed. "Candy, however, is on her fifth."

"But the class is called Drama for the First-Time Film Writer."

Laurel shrugged. "Doesn't matter. Every time I teach, it's a different class. People take away different lessons at different times. Writing is one of those things that's constantly evolving. Like people." She looked at me and then at my sketch of her breasts. "Like most people."

"You don't even need to be in her classroom to learn," Janet informed me. She bent down below the register as she continued to speak. "I know everything from just listening to Miss Laurel while she eats." She stood up holding a red binder. "See, here's my script. It's sci-fi." She said she'd been working on it for two years, it was her ticket out of the 3 Woos.

"I need a ticket out of the 3 Woos," I said.

"Don't look so worried," the Mormon Rodeo said. She patted her stomach. "I'm full. I feel good. I'm going to teach you a thing or two." She told me to pay attention, and then she began. "These here are slug lines." She pointed to what she'd written on my sketch. "Every scene starts with them. Put them in all caps. Below the slug lines come stage directions, and dialogue follows that." She pushed a clean napkin in front of me. "Drawing out each scene is a perfectly good way of working. Many film writers do it. If sketching works for you, I'm all for it. Anything that helps you visualize your story. Let's start off your next scene together."

"I thought we were here to figure out my catalyst," I said.

She plunked the jar of sweet sauce over the breast portion of her caricature. "I think that ought to take care of your catalysts."

"I thought you were here to eat egg roll," Janet interrupted. "Why don't you eat?"

I told her it was still too hot.

"Dip it in the sauce, Chuckerman. Sauce cools it down."

"Yeah, Chuckerman," Laurel said. She laughed and hit my shoulder. Her first use of Chuckerman. Her first flirtation. She dropped her guard long enough to let me see her in a different light, and in that moment, in the dark, dingy light of the 3 Woos, knowing that soon she'd be forced to abandon her following to move to Los Angeles, I felt sorry for her.

But only for an instant, because suddenly she was back to business, assuring me that my catalyst would reveal itself as long as I wrote honestly. She'd prefer to spend our time teaching me some basics so I could move forward. She wrote SCENE 3 at the top of the empty napkin. "Okay, so Scene 2 took place in the card room. Where does your next scene take place?"

"It takes place in three different spots," I said. "So divide the napkin into three sections."

She shook her head. "If it takes place in three spots, its three scenes."

"A sequence, actually," Janet, now munching from a bowl of fried rice, clarified.

Laurel agreed with Janet.

I told them they were wrong. "The next part of my story is one scene called What Went Down in the Building after the Brawl." I pointed to my sketch of Big Sid lying on the ground to clarify.

Janet shook her head in dismay. "He is a very remedial student."

Again, the Mormon Rodeo agreed. Then she said, "Let me give you the nuts and bolts, Chuckerman. A scene is like an atom, the basic building block of a movie. Related scenes link together to tell a piece of your story. These are called sequences. Every time you change either location or time of day, you have a new scene, because the crew has to adjust either location or lighting. So, if the next part of your movie takes place in three different places, you've got three scenes, or a sequence." She said not to get hung up on sequences now since next week's class would be devoted to them. However, she wanted me to get comfortable with scenes and slug lines. "Scene 3. Give me the slug line."

I told her that the scene starts with me charging through the doors of the game room to find my sisters. "Does the through-the-door motion count as interior or exterior?"

Laurel rolled her eyes. "Try not to get bogged down in the nitty-gritty. Just do the best you can and we'll fix it later."

"Fine. Exterior and/or Interior of Game Room of Imperial Towers Building 100. Late evening."

Laurel wrote my slug line on the napkin and told me to keep going with my story. She'd sketch it, break out the scenes, make notes, suggestions.

"Here? At the 3 Woos?" I'd never told the story to anyone besides Estie and Ryan. To jump straight to the Mormon Rodeo—not to mention Janet—was a leap.

Janet obviously sensed my panic, because she was filling a plastic cup with some sort of Chinese wine. "Take a sip," she said. "It will settle you down."

"Does Miss Laurel often drive her students to drink?" I asked her.

"No, Chuckerman. You are a first."

Comforted by that knowledge—that this scenario was as new to the Mormon Rodeo as it was to me—I spoke and she wrote, and maybe because she was looking at her napkins and not me or maybe because I was drinking Janet's wine, I felt okay.

I started by explaining that when I banged through the doors of the game room after the fight that night, Rachel was going for high score on Toledo, the room's most challenging pinball machine, with crowds around her two layers deep, thick enough to insulate her from me and our family trouble. I told Janet that Rachel was my other sister, and even today, if you need Rachel's help, as I often do, you've got to practically shove down her front door and wade through her four kids and all of their crap to get it.

Marcy, however, who is and always has been only one year older than me, is and always has been readily available to me, although hers is and always has been advice that one should not be too quick to follow. When I charged through the door of the game room, Marcy, who'd been playing herself in a game of ping-pong, was, as usual, the only one who both noticed and took interest in my presence.

The soundtrack from *Saturday Night Fever* had just been released and played relentlessly in the game room that season. Over the blare of "Jive Talkin'," I gave Marcy a rundown of the card room events. She tossed her paddle on the table and, through repeated nods of the head, indicated her agreement that we should get our parents as quickly as possible.

I explained to Laurel that for me, the urgency came from a sense that death loomed large over Imperial Towers 100—a sense that stemmed, in part, from our family breakfasts, which began with the obits. "See who died?" was the phrase that kicked off my day.

"Try not to talk so much," Janet interrupted. "Movies are a visual medium."

"Think in terms of dialogue," the Mormon Rodeo said. "What did you say to Marcy to convey this urgency?"

"Hurry up," I said as Laurel stuffed egg roll into her mouth—similar to how Marcy stuffed the ping-pong balls into the pockets of her yellow satin disco jacket as she ordered me to run to the stairs.

"Then what?" Laurel asked.

"I followed her," I explained, "because I was younger, and politics and power were age-based then. Had I the presence of mind or the courage, I might have questioned why running down the back corridor of the building and then up eighteen flights of stairs was speedier than heading into the lobby and taking the elevator."

Laurel cut me off. "When you go into the staircase, where does the camera go?"

"Into the lobby," I said. "So the audience can see the ambulance come for Big Sid and the building manager come for my grandfather."

"Then the lobby is a new scene." Laurel pulled out a new napkin and picked up her pen. "Do the slug lines."

Janet couldn't help herself. "SCENE 4. EVENING. INTERIOR LOBBY OF IMPERIAL TOWERS 100. Wherever that is," she added.

I raised my glass in thanks.

"Now give me stage directions," Laurel directed.

"I think I get it now. I'm good to do the rest on my own." I stood up to leave, but the Mormon Rodeo pushed me back down.

"Not so fast. Paint the scene in the lobby."

I couldn't work from memory here because, thankfully, I hadn't seen or heard the circus unfolding in the lobby that night. The noise in the game room had eclipsed the sounds outside, which was a good thing—a great thing—because of all of my fears, the sound of sirens, an advertisement for imminent death, topped my list.

"I wasn't in the lobby that night," I told Laurel. "I can't tell you what happens."

"Make it up, Chuckerman," she hollered. "That's the whole point. Or should I do it for you?" She continued on. "After Marcy and I disappear through the back door of the game room the cameras will head into the lobby, which will be a-brew with the type of chaos audiences love, like people rushing out of card rooms and paramedics rushing in. The audience will enter the lobby as the Miami-Dade ambulance crew storms into the building with stretcher in hand, issuing commands over a megaphone, like, 'Folks, please keep it down and keep out of the way.' The directive will fall on deaf ears—literally and figuratively—as sirens and spectacle overshadow the command." She raised her brows. "I wasn't in the lobby either. How'd I do?"

I told her I understood why she had a following. "Do you want to write the rest of it?" I asked. "That way, if the suicide movie doesn't sell, you'll have a fallback."

The Mormon Rodeo rolled her eyes and asked Janet to refill my glass. Then she ordered me to give the next part a whirl. "Try not to talk in past tense."

I did my best. "Eileen, the building manager, on her own megaphone, will order the crowd to disperse. She'll holler something like, 'Clear the way. There is no loitering allowed in the lobby. If you have nowhere to go, return to your units.'" I paused and looked at Janet and Laurel. "How'd I do?"

They nodded affirmatively, so I went on with the story.

"But megaphones will not be honored that night. Instead the criminal, my grandfather, will carve his path through the throngs as he is ushered towards the elevators. 'Get the hell out of the way,' Slip will tell his peers. To Eileen, he'll say, 'Get the fuck away from me.' Every so often, he'll stop to adjust his cigar or to wink and smile at some of the better-looking women in the crowd.

"The best-looking woman in the building will be there, too. Lucille Garlovsky will be the only resident sporting a bright red miniskirt and five-inch heels and standing separate from the pack. She'll be leaning casually against the door to the building, talking to a paramedic. The audience may glimpse and wonder about her, like the rest of us always did, but they won't get any closer to her until later on, when I do. Instead, another woman will holler, 'Where they taking you, Slippy?'

"'None of your business,' Eileen will answer as the stretcher carrying Big Sid emerges from the game room.

"'No one's taking me anywhere, Belle baby. Don't you worry,' Slip will answer, and as his finger gives the UP button a shove, he'll add, 'I'm going home.'

"As word of Slip's destination reverberates through the lobby, the elevator door will open. Slip, Eileen, Jack Glassman, and as many others who can squeeze into the car without exceeding capacity will load themselves on, and off they'll go."

I slammed my cup down and took a bite of the last egg roll. "There you have it. End of scene. That's a wrap."

Laurel applauded.

"I like it," Janet said.

So, with unanimous approval and another gulp of wine, I moved on to Scene 5.

An hour later, I was standing in front of the Mormon Rodeo's walk-up. We'd said goodbye to Janet, whose constant commentary had gotten to be too much for me, and Laurel had done away with the napkins and instead listened as we walked the ten blocks to her building. She sat down on the steps in front when we arrived, and I kept talking. She had comments, she pointed out scene changes, but by and large she listened until I reached the end.

"You tell quite a story," she said.

I took a little bow. "Thank you."

She was staring at me. She was going to invite me inside. I had no idea the way to a woman's heart, or at least into her apartment, was through my grandfather's story. Who knew stories were aphrodisiacs. If only I could bottle them.

She started to stand. I offered my hand and pulled her up, wondering if the gesture would lead to a kiss—a natural assumption, given our face-to-face positioning.

"Now," she said. "Go home and write it down."

"What?" I told her I thought she was going to invite me inside. I couldn't mask my disappointment, I was too tired. I let it ooze all over my face.

She didn't care. "While everything is fresh in your mind, put it on paper."

"It's eleven o'clock at night, I'm exhausted."

"You'll feel good when you're done."

"How am I supposed to just go home and write it? I only learned about slug lines an hour ago. We didn't even get to dialogue."

She put a hand on my shoulder. "Relax, Chuckerman. Write out the Sentencing Scene exactly like you told me. Start with what happens after your grandfather gets on the elevator with Eileen, since I didn't write down any of that."

I pretended to contemplate her advice while I actually contemplated her hand on my shoulder and the filth that had accumulated on the bottoms of her white pants. "Let me ask you this: are you going to show up at Marcy's bakery on Sunday?"

"Probably." She removed her hand and crossed her arms. Suspicious, and rightfully so.

I told her I'd make her a deal. "If I hand in my scenes to you there, will you go out with me afterwards?"

"On a date?"

I shrugged. "You can call it a date, but I prefer to think of it as a meeting."

As I sat in my kitchen at 11:30 p.m., exhausted, wanting nothing more than to get into bed yet feeling compelled to fulfill my orders from the Mormon Rodeo, I felt like I was in my own personal sentencing scene. NIGHT, the slug line of my life would begin.

INTERIOR OF APARTMENT 22B. FOOL SITS AT KITCHEN TABLE. HE WEARS SWEATPANTS AND SCRATCHES HIS STOMACH WHILE MULLING OVER THE EVENING'S EVENTS, INCLUDING BUT NOT LIMITED TO WHY HE ASKED THE TEACHER ON A DATE AND WHY HE IS LETTING HIMSELF BE BULLIED INTO WRITING A "MOVIE" WHEN HE ISN'T A WRITER AND HE WANTS TO GO TO BED, AND HE SHOULD GO TO BED BECAUSE HE HAS A MEETING IN THE MORNING. WITH A POTENTIAL NEW CLIENT. A BIG ONE.

The truth was, I was too anxious about the meeting to sleep. If I closed this deal, if I landed this client, my whole life would change.

It turned out that the writing, once I got started, was a solid distraction. Somewhere else to put my mind.

SENTENCING SCENE

NIGHT. INT. OF ELEVATOR TRAVELING FROM THE LOBBY TO THE 18TH FLOOR FOLLOWED BY INT. APARTMENT 1812

Maybe, had I not followed Marcy to the stairs, I would have been on the elevator that carried Slip and Eileen. Or, better yet, I might have been on the elevator before Slip's—the one that carried my Grandma B, my other grandmother, my mother's mother, who smoked Marlboros, like my mother, and who happened to be doing so while playing canasta in the Women's Card Room when all hell broke loose in the Men's.

While the elevator lifts, the narrator might explain that to have both sets of grandparents living in Imperial Towers 100 was not the norm, but not unheard of, either. For many similarly situated children, deciding which set of grandparents to stay with each visit was an issue. Some rotated apartments by year, others divided up the single stay, schlepping midway through the vacation on the elevators—like children of broken homes—from one floor to another, suitcases and stuffed animals in tow.

This issue of custody was one that we didn't have to contend with, as Grandma B was a widow and lived with her sister, my mother's aunt BoBo, for the winter. During vacation, Aunt BoBo's apartment was filled with her five grandchildren. She barely had room for Grandma B, and certainly no room for us or the Marlboros. Aunt BoBo (who refused to go by her real name, Barbara, because she felt it was too modern) didn't allow smoking with the kids around.

Consequently, Grandma B spent a lot of time in Apartment 1812. She didn't have a key, but she didn't need to knock, either. If I'd jumped right on an elevator that night, I might already have been in the apartment when she burst through the door a step ahead of Slip, unaware that Gladys Greenberg—Big Sid's sister and a bigwig on the Board—was sitting at the dining room table, poised to listen and hold her every word against Slip. Had I arrived first, I might have had a chance to set the record straight. At least I would have been able to head off the storm.

"Slip just about nearly killed Big Sid. Almost beat him to death. It was vicious." This will be Grandma B's introductory line.

Let me take a minute here to add that the role of Grandma B will have to go to someone under five feet tall, and ideally she will be shot in black and white. The whole scene won't be in black and white, just the character of Grandma B. This will really make a statement, express my grandma's grayness. I know, I digress, but I must make a note to ask Laurel whether this has ever been done in cinematography. If not, I could break new ground. I'll de-color Grandma B—and all of her sisters, for that matter.

Grandma B's introduction was followed immediately by the entrance of Slip, Eileen, Jack Glassman, and eventually all of the onlookers from the lobby, so that by the time Marcy and I climbed our way to the eighteenth floor, it was standing room only outside the door to Apartment 1812.

When I told Laurel this part of the story on our walk to her house, she laughed. She said my childhood sounded crazy.

Maybe it was. I had no idea. I was a kid, and when you're a kid, everything is normal. At least that's the David Robert Melman definition of being a kid. Total acceptance that the events going on around you are par for the course if the adults around you treat them as such.

Anyhow, I easily digested the events of that night in Florida. Yes, they were more exciting than a typical lobby night, but I didn't think they warranted anything like study in a sociology seminar—which Laurel said they plainly did.

Aspects I wouldn't consider twice struck Laurel, like the familiar small talk and platters of food that were disseminated among the crowd. (Several of the neighbors, upon sensing the length of the evening, had run into their kitchens for refreshments. Plates of rugelach and cookies circulated. So did a black forest cake.)

But mainly, Laurel pointed with jealousy to my mother, declaring that her mother was not the type to be caught dead having company with her hair wrapped in a towel.

To my mother, this crowd did not qualify as company. So she did not care how she presented herself, if she presented herself at all. When the people began to pile into the apartment, she hid herself in the bathroom, so when Marcy and I finally burst through the crowds, we couldn't find her. Instead I caught the reflection of my Grandma Estelle in the dining room mirrors. She was tall, especially among that crowd, and standing next to the chair that held Slip. I couldn't see his face or his legs, but every so often a piece of his salmon-colored sweater poked through gaps between bodies.

My father stood next to my grandmother. In the movie, he'll stand over Slip with his hand on Slip's shoulder, pressing him into his seat. His face will be red with anger, and he will be hollering.

At the time, I assumed he was angry with my grandfather. However, I couldn't see Eileen and Gladys Greenberg powwowing in the front corner of the dining room, and I couldn't hear my father's words, since most everyone was hard of hearing and therefore hollering as well. The audience will not be able to make sense of my father's words, either.

Marcy and I shouted back and forth to each other, negotiating our way under elbows and over kitchenette chairs, fighting for air and access to my father. In the movie, cameras will pan the dining room to capture the scene as I recall it: the giant bosoms on the women; my father's dental pick waving in his hand; Ida from 27 sitting in the dental chair, the dental bib still hanging around her neck; my grandmother's solitaire cards frozen mid-game on the dining room table; and her pewter tray, now empty, resting next to it.

The air that night was filled with smoke. And where there was smoke, there was my mother.

"Your grandfather got himself into trouble again," she said, grabbing hold of us from behind and pushing us into the hallway that separated our sleeping area from the kitchen.

"We already know! Davy saw the whole thing," Marcy informed her. "He was in the Men's Card Room the entire time."

My mother wasn't as impressed with this information as I'd anticipated, and it dawned on me that my nightly trips to the card room were not as secret as I'd thought.

I looked up at my mother. "It wasn't Papa's fault. I saw the fight. Big Sid started it. He said bad things about Papa. He asked for it." I felt confident that as an eyewitness, I'd have more credibility than usual. I was wrong.

"Is that so?" My mother raised her brows. The towel lifted slightly too.

"Yes, I swear. I am telling the truth."

She put a hand on my shoulder. "I don't doubt your account of whatever nonsense went down in that card room." She paused and set both hands on her hips in typical mother fashion. "Although, Davy, you had no business being there in the first place."

"Papa says it's fine."

"I'm not interested in what Papa says. I see no reason for you to spend your evenings watching grown men behave like animals. A fine example they set."

Now Marcy's hand went to the spot where she assumed her own hip would one day be. "But since he did witness it, shouldn't he tell everyone what happened? I mean, they'll believe him because he's just a kid."

"Oh, really? Why is that?"

"Kids don't lie."

"I didn't realize." My mother tugged at one of Marcy's pony-tails. Marcy had a reputation for bending the truth like no one's business.

"At least *Davy* doesn't lie," Marcy qualified. "Not about serious stuff like this."

My mother looked at me. "I appreciate you wanting to save the day. But before you take the stand, let me ask you this: Who threw the first punch?"

I looked towards the carpet, not willing to incriminate my grandfather.

She lifted my chin toward her. I murmured my answer so softly that in the movie, the audience will only be able to read my lips when I say, "Papa."

"He shouldn't have hit Sidney," my mother said.

"I don't see why not," Marcy chimed in.

"Basic playground rules. We don't hit."

"There should be an exception to the rule," I whined.

"Go tell that to Gladys Greenberg," my mother said.

"Papa's not going to get in trouble, is he?" I asked. "It's not fair." I leaned into her robe.

"Davy, I wouldn't worry." She pulled me closer. "This isn't prison. Well, in a way it is"—she paused to laugh at her comment—"but your papa's already been to a real one. What kind of punishment can be worse than that?"

In the movie, at these words, the shot should probably cut straight to Gladys Greenberg and Eileen at the dining room table, preparing to hand down Slip's sentence. In real life, however, the conversation continued with my mother running her hands through my hair. "Why don't the two of you put on your pajamas and get in bed?"

"Bed?" Marcy protested. "Everyone will be able to see us lying there."

"And it's so noisy," I added.

My mother reached behind her into the bathroom, where her cigarette had been resting in an ashtray on the countertop. She took a puff and glanced around the apartment.

"I can't argue with that. Watch TV as late as you want, as long as you keep the partition closed."

We did as we were told. We were good kids, amazingly good kids, something my mother never appreciated until Rachel had kids. Marcy and I changed our clothes and yanked on the TV, which was temperamental and showed a picture only when the antenna was tilted just so.

The movie will pick up here with the voice of Eileen, again on her megaphone, screeching through the rooms, reeking with self-imposed power, "Order in the apartment. May I have it quiet, please?"

As Eileen whistles through her fingers, and the crowd draws toward the dining room table, the narrator will explain that vacation seasons were glory days for Eileen, rife with guests and therefore limitless opportunities to impose the limitless rules of Imperial Towers 100, rules that hung on the doorways to every rec-reational potential, rules that were created largely by her.

"I said, *order in the apartment.* This is not a cocktail party, it's a Board meeting." Eileen will nod at Gladys Greenberg, stand-ing at her side with a posse of three other board members. "An impromptu Board meeting."

With a vigorous pushback of her poncho, Gladys Greenberg will say, "A majority of the Board happens to be present, which is enough to proceed." She'll glance around the room and clear her throat. "Violent behavior like this cannot go unpunished. Use of physi-cal force for any reason on the premises of Imperial Towers 100 is a violation of the Condo Association Code, not to mention a blemish on the good name of all our residents. Property values will plummet if such antics continue unfettered. So, after considering the evidence, including the statements of witnesses"—here Gladys Greenberg will pause and gesture to the key witness, my Grandma B—"the Board finds Slip Melman guilty of assault and battery in the Men's Card Room."

"You haven't even seen the assaulted party," Jack Glassman will call out. "Don't you think you should go check on him? He is your brother, after all."

Gladys Greenberg will tell Jack to mind his own business and then give Eileen the floor.

"Punishment for such an act is expulsion from the Men's Card Room for the duration of the seventy-seven season," Eileen will say. "The sentence will begin immediately. The Board will not hear appeals, as we are acting in the best interests of all." She'll turn and raise her hefty brow at Slip.

Slip's expulsion did not occur without protest, a sit-in of seniors. The movie cameras will capture the outrage in full. Above the flying profanity and pounding fists, the audience will hear my Grandma B call Gladys Greenberg a dirty double-crosser and apologize to Slip, promising that she was just telling it like she'd heard it and that she'd meant no harm. They'll hear booing from Ida from 27, who, still stuck in the dental chair, will be capable of nothing more. They'll hear Mickey Leonard, a former lawyer, posit that Slip should not be punished for what amounted to self-defense, and that Grandma B's statement should not have been used against Slip, as it amounted to hearsay. They'll see my eyes, and Marcy's, peering through the partition that separates us from the adults, and they'll see my Grandma Estelle's tears—tears brought on by humiliation and also fear, I see now, at the prospect of Slip without his card room to occupy his days.

Finally, they'll hear the threats of my father, who, unlike my grandfather, has always been soft and measured with his words.

"If I may offer my opinion," he began.

Probably because she needed dental work done, Gladys Greenberg gave him a nod, the okay to proceed.

"This business of sentencing is absurd. Residents cannot be banned from areas of the building for entire seasons."

Eileen and Gladys Greenberg shook their heads, indicating my father was wrong. Crumbs exploded from Gladys Greenberg's mouth as she said, "There's really nothing you can do about it. It's Code."

My father raised his voice. "Is that so? Because I already have an idea about what to do about it." We'll do a close-up here of his eyes (narrowed) and pick (pointed at Gladys's face).

I'd never seen my father in action this way before. To see a little of my grandfather in him made me smile.

"If you even attempt to go through with this," he said, "you can kiss goodbye my days of providing free dental services to your residents."

As the masses flew into a rage at this notion, Slip stood up and shook a fist under Gladys Greenberg's chin. "You wanna know what I'm going to do about it? Why don't you go have a look at your baby brother? That'll give you some idea."

"Slip, enough. Let's put this day to bed. We'll figure out the rest in the morning."

This was my grandmother. Her voice was calm, but she was blotting her eyes with Kleenex, and her long legs wobbled in her heels. "Let's not ask for any more trouble."

Gladys Greenberg laughed. "Isn't that what Slip does best? You ought to know better than any of us, Estelle. I don't know how you put up with it all. The bookmaking . . . the gambling . . . the wandering eye. . . ."

At the mention of the eye, all of the women gasped.

I gasped, too. Then I looked at Marcy. "What's a wandering eye?"

"It's when one eyeball rolls into the other." She crossed her eyes to demonstrate. I watched and accepted this definition for about three more years, until I was old enough to have a wandering eye of my own.

"How dare you," I heard my father say. "How low are you going to sink in order to justify what you are trying to do here?"

I saw my grandfather move his bruised hand open and closed like a mouth. "Let her blah, blah, blah, blah, blah all she wants," he said.

I can hear Slip's voice now as I write, clear as a bell, and since Laurel said to think in terms of dialogue, I think I'll end this scene with him.

"I know what is and what ain't. And I ain't no goddamn cheater."

CHAPTER 6:

The Outing

I strolled into the bakery a few days later, my homework in hand, though no idea in my mind as to what Laurel and I would do on a Sunday morning. I hadn't spoken to her since the 3 Woos. I still didn't understand what had possessed me to ask her out. I figured I'd show up, we'd meet up, and I'd wing it. Nothing big. Nothing anyone else needed to know about. A walk. A bite to eat. As I'd never spent a Sunday morning in the city with a Mormon, I'd see what she wanted to do.

Marcy interrupted my mental planning. "Can we please have a word?" Before the door chimes quieted, she grabbed my arm and pulled me through the crowd of women—women who, surprisingly, remembered me from my reading the previous week. As I passed, they asked me about my movie, if the papers I carried were this week's scene. Who knew I'd become somewhat of a celebrity at the bakery? Nothing to warrant my own perfume, sure, but I'll be honest, as I got yanked by Marcy into the back room, I was sorry to recede from view.

Estie and Ryan followed us, and a few seconds later, the Mormon Rodeo surfaced. She hung back, resting her shoulder against the doorframe, crossing her ankles. Her legs were bare above her boots. Her lips wrapped around a straw that reached into a to-go cup of coffee. The largest-size cup.

Clearly we will not be going for coffee on our date, I thought as I waved to her and held up my papers. "What would you like to do today?"

"I thought we were going to the *Saturday Night Fever* bridge," Ryan said as the Mormon Rodeo executed a series of gestures—a head tip, a brow raise, and a small wave—all while sipping coffee through the straw.

The *Saturday Night Fever* bridge is the Verrazano-Narrows Bridge, the massive suspension bridge that connects Brooklyn to Staten Island, the upper section of the Narrows to the lower, the bridge that Bobby C falls from in *Saturday Night Fever*. The bridge is one of our regular Sunday destinations because *Saturday Night Fever* plays a role in the story of the Cadillac. Visits to the bridge are like field trips: they help give life to my story.

"It seems you double-booked," Marcy said, resting her gloved hands on her stringy hips and pointing her netted head in the direction of the injured parties.

She didn't need to explain. The minute Ryan mentioned the bridge, I registered my mistake. The previous Sunday, the Sunday of my reading at the bakery, I had promised Ryan a trip to the bridge because, due to my debut, I hadn't had time to take him out. At the time I made the deal with Laurel outside her apartment, I'd forgotten my promise; in fact, I'd forgotten until right now. Ryan, of course, had not.

Everyone stared at me. The females, Estie included, smirked. Already, without even leaving the bakery, my Sunday morning had become an outing—not the literal but the figurative kind, the kind that means you've been exposed, that family members now know that you've been carrying on in some way, no matter how innocent, with someone no one would ever have suspected you'd carry on with, like a member of your same sex or of a different religion or, in this case, your sister's friend from yoga, your Mormon teacher from Utah, the one moving to Los Angeles, the one with whom you have nothing in common and no future and who, as a favor to your sister, gave you a seat in her class in effort to help you grow up, settle down, and get serious.

"You promised," Ryan said. Then he added that too many girls were in the bakery, he needed to get out. "They're making me dizzy."

"Let's all relax," I said, palming my nephew's head with my free hand. I shook Marcy's hand from the wrist of my other and motioned for the Mormon Rodeo to come on over. "How does everyone feel about going together?" I asked. Like the best ideas do, this one came to me off the cuff, the way Share 'N Share Alike, Share's fragrance, had come to me while listening to Marcy discipline her kids.

As I made the suggestion, I realized that I felt great about the idea. Not only did it give us a destination, it gave me a buffer, in the same way that when I was a kid I preferred to have my sisters with me when I was in the company of Grandma B.

"Are you out of your mind?" Marcy now asked. "You'll take the kids to the bridge next week. Today, you'll take Laurel on your date."

"Did you say 'date'?" I asked. "I think you are mistaken." I looked at the Mormon Rodeo. "This is not a date, it's a meeting. Isn't that right, Laurel?"

She uncrossed her legs and then recrossed them the opposite way. "Yes, by prior agreement, it is only a meeting."

"Well if it's only a meeting," Estie said with finger quotes around *meeting*, "we can go, too."

Ryan agreed, and Laurel said she didn't mind going to the bridge. With that, the figurative outing became a literal one. A family one.

"Not so fast," Marcy said, grabbing my wrist again. With the other hand, she motioned for the others to go on without me. "Go with Laurel to the car," she told the kids. "David will be there in a minute."

During that minute, Marcy made clear that I was not to start up any sort of romantic relationship with her friend Laurel.

"Then why were you encouraging our date?"

She let go of my wrist and stuck her head in an oven. She removed her head and a tray of muffins simultaneously. "Because I thought a date with a mature woman would be good for you. That doesn't mean I think a date with an immature man would be good for Laurel."

"For your information, I hadn't planned on starting up any sort of relationship with the Mormon Rodeo. Especially with your children in the car. I'm only looking to get through the day."

"You actually call her the Mormon Rodeo?"

"Not to her face."

Marcy rolled her eyes. "Well that just proves my point."

"Which is?"

Our conversation paused as the teenage helpers came into the back room to get both more pastries and Marcy. Her friends, they said, were looking for her. They made no mention of my fans missing me. Apparently my fifteen minutes were up. Marcy, however, still had one more minute left. She told the girls she'd be out in sixty seconds and continued.

"You couldn't possibly have any genuine interest in her, and she's in a delicate place right now, so stay away."

"I love the way women talk. A delicate place—what does that mean? Are you trying to say that she's moving to Los Angeles and she's not thrilled about it?"

"It's a little more complicated than that," Marcy said. "But she told you she's moving?"

I asked her why Laurel's situation was more complicated.

"All I'm saying is that she's trying to figure some things out, she's seeking clarity, and you have a tendency to muddy the waters. So just . . . just stick to Share or whatever teenager you're currently making up from scratch."

"Words I never thought I'd hear. You must mean business." I told her as I turned to go that she had my word, but then I turned back. "Why do you think I couldn't have any real interest in her?"

"C'mon. Anyone who finds Share appealing is not going to like Laurel. Venn Diagrams, David." She held up two chocolate donuts. "You've got the circle of bright women with dysfunctional families and horrible hair and then you have the circle of starlets with their own perfume lines. The two circles don't intersect."

"Is that so?" I said, grabbing the donuts. "We'll see about that."

She told me to leave the donuts, which I didn't, and get out of the bakery, which I did.

⁓————

The air was hot. It was going to be a doozy of a Manhattan day. A perfect day for a ride. An ideal day to roll down the windows, crank the radio, sprawl across the backseat, like Estie and Ryan did, and head to Brooklyn.

Even under the best conditions, the bridge is not a quick trip. We are usually in for a thirty-minute haul. We go Houston Street, to West, to the Henry Hudson Parkway, through the Battery Tunnel into Brooklyn, and across Brooklyn to the bridge. We cross over the bridge to Staten Island—screaming as we go, because I'm scared to death of bridges, of the water beneath, of the space in between. Then we return, sometimes coming to rest in Brooklyn on the grass near the bridge, just like Tony Manero and Stephanie did in *Saturday Night Fever*. We get hot dogs, play cards, and toss rocks in the water until a cop asks us to stop.

Laurel did not seem to be as comfortable in the Caddy as were my other passengers. One hand clutched her coffee cup, the other pressed her messenger bag to her side. Her hair blew wild, her words barely escaped her mouth without strands of hair blocking them.

"This is not what I imagined," she hollered.

"What's not?" I asked, turning down the radio.

"Your Cadillac," she said. "The shrine. I thought it would be a little more grand, a little less cluttered." She pulled an empty Frito bag from the heel of her boot.

I grabbed the bag and tossed it into the backseat. "Based on what?"

From the backseat came Estie's voice: "From your movie, duh."

"Right," I said. The concept that those who read my work would gain insight into my personal life without me telling them a thing had never dawned on me until this moment. I shook my head slowly, like one tends to do when the light bulb goes on.

"Did you like it?" Estie asked. She told Laurel that she'd read the scene that introduces the car in the bakery.

Laurel said she'd heard about the reading that morning. "I wish I could have heard it," she added, noting that as far as she knew, a public reading was a first for any of her students. "But I did read it and yes, I liked it." She leaned toward me. "I gave you an F for format but an A for description."

"I'll take it," I said.

"You painted quite a picture. There is clearly a disconnect between the reality of the car and what lives in your mind."

"I beg to differ," I said, quickly brushing onto the floor some crumbs left over from the annual Slip Melman Birthday Ride cake.

"Don't be offended," Laurel said. "That's one of the reasons we write."

"To misrepresent?"

"To immortalize. To remember a time, a person, an object, maybe all of the above, as we want them to be remembered."

"Why do we need to remember the Cadillac?" Ryan asked, finally interested enough in the conversation to sit up. "She still runs like a son-of-a-gun. Doesn't she, David? Even with 200,000 miles on her."

"I'm sure," Laurel said. She sipped her coffee through the straw, seemingly eager to drop the topic. But her silence just got her further into the hot seat.

"You want to drive it?" Ryan asked.

She shook her head and said that she was good where she was.

"Go ahead," I said. We were still in the city. "I'll pull over, you can take it a block or two. Maybe it will enhance your appreciation of it."

"You should give it a try," Ryan told her. "Uncle Davy doesn't let many people behind the wheel." He paused to throw his torso into the front seat. "I've been behind the wheel," he said, and he explained how he and Estie sit on my lap in empty lots and steer while I press the pedals. "But my mom's never driven it. Neither has Aunt Rachel. No one has. Not even Share."

"Share can't drive anything," Estie offered. "Mom says she's not old enough to have her license."

"Of course she is old enough," I said, more in defense of myself than Share.

"Well I'm old enough," Laurel said. "But I don't have my license."

The three of us stared at her.

"You don't have your license?" Ryan asked.

Laurel shook her head, oblivious to the outrage of her fellow passengers.

"Why not?" I asked.

"I don't drive," Laurel said.

I almost ran off the road, right into the Hudson River.

"What do you mean, *you don't drive*?" Estie took the words out of my mouth. My niece and nephew were as shocked as I was. The Melman family learned the importance of driving during the Christmas season of 1977, and I've made sure that all subsequent Melmans have understood that lesson as well.

Laurel explained without embarrassment that she only possessed an expired Utah driver's license, and she hadn't driven since she moved to New York. "New York has everything I could ever want, and I don't have to get behind the wheel of a car to get it," she said. "Last summer, over the Fourth of July holiday, I had the corner grocer deliver of a bag of marshmallows—a single bag—because I had writer's block and a sweet tooth, and it was raining."

"What's the point of living in New York City if you're not going to go outside?" I asked.

"That's the whole point," she said.

"If that's so, then you have no business moving to Los Angeles," I said. "You're going to have to take three highways to get that same bag of marshmallows."

Laurel shrugged and sipped her coffee.

"You're moving to Los Angeles?" Estie asked.

"I'm planning on it," Laurel said. She explained to Estie, as she had to me, that if she could sell her movie, she could stay in New York. She also explained, in more detail than I'd heard before, that in the movie she was writing, the father of a wealthy Utah family loses his fortune and then commits suicide in order to free up insurance money for his family. "Before he commits suicide, he comes to New York to say goodbye to his estranged son. He kills himself by throwing himself off a bridge. I was thinking of using the Brooklyn Bridge in my film, but I suppose the Verrazano will do."

"The Verrazano Bridge is actually better than the Brooklyn Bridge for your movie," Estie said. "It gets way more suicides. There's even a sign at the bottom that says 'Life is Worth Living.' But it doesn't work."

"I don't think the issue is which bridge, I think the debate should be about whether jumping off a bridge is a realistic method of suicide," I said. "No one in their right mind would throw themselves over the side of a bridge."

"Plenty of people kill themselves with bridges," Laurel said.

"That's why there's a sign," Estie added.

"Well, they're all nuts," I said.

"Exactly," Laurel said. "They are committing suicide."

"If I were to commit suicide, jumping off a bridge is the last thing I'd do," I offered.

"You don't strike me as the suicide type," she said.

"Why not?"

"You're wearing a Cubs shirt and Air Jordans. You're way too young at heart." I didn't offer, because I didn't want to ruin my image, that I'm way too faint of heart as well. I like to play it safe. I couldn't fathom stepping onto and looking over the side of the Verrazano, which was what Laurel planned to do once we reached the bridge. Research, she called it, getting in touch with her father-character's mindset before he takes the plunge. She wanted to touch the edges of the bridge, observe the water "roil" beneath, feel the rush of the cars as they passed, hang over the side.

"You're crazy," I told her.

The Verrazano-Narrows Bridge is a two-story structure. It has six lanes on the bottom, six on top, all for cars, none for pedestrians. So on our return trip out of Brooklyn, I pulled into the far right-hand lane, put on my hazards, and prayed as Estie and Ryan hopped out with Laurel, who took them where no Melman—except for one—whose exploits were about to be a major motion picture—had gone before: to the edge.

The kids, like the Mormon Rodeo, viewed the outing as an

adventure instead of an accident waiting to happen. I watched them disappear from my side mirror. The second hand ticked away on the dashboard clock as I waved traffic around me and waited. Cars passed; my car trembled. So did my hands. The wind blew, steamy and strong—which was, apparently, why Laurel's immediate takeaway from her near-death experience was that her hair totally frizzed.

"Look at me," she said, hopping back into her seat and pulling down on the sun visor to get to the vanity mirror.

I couldn't tell the difference between her hair before and after, but I knew enough to keep that to myself.

"I should have wrapped my hair in a towel first," she said. "Like your mother." She rummaged through her bag and cursed the fact that she didn't have anything with her for her hair.

Looking at me through the rearview mirror, Estie again reminded me, "From the first scene of your movie." Then she reached into her purse and pulled out a thick, hot pink ponytail holder with blue and purple sequins around it. She handed it over the seat to Laurel, who thanked her, gathered her hair onto the top of her head, and secured it there, like a pompom.

As she wrapped her hair, and I attempted to merge us back into moving traffic, I said, "You know, you know more about me than most people, including most of the people I've dated, and I've hardly had to speak a word to you." I had to yell to be heard, so I paused while I rolled up my window, hoping the glass would keep the noise of the expressway from interfering with my profound statement. "I think we're onto something. Everybody ought to show up on dates with scripts. They'd save a lot of time and talking."

"Most people's scripts aren't as autobiographical as yours," Laurel said.

"It isn't even really a script," Estie said. "It's more like a story that he is calling a script."

"Estie, my dear, let's not waste our time trying to pigeonhole," I said, elbowing Laurel. "The teacher says we're not supposed to get bogged down in semantics."

Laurel laughed. "I can't stop thinking about your mother in

that towel. My father would never have allowed my mother to walk around in public with her hair wrapped like that."

"Why not?" Estie asked.

"He's an asshole." Laurel offered the information no differently from how she answered questions in class. Straightforward. Matter-of-fact. She apologized to my niece and nephew for her language and added, "A real spare-the-rod-spoil-the-child type of guy." She busied herself with a few seconds of scenery watching before adding, "He'd have been better off, we all would have been better off, had he done like Bobby C and thrown himself off the Verrazano-Narrows Bridge."

This information was more than I'd bargained for on a Sunday outing, especially a family one, but Laurel did not seem to feel sorry for herself, so I decided to not feel sorry for her either, although that was my instinct.

"Bobby C didn't throw himself off; he was drunk and he fell," Ryan said. "It was an accident."

"No, he killed himself," Estie said. "He got the girl pregnant, he didn't want to marry her, the priest wouldn't help, so he had no choice. He was Catholic."

As they went back and forth as to whether Bobby C committed suicide or not, Laurel said, "Aren't they too young to be studying *Saturday Night Fever*?"

"No such thing as too young. Not when you're studying under Uncle David."

"Well, if I ever need a sub to teach my class, I know who to ask."

"Sure," I told her. "I can step in this week if you're covering *Saturday Night Fever*, *The Big Lebowski*, or *Caddyshack*."

"How about *Schindler's List*?" Laurel asked. She explained that she was using a clip from *Schindler's List* in our next class to demonstrate sequences. "The Ghetto Liquidation scene," she said. "The part where—"

"Sorry, can't help you there," I interjected.

"You never saw *Schindler's List*?"

I shook my head.

"Oy."

Objectively speaking, Laurel—a six-feet-tall (with the pom-pom) Mormon in cowboy boots with an abusive dad and no ability to drive—was as foreign as foreign could be. Yet if I closed my eyes and changed Laurel's rasp to a slightly higher pitch, I would have sworn I was sitting next to my mother.

"Is that something else they teach you in conversion class? How to make your fellow Jews feel guilty about not seeing *Schindler's List*?"

Laurel said her disapproval had nothing to do with religion. "*Schindler's List* is a classic. As a film writer, you should see it. I don't care what you do as a Jew."

"My grandmother does," Estie offered. She hung her torso over the front seat and explained how happy my mother would be if Laurel showed the movie in class because she's been trying for years to get me to see it. "She even sent him a copy of it in the mail."

"You can borrow it for your class," I told Laurel as I shoved Estie back onto her seat.

Laurel laughed. Then she sighed and sat back against her own seat. For a while we traveled in silence, everyone content to look out their respective windows. Laurel still had her cup of coffee tucked in between her legs. Every so often she'd take a sip, and I wondered how she could bear to drink cold coffee. Mostly, she rode with the side of her head pressed against the window. I couldn't tell if she was thinking about something—her movie, maybe—or just watching the scenery.

I thought about asking her what was on her mind, but I stayed silent and kept my eyes on the road, which was congested. The Cadillac was nothing if not hard to maneuver, so focusing on driving was probably not a bad way to go. Besides, I figured, maybe she wasn't thinking about anything. Maybe she was just enjoying the ride—something I've never been able to do. My wheels are always spinning. I've clocked more miles in my head than my Caddy will ever see on the road. In this moment, for instance, I was thinking about how Laurel could move to Los Angeles without a license, a car, or the desire to drive.

So, after we dropped Estie and Ryan back at my sister's Union Square apartment, I shoved my car into a spot on 14th and offered to buy the Mormon Rodeo a pretzel in Union Square Park. I also offered to give her driving lessons.

She said yes to the pretzel but no to the driving lessons. Later on, Marcy would say that in her opinion, getting experience with women who eat carbs was more important for me than spending time with women who drive. I, however, found Laurel's decision disturbing. What kind of woman doesn't want to drive?

We walked into the park and talked. Laurel learned about my day job, my business, and my latest project—the big deal I was about to land—branding perfume for a pop star whose identity I could not reveal to Laurel due to a confidentiality agreement. She shrugged and said she'd probably never heard of her, anyway. I told her, as I pointed us in the direction of the statue of George Washington and his horse, that she may not have heard of her, but she may soon smell her. "She wants me to create a signature scent," I explained. "Its distinguishing aspect, what will set it apart from the pack, is that it will mark everything. Her CDs, concert tickets, the T-shirts she sells at the concerts. We're going to call it Omnipotence." I shouldn't have divulged the name of the campaign, but Laurel didn't strike me as the gossipy kind.

She didn't strike me as that interested, either. She laughed and called the concept cheesy.

I told her I didn't disagree. "It is cheesy."

"Then why is this mystery pop star going through with such a campaign, aside from the fact that her ego is obviously out of control? Doesn't she care that her handler, or whatever you are, thinks her idea is lousy?"

I shrugged, took a sip of my Coke, and sat on the stone wall across from George. "I don't know, I didn't tell her." As Laurel sat down next to me, I added, "Sometimes you have to make room at the table for the little white lie."

"Not in my business," she said. "Writers need to tell it like it is."

"I thought writers weren't supposed to tell it like it is. I thought we were supposed to live somewhere in between writing what we know and what we don't."

"Factually, yes. But you have to come from a place of honesty.

Your characters don't have to be honest, but you need to be honest about them."

"Is that so?"

Laurel pulled her knees to her chest and her boots onto the edge of the wall. My eyes went to her boots. They were beat up, I could see now, and faded to the color of the stone base on which George Washington and his horse were resting. This was, I realized, the closest I'd been to the boots, probably to Laurel herself, and I'd be lying if I said I didn't feel like touching her. On her arm, her leg—which was only an inch or two away—it didn't matter. Not because of any feeling of affection towards her, I told myself, but just because I was a guy, she was a girl, and there she was. But she was moving to LA, and Marcy had told me not to start with her, and so I didn't. Instead, as a hacky sack flew over Laurel's head and into the bushes, I touched her boots.

"You think you are telling it like it is when you say it's not a problem to live in Los Angeles without knowing how to drive?"

She didn't answer. Instead, she asked, "Why do you care so much?" Her head was bent over her pretzel, which she'd been separating into miniature pieces that she was eating one by one. She was more reserved with the pretzel then she'd been with her egg roll, which I found disappointing.

"Good question," I said. And it was. Why did I care? Because I grew up caring? The story of my car, she would soon see, if I kept writing and she kept reading, was caused by my caring about my grandmother—who, like Laurel, was scared to drive. "Let's just say the idea of a woman not being comfortable behind the wheel of a car doesn't sit well with me. It makes me anxious."

"Interesting," she said. She popped another piece of pretzel into her mouth. "You're really layered, Chuckerman."

"What does that mean?"

She said she'd give a whole lecture on layered characters in class in a few weeks.

"I'm not a character," I told her, taking a piece of pretzel. "What does layered mean in real life?"

"It means that you are a piece of work."

Maybe I was. Hadn't Marcy expressed essentially the same

sentiment on the day of the Birthday Ride? Hearing it from Marcy's mouth, however, I'd been insulted. From Laurel, I felt proud. "Talk about the pot calling the kettle black," I said. "You are floating between religions and between coasts, and you wish your dad had flung himself off a bridge."

"So you see now why driving a car is the least of my issues."

"I think, actually, it might be the key to your salvation."

"Yeah, as much as your mother believes that *Schindler's List* is the key to yours."

I told her we would see, and that I might not even attend the next class, given that I had no desire to see *Schindler's List*. Nor did I see a need, given that she'd already taught me about sequencing at the 3 Woos.

"That was just an overview," she told me, and added that based on the pages I'd handed over to her at the bakery, which she'd apparently looked at when I ran Estie and Ryan into their building, I didn't even grasp the basic concept. "You can't just schlock scenes together and call it a sequence."

"Schlock?" I asked. "Is that a technical term?"

"I used it well, didn't I? The rabbi says I have a flair for Yiddish vocabulary. He's teaching some to me on the side. A *biseleh*—a little bit," she translated. "It's very onomatopoetic." She crossed one leg over the other so that her boot came to rest on my leg.

I stared at it. Marcy had said to not lay a hand on her, but she'd left unaddressed a scenario in which Laurel set a foot on me. Slowly, as if to sneak by myself, I wrapped my hand around the ankle of the boot. Not wanting to see her reaction, I stared at my hand, at the scar running down my pinkie. When I was four, my finger got jammed in the door of a Tilt-a-Whirl car. My finger's extraction required the ride to temporarily shut down. Its repair required five stitches. Sometimes I wonder if this calamity at my first carnival wasn't the catalyst, to borrow a term from Laurel, of my doom-and-gloom mindset. Or maybe mindsets are genetic. Who knows?

What I did know was that Laurel had a striking command of Yiddish, as she was now throwing around Yiddish expressions with the fluency of the folks in Imperial Towers Building 100.

"What kind of rabbi teaches Yiddish on the side?" I asked as I removed my hand and returned it to my own lap.

Laurel, who seemed far more interested in her pretzel and her language skills than in me, showed no reaction to this move. She was now pulling off even tinier pieces than before and tossing them to the birds. As she did so, she explained that the rabbi was a former student of hers. "He gave me permission to take the conversion classes for research. But now he's really pushing me to convert."

"Interesting. You'd be a Jew in cowboy boots," I said, gesturing toward her feet. "Actually, that's not a bad title for a movie, *Jews in Boots*. Maybe you should try that instead of the Mormon suicide flick."

Laurel rolled her eyes. "Don't you take anything seriously?"

I stirred the straw in my Coke as I explained to her that I take everything seriously. I told her my theory, that history repeats itself. "I'm sure another Holocaust is somewhere around the corner, which is why I refuse the catharsis of *Schindler's List* and why I make the jokes. In the end, what else can you do? Life is going to play out the way it's going to play out. One can only hope to survive the ride."

"Wow," Laurel said. "Catharsis." She stared at me for a few awkward seconds. "It's dark beneath your Cubs hat." She hit its brim. "Chuckerman has a dark side. Who would have thought?"

I repositioned the hat on my head. "Practical, not dark," I said. "Which is why you really ought to know how to drive. Forget getting groceries, you never know when you might have to get out of town quick."

A year earlier, we might have bantered about emergencies, discussed them as fictional scenarios. The kind of thing that happened in movies. We knew better now.

"What if there's another 9/11? A nuclear attack?" I asked. Amid the green of the trees, the spray of the fountains, the blue of the sky, a nuclear attack admittedly did not seem imminent. But then again, neither had 9/11.

"If there is a nuclear attack," she told me, "I'll be throwing myself off the Verrazano Bridge."

"Really?" I asked. "It was that good, huh? Well, I'll be in the Caddy. Windows up, doors locked, because if there's one thing that can survive the big one, it's that car."

Laurel adjusted her pompom of hair atop her head and raised her brows. "So we won't be going down together? No *Titanic* ending for us?"

"Almost," I told her. "Except that in our movie, you'll be jumping in, and I'll be going down with the ship. If we're lucky, we'll meet up on the other end."

"Romantic."

I shrugged. "That's me."

CHAPTER 7:

Sequencing and Seeing the Forest Through the Trees

⟋⟍

"*I*f you just string together scenes, your movie won't move," Laurel told us during Class 3, the one to which I am now referring to as The Holocaust.

"To keep things forward-moving, your scenes need to flow so seamlessly that the audience doesn't notice where one ends and another begins."

I felt like she was speaking directly to me, as we both knew stringing had been my plan of attack. Her ponytail swung with enthusiasm as she fiddled with the VCR, readying the class for the much-anticipated film clip, our first visual of the session.

Curiously, she was wearing a bathrobe over her clothes, a bright pink number with colored flowers scattered around it. Even more curious, Estie's sequined hair band secured her sky-high ponytail. The getup did not say "*Schindler's List* Day" to me, and as

I watched her adjust the TV, I prayed that she'd decided to switch the movie to *Grease*. *She definitely resembled Sandra D*, I thought, as she continued talking.

"In order to flow, each scene must have a reason to exist," she said.

"How do you know if a scene has a reason to exist?" I might have asked had I not been distracted by her outfit and work.

I'd had a rough day at the office. My fragrance chemist—a woman named Ezmerelda Rich, a perfume pro who used to work for Chanel, had a gift for essential oils and a sniffer like you would not believe, and was the genius behind all my scents—was having a problem with the Omnipotence concept. She, like Laurel, felt the concept was cheesy, and she didn't want to attach her name to the project. According to Ezmerelda, her process was an art. Using her oils and odorants on anything other than human skin—like concert tickets—would compromise the integrity of her work and, ergo, her good name—which, by the way, I created for her.

I begged Ezmerelda, formerly Lizbeth Klonsky, to take the chance on the concept and if the venture went south, we'd get her a new name. She told me that this wasn't a joking matter. "You either need to find another chemist or get me a lot more money," she threatened before she walked out the door.

As I thought about all this, Candy stole my question. "How do you know if a scene has a reason to exist?"

With a shove of a tape into the VCR, Laurel answered. "Ask yourself this: 'How does my scene fit into the big story I want to tell?' A movie is about relationships, not just between characters or between various plots but between the whole story and the individual scenes. Whether your movie flows depends on how well each scene fits in with the one that comes before it and the one that follows." She yanked the strap around her waist tight and began to walk up and down the aisles. "Take a close look at my robe as I pass by you," she said as she paced.

As the student body admired hers, Laurel explained that her mother, a woman named Darlene, knit and embroidered as a hobby. "She makes her stuff during the winter, and during the summer, she travels around to art fairs to sell it. That's basically all she does," she said, "except for going to church every Sunday."

Laurel picked up the bottom of the robe and lifted it straight out. "The robe is made up of thousands and thousands of stitches, but you can't see them, can you? That's because my mother is an expert, the Steven Spielberg of seamstresses. You only see a robe, or an afghan, or whatever it is she's made. No stitches. No seams." She made her way back to the front of the room, where she dropped her arms, grabbed her copy of *Schindler's List* from her desk, and waved it at us. "The same is true of a well-made movie. When you write, your eye needs to stay focused on the big picture. The individual scenes should be so fluid that they are not noticeable. Sequencing helps with this." She picked up the remote and started pressing buttons. "It helps you see the forest through the trees."

I groaned. Internally. Seeing the forest through the trees has never been my forte. Where I come on strong is getting ensnared in minutiae. I glom onto occurrences that are insignificant to the normal human eye—random remarks or behaviors, like Laurel's use of Estie's ponytail holder. I retrofit. I take trees and I build a forest around them.

Flash forward, for example, to our family dinner on the Sunday following this class, where I declared that Laurel's choice of dress and film clips proved that she could never assist me with personal growth. "Talk about the blind leading the blind," I told Marcy and Broc. "She's definitely got screws loose. She wore a cheery pink bathrobe and Estie's matching ponytail holder while she showed us clips from *Schindler's List*. Including the worst part, the Ghetto Massacre, when the Nazis liquidated—"

"I know the part, David," Marcy said.

"Not only did she play it," I said, "she *replayed* it." Then I explained the whole rundown of events.

Well, not the entire rundown. I left out the part where Don asked me if I'd scored with the teacher. This question came as the first clip got underway, as smoke from a lone Sabbath candle morphed into smoke from a steam engine and the picture shifted from color to black and white. I didn't answer Don. I pretended I was watching the screen but in reality I was squirming in my skin, preparing myself for the Liquidation, which didn't come as quickly as I'd anticipated. I squirmed as we watched a few other sequences that were supposed to shed light on Schindler's character and show his evolution from self-serving asshole to savior. Laurel, all the while, sung Spielberg's praises as a master of imagery and character development while Don sang his own praises as master of the opposite sex. He yakked about how he and I were cut from the same cloth, we were both players, and if I had any sense, if I could see the forest through the trees, I'd have a fling with the teacher.

I nodded but stayed quiet, primarily out of respect for the millions about to get massacred on screen but also for myself. No need to tell Don that I wasn't much of a flinger. He wouldn't believe me. Based on my bachelor status, the girls I've dated, the clothes I wear, people often assume that I conduct my personal life in the same slapdash manner in which I'm writing my movie, that I string one girl after another without thought. But that's not the case. I'm not a one-night-stand kind of guy. I date my clients, generally, and although they are in no position to get serious, that doesn't mean I don't take our relationships seriously. I'm invested in their careers. I care about them as people. The sex eventually ends, but our relationships carry on ad nauseam. Just this week, I gave hours of free counsel to Share and to Mini Francis, my first discovery, who is now debating whether or not to star in a Broadway revival of *Annie Get Your Gun*. Beneath the expensive suit, I'm a softie who tends to carry the weight of everyone else's worlds on his shoulders—which was why the Liquidation sequence was too much for me to bear.

I told this to Marcy. How for sixteen minutes, we watched a sequence depicting the deportation of Jews from the Warsaw Ghetto. How, a few minutes in, Candy started crying. How Judd, the dude with the long hair who sits next to her and now apparently dates her, squeezed her hand and wiped a tear from her face. How the class sighed. How at Candy's request, Laurel replayed the Ghetto Liquidation sequence for closer study. How at my request, Laurel allowed me to sit in the hall during the replay, because once was enough. I didn't need to see any more.

"It was awful," I said as I sat at Marcy's kitchen table and helped Estie spread paper plates around it.

"So awful that when she came to check on you in the hall, you asked her if she wanted to make out," Marcy said.

Laurel must have told her this tiny detail, because I certainly hadn't.

"I was just lightening the mood," I told her. "Making a joke."

"David, it was *Schindler's List*."

"Exactly," I said as the pizzas descended upon the table. Estie, Ryan, Marcy, Broc, and I gathered around, as we did every Sunday night, for slices and a conference call with the faction of my family that remains in Chicago. "I assumed she'd seen *Seinfeld*. Who hasn't seen *Seinfeld*?"

"Laurel, obviously," Marcy said.

"I don't see how it's possible for someone to not know *Seinfeld*. It's like someone from Elizabethan England not knowing Shakespeare."

"Maybe Mormons don't watch TV," Broc suggested.

Marcy told her kids not to listen to their father.

"If you ask me," I offered, "it's in poorer taste to make out during *Schindler's List* if you haven't seen *Seinfeld*. At least if you've seen it—"

Broc told his kids to tune out the entire conversation.

"She didn't make out with you, David, she gave you a peck." Clearly, Laurel had gotten to Marcy.

"I don't know where you are getting your information, but that kiss was full-on. Lips. Tongue. The works." I took a bite of pizza, and with a full mouth, continued with my interpretation of events. "She was all in. I didn't know what hit me."

This was true. One minute I was making a wisecrack, and the next Laurel's hands were on my shoulders and her lips were pushing against mine.

"By the time my mind caught up to reality, the moment was over. The door was opening, and the Mormon Rodeo was guiding me through it." I told my family that I watched the final minutes of the Liquidation oblivious, numb, anesthetized to the gunfire lighting the sky, to the bullets ringing out. Estie and Ryan laughed, but I was speaking the truth. Amid the cacophony of ghastly sights and sounds, while Laurel lectured about how Spielberg used the sequence to contrast Schindler to Goethe, how he used cinematography to illustrate the turning point for Schindler, while my classmates dabbed their eyes, there I sat, stunned and thinking about sex with the Mormon Rodeo.

"God cannot not be pleased," I said as I helped myself to another slice of sausage and onion. "He'll find a way to punish me. It wouldn't surprise me if He tanked the Omnipotence deal."

"You are pathetic if you think that souring a business deal is the worst thing God can do."

No one listened to Marcy. The jokes about the demise of Melman, Inc. due to a botched *Seinfeld* reference kept rolling. We were still laughing when the rest of the Melman family—my parents and my sister Rachel and her family—rang in from Chicago, as they do every Sunday night. "What's so funny?" my mother asked.

And just like that, my relationship with Laurel became a family affair. This, obviously, was the worst thing God could do.

I groaned again. This time externally. I didn't need a sequencing class to see that my personal life had become a sequence run amok. My class, my teacher, my family, even my movie were all starting to seem like a seamless flow.

"I love her already," my mother said after Marcy filled her in on the necessary details.

The phone rested on the lid of the pizza box in the middle of the table. I leaned over it and questioned my mother. "What do you mean, you love her? You don't even know her."

"What else do I need to know?"

"For one thing, she's Mormon."

"So what?" my mother countered. "She's seen *Schindler's List*, which is more than you can say for yourself. And she was bold enough to make the first move, which shows she's comfortable in her own skin." My mother, queen of the quick fix and, as such, a lover of platitudes, has always been big on being comfortable in one's own skin.

"She's also moving to Los Angeles," I announced. "So let's not get too excited about her."

Broc interjected that he thought the move to LA was reason to get excited about the Mormon Rodeo. "No strings attached. Right, Pete?"

Peter, Rachel's husband, asked Broc who the Mormon Rodeo was while Marcy yelled at Broc for egging me on.

Ignoring them both, my mother asked when she was moving. "I hope she'll still be in New York when we come in October for Yom Kippur."

Now my father joined the conversation. "I didn't realize Mormons had flings."

Peter, the head of the US Attorney's office in Chicago, a man with an answer to everything, said, "What else is polygamy if not a permanent fling?"

"This is all wasted conversation, anyway," Marcy said. "She's converting."

"To what?" Rachel asked.

"Judaism," Estie answered as she pulled off the cheese from her pizza and handed it to Ryan—another reliable part of the dinner routine.

"She's not really converting," I said. "She's just taking conversion classes."

"Who bothers to take conversion classes if they aren't going to convert?" my mother asked.

"The classes are just research for a movie," I explained.

"Isn't that like fraud?" Rachel said.

For reasons having more to do with my relationship with Rachel than with Laurel, I felt the need to prove that Laurel wasn't acting in bad faith. I shared some of what Laurel had told me during our conversation in Union Square Park—that the rabbi, a former student of hers, had suggested she sit in on his classes and participate to any extent she deemed helpful to understanding the character of the gay son's boyfriend in the movie she was writing. "She made clear she wasn't going to take her research as far as the Mikvah," I said. "But she's now six months into the process, she has a Passover under her belt, and she's tossing around the concept of keeping kosher. The rabbi is also teaching her Yiddish on the side," I added to bolster my case.

My mother squealed. The news of the conversion combined

with *Schindler's List* was as glorious to her as the meringue and apple pies Estie and Ryan were now pulling from the freezer.

Marcy got up to help them with the pies and motioned for me to follow. "Yiddish, apparently, isn't all he's teaching her on the side," she whispered.

"What do you mean?" I whispered back. Meanwhile, the conversation was still going on over the phone. I heard my mother comment that even if Laurel didn't convert, she obviously felt some affiliation, since she used *Schindler's List* as a teaching tool.

Marcy shrugged. "That's the rumor, that's all I'm saying. It's not my place to say anything more." She picked up the now sliced pies and handed them to me. "But when I told you to stay away, there was a reason."

"*She* kissed me," I reminded her as we headed back to the table and Rachel said, "I still think it's odd to use *Schindler's List* as a teaching tool."

"If I were teaching the class, I'd use Steven Spielberg, too," Marcy said.

"I'd use the Coen Brothers," Broc interjected. "I'd have shown *The Big Lebowski.*"

I laughed. So did Peter.

My mother ignored us. "Marcy is right. If this girl teaches at NYU, I'm sure she knows what she's doing. Anyway, at least now you've seen a clip of *Schindler's List*. I'm just happy about that."

Irritated by the news that the Mormon Rodeo might be sleeping with the rabbi, I decided to jump on Rachel's bandwagon. "It's not like Steven Spielberg only made one movie. She could have picked a clip from *E.T.*—or *Jaws*, even."

At the mention of *Jaws*, my nephews in Chicago started to make the shark noise. Na-na. Na-na. I heard Rachel tell them to be quiet and my father ask my mother, "Why is he taking a film-writing class in the first place?"

"You guys are reading too much into this," Marcy countered. "Laurel showed *Schindler* because it was the best movie for what she wanted to teach. Mormons just aren't as emotional as Jews. Plus, she had a rough childhood."

"Who didn't?" Rachel countered.

"Oh please, yours was a cakewalk," my mother told her. For once, Rachel did not argue. We all knew that my mother, raised by Grandma B, felt she'd cornered the market on rough childhoods.

"Forgive me for changing the subject," my father chimed in, "but David, why do you want to get involved with a girl with a screwy past?"

"You got involved with me, didn't you?" my mother said.

"I'm not involved with her. We kissed once. I haven't even spoken to her since."

"You should be ashamed of yourself," my mother said. "How could you not follow up after she extended herself like that?"

"Extended herself?" I said. "Showing the new kid in class where the gym is. That's extending oneself. Foisting yourself onto another human being is assault."

"Don't be insensitive, David. She put herself out there. That takes courage."

"Insensitive? Oscar Schindler was insensitive. I was ambushed."

"I don't understand what her rough childhood has to do with her decision to use *Schindler's List*," Rachel said.

"I'll tell you, if you will all shut up long enough to listen." Marcy put down her fork, rubbed her hands over the apron she wears even when she doesn't cook the meal, and raised a finger into the air. "Number one. Laurel grew up on a farm with an abusive dad. Her skin is thick. She can look at *Schindler's List* and just see the mechanics of it, the progression of the scenes or whatever."

"Sequencing," I corrected.

"Well look at you, all up on the film lingo," Rachel said. "Maybe you actually like this woman."

"Is there a number two?" my father asked. At the mention of number two, the kids started to laugh.

"Yes, actually," Marcy said. "There is." She put her hand back into the air and raised an additional finger. "Number two. The Holocaust is probably not as shocking to her since her expectations of humanity are so low."

"Clearly," Peter said. "She's willing to date David."

"We're not dating," I said again, though no one was listening. They were laughing.

"I'm not kidding. Again, I don't know her that well, but it doesn't seem to take much to make Laurel happy," Marcy answered. "All she wants is the basics. A roof over her head. A good family—"

"Well then, you better not tell her about us," my dad said.

"Too late," Ryan answered. "The movie David is writing is about us."

"What's there to write about us?" Rachel asked.

"It's about Florida," Ryan said.

"Who's playing me?" my mother asked.

"You're actually writing a movie?" Peter asked.

"How about Debra Messing?" my mother continued, mostly to herself. "I love Debra Messing."

"Not really," I responded to Peter. "Just scenes."

Or, in this case, a sequence.

THE ESTELLE LIBERATION SEQUENCE
MORNING AFTER SLIP'S SENTENCING. INT. APARTMENT 1812

I think we'll kick things off with David waking up, just as I did the day after Slip's sentencing, to an apartment filled with solemnity. I remember that things got rolling early that morning, like always, just as you'd expect in a tiny space filled with insomniacs.

Initial talk of the day usually concerned the movies caught at odd hours of the night—*The African Queen, All About Eve*. But talk was different that morning. I remember waking to the low whisper of voices—my father's and my grandmother's. The minute I heard the whispers, I knew something was up. As I might have already mentioned, whispering was as unheard of in Imperial Towers Building 100 as leaving leftovers at a restaurant. It just wasn't done.

Mornings were generally filled with screaming. My grandparents (and everyone else's) belonged to the breakfast club at the Rascal

House, the world's most famous deli, visited by folks from near and far. We had to be up and out of our apartment by seven each morning in order to take advantage of all that a Rascal House Breakfast Club membership had to offer, which was mainly the privilege of bypassing the line between six thirty and seven thirty for immediate seating. Membership was the equivalent of a get-out-of-jail-free card.

So every day, we were woken by hollers from Slip and my father to get up, get dressed, and get into the car for breakfast. Then they'd issue follow-up calls of "move it" to my sisters, who were not as good as me at popping out of bed in the morning and not as willing as me to go to the Rascal in their pajamas.

No wake-up calls came that morning. Instead, as the camera opens on the sitting room, I will lie in bed and strain my ears to hear what the whispering is about. Then the audience will see me kick my sisters. "Listen," I'll say.

They'll kick me back and mutter, "Shut up, Davy."

At this, I will slip through the partition to find my father sitting in a dining room chair, my grandmother next to him, my mother on the pullout sofa.

"Did you guys stay here all night?" I remember asking, as their positions seemed remarkably unchanged from the night before.

"Get your clothes on," my father barked.

"Where's Papa?" I asked. Neither my grandma nor my mother had gotten dressed, so I didn't feel any sense of urgency.

"He's at the Rascal."

"Alone?" This was a first.

"He went early today. He was hungry."

I remember that the clock above the pullout sofa said it was six forty-five. I wondered how early "early" was.

"All the fighting and everything," I offered. "He probably worked up a real appetite."

In the movie, my mother will chuckle from her bed. My grandma will roll her eyes, an acknowledgment of the absurdity of the circumstance rather than a look of annoyance, and my dad will repeat the command to get dressed, with the addendum to get my sisters out of bed and dressed, too.

"Are we going to meet Papa at the Rascal?"

My father will shake his head no and return to lecturing my grandma in undertones, leaving me to get dressed and wonder from where our next meal will come.

CUT TO: THE BAGEL BAR. At this point, the director will cut so seamlessly from the living room of Apartment 1812 to the waiting area of The Bagel Bar Delicatessen that the audience will barely realize the change of location, but for the strangers and giant pastry case now in our midst. The Bagel Bar, an age-old, barebones establishment in Miami Gardens, not unlike the 3 Woos in its bland decor, was our natural fallback for when we missed breakfast club hours at the Rascal, or when my mother felt like chopped herring, because no one's herring could hold a candle to the Bagel Bar's. (These words, naturally, were my mother's, not my own. I was and still am a bacon-and-eggs kind of guy.)

"If I ever again set eyes on your grandfather, I'll strangle him to death," my grandma will declare as we wait for our table to be set.

We'll be seated around eight o'clock, as indicated by the knife and fork hands on the Bagel Bar's tea-pot clock, which will come into focus as the audience hears my father begin to explain to us that Eileen refused to give in on Slip's expulsion. "So it seems," he'll say as a waitress shoves paper cups of water in front of each of us, "Slip can't play cards for the rest of the season. Unless we find some way to change her mind."

Rachel will shake her head. "How embarrassing." Rachel's only interest was the family reputation and how this latest to-do would impact her own wheeling and dealing in the game room. The character of Rachel will be played by one of those wunderkind teens, the ones who can act, sing, and walk a tightrope by the age of three—a little perfectionist, albeit with a gargantuan nose.

"How can you say that?" The script will direct my father to look at Rachel with dismay while my grandma winks—another subtle show of understanding. My mother will be too busy doctoring her coffee to react.

"C'mon, Dad," Rachel will say. "You can't pretend that this situation is not humiliating. Everyone in the building is talking about us."

"I don't care what everyone in the building is doing. For one lousy minute, let's try and think about somebody else besides ourselves. Let's think about what this predicament means for your grandmother and grandfather." And off my father will go on his favorite type of lecture, the "let's think" lecture.

The second phase of the lecture, the acceptance phase, coincides with the arrival of our meals, and so in the movie, as the camera closes in on the central visual object of this scene—my mother's mound of herring—the audience will hear my father drone on with a tortuous monologue that I will have to make up, because I don't recall the original. I'd tuned it out, as I imagine the audience might do as well.

"We must recognize the crossroads that Slip and Estelle now find themselves at, with life having thrown them a curveball. It may not seem significant to us, and may even seem funny"—this line he'll direct at the laughing sisters—"but at their age, with routine being such a big part of getting by day-to-day, the fact that Slip has nothing to do with himself, nowhere to go, is detrimental to the well-being of our grandparents' happiness and, for that matter, their health."

"Let's not get carried away." My mother, as she chews, will say something to this effect.

My grandma will agree. "I feel just fine," she'll assure us. "My health is good, and you kids are not to worry. Let's have a jelly donut." She'll rub her stomach and point in the direction of the pastry case. She eyed the jelly donuts every time we came in the Bagel Bar.

"Bad idea," my father will say, as he always did.

My grandma will shrug her shoulders, letting us know that she'd tried. To me, she'll whisper—and the camera will capture it—"One day I'm gonna get my hands on one of those donuts, Davy. You just wait and see."

I remember studying her as she spoke, trying to evaluate who to believe regarding the status of her health. Who knows how old Estelle looked objectively. In calendar years she was seventy, younger than my father is today. But through my young eyes, she looked ancient. Her skin hung loose on her neck. Her eyes watered regardless of her mood, and her "stomach troubles," as she called them, kept her away from jelly donuts and dependent on cortisone, which I knew from my father wreaked havoc on the body. Could banning Slip from his card room really play with my grandma's lifespan? From the perspective of someone to whom it seemed dicey that she would live to finish her bagel, this outcome seemed possible. I was concerned, so I listened to the rest of my father's speech, which was in essence a call to action:

"Let's all do what we can during our days left in Florida to help keep Slip busy so his irascibleness doesn't bleed over, and let's all help keep Estelle occupied in her usual ways. Does everyone understand?"

We'll nod our heads. Mine will nod the most. I was on board. If I could do anything to extend my grandparents' lives—for any amount of time, but certainly through the duration of our visit—I was up to the task.

Marcy's head will tip slowly and with a little groove, as if "Jive Talkin'" was still playing in her head—which, probably, it was.

Fourteen-year-old Rachel, savvy enough to see that we could never save our grandparents from themselves, will give a single nod and a sarcastic thumbs-up. "Whatever you say, Doc."

"Good," my father will answer, happy to have even a half-hearted consensus. "In the meantime," he'll finish, "I'll work behind the scenes to see what kind of strings might be pulled to get Slip back into the card room."

From here we'll cut seamlessly again, but I'm not sure where we'll go. At this point, I'd be better off with a director than me calling the shots. Maybe I'll bring in Steven Spielberg, as clearly he is not only the master of the sequence but of capturing throngs of Jews flooding out of their apartments, fighting for survival. At the risk of offending my fellow Jews, I have to say that the scene on the Imperial Towers pool deck every morning and the Ghetto Liquidation scene are not without commonality. As I think about it, perhaps I've never been able to bring myself to see *Schindler's List* because it touches too close to home.

Based on the BASIC CAMERA SHOTS poster that hangs in Laurel's classroom next to the poster on SCREENPLAY DEFINITIONS, I should start with a wide lens in order to get a view of the Intracoastal surrounding the pool deck. Maybe an aerial shot's the way to go. An aerial will give us the Intracoastal with its boats and the 163rd Street Bridge, as well as the pool deck and the building. We'll see the pool, the shuffleboard courts, and the dance floor. We'll see the hundreds of yellow lounge chairs covered in the same number of yellow towels. We'll see the movement of people. We'll miss the smell of the suntan oil, but we'll hear the howl of the wind.

The placement of the buildings in relation to each other and the Intracoastal created a wind tunnel so that even when the weather was perfectly pleasant, we felt like we were on the heels of a hurricane. When you understand the wind you understand, too, why all the women wrapped their hair in scarves, brightly colored things, and why, when the aerial view comes in for a landing—I'm sure there's a technical term for this, I'll have to ask Laurel—the audience will see a disproportionate number of sunbathers crowded into the wind-blocked corner in which we stuffed ourselves each day, every day, for sunbathing, sitting, and smoking.

Every once in a while, someone would actually move from a chaise—like my Grandma Estelle, who was a big pool deck walker. At least she was while we were visiting, most likely because my father was a big nag about it. "You gotta do it," he'd remind her. "You gotta get the blood flowing." Because he was a dentist, close enough to a doctor to satisfy my grandma, she listened. And she walked. In heeled sandals, nylons, and slacks, and with a two-ton purse dangling from her arm, she did her circles around the deck. Usually slowly (more due to her outfit than her age), and with stops to pull Kleenex from her purse to dry her eyes or wonder about an interesting boat waiting to pass under the bridge.

On this day, the morning of the Bagel Bar, she walked for hours, with each of us taking turns accompanying her. I was, on the totem pole of walking accompaniment, her most frequent partner. I wasn't in it for the exercise but for the childhood stories my grandma would tell while we walked.

As the camera comes to rest on Davy and Grandma Estelle walking and talking, perhaps the narrator will explain that it was Tuesday, the day of the week that Estelle usually went to the Marco Polo, this colossal hotel with a neon sign that lit Collins Avenue for miles. Every week Slip drove Estelle to the Marco Polo, where she met her friend Ruth in the lobby to play duplicate bridge. Every Tuesday evening at dinner, Estelle recounted to my mother, hand by hand, how things had played out.

But on this day when things were playing out so poorly, we walked and walked, and my grandma talked not of the past but about how silly it was to make yourself so reliant on one person.

The day was one of the few genuinely nice ones of our visit, and the deck was loaded, to borrow my grandma's phrasing. I remember looking around as we walked, scanning the crowds for Slip, particularly when we got toward the shuffleboarders. If he ever hit the deck, the shuffleboard area was his spot. I didn't see him. My grandma didn't see him, either. She didn't say she was looking, but I knew she was.

The audience also will notice her glancing around for him as she says to me, "Marriage, my Davy, is hard no matter how old you are. If you ask me, love matters a little, but luck matters more."

I will watch my grandma's feet turn out like a ballerina's as she talks.

"It's all one big crap shoot. You never know how things are gonna end up, and there's no good way to hedge your bets." She'll sigh and stare out over the water before adding, "But I imagine it is a bit easier for girls nowadays because they have more choices and independence. They call it Women's Lib, Davy. And between you and me"—she'll pause again here to tug my shoulder toward her thin body—"if I knew where they were selling it, I'd go get me some."

I did not have enough zinc oxide on my shoulders, and I was aware of both the feeling of them burning and the awkwardness one feels when one momentarily, like a flash in the pan, glimpses a person as just that—a person—and not a parent or grandparent. "I don't know where to find Women's Lib, either," I'll tell her.

I didn't. But I did know that I had to help my grandma. I saw it as my responsibility. She had, after all, confided in me.

"I guess this is why they tell you to not put all your eggs in one basket," she'll say.

"Why?" I'll ask.

"In case the basket turns out to be missing marbles," she'll say, and then chuckle at her joke.

I don't care how he does it, but at this point, the actor who plays me will have to let the audience know that the wheels in his brain have begun to spin. I remember that day feeling the vibrations of the deck, like barely perceptible earthquakes, each time a car pulled in or out from the top floor of the parking garage below us. Perhaps the vibrations subconsciously gave me the idea.

I have no clue how to translate this osmotic creation of an idea onto the big screen. In the movie, as I saunter barefoot over the cement, perhaps the narrator will explain that below the pool deck was the parking garage. Every apartment came with two parking spaces. My grandparents' top-floor slots, however, housed only one car—my grandfather's brand-new Cadillac—which he gladly parked in the middle of both spaces.

Why did Slip have a free space? Simple: my grandmother couldn't drive.

As the Davy character thinks, his grandma will say something like, "I bet Rachel and Marcy will get to be anything they want." She'll bet that Rachel becomes boss of something big, like the whole country. "But Marcy . . ." She'll shake her head and sigh. "I don't think she'd make her way through steno."

Steno, I knew from previous walks, was short for stenography class, where my grandma was sent after she finished high school. The classes, along with ballet, were offered free at the Association House where she met my grandfather. By then he already had a car, and my grandma had legs, long dancer's legs, which my grandfather would drive home every afternoon. They'd been driving together ever since. Estelle had never had any need to learn to do it herself.

Until this day, when Slip did not come home after breakfast to drive her to bridge before moving on with his afternoon. Today was a first, and I think that with this failure, my Grandma Estelle began to worry in earnest—because when I casually suggested, "Maybe you can learn to drive so you can take yourself to the Marco Polo," she didn't dismiss me or laugh at me the way I'd expected, the way that Laurel did when I suggested that she get a New York driver's license.

On our next swing by the yellow chairs, my grandma and I asked my father to join us on our walk.

"There's a cool boat I want to show you," I hollered to him, and my grandma winked at me.

When the three of us reached the far side of the deck, I hung over the side of the cinderblock wall, studied the waves rolling into the bottom of it and the cars parked against it, and told my father my plan.

"It's a good one," my father declared. He patted my grandma's back, and then replaced his own few strands of windblown hair as he explained that lessons would begin the very next morning in the Publix parking lot. "Early," he told us, "before anyone sets out to do their grocery shopping for the day."

My grandmother raised her brows in excitement. I slapped her a high-five. Then, while she was busy bantering about what fun the lessons would be, I quietly pointed out to my father that my grandfather's Cadillac was still not in its space. My father shook his head. He was already aware.

CHAPTER 8:

Objects and Affections

W hen I rang Laurel's buzzer on Sunday evening after our family dinner, I was nervous. My decision to go to her place was spur of the moment, propelled by guilt from my mother and curiosity ignited by Marcy's remarks about the rabbi. I didn't mention my plan to Marcy, I just left her house at my regular time, a polite interval after finishing two slices of apple pie.

I don't do drop-ins, even on people I know. A lawyer like Rachel would classify the drop-in as an invasion of privacy. To a branding guy like me, it's just plain Rude.

Hence, when Laurel asked through the intercom who was there, I identified myself as my alter ego, Mort Chuckerman. He was already dead, I figured, so how embarrassed could he be?

"This is a surprise." Her raspy voice was garbled further by the speaker. "Is everything okay?"

I told her yes, that I'd just had a little trouble understanding some things that went on in our last class.

She said okay and buzzed me in. "Walk slowly," she added. "I need time to put away some stuff."

I wondered as I paced myself up the three flights whether "stuff" included the rabbi. The possibility that the two of them might be up there doing Yiddish on the side didn't cross my mind until I was two flights into the climb. I was even more nervous by the time I reached the top than I'd been at the bottom.

But my angst was for naught, because the minute the Mormon Rodeo opened the door and I stepped into her foyer, I realized that ten rabbis, an entire minyan, might be holed up in her house and I'd never know it, the clutter was that bad.

The foliage was worse. Ferns and some sort of hanging stuff draped over the windowsill. An orchid was in the mix, along with a rose bush and vegetables. My eyes darted from them to the plates and pans filling the sink to the stacks of papers covering her couch and coffee table to the mounds of books and videos lined on shelves to a white cat (which Laurel later introduced as Chloe) sitting smugly on the end of a bed and then to Laurel, standing before me in shorts, a T-shirt, and the same horrible robe she'd worn in class.

I don't know what I was expecting when I decided to drop in on her, but this scene was not it.

"I guess I should have walked slower," I said, looking past her and into her natural habitat. I'd pictured neat white walls, or maybe pale pink, with an old-fashioned desk and papers tucked in files. I'd pictured shelves organized like a library, with a section for audio/visual and a section on Judaica. I'd figured she'd have, as Marcy does, a piece of her floor designated with a mat for yoga and meditation. I'd imagined a poster, one of the vintage SKI UTAH ones they're using for the Olympics, on the wall.

She rolled her eyes at me and said, "I've been busy, I've been gone, and I wasn't expecting company."

I nodded and smiled as I took in Laurel's Sunday night routine—which, from what I could tell, included eating grilled cheese, drinking a beer, and grading papers in her robe with all the windows wide open and the air conditioner unit blasting.

"You sure do have the air flowing."

"It gets hot in the robe," Laurel said before holding out her grilled cheese and offering me some.

"Well, it is the end of June," I said. "It might make more sense to take off the robe." I then said no to the grilled cheese; I was still full from the pizza at Marcy's, and Laurel's kitchen looked so cluttered with pans and mugs and watering cans, I didn't know how she'd find space to cook.

"I always wear the robe on Sunday nights," she said, and before I had a chance to ask why, she put a hand to her hip and followed up with, "So, what brings you here?"

She motioned me toward her couch, a brown leather love seat that looked like it might have been cut from the same cloth as her messenger bag. She plopped herself down and began to scoop scripts from a cushion to make room for me.

"I wanted to apologize for running out of class without acknowledging our make-out session," I said.

"I wouldn't exactly call it a make-out session, Chuckerman. It was a kiss." She propped her heels on the edge of her coffee table, leaned back, and pulled the crust from the body of her sandwich. "I didn't mean to throw you." She paused. "Well actually, I suppose that's not true. I guess I did hope to throw you. I wanted to get you out of your head so you'd go back and watch the movie. Shock therapy."

"Creative," I said and ran a hand through my hair, as I tend to do when regrouping. I had expected more of an I-just-couldn't-help-myself response.

"Thank you," she said.

"Just to be clear," I went on, my hand still in my hair, "the purpose of your kiss was to get me to watch *Schindler's List*?"

Laurel nodded. "Correct."

"So let me ask you this," I said, pushing around a few of the papers on the table in search of mine. "If Judd, or say Don, had run out of the room because they didn't want to watch the massacre, would you have redirected them the same way? French kisses for all?"

She laughed—a breezy laugh, as if she were in a conference room and her breasts were in a business suit, not hanging loose beneath an I HEART LA T-shirt. As if they hadn't been pressing against me just a few days earlier. Apparently, our exchange in the hallway had had a larger impact on me than her.

"No, probably not," she admitted. "Although neither of them asked me if I wanted to make out in the hallway."

"I didn't think you'd take me seriously. It was a *Seinfeld* reference." I explained the episode, the one where Jerry tells Elaine that he didn't get to see all of *Schindler's List* because he was making out with his date.

Her head pivoted in ignorance. "I've never seen *Seinfeld.*"

"How is that possible?"

"How is it possible that you took that kiss seriously?" She picked up her beer to take a sip, but it was empty, so she set it back down and kept talking. "Regardless, you don't need to apologize for running out. That's what men do. They bail. I wouldn't expect anything more."

"What men are you referring to?" I asked. Perhaps she had the rabbi in mind, though I couldn't imagine a rabbi would bail.

She didn't name the rabbi. She named her father, who cheated on her mother, and her old boyfriend, some dude named Hal, whom she met in her MFA program and dated for three years. He drove a motorcycle and apparently left her for a woman in his riding group. "He's the one who gave me my cowboy boots," she said.

I nodded. "You dated a guy who rides a motorcycle and yet you won't drive a car?"

"If you came here to nag me about the driver's license, you can leave now. Besides, *I* never drove the motorcycle."

"I didn't come here to nag you," I said, unsure of exactly why I was there. If memory served, I had come hoping for clarity as to how everyone involved felt post-kiss, but now I felt more unsettled than before. Her confidence and lack of emotion threw me. I continued with our relatively safe line of conversation. "However, I do think that anyone who is willing to get on a motorcycle should be willing to drive a car."

"Hal didn't drive a car."

"Well, it doesn't seem like Hal and I have a lot in common, then. I'd never ride a motorcycle." I leaned back against the couch and tucked my hands behind my head. "I'd also never bail."

"How do you know that?"

"I'm a loyalist. Once I take something on, I never get rid of it. Don't I still drive my grandfather's car?"

"I don't know why you do."

"I told you, loyalty to my grandfather."

"You know, your grandfather wasn't such a great guy either. He bailed."

"My grandfather?" I asked. "No he didn't."

"Of course he did."

"Did Marcy tell you this? 'Cause I know how girls talk. For instance, I know that Marcy somehow knew about our make-out session without me telling her"—I paused while Laurel mumbled a halfhearted apology for providing details to my sister—"but I also know that Marcy doesn't always know what she's talking about."

She handed me her grilled cheese and began to file through the scripts on her table. After a few seconds, during which I sampled the sandwich and wondered how Laurel had gotten the upper hand on my family history, she located what she wanted. "Your Sentencing Scene," she explained, waving it in the air. She flipped to the end of it, to the remarks about the wandering eye and the gambling. "You said so."

"I told you what happened that night, what other people who did not like my grandfather said about him. But I never said he did those things."

"C'mon," Laurel said. "Do you really believe that your grandfather had an undeserved reputation?'

"I think a lot of people have undeserved reputations."

"Like who?'

"Like my grandfather," I said. "And Oscar Schindler," I added, echoing my mother's earlier example.

"For God sakes, Oscar Schindler couldn't keep the women out of his bed."

"Okay, well, aside from the philandering. People thought he was bad but in the end he turned out to be good. So in that sense, his reputation was undeserved." I nudged her. "See? I paid attention in class. The kissing worked."

"I'm so glad," Laurel said. She brought her knees up to her chest and pulled the robe down over her knees. "You know, there's another side to that story. According to the rabbi, plenty of people think that Oscar Schindler never had pure intentions—that he decided to spare the Jews only after he saw that the Nazis were going to be defeated. Basically, he was only out to save his own ass."

"Well if that's the case, what's the big fuss over the movie?" I began to mimic Laurel's teaching persona—the excited voice and wild hand-waving—and said, "Pay attention to the girl in the red dress, everyone. This symbolizes Schindler's ultimate transformation." In my regular voice, I asked, "Then what was all that about?"

"It's a movie, Chuckerman," Laurel said, downing the last of her sandwich. "Like I said in class, if you want to make a good movie, you need to create characters who are complex, who evolve. Otherwise, we wouldn't want to watch them. The same cannot always be said of people. *A volf farlirt zayne hor, ober nit zayn natur.*" The unintelligible sounds rolled off her tongue as if *she* were the Jew on the couch. She threw one leggy leg over the other, smoothed her hair, and smiled.

"I love when you talk dirty to me," I said.

She tossed my paper back onto the table. "It's Yiddish, Chuckerman." She popped to her feet. "It means you can't make a leopard change its spots."

"Thank you for translating," I said. "I recognized the language, but did not expect your command of it. I assumed you only knew words, the usual—*oy, schvitz*. Not full sentences. You must be working a lot with the rabbi." I said this hoping for some explanation, but none came; she just shrugged and said she was a quick study.

Then she pulled the tie around her robe tighter, headed toward the kitchen, and asked if I wanted a beer. She told me that she usually has only one beer on Sunday nights, but tonight, due to the unforeseen circumstance of my visit, she was having two. I told her yes, if she could find one. She said "very funny" and then, as she sashayed into the kitchen area, reminded me again that she hadn't been expecting company.

Laurel returned with two more bottles of Red Rock Amber Ale. "Utah's finest," she told me as she handed one to me and sat down again.

I took a sip and said, "I would like to point out that your Yiddish belief that people don't change and the David Melman philosophy that history repeats itself are essentially one and the same." I raised my bottle. "A toast to similarly bleak views of mankind."

"Cheers," she said, clinking her bottle to mine and again crossing one leg over the other. Between our outing last Sunday and our evening so far, I'd become fairly well acquainted with Laurel's legs from mid-thigh down. Her calves were fairly built up, and I wondered, as I studied them again, whether the muscle was due to skiing as a child or if heavy calf development was indigenous to the Mormon population, the same way big hips are for Jews.

Laurel was busy talking now, telling me that as much as she'd like to agree that our views were similar so we'd have at least something in common, there was a critical difference between them. The only critical difference I was aware of was the disproportionality between her slender thighs and the calves. *Maybe that's why she wore the boots*, I thought. *Maybe that's why cowboy boots are popular out West, because Mormons have big calves.*

I felt a finger under my chin and then my head lifted. "Would you like to go ahead and touch my leg so we can get that out of the way and move on to the listening portion of our evening?"

I apologized for my own wandering eye. "You know what they say."

She stared at me.

"A wolf cannot change its spots."

"It's the leopard, you fool." She slugged down some beer like we were buddies at a bar and said, "And while the leopard cannot change its spots, you can change the way you react to the leopard. That's how you keep history from repeating itself, Chuckerman. Change your own actions and reactions. My father, for example, was mean and unfaithful, and he never changed." She told me that just last year her mother, who's a blond, found several long black hairs in her bed. "On white sheets, as if he was asking to get caught." She shook her head. "There was a fight—yet another fight—but in the end, she stayed." She took another drink and slumped backwards into the corner of the couch. "One thing is for sure, Chuckerman. As much as I love my mother, I am going to be the opposite of her."

"If you want to be the opposite of your mother, why do you spend Sunday nights in her robe?"

She shrugged. "Objects of affection, Chuckerman. Some things defy explanation. Why do you hang on to that car?"

I told her I'd already told her why: out of loyalty.

She told me that she didn't buy that explanation; she thought there was more to it than I was willing to admit.

Before I could argue, she went on to explain that the robe was one of the first ones her mother made. Now, her business was booming. "She calls herself Lazy Daisy. She puts daisies on everything she makes." Laurel pointed out the daisies on her robe, as if I hadn't noticed them. "But she doesn't just travel around to fairs and craft shows for a hobby, like I told the class. The real reason she travels is to get out of the house. It's her escape."

"Just another woman looking to get away from her man," I said, thinking of my grandma and the driving lessons.

"My father is not your typical man," Laurel said. "His temper has mellowed a little with age, but he rarely has a nice word to say. As soon as the eight of us left, my mother hit the road with her stuff. I'm proud of her for that. Maybe that's why I keep the robe."

"You have seven siblings?"

She told me they were all still in Utah, except for her and her youngest brother, who was gay and would have been locked in the proverbial closet as long as he stayed in Utah. He lived in San Francisco now.

"I don't know," I said. "Your mother doesn't seem so bad to me."

She shrugged. "I would have left my dad," she said. "I wouldn't have stuck around."

"Maybe she didn't have a choice." I didn't know why I was defending her mother. Maybe because her embroidery was worthy of sympathy. (Now that I'd been close to the robe for an extended period of time, I could see it wasn't seamless.) Or maybe I just didn't like the idea of leaving. Melmans never leave.

"That's the thing, Chuckerman. There's always a choice. There are always deal breakers, and there is always a choice."

My beer was almost finished, and so was I. The discussion had taken a serious turn, and the clock, which now read past ten, was moving quickly toward Monday morning, and with it the dilemma of Ezmerelda Rich and my Omnipotence campaign. If I couldn't get Ezmerelda on board, there'd be no campaign. I scooched to the edge of the couch—a signal, albeit my own personal one, that the drop-in was ready to depart.

The Mormon Rodeo, oblivious to the significance of my move, just kept on going. "That's one of the things I like about Judaism," she was now saying. "The rules aren't as rigid as they are in my religion. They make more sense. For example, in Reform Judaism—which is what I'm studying—the rabbi has jurisdiction over marriage, but divorce is governed solely by civil law. So here in New York, where the law is no fault divorce, all you've got to do is file, no questions asked. Mormons have never heard of the concept of 'no fault.' The Mormon mentality is that divorce happens because of sin, and while you can get divorced if you want, you will be shunned from the Church and screwed forever after."

"So your position is that a person should convert to Judaism in case she wants a divorce one day?"

"No, all I'm saying is that Judaism offers freedom and flexibility. I can drink coffee if I want without feeling guilty. I can have this beer." She held up the bottle and took another long swig. "And, I can have another, if I want. Which I do." She stood up again.

"The Jews are low in numbers," I said as she took off into the kitchen, "so we throw in some nice perks."

She returned with two more bottles and bright eyes. "It's liberating, really. To be able to act without strings attached. Like, I could take you to my bed right now without any concerns of eternal repercussions."

My eyes widened. Here was a twist I hadn't expected. I took a drink of my new beer and leaned back. "Maybe not for you," I said, and then I explained how I'd been forbidden from touching her by someone more frightening than God.

She sat up. "Who?"

"Marcy."

She sighed. "And yet here you are. Dropping in at nine thirty on a Sunday night. You can't be too frightened of her. Or maybe she wanted you to come by, and that's why she told you not to." She put her hand on my thigh.

I hadn't thought of that. "I don't think Marcy's that smart," I said, staring at the hand and wondering what to do with my own. I decided to take temptation off the table by tucking both my hands in the pockets of my sweatshirt. "I didn't come by for sex," I told her.

"Oh, really," she said. She moved closer to me. The tie of the bathrobe flopped onto my leg.

"Really." I moved away from her, intent on walking the walk of someone who only came by out of guilt. Sure, I had entertained the possibility of getting lucky, but I'd defined lucky as a repeat performance of the hallway kiss. Maybe a little longer, maybe involving a little second base if my stars were aligned, but nothing more, and certainly not this. I was ill-prepared. "I've got news for you," I said. "I don't hop into bed with every girl I meet just because the Jewish God isn't going to send me to hell when I die for doing so." I slid my palms, damp from sweat, over my pants and, out of nerves, kept talking.

"The coffee thing, great. No downside to going hog wild with the coffee. If you want, I'll buy you your own coffee maker so in case one day you can't find the door to get out of this place due to clutter, you can still have your coffee. But if we start in with sex, then we're in a relationship, and even though the Jewish God says I can bail at any time, my own personal Big Guy is a little more Mormon. He says 'strings attached.'" I stopped to take another drink. "And why would I want strings attached to a girl with whom I have nothing in common and who is moving away? Besides," I added, "you're not even Jewish yet. Actually, I thought you weren't planning to convert. You said you're just doing 'research'"—I paused again to finger-quote. "So isn't all this free love business a little cart-before-the-horse?"

"Wow," she said, sitting up and digging the palms of her hands into the small of her back the net result of which was to force her chest toward me and me further back into the couch. "Before this outburst, I wasn't sure you could utter more than a sentence at a time."

"Monologues happen every so often," I said.

"Good to know," she said. "To continue on with your horse theme, I guess you could say I'm sowing my oats. I'm experimenting. Whether I'm out from under the reach of my father or the Church, who knows. But for the first time, I feel free, and I'm playing with my freedom. I even whitened my teeth when I was in LA." She tapped her bottle against her teeth. "Six months ago, I never would've had the guts to whiten my teeth. My father doesn't believe in it. He says our bodies aren't really ours to tamper with."

In search for common ground I told her my father, professionally speaking, doesn't believe in it either. "He says it weakens the enamel."

She nodded with little interest and kept talking. "Do you realize that if you'd dropped in on me six months ago, you'd never have found beer in my fridge? Actually," she said, talking more to herself than to me, "a guy as good looking as you wouldn't have dropped in on me six months ago; I was too buttoned up. But if you had, you'd never have found as much as a crumb in my kitchen, a book out of place. You'd have found me in the robe—some habits die hard—but you'd never have found me half-naked beneath it." She gestured, unnecessarily, to her chest. Then she raised a brow at me and, as she began to speak again, got to her feet. "You'd never have heard me talk about taking you to bed, or seen me stand over you like this and say anything like, 'I'm attracted to you, you're attracted to me, I'm moving to LA, you'll never see me again, let's just go at it without worrying about where it's going.'" She put one leg on either side of me. "Before," she explained from her straddle position, "I'd have saved lines like that for my characters. But not anymore." She undid the tie on her robe and let the robe slide off her shoulders to the floor. Her hand went to her hip. "And what are you gonna do in return?"

As I stared in awe at the scene unfolding before me, she began to play with the tiny Jewish star around her neck. She smiled. Then she let her hand move slowly over her chest, raised her brow, and said, "Who are you going follow in this scenario, Mort Chuckerman, my God or yours?"

———

I'm a private guy. I only discuss personal issues with a few people, all of whom are related to me, and I can't think of anyone on the planet with whom I will comfortably discuss the subject of sex. Don't get me wrong. I'm a guy's guy. I can trash talk with the best of them. I just don't like to talk about sex as it relates to actual relationships, mine or anyone else's. But I was going to have a hard time keeping my night with the Mormon Rodeo to myself.

As I sat in my own leather chair and stared into the darkness, waiting for the sun to give life to Riverside Park, I realized I had to tell Broc. He was a finance guy, they all start work early. I could probably call him at five, although then Marcy would want to know why I was calling, and I didn't want to tell her about my night with her friend. I wanted to tell Broc, because he deserved to know that he'd hit the ball out of the park, the nail on the head, when he named Laurel Sorenson the Mormon Rodeo.

It was something to experience. The whole time things were happening to me—and things were happening to me the whole time, it was an insane, six-hour free-for-all of groping and thrusting and screaming my name—two words were going through my mind: Mormon Rodeo. Broc deserved to know that. I wouldn't give details, I was too worn out for details. But how much detail is needed when you say that the Mormon Rodeo earned her stripes in bed? The name speaks for itself. *Res ipsa loquitor*, as Rachel would say. To a marketer like me, it's plain old onomatopoetic. She put all the young women I've been with, from Share on down, to shame.

I began to consider Don's concept of a fling in a more positive light as I stared into the darkness and studied my reflection in the glass. Looking back at me, I saw a man with a movie script on his lap, watching the clock, waiting to call his brother-in-law to talk about his booty call, and though he looked vaguely like David Melman, I didn't fully recognize him. Could it be that I was evolving, albeit in the wrong direction? *Maybe I should call Marcy*, I thought, *and tell her that I actually wasn't at rock bottom when she signed me up for the class, but I'm there now. Perhaps people do change.*

I stared at my reflection some more.

But what did it mean to change? Having a one-night stand with your teacher, was that change? It was new, but it wasn't change. If I had come home afterwards and gone to sleep without analyzing whether I'd changed, without worrying about whether the Mormon Rodeo carried any sexually transmitted diseases, without rehashing my performance—that would have been change. No sir, I concluded to myself in the glass as I picked up my pen and prepared to kill some time with my movie, a person's fundamental character doesn't change. Spots—my own, Laurel's father's, my grandfather's—are in fact spots.

Although I suppose one's spots can appear different at different points in time, depending on the other person's angle or even just the time of day.

$$\text{\sim}\!\!\text{\rule{2em}{0.4pt}}$$

THE CADDY AND THE LOOSE CANNON

LATE AFTERNOON, SAME DAY AS WALK ON POOL DECK. INT. RASCAL HOUSE. IN THROES OF EARLY-BIRD SPECIAL DINNER RUSH

When he finally shows up at dinner that afternoon, Slip will look abnormally askew. Silver strands of hair will stray over his forehead. His white shirt will no longer be tucked into his pants, and his loafers will be coated in sand. The audience will watch as he pulls a handful of sea glass out of his pocket and offers it to us kids. To my Grandma Estelle, he'll offer his version of an apology: he'll whack her on the back and say, "I screwed you up today, huh?"

I remember that we had been waiting in line for a while when Slip arrived. The air was heavy with heat, uncertainty, and grease (not unlike the atmosphere in Laurel's apartment). The room was thick with people; we'll need a lot of extras, old ones, for this scene. We were packed so tightly together that I was beneath my grandma as I played with the plastic beads around her neck and watched the skin under her chin jiggle as she spoke.

Estelle will answer Slip calmly. "Actually," she'll say, "I had a lovely day. I got to spend it with my Davy boy." She'll tap my head, then add, "But you might want to apologize to Ruthie. She waited an hour at the Marco Polo for me. Thought I'd died. Poor thing was scared out of her pants."

"That Ruthie can kiss my you-know-what," Slip will declare. He'll pause to pardon his French in front of us and the other families in earshot. "If I had a nickel for every time she's opened her fat trap to you . . . That broad deserved to be stood up."

My father, who will be helping my sisters pick up some fallen sea glass, will suggest that two wrongs don't make a right.

"But," my Grandma Estelle will reply as she rests her purse on the silver railing, rifles through, and hands my sisters a baggie to hold the sea glass, "two Wrights make an airplane." She'll laugh. So will we. Then she'll look at my mother and say, "You know, Ruthie *does* have a big mouth."

My mother will agree.

My father will ask my grandfather, "Where the hell you been all day?" and my grandfather will reply, "Out walking."

I remember overhearing my parents, as I sat on my sofa bed later that night, discussing Slip's day. Perhaps we'll CUT straight from the Rascal House's waiting room to our own sitting room. The audience will see the open window above my pullout chair and the stack of quarters on the table next to the chair. I'm guessing I had about six or seven dollars' worth. Not that much, but to me, a fortune. Enough for a few Matchbox cars or, if I kept saving, a pair of Adidas. The leather ones with the blue stripes. Roms, they were called. Talk about objects of affection. I was dying for a pair.

"It's ironic, isn't it?" I heard my father say. "Each of them spent the day walking—my ma at the pool, my dad at the beach. That kind of synchronicity must happen to people after fifty years of marriage."

From my pullout on the other side of the partition, I agreed with my father until my mother chimed in with something like, "It's a little less ironic when you consider that neither of them had anything else to do all day."

Then I agreed with her.

Slip was in his bedroom watching television. My sisters and Grandma Estelle were downstairs. Rachel was playing pinball. Marcy was watching the kick-line's rehearsal for the Vaudeville Review—which, come to think of it, the audience should see for themselves. No better entertainment than eight old ladies dancing to "I've Got Rhythm" in mini dresses as blinding as Laurel's robe. Relatively speaking, back in Apartment 1812, the atmosphere was downright dull—which I didn't mind at all. I liked the peace and the smell of the salty ocean air.

I fingered the brand-new quarter my grandfather had left next to my bed to make up for the one I'd blown in the game the night before. Even in the "tumult," as Estelle referred to it, he hadn't forgotten that just before he'd lost his card room privileges, I'd lost a quarter.

During our last film writing class, when Laurel was singing Steven Spielberg's praises, she'd said that he always started with character because good characters were at the heart of any good drama.

"Good characters are layered," she told us. "So layer your people, people!" She used a voice that was almost a scream. I think of it now as her bedroom voice. "Dig deep, let your characters come to you organically so they ring true, so they sing on different levels." She motioned upwards with her hands, as if to imply that our characters would appear out of nowhere if we willed it to happen.

Well, no deep digging was required to get to Slip's character. It was right in front of me, a shiny quarter in the palm of my hand.

The camera will close in on the quarter. Then music, the subtle tinkling of piano keys, will kick in as the narrator says, "Had I an ounce of character myself way back when, I'd have taken the quarter he'd left me to the lousy Condo Association Board as evidence of my grandfather's good character. I also would have explained that I'd seen the fight in the card room, and Slip had been provoked. I would have lost my case. However, it wouldn't have cost me to try. And had

I won, what a victory! Not to mention, what a simpler, and indeed safer, fix to the problem than putting Estelle in the driver's seat."

Not everyone shared my same lofty opinion of Slip's character. As a matter of fact, while I was upstairs musing his praises, my grandmother's kick-line crew was turning his name to mud eighteen floors below. The camera will follow the music playing in Apartment 1812 to its source: the piano in the back of the multi-purpose room.

A group of women, all dressed in costume, will be gathered around it. Morry Pine, the show's accompanist every year, before his stroke and after, will sit on the piano bench. His fingers will do a shaky several bars of "I've Got Rhythm" as Estelle stands on stage demonstrating the next eight-count, which will include a pivot and a kick-ball change, her signature move. As Estelle dances and Morry plays, the rest of the ladies will perform their own signature move: they'll gossip.

"You know Slip wasn't walking on the beach today," Gloria from 14 will say. "He was taking bets on those paddle games that go on there. He lost thousands." She'll mimic Estelle's quick kick-ball change and again say, "Thousands," using jazz hands for emphasis.

"He didn't mention anything at dinner about losing money," my Grandma Estelle will counter as she dances.

"Of course he didn't," Gloria from 14 will say. "He's not an idiot."

"He's a menace," Florence from 9 will say.

Grandma B will add, as she presses her cigarette into the ashtray on the top of the piano, "He's a bag of trouble."

Without pausing his music, Morry will say, "You're wrong, he's a saint."

"Oh, please," Viv from the Lobby Level will say. "He's a loose cannon, and Estelle should either walk out or set up some ground rules."

Marcy overheard this conversation in real life. She sat in the corner of the stage in her yellow satin disco jacket studying both the dance moves and the talk so that the next morning, as she, Rachel, and I rode the elevator into the lobby, she was able to repeat both verbatim.

"He didn't seem like he'd lost thousands last night at dinner," Rachel countered. "He was in a good mood."

"Yeah," I added, understanding little of what I'd heard and liking none of it. "And he had sea glass, so he had to have walked on the beach."

"What did Grandma say?" Rachel asked.

"Heavens to Betsy," Marcy said, rolling her eyes just like Grandma Estelle did whenever she used any of the "heavens" expressions. "She said, 'He is who he is, and his bark's worse than his bite.'" Marcy studied herself in the mirror as she performed some of the previous night's dance routine. Whoever plays Marcy—Estie would be perfect—will have to execute a few high kicks and pivots at this point and then belt out at the top of her lungs, "I've got my man, who could ask for anything more."

"Shut up," Rachel will yell.

"Yeah," I'll add. Taking Rachel's side was and still is a reflex for me.

"Okay, fine," Marcy will say. She'll do exaggerated jazz hands in Rachel's face and pull the lip-shaped sunglasses off of her head.

As silence falls over the elevator, the narrator will explain that we were on our way to the Rascal House for breakfast in the company of my grandfather only.

That morning, my mother, father, and grandma had headed off early, as planned, to the Publix parking lot for driving lessons. This scenario—me, Marcy, Rachel, and Slip on the road alone—was a first. Not only had we never driven with Slip, we'd never ridden in the Cadillac. Ours was a maiden voyage in many respects, and the excitement was palpable.

Marcy will continue, "Then let's discuss what went down *after* grandma's rehearsal."

"What happened?" I'll ask.

"You shouldn't spread rumors," Rachel will warn.

"But you already know," Marcy will announce. "I'm not spreading anything."

"Davy doesn't know," Rachel will answer, pulling her glasses away from Marcy.

"Davy doesn't count," Marcy will respond, and without pause she'll announce that at some time during the previous day—probably when I was walking around the deck with Estelle—my father and his dental patients had appealed separately to the Board of Directors to pardon Slip. They felt hopeful they'd succeed, but at the end of the evening's rehearsal, Gladys Greenberg came into the room and announced to Gloria from 14 that both pleas had been rejected. When Gloria from 14 asked Gladys if they could do anything to change her mind about the pardon, Gladys nodded in the direction of the stage and said, "Estelle knows what she can do."

"Grandma ignored her," Marcy will say as the numbers above the elevator light up one by one, marking our descent. "Instead she just ordered the dancers to take it from the top."

"Why did they reject the pleas?" I will ask in my worried voice.

"'Cause Gladys Greenberg said to reject them," Marcy will explain.

"Probably because she hates Grandma for not giving her a spot in the kick-line. Either way, Dad's never giving free dental services again," Rachel will inform me. "Not even to Ida from 27. There are going to be a lot of people mad at Dad." Not even her lip-shaped glasses will detract from Rachel's credibility in this moment.

"Yeah," Marcy will say. "And it's all Papa's fault. He's a loose cannon."

At this, the elevator door will open and the audience will see Slip waiting on the other side of it.

As we head through the heavy doors to the parking garage, background music will kick in again. This selection will have to be stirring, with a chord of anticipation and a note of tension—something like "Chariots of Fire"—as we head, perhaps in slow motion, toward the Cadillac, which will gradually come into focus. And what a shot this will be.

Flawless, shining with polish. Yellow exterior with white leather seats. A beacon compared to the cars around it. A symbol of status. The ultimate object of affection. The American Dream. The fanciest thing Slip had ever owned.

Somehow, whether with a slow pan over the car or over our enthralled faces, the camera will give the Caddy its due.

"Wait a while, wait a while," Slip will holler as we tear toward the car. We'll gather at the door as Slip, dressed in a pale blue sweater and matching cap, moves toward us at a mile a minute, keys in hand. We'll watch as the silver key, the same one I have on my key ring today, slips into the slot. With an authoritative click, the door will unlock. Then it will open.

"Whatcha waiting for?" Slip will say, motioning with his hand. "Go on. Get in. I ain't got all day."

We'll climb in and sit down three in a row, no fighting for position. I will finger the power window control and feel the soft leather seats. I remember the air inside already smelled strong and smoky like my grandpa who, in the movie, will slam the back door shut and tuck himself behind the wheel. "You ever see anything as pretty as this, ladies and gentleman?"

"No," we'll say, as if there was any other answer.

"It's high time those folks of yours handed you over to me. You're in for a real ride."

"Hang on," Rachel will whisper to me, grabbing my arm.

She didn't need to offer me this instruction. My Superman T-shirt belied my true nature. I'd been fearing the worst since my father had announced the morning's plan.

Slip had a reputation as a reckless, practically blind driver. A reputation bestowed by my mother and grandmother, who until that day had not allowed Slip to drive when we were along for the ride. A reputation that was rightly deserved, we knew, the minute the Cadillac screeched off, reaching sixty in five seconds and going back down to zero in two more as Slip slammed on the brakes and skidded past the stop sign at the garage's exit.

No one wore seat belts back then, I explain to my niece and nephew, so the three of us flew toward the front seat and screamed stuff like, "We're going to die!"

In the movie, I'll bang into Rachel, and Rachel will bang into Marcy so that Marcy, with her hood over her eyes, will get shoved onto the floor.

There'll be a moment of silence while we climb back onto our seats and come to the realization that we survived. Then we'll start to laugh. And here's what I remember: I remember looking up into the rearview mirror and seeing Slip looking back at us. He was laughing, too. Not out loud—he couldn't or else his cigar might have dropped out of his mouth. But he smiled, and his blue eyes danced. In the movie, the camera will have to be placed in the back seat (a POINT-OF-VIEW shot, according to the poster over the classroom clock) so the audience can see Slip just as I did.

Immediately, my worries went away. Mine had stemmed in part from being a passenger in Slip's Caddy, but more so from being alone in the company of a loose cannon. I didn't know what a loose cannon was, but, like a wandering eye or a coma, it didn't sound good. However, as soon as I saw the dancing eyes in the mirror, I felt certain that Estelle had been right. At least as far as we were concerned, I decided, Slip's bark was worse than his bite.

Today, as the reliable narrator, I'll tell you that I'm not sure what to make of this whole scenario. Back then, explanation seemed easy. We were a family. A unit. A tight and tiny one-bedroom convertible. We fought. We forgave and forgot. It never crossed my mind that the adults had ended up in Apartment 1812 by choice, or that Estelle might have reacted to Slip's behavior in any other way than with acceptance.

But now I wonder, what makes some people stay and others go? Did Estelle, like Laurel's mother, crave an escape from her loose cannon but lack the means? Did the Depression-era mentality that caused her to keep every doggy bag prevent her from getting rid of her husband? Was walking out what the driving lessons were all about? And what about ground rules? Did Laurel's mother set ground rules in the beginning? Did Estelle? Did her rules erode over time as she got tired of spinning her wheels, or is it possible that rules were never needed, that Estelle didn't mind the gambling or whatever else Slip did as much as she enjoyed being married to him? I don't know. The sun can rise a million times over Riverside while I sit and wonder, and I'll never have answers. But I can choose to believe that Estelle just loved him, plain and simple, spots and all.

CHAPTER 9

Parallel Journeys

w

A s I've said, I'm not a kiss-and-tell kind of guy, but I had to talk to someone. If I was going to confess or brag about our night together, my confidant had to be Broc. After all, he'd named her.

"Davy, she's from Utah and she wears boots. It isn't rocket science. The name wasn't about sex," Broc said, laughing, when we met for lunch at the health club. "I was never attracted to her."

"She's not my type either. I think that's the whole appeal," I explained to him, because he was now looking at me cock-eyed. "We're two ships passing in Union Square, one headed to Los Angeles, the other back home to the Upper West Side," I said. "We have nothing, absolutely nothing, in common."

"Marcy and I had nothing in common when I started sleeping with her." Broc explained, not for the first time, that he'd been the big-shot editor, she'd been the idiot freshman posing topless for a women's studies' art expo he'd covered. Marcy was supposed to be a distraction until he got his degree and headed back to Raleigh, where he would dabble in local politics while living off the fat of the family business, Meester Foods. Broc, né Louis Meester, gestured toward his bald head, his belly. He took his billfold out of his pocket and tossed down its contents. "And now look."

We stared at his stock exchange badge and three dollar bills. Now it was my turn to laugh. Broc laughed too. One of the girls seated next to us handed him a napkin with her phone number written on it. We laughed harder. Then Broc said he had to get back to work.

On the escalator down to the lobby, I asked him if he was sorry about the road not taken.

"I ended up on the Melman road," he said. "How could I be sorry?"

I nodded in agreement. "Life on the Melman road is a good one. Especially for me, right now. My career is about to skyrocket; I've got a regular girl, not a starlet, who eats normal food and has no expectations of life, let alone me; and pretty soon I may even have a screenplay."

Broc told me that he was happy for me and didn't mean to take the wind out of my sails. "My only point is that at some point, if you're not careful, the road you think you're not taking can become the road you're actually on. So eyes wide open, brother."

I took the advice to heart, and made a concerted effort to pay close attention to all that transpired between Laurel and me over the next few days to make sure we stayed on the right road. By the time I walked into her class on July 23, I was fully aware that exactly twelve nights, eleven days, five movies (four rentals, one in the theater), two dinners, and a trip to Macy's had passed, and I was feeling only slightly less free and easy in the new shoes I'd bought at Macy's, where we'd had the first real talk of our relationship and where we'd bought Laurel a coffee maker for my apartment.

Might one consider a jointly owned coffee maker—a gargantuan contraption, it turned out, that now sat on my kitchen counter, looming over me every time I ate—something to throw a man off his intended road? Yes, I suppose. But, I'd rationalized, the machine was not so much a gift for Laurel as for myself, so she would be willing to spend the night at my place—so we could both have our cake and eat it too, so to speak. For the time being, everything was under control.

Good thing, too, that I wore the new shoes to class, because they had soft soles, and I was late. When I arrived to the classroom, I gently set the bottoms of my new shoes—moccasins to match her boots, as I'd told her in Macy's—on the vinyl floor and slipped through the door.

Given the events of the past twelve days, I was not as concerned about being tardy as I previously might have been. I'd missed the last class entirely. Although, truth be told, I would have missed that class regardless of my status with the teacher. I'd been in the thick of dealing with Ezmerelda, who wouldn't budge from her position on Omnipotence without an advance fee. The sum was a substantial one, too much for me to articulate without triggering the heart attack that is eventually headed my way, but I didn't want to rock the boat with my still-to-be-locked-down, signed-on-the-dotted-line client—not *this* client—so I paid Ezmerelda what she asked, out of my own pocket.

Laurel, in a brown mini-skirt and the same I HEART LA T-shirt that had done me in a couple of weeks ago, was standing next to the blackboard, where she'd written in giant chicken scratch: WHAT'S YOUR TYPE?

The sentence, apparently, had set off a sixth-grade response. Judd was winking and pointing at her. The guy near the window hollered out that his type was Angela, this tall brunette who sits next to Rhonda. Rhonda said Angela was her type too. I thought of my pronouncement to Broc that Laurel was not my type, and chuckled as I slipped into my seat. Did her decision to wear the T-shirt, I wondered, have something to do with me? Or was it simply the only shirt she could find in the clutter?

"That's not what I mean," Laurel said. She added that she was glad she'd grabbed our attention and clarified that she was talking about story type. "Good film writers know what type of story they want to write when they begin to work." She threw on the board examples of what I assumed were story types—Spiritual Quest, Mystery, Romance. "Different types of stories have different types of arcs. You need to know what type yours is so you know how to tell it."

Moving into the center of the room in her mini-skirt, she announced that we were to go around and say our story type so she could make sure we each had a handle on the concept.

As I listened, I was shocked by the level of thought my peers had put into this. Revenge, War Romance, Unexpected Visitor, Loss of Love, and, of course, Candy's Parallel Journey. Whatever that was.

One by one we circled the room, much like we had on the first day of class. How far I'd come since that day, I thought. As the class members pigeonholed their scripts, I laundry-listed the actions I'd taken toward personal growth in the past six weeks. I'd committed to a class. I'd written seven scenes. I'd changed up my footwear. I'd casually slept with the teacher, and to boot, I'd had a public reading of my work—a success, even if it did take place in a bakery. In fact, at dinner this past Sunday night, just after Broc (in person) and Rachel (by phone) berated me for buying the coffee maker, Marcy had said that the Sunday bakery crowd had been asking for an encore, and Estie had said that she was eager to do one. In fact, she said she'd like to stage this one more formally, with different people reading different characters' parts. "A table read," she said.

"Where'd you pick up that lingo?" I asked.

"Duh," she said. "Laurel."

I didn't share with my niece that she wasn't the only Melman who had Laurel to credit for enlightenment. Thanks to the Mormon Rodeo, I now wrote, drank coffee, and slept around. I was practically a Renaissance man.

Laurel tapped on my desk. "Mr. Melman, what would you call your story?"

I shrugged. I had no idea what kind of story I was telling. I hadn't written a word since the morning after the drop-in. Not that I didn't intend to continue, but between working and flinging, I hadn't had time. "I'd call it entertaining."

The class chuckled—except for Candy, who turned up her tiny nose.

To my surprise, Laurel did not. "Actually, that's a great point. Any movie, no matter the type, must entertain," she said. "After all, there are only so many story types. In the end, what will set yours apart is the way you tell it. It's your voice and your vision that really count." She thanked me for my contribution.

I sat back in my chair, gloating at Candy.

Laurel looked at me. "That said, can you be more specific about yours?"

"Sure," I offered. "Mine is a Parallel Journey story too." I smiled at Candy.

"Oh, please," Candy mumbled.

Laurel crossed her arms. "Is that so? I haven't picked up on that from what I've read." She was annoyed. I could tell by the way she smacked her lips together. I studied her for signs that she and the woman I'd been spending my nights with, the owner of my coffee maker, were one and the same. I came up empty-handed. "I see it as more of a Coming of Age," she said.

I proceeded with more deference. "I like it," I said. "The designation adds a certain credibility. But I'm not sure how a story about two old folks can be a Coming of Age."

"I think it might be about more than two old people," Laurel said.

"Even if it's about a bunch of old people, it doesn't seem to me that—"

She told me to stop talking. Then she walked to the blackboard and scrawled a word. Bildungsroman. She asked if anyone had heard of it before.

"Is it Yiddish?" I asked.

Laurel rolled her eyes while Rhonda spouted off that the word was German, coined by a man named Karl Morgenstern in the late 1800s. Laurel thanked her and then explained that the term Bildungsroman described a story characterized by the growing up of a stunted person who is pushed by a childhood event to go on a journey until the light bulb goes on one day and he gets it.

"Gets what?" Don asked.

"Gets what it takes to be a grown-up in the real world," Laurel said. "It's a fancy word for a Coming of Age."

"How can a guy who's this immature write a Coming of Age?" Candy demanded.

"I'm not," I said. "It's a Parallel Journey."

Don gave me an elbow in the side for my quick comeback, and Laurel gave Candy and me warnings. One more snide comment out of either of us and we would be asked to leave. Clearly, I was getting no special treatment in the classroom.

The couples club, however, was. When their turn came, Helene revealed that they were having creative differences over whether their film, now called *Not Totally the Titanic*, was an Adventure or a Journey. Susan felt that the story was a Journey. The rest of the group disagreed, and no one would relent.

After five minutes of bickering, Laurel asked them to form a circle with their desks. She pulled up a chair to mediate and told the rest of us to take out our notebooks. "You are going to spend the remainder of class doing an exercise that will help you get the feel for the trajectory of various types of movies. You can spend your time testing how well your individual stories fit into an outline for the type of movie you are writing, or you can pick any of the story types listed on the handout and write a new outline for it." She asked Candy to distribute the handouts. "Who knows," Laurel said to the room as she took a seat next to Susan, "maybe you'll get an idea for another great story."

I accepted my paper without glancing at Candy. I barely glanced at the handout, either. The last thing I needed was another great story idea, and I was unconcerned with whether mine fit into an arc. So, ignoring the worksheet, I opened my notebook and began to sketch my next scene.

GRANDMA ESTELLE'S FIRST DRIVING LESSON, I wrote at the top of the page. I hadn't planned to include a shot of my grandma's first driving lesson. I was headed straight to the Introduction of Lucille Garlovsky. However, now that I was writing a Parallel Journey, I figured my next scene should open with one. So, I drew a line down the center of the page and on one side of it I drew a picture of Grandma Estelle and my folks skidding down Collins Avenue toward the Publix parking lot in our rental car. On the other, I drew Slip, my sisters, and myself racing down Collins to the Rascal House in the Caddy. Then, for clarification, I wrote, SPLIT

SCREEN. VIRTUALLY THE SAME SCENE IN BOTH SCREENS.
EARLY MORNING, COLLINS AVENUE

Of course, a split screen wasn't necessary here. Publix and the Rascal House were only a shopping center apart, one just north of Imperial Towers, the other just south, close enough to be shot on a single screen. But I decided—for no other reason than to outdo Candy—to go with the split.

I added identical palm trees and balls of sun on each side of the paper. Then I made musical notes escaping from the windows of both cars, because I was also going to throw in music. Laurel had taken me to see *Road to Perdition* a few nights earlier—my first movie in years, perhaps my first drama since *Saturday Night Fever*. I'd protested, but she'd promised I'd like it because it had similarities to my movie, like father figures, gangsters, and cars. As we took our seats and she ripped open a bag of licorice with her teeth, she told me to watch the movie as a film writer, not just an audience member. "Pay attention to what makes it work and incorporate those things into your own project," she advised. I was doing just that, which was why my film would now be featuring Tom Hanks and Paul Newman, as well as a high-class soundtrack, though nothing as bagpipey as in *Road to Perdition*. I was thinking more along the lines of "My Life" by Billy Joel.

I did my best to depict my mother convulsing on the floor of the rental car as my grandmother, going five miles an hour, hugged her head to the windshield and her tires to every inch of yellow line. I crossed out the musical notes coming from her car after deciding that the radio was probably not playing. My grandma didn't need any outside distraction. Then I doodled oversized smiles onto the faces of the kids in the Caddy. On the other side of the page, in bubbles next to my father in the passenger's seat, I added the instructions he gently issued to my grandma above my mother's laughter.

"Relax your grip, Ma."

"A little bit more on the accelerator, Ma."

"Ma, open your eyes."

According to Melman lore, the "open your eyes" remark pushed my mother's bladder over the edge, and her wet pants brought an immediate end to the morning's driving lesson. So I decided to FADE OUT on my mother strewn across the floor of the rental car's back seat and FADE IN on my father talking to Slip in the kitchen of Apartment 1812, where the parallel journeys came to identical ends.

I flipped my page and began a quick sketch of the kitchenette, of the small round table tucked into the corner, my father and Slip seated at it. I labeled it: MORNING. INT. APARTMENT 1812. TENSION MOUNTS AT THE KITCHEN TABLE.

Tension was mounting, too, around the couples club circle. Susan was now admitting that long before this class exercise, she'd stumbled on a new project idea. "I've been tossing around the concept of a twilight years Rom/Com about old high school sweethearts who reunite decades later in the hospital, where their respective spouses are recovering from hip replacement surgery," she told Laurel. "I think I'd like to sever ties with the *Not Totally the Titanic* crew to pursue this story."

The entire class now turned to watch the group. Tears began to stream down Susan's face.

"I commend you for your bravery—and for daring to go where no Rom/Com has gone before," Laurel told Susan as Helene handed her Kleenex left over from *Schindler's List*.

Don was griping that this whole thing—the movie, the class—had been Susan's idea. "We all signed on to help you rise out of the haze of Harold's death," he said, "and now you're leaving us high and dry."

Laurel glanced over at me and saw me staring at the couples club meltdown.

"Keep your eyes on your own work, Mr. Melman."

I told her no one's eyes were on their own work.

"It's okay if he listens," Susan said, but then she began to cry again, and I decided that I'd actually prefer to be back in Apartment 1812. I picked up my pen and put down my head.

I drew the doggie bag of bagels that sat on the kitchen table. We always brought home the extra bagels and rolls from breakfast and every other meal, but I remember my father accepting the bag of bread from Slip that morning like he'd never seen anything so delicious.

In the movie, he'll say, "Thank you, I wasn't sure I'd live to eat again," like he means it. In this same earnest way, he will also say, "There's gonna be an afternoon lesson, too. We'll need two a day to get her up to snuff."

"You ain't getting her ready for the races," my grandfather will reply. His fingers will push an ace-of-spades ashtray back and forth on the table.

I added the ashtray to my drawing. Then cigars. Then smoke.

They were able to speak freely because my grandmother was soaking her feet in the bathtub. Word was that her sandals had pressed awkwardly into the accelerator and against her feet as she drove. She was blaming the sandals for her poor performance.

In the movie, my father will slather cream cheese onto a bagel as he says, "Twice a day will ready her for just the ordinary road." He'll pause to take a bite, then add, "It's going to be an uphill climb. She doesn't come by it naturally."

"Naturally?" Slip will chuckle and puff a bunch of air through his pursed lips. "She didn't come by it naturally when she was twenty. What makes you think it'll be any different at sixty-eight?"

My father will shrug. "Well, maybe lessons will do some good."

My grandfather will shake his head. "You don't get it, Allen. Driving just ain't in her."

I understood what my grandfather was saying. Rachel had been taking piano lessons for about five years at this point, and even Mr. Tavollis, the teacher, called her Lead Hands. My grandfather's confidence, however, surprised me. Driving seemed easier than playing the piano.

I added to my sketch three kids—two girls and a boy—dressed in bathing suits and standing in the doorway to the kitchen, since by this time, say nine o'clock, my sisters and I were suited up and waiting to go down to the pool. I also attempted a rendering of Marcy's white hat with the orange plastic sun shield hanging from the sides and the red propeller on top.

I remember shouting as we stood there, "Can someone please take us downstairs? Mom's not ready yet."

Confirmation came from the hall bathroom. "Can you please

take them down today? I need a little more time. I'm washing out my pants and underwear."

As everyone assembles for the trip downstairs, the narrator will explain that his mother often washed clothes in the bathroom sink. She hated doing the laundry in Imperial Towers 100. The laundry room was communal, which meant you not only had to schlep your baskets to the basement, you also had to pay to use the machines. Four quarters per load, plus my mother paid an additional twenty-five cents to me to stand guard for the duration of the wash because residents had no problem pulling someone else's load mid-cycle to accommodate their own.

As I'd explained to Laurel at Macy's the other day, the culture of Imperial Towers 100 was dog-eat-dog. Neither civility nor mercy existed. It was like *Lord of the Flies* with old people.

Who knows why the place was so rough and tumble. My theory is that the survival instinct that led the Jews to claw their way through the deserts of Egypt and the doors of Ellis Island no longer served a function. Instead it had, like a sociological lupus, turned folks against each other.

Which was why my sisters and I liked to do the initial pool visit of the day together. Grabbing those chaises, enough for your whole party, and marking them with your respective monogrammed towels was like going to battle, and we felt power in numbers.

I began to sketch the chaos on the pool deck: grandmothers hell-bent on assuring their kids a nice vacation and young girls hell-bent on going home with a tan pulling and tugging at chairs the same way that Laurel and I saw them tugging on wedding dresses at the annual Macy's bridal gown sample sale. Now that I thought about it, my experience with Laurel in Macy's and the scene on the pool deck were nothing if not Parallel Journeys. I might have pointed out this realization to Laurel now, had she not been so embedded in Susan's breakdown.

"They have Vera Wang up there," Laurel had said to me as we walked into Macy's. She'd nodded upwards, five or six floors so, in the direction of violent screaming and yelling.

"They must be holding her hostage," I'd replied, though I knew what she meant. Luckily, we were heading in the opposite direction of the bridal frenzy. Housewares was in the bottom of the massive store.

"Her dresses, fool," she said. "Everyone wants her dresses." She went on to say that she, too, wanted to get married in one of those dresses, like a real New Yorker, except she didn't want to pay full price. "You know what I mean?" she asked.

I choked on my blueberry smoothie. The whole reason I liked her, the secret of our relationship success, was that she wasn't like a real New Yorker. And what Laurel didn't understand, like my father didn't understand about my grandma's ability to drive, was that she just didn't have it in her. "You mean to tell me that every person who wears a Vera Wang dress is a real New Yorker?" I asked. Then I took a page from Marcy's playbook: "Where were you the day they taught Venn diagrams?"

By this time, we'd found our aisle and Laurel was lowering two boxes to the floor for examination. "I don't know, Chuckerman," she said as she lowered herself after them. "I was probably absent that day."

"You know, *Venn diagrams*. The circles. Some intersect. Some don't. Subsets." I drew in the air, trying to explain. I had a circle of girls from Utah and another of real New Yorkers, the kind I knew from Imperial Towers Building 100, the kind who tugged on pool chairs, the kind whose grandchildren were probably the ones six floors above us, tugging on Vera Wang. "Most of the Imperial Towers 100 women were widows for a reason. They pulled and tugged their husbands to death. The two circles don't intersect."

"I have no idea what you're talking about." She yanked open one of the boxes to have a closer look.

"I'm saying that there cannot possibly be any overlap between the circle of real New Yorkers and the circle of Mormons with eight siblings, two horses, and a homemade daisy bathrobe in the closet. You can wear Vera Wang 'til the cows come home and you still won't be a real New Yorker. It's not in your genes." To punctuate my point, I gave a long slurp on the last bits of my smoothie.

Laurel looked up from the boxes and smiled wide. "That's quite a theory, Chuckerman. Let's make sure I understand. Are you saying that our circles cannot overlap or that you don't want them to overlap?"

"Both," I told her. "I wouldn't want the circles to overlap, but luckily, overlap in our case is genetically impossible."

Laurel stood. "And you wouldn't want them to overlap—by, say, me converting to Judaism—because if I converted and we stayed together in some crazy, hypothetical world, I'd eventually end up killing you?"

"Cause of death would be more of a gradual erosion of spirit than murder in the first degree, but yes, that's the basic gist. I've seen it happen. Which is why I'm so happy that my circle and yours do not overlap. Our relationship is working because we have nothing in common. Aside, now, from this machine," I kicked the box containing the Krups 888 Cafe Centro Time 10-Cup Coffee/Espresso Machine.

She did her single eyebrow raise, something I've never been able to do, and pushed on the brim of my Cubs hat. "Trust me, Chuckerman, you never have to worry about me being anything like you."

I nodded, confident that I had made myself clear, and went on to buy the machine and then the moccasins.

However, when I ran the Vera Wang incident by Rachel later that day, she told me I was wrong. "A woman can transform herself into anything she wants, depending on what she wants. Genetics have nothing to do with it," she informed me. "As far as women are concerned, you never can be sure who you are dealing with." From her prosecutor's office in Chicago, she suggested I proceed with caution. "It could be," she continued, as I stared at the Krups Caffe Centro on my counter, "that she's one of those who's just pretending to be all natural, all T-shirt and jeans, until she lures you in and the ring appears." She gave one of her long, closing-argument, nail-in-the-coffin pauses. "You may be on a slippery slope to Lucille Garlovsky."

This is the way the Melmans express affection. We devil's advocate. Second-guess. Rain on each other's parades.

I told her slippery slopes didn't matter. "I'm only concerned with who Laurel is now. By the time she transforms in the way you are talking about, she'll be long gone."

Rachel told me to mark her words.

I told her she was wrong.

As I sat in class and watched the Mormon Rodeo throw a foot on her chair and a hand on her hip and rasp to Susan that life without Harold would give her opportunities to discover new creative, emotional, and sexual sides, I couldn't help but think of Rachel's warning about transformations, slippery slopes, and the dangers of dealing with women. Which led me, suddenly and seamlessly, back to not just my movie but also the scene I'd originally planned to start off with: The Introduction of Lucille Garlovsky.

CHAPTER 10:

Introducing Lucille

~~

I ended up writing the Lucille scene a few days after class at the Grey Dog Cafe, a crowded NYU hangout with tiny tables and fabulous food. I'd never have pegged a place of such utter action as a solid writing spot, but Laurel convinced me otherwise. She explained that she'd written her previous script there—*Deep in the Heart of Daisy*, a drama detailing the life Laurel's mother would have had if she'd had the courage to leave her husband.

"She marries a real estate developer and relocates to an estate in the Ojai Valley. A life of love and leisure," Laurel explained as we walked down Broadway toward the Grey Dog. "It's a Spiritual Journey story." She winked.

I'd been fixated on story types since her last class. At the end of it, Laurel had told Susan, as part of her pep talk, that a person is never too old to come of age. She told Susan to give herself the freedom to grow, adding, "I say we call it your second coming."

Don responded with, "I say we call it horse shit."

I didn't disagree with Don, but still, I'd taken to labeling the kind of stories we all were living. Broc, according to the picture he'd painted at lunch, was living a Horror or maybe a Tragedy.

Share was living a Rags to Riches. I couldn't decide if Laurel was on a Spiritual Journey or, as Rachel would contend, a Quest. But wasn't everyone's story in some way a Quest? Weren't we all trying to attain or achieve something or someone? Marcy, a woman who didn't set goals and lived according to whim, was on a Quest to find me a wife and kids. Even I, a person accused of having no interest in personal growth, was on a Quest to acquire a new client and to live a life free of major illness, entanglement, or catastrophe.

"*Deep in the Heart of Daisy* sounds to me like a Quest," I now told Laurel.

"Spiritual Journey," Laurel repeated, explaining that the focus was on the main character's self-discovery.

Regardless, New Line Cinema apparently had optioned the script for a decent amount of money, which was why Laurel believed the Grey Dog gave "good pages."

The Grey Dog also gave Laurel good service. They knew her like the Reebok Club knows me, and so she was allowed to sit and write as long as she wanted—which, that Saturday, was hours. She was preparing final changes to her suicide script, currently entitled *Mormons Don't Die.* I, left with nothing better to do, analyzed the food and the crowd while jeopardizing my life by downing a club sandwich (copious amounts of turkey, a side of Thousand Island dressing, and buttered rye). Eventually, with nothing better left to do, I wrote. I decided to sketch this scene out in words rather than images. It would be a perfect one, I thought, for Estie's table read.

———

THE INTRODUCTION OF LUCILLE GARLOVSKY

The scene will open on the pool deck, where our arrival will be met by a group of my father's dental patients.

"Dr. Melman," they'll holler, smiling and waving like genuinely pleasant people. The audience will see faces they recognize from around our dining room table: Ida from 27, Gloria from 14, Jean from 22, and Lil Sharp, who, everyone knew because she was always complaining about the noise coming from the game room, lived on the Lobby Level.

The narrator will explain that everyone in this group was in desperate need of dental work. They were motivated by pain rather than principle, and their plan to get Slip back into the card room will eventually reflect this lack of moral compass.

"Hello, ladies," my father will call out as the zealous flow of sunbathers carries us past the patients.

Jean from 22 will speak first: "Allen, we've got another approach. We were playing too fair and square yesterday." She had a voice as rough as the Bronx that carried beautifully over the howl of the wind and the hysteria of the crowd.

Next, Gloria from 14: "Got to fight fire with fire."

Again, Jean from 22: "It won't take long to explain. You'll get back to your family soon enough."

Who knows what else they said, as we were by now caught up in battle, tossing towels and tubes of Bain du Soleil at empty chaises to claim them. In the movie, other folks will tell the ladies to shut up, and my father will say to Slip, "For people with teeth trouble, their mouths never stop moving. I can see why you like the card room."

"Do me a favor, Allen," my grandfather will say, putting a hand on my father's shoulders. "Tell all them babes to go tan their fannies."

My sisters and their friends, already lumped onto a single chair, will break into fits of laughter and throw around the phrase for the rest of the day.

"Why would I do that?" my father will answer. "They mean well. They're just trying to help."

"We don't need any help," Slip will tell him. He'll point to an ashtray a couple of tables over and ask if I can grab it for him.

As I climb over a row of lounge chairs to reach it, my father will say, "I beg your pardon? We don't need help? I think Ma would disagree." He'll shake his head in disbelief and help me down from the chairs as I return and hand the filthy black plastic tray to Slip. "By anyone's account," he'll add, "you are up to your ears in trouble."

Slip will chuckle as he sets the ashtray on a table and sits himself in the chaise next to it. Then he'll look up into the sun and sigh like he's poolside in paradise. "Trouble? Are you kidding me? I've never been better." He'll pull a cigar out of his shirt pocket. "Even if they let me back into the card room, I may not go." His hand will slap the chaise holding Marcy and Rachel. "This is the life. Right here."

"You're talking nonsense," my father will tell Slip. He'll toss his baseball cap on a chair in frustration and flash a fake smile at the dental patients. He'll signal with his finger that he'll be with them in a minute.

"You want to talk nonsense, go have a word with your following over there." As Slip speaks, he'll peel his cigar out of its plastic.

My father will stretch his sore back—the onset, I see now, of a bad case of arthritis. Then, with a shake of his head, he'll walk toward his patients.

But the scene will continue, as it did that day, with me and Slip. I remember he pulled a lighter out of his pants pocket before he said, "Your father's too goddamn loyal." Then he tried to get a flame to hold long enough to light his cigar, but the wind wasn't cooperating.

I sat on the chair next to him, as far away as possible from my sisters, their friends, and their conversation about how old you had to be to use a tampon, and asked, "What do you mean?" I hadn't realized that you could overdo it in the loyalty department.

"Have you heard the expression 'loyal to a fault'?" my grandfather asked me.

I shook my head no. They were quick shakes, as I hated to admit ignorance to my grandfather.

He threw me a towel and instructed me to hold it over his body like a fort so he could light his cigar without disruption and lecture me. "Let me put it to you this way, Davy boy. Too much of a good thing ain't no good neither." He pushed away the towel and took a puff. "You get where I'm coming from?"

In terms of cookies or TV, I did. But I'd never applied the concept to character traits. Especially ones that my parents, my father especially, were always talking up.

"No, not really," I said under my breath. I stared in the direction of my father and his people. He had people for a reason. His arm looped around Ida from 27. Lil Sharp tossed her head like a teenager. Jean from 22 laughed and put her crown back into her change purse. I couldn't hear the conversation, but based on the way my father's head nodded and his hands waved, I knew he was telling them not to worry, he'd take care of everything. He hollered over to us that he was going with the group to track down Gladys Greenberg and Eileen to make another appeal. Whether or not this was too much loyalty, I didn't know. But I didn't see a downside.

Slip, on the other hand, saw things differently. "He's a dentist. Not a keeper of world peace. At some point, a guy's gotta start looking out for number one. That's all them ladies are doing. They don't give a shit about me or your father. All they care about is getting something for nothing." To make clear what the ladies were after, he smiled wide and banged the end of his cigar into his teeth. Then he took a long puff and inhaled deeply as I jammed my hands between the yellow strips of plastic that ran across my chaise. I didn't know what else to do.

Generally Slip didn't issue more than a sound bite at a time, but today, he kept on going. "Take it from me, Davy boy, a man can't let himself be taken advantage of like that. He's got to be willing to make a few enemies. Because if you're not willing to make enemies, how the hell are you supposed to know who your friends are?"

His question was a good one. I still have no answer. Making enemies has never been my strong suit (although I seem to be making strides with my film colleague, Candy).

"He's only trying to help you get back to playing cards," I said.

"He's wasting his time," he said. Lifting his hips up from the chair, he reached in his pocket and pulled out a handful of change. He began to pick out the quarters. "If I felt like it, I could muscle my way back in that card room in two minutes. But I'm happy here. So let's relax. Things like this have a way of working themselves out naturally." He gave my chair a friendly kick and, without skipping another beat, moved on to making quarters appear from behind the ears of all the kids around us.

It was then that Lucille made her entrance. The script will capture the moment with the fanfare of all caps: LUCILLE GARLOVSKY BUSTS THROUGH THE GLASS DOORS TO THE DECK.

Suddenly, the magic tricks ended and, it seemed, another kind of magic began. Did I understand this then? Did the "loose cannon" remark float back into my head? No, don't be silly. I was ten and upset that I couldn't figure out the coin thing.

Rachel has always claimed that she understood. She probably did, but she didn't say anything at the time. Like the rest of us, she just stared. As will the audience, because the sight of Lucille (played by Susan Sarandon or maybe an aged-up Catherine Zeta-Jones) will, as Laurel likes to say, hijack the screen.

Unlike the rest of the women, who either left their hair a natural gray or dyed it yellow, Lucille's was jet black. It was thick. It was long.

Also unlike the other women, who came to the pool in frumpy cover-ups they rarely removed or in slacks like my Grandma Estelle, Lucille Garlovsky strutted onto the deck every morning in a brightly colored, high-cut suit and heels.

Legend had it she arrived on the deck every day, hurricane or shine, at the same time, which was about fifteen minutes after the melee from the lounge chairs quieted and everyone was reclined and free to stare. She always gave the door a tremendous fling, so it opened to it fullest, gave the group a voluptuous, "So how are we all this morning?" and then, when she'd gotten front and center, separated the handles of her rope and began to jump.

I never paid Lucille much attention, other than as a signal, like the rising of the sun, that the day was officially underway and it was permissible to go into the pool. Never, that is, until that morning.

"Well, well, will you look at what the cat dragged in," Lucille will announce in place of her usual greeting. "To what do we girls owe this honor?" She'll say "awna" instead of honor, but we'll understand. She'll stand, arms akimbo, hip out to the side. With her still-folded rope, she'll tap Slip's knee. "So you think you're gonna join our crowd now, Slippy boy?" She'll laugh.

Laughter will come, too, from the ladies. At least a dozen women will be watching, including my Grandma B and Aunt BoBo. One of the women will holler, "You tell him, Lucille."

Slip will smile, clearly enjoying being the center of attention, the object of the head cheerleader's affection. I, too, will sit in awe, my head bobbing up and down.

"Beggars can't be choosers, Lucille," my grandfather will respond. Then he'll wink at her and put his cigar in his mouth.

"Always with the wisecracks, aren't you?" she'll say.

The cigar will come back out. "I'm just telling it like it is."

"Well, since you're so honest, I guess you can stay." Lucille will tap the rope on Slip's head. "As long as you promise not to beat the crap out of any of us."

At this, the script will direct the women to hoot with laughter and Slip to take the rope out of Lucille's hand and wave it in front of her.

"Watch your language, Ms. Garlovsky," he'll say. "I got my kids with me."

Lucille will look my way and tousle my hair. Laurel likes to do this too. "You've got fabulous curls, kiddo. Wear it long and you'll never have trouble with the girls." She'll give a quick wink. "You can take that to the bank."

At this point in the movie, the actor who plays me should be replaced by a mannequin, because that's what I'd become. I didn't move. I didn't answer. I couldn't. I'll tell you, as a celebrity fragrance man, I meet stars all of the time. Yet never in my professional career have I been as bowled over as I was by my encounter that morning with Lucille Garlovsky. Whether the feeling came from proximity to the legendary widow herself or to the breasts that poured over the top of her suit, I'm not sure. What I do know is that I—borrowing my mother's litmus test of love—heard bells.

Consequently, I didn't notice, like Rachel did, that Lucille's toes were painted the same red as her lips and that both lips and toes matched her suit. And I didn't notice, like Marcy did, that the handles on her jump rope had LUCILLE painted on them in pink nail polish. When Marcy also observed that the skin on Lucille's knees looked like a lizard's at lunch that day, however, I realized that I had noticed that.

The camera will follow us upstairs for lunch, and so the audience will see my mother tell Marcy, "Be nice. It will happen to you one day."

"No it won't," Marcy will answer. She'll snort, her natural reaction to any preposterous suggestion.

My mother will move away from the counter, where she's been making peanut butter sandwiches out of leftover breakfast rolls. She will then throw her forty-something leg onto the kitchen table.

Borrowing from Laurel's BASIC CAMERA SHOTS poster, I'll use a CUT-IN shot here, so the camera zooms in on the leg amid the sandwiches and follows my mother's fingers as she points to veins and other apparent eyesores I'd never noticed prior to this demonstration.

"Do you think my legs looked like this when I was your age?" she'll demand. "I got news for you. My legs are halfway to Lucille's, and yours are on the road to mine." She'll mutter, as she still does today, about the ravages of time. Then she'll pull her leg down and instruct us to appreciate our youth while we're young.

Marcy and I—more interested in the leg lift than the lesson—will laugh, but Rachel will make a face like she's seen the devil.

"I pray to God I never get lizard legs," she'll say, stretching the skin down around her thigh, looking for signs of things to come. "I pray, I pray." It's a prayer she's attempting to answer herself today with regular use of cellulite creams and a refusal to consume sugar or animal products.

My mother will try to give her a head's up on this. "I don't think God's going to answer that prayer."

"Why not?" Rachel will ask.

"Because he's too busy," I'll offer.

"Or maybe he likes lizard legs," Marcy will suggest. "Maybe God *has* lizard legs."

Unlike Rachel, my mother never had any dietary restrictions and always waited faithfully through lunch, hovering like a seagull over the Intracoastal, for any morsel we left behind. Her pride was never too big and no crumb was ever too small.

She'll pick up a piece of Marcy's crust. "You are who you are. You get what you get. The trick is to like your skin whether it holds up or not."

"Like Lucille," Marcy will say. "She wouldn't jump rope in lizard skin unless she liked it."

"And she wouldn't flirt, either," Rachel will whisper.

She and Marcy will laugh. My face will redden beyond my sunburn. To me the word "flirt" was synonymous with my limited knowledge of sex.

"What does that mean?" my mother will ask.

As my mother enjoys her scraps, Rachel will tell her everything that transpired between Slip and Lucille that morning, including "flirting." Rachel will speak the word slowly and with excessive enunciation as she bites the string from the hood of her bathing suit cover-up.

At this point, I bolted down the hallway. Be it about the birds and the bees or my grandfather and Lucille, I did not intend to discuss this topic or even witness it being discussed. From the hallway floor a few steps from the kitchen, I was able to hear the evil but not see it. And what I heard was my mother spitting out her sandwich when Marcy offered up, "Grandma B says Lucille's itching to have an affair."

As tantalizing a remark as this was, I must pause to explain that my sisters' story was as much news to me as it was to my mother. Earlier that morning, the minute after Lucille had messed my hair, I'd headed for the pool, never to return until I saw my mother hanging over the balcony waving a dish towel—the well-established signal for families with poolside exposure that lunch was ready.

Of course, in the movie, the audience already will have seen this activity unfold. They'll have seen the boy head to the pool. They'll have seen the mother call for lunch. They will not have seen the flirting between Slip and Lucille, because I don't think I can bear to write it.

But they will eventually see the boy who plays me hiding in the hallway on his hands and knees, listening intently to the conversation about the flirting, which will go something like:

"Grandma B said what?"

"She said that Lucille wants to have, you know . . . an affair."

My mother will put down her plate and take a seat. "Marcy, take your head out of the box of cookies. Do you know what that means?"

I, for one, having no idea, will crawl closer to the kitchen, still not wanting to be a party to the conversation but sure that I'd better grasp its gist.

I'll see first that Marcy has stacked her finger with Salernos. (I remember they looked good.)

"I know what it means," she'll assure my mother.

My mother will signal with her hand for Marcy to cough up some sort of definition.

Marcy will comply. "It's when you go on a date with someone else even though you are married." She'll stick a full cookie in her mouth, as if to formalize that she has hit the nail on the head.

"No, idiot," Rachel will say. "It's when you kiss someone even though they're married. It's cheating."

"Well either way," Marcy will say, "it should be called an *un*fair instead of an *a*ffair."

"Yes, it should." My mother will pull Marcy's ponytail—which, I remember noticing, was the same color as the butter cookies.

"Well," Rachel will say, "Lucille can have one because she's a widow and she's bored."

"How do you know she's bored?" my mother will ask.

We could always tell when my mother was trying to not laugh in our faces; she'd push her tongue through the little space between her front teeth. The script will direct the actress who plays Paula Melman to do so now.

"Grandma B," Rachel will say.

"Grandma B told you this?"

"No," Marcy will admit. "She told Aunt BoBo, but we could hear."

I will lie on the carpet, predicting my mother's response: "You should not be listening in on other people's conversations."

Her words will come just like that, but then she will cough and continue, unable to help herself, "Did Aunt BoBo answer Grandma B?"

Rachel and Marcy will look at each other. Silence.

My mother will ask again.

Rachel, still chewing on the string, will nod her head yes.

"And?" My mother's hands will again gesture for information.

"She said Lucille was nothing but a two-bit hussy and Estelle should watch out."

"Oh fabulous," my mother will respond.

Rachel: "Is it true?"

My mother: "Is what true?"

Rachel: "Is Lucille a two-bit hussy?"

Marcy: "What is a hussy?"

I, also wanting to know, will hold my breath on the hallway carpet.

My mother will not define hussy but simply clarify that Lucille is not one. "No one is to use that word again," she'll instruct. Then she'll order my sisters to finish their cookies as she helps herself to one of her own and mumbles that the whole conversation has been nothing but disturbing.

I, to the contrary, found it overwhelming and mesmerizing.

While the kids finish eating, the narrator will explain that when you're a kid, you know a whole complicated world exists out there—the world of adults and their dealings, coinciding with yours but distant as the moon. I could feel its vibrations in the nighttime chatter and low whispers, in the "tsks-tsks" and the "isn't that a shames," in the "God forbids," in the "knock on woods," and naturally, in every "did you hear who died?" But I (maybe because I was male, or maybe because I was human) never had the desire to delve any deeper. It always seemed so complicated, so much easier to stay out of the fray. In fact, the closest I'd come ever to getting involved in making sense of the mess was in writing this silly movie.

Not so with Rachel and Marcy. They were like the Woodward and Bernstein of Imperial Towers Building 100, although not as on the mark—eavesdropping, spying, and piecing together and reporting (mostly to each other) the news from the adult world. I liked to be, and mostly was, left out. But on that day, the idea that they'd amassed such a load—not just the news itself but the vernacular—while I was doing cannonballs off the low dive caused me to sit up and come out of hiding.

When I do this in the movie, my mother will say, "You heard all this, too?"

A response will not be necessary, of course. Mothers know the answers to these questions automatically.

Another "oh fabulous" will issue forth, followed by a command to go back to the pool. "Stay away from the gossip," she'll holler as we head down the hall, and in the pre-SPF era of optimism, she'll add, "Try to keep your faces out of the sun."

CHAPTER 11:

Transitions

~~~

I assume, as Laurel instructed us to do, that my viewing audience will be intelligent and therefore will have inferred that we are on the cusp of Christmas from the strands of colored lights and preparatory hubbub around the pool deck. But at some point, like when the kids go back to the pool deck after lunch, the narrator should probably say something like, "It was Christmas Eve Day."

He will add that the pool deck is humming with excitement because the next day, Christmas, will bring the annual Christmas party—the centerpiece of the vacation, as reliable as the seasons themselves, as festive as two hundred boiled hot dogs can be. Nonetheless, he'll continue, we were kids, and to us the preparations for the event created a buzz that reverberated up to the highest balcony and as low as the deepest depths of the pool. As if we didn't know exactly what the next day would bring. As if the games might include something beyond ring toss and Bozo buckets. As if the dessert might stretch beyond red popsicles. As if Santa Claus might pay us a visit. As if any of us actually celebrated Christmas as a religious event.

But an event it was, and you can be sure that the prior scene will be shot so that the party setup is visible, prominent even, in the background.

I'm sure the director of the film will be able to figure this setup out for himself (or herself, as Laurel would have me emphasize). No special effects involved, just a lot of hauling. As the camera lingers over the afternoon activity, the audience will see the hauling of card tables, of metal vats for the hot dogs, of cardboard boxes labeled Buns, of oversized snowmen and matching Santa Clauses, of the record player and the albums of holiday songs.

The hauling will be done by Franklin, the building custodian and security guard, along with the evil Big Sid and a few of his cronies. The directing will be done by Eileen and her whistle, a typical silver instrument that she wore around her neck and blew in various patterns, like a shofar, to command her troops. The whistle made Christmas at the pool deck an unpleasant experience for adults (even those hearing deprived), which, my Grandma Estelle explained to us on our way to dinner that evening, was why she hadn't minded the crowds at the mall a bit.

Talk about omitting a key detail! I also forgot to explain in the last scene that as I did my cannonballs, my father had returned to the pool deck to report that he was finished with his dental patients and was taking my grandmother for gym shoes. "Nobody should be driving in those heels," he'd said, and speculated that they were part of Estelle's problem.

By dinner that night, he'd modified his position. And here is where we'll pull the camera from the pool deck and plop it down at the Rascal House using one of the techniques listed on the Basic Film Transitions handout Laurel had left on my kitchen table on Tuesday morning. She was going to distribute the handout later that night in class, which I had to miss due to work. With the handout, she had also left me a note saying the terminology was self-explanatory, I should be able to figure it out on my own. She gave me too much credit, I saw now, days later, as I sat at my desk and looked over the terms.

Laurel was asleep. Had it not been late, the middle of the night,

I might have woken her to tell her that I didn't see any difference between a CUT TO, a QUICK CUT, a FADE OUT, or a DISSOLVE TO. Only the SMASH CUT, described as an abrupt a shift used to startle the audience, like when a person wakes up from a nightmare, stood out to me. A notation next to the term said to use the SMASH CUT sparingly to avoid looking like an amateur. Since an amateur I am, I make no promises. In the meantime, however, we'll simply DISSOLVE TO the Rascal House's enormous and overstuffed waiting area.

Holy day or not, we were at the Rascal as early as usual, packed as tightly as usual in a line that extended much longer than usual, as no Jew likes to eat at home on Christmas Eve. My theory is that misery loves company, and the knowledge that everyone in the Western World but you is caroling and nogging forces minority religions to band together in a way you don't see any other time of year.

As the camera closes in on the Melman family, the audience will begin to pick up from the conversation between my father and mother that Estelle's afternoon driving lesson didn't go so well. Even in her new Adidas, which she will wear proudly as we stand in line.

"Whether or not they help her driving," my father will say to my mother, "the gyms are better for her to be walking around in."

"They are so comfortable!" Estelle will comment as the camera pans down to her Adidas-clad feet. "Now I can stand with you guys the whole time instead of sitting with Slip." She'll nod toward the senior waiting area, where Slip will be lined up on a rickety brown chair, winking at his favorite waitresses as they walk by him. "Merry Christmas to me," my grandma will exclaim. "Thank you, Allen. This is the nicest gift I ever got."

From our line—Parties of Five or More—Estelle will hike up her slacks and lift her leg to show her shoes to her friends in the adjacent line, Parties of Three or Four. Eventually, a big to-do will brew around the shoes. One friend will tap another, and gradually they'll all lean over to see Estelle's Adidas.

As the women bend down toward the shoes, the rest of the crowd will clamor skyward toward the finger sandwiches—mini corned beef and grilled cheese—that are being handed out to appease the Christmas Eve crowd. A panoramic shot will best capture the competing interests at work.

"Are they really that comfortable?" one of the women will ask Estelle.

"Yes, they are so comfortable, like standing on cotton balls."

"How much did you have to pay?"

"I haven't the faintest. They were a gift from Allen!"

My father will keep saying, "Enough, Ma. Take your foot off of the bar."

My mother will laugh and her mother, my Grandma B, who always joined us on Christmas Eve (a splitting of hairs, really, since Aunt BoBo and her crew were the party behind us in line), will ask my mother if she's getting shoes, too.

"No," my mother will answer.

"Good," my Grandma B will reply. "They're not my style." Any shoe that promoted physical activity was unlikely to be her style. Grandma B was, by anyone's account, the laziest woman alive. House shoes were her style.

Adidas, now they were mine. These were the exact shoes I'd been coveting. I'd spent the whole summer campaigning for a pair. As I've already mentioned, I wanted blues too—the Roms—but to no avail. They were leather and deemed too expensive for a ten-year-old boy. But they were perfect, apparently, for a sixty-eight-year-old woman.

The audience will see Davy's eyes fix on the blue-striped shoes and his eyeballs pop out of his head. The directive in the script will read, *Davy is speechless, but his face conveys jealousy toward his grandma and frustration toward his parents.* This seems to me like a tall order to fill with one person's face, but hey, I'm no actor. I'm sure whomever we hire will nail it.

In the meantime, the Melman party will inch its way up the line.

"One more and then us," Marcy will announce.

"No matter," my Grandma Estelle will reply, "I could stand forever."

At the same time, Grandma B, dressed in a sequined tracksuit, will chew methodically on a grilled cheese. "Does Slip know about the shoes?"

My mother will shrug.

Grandma B will press further. "Why does Estelle need them?" She'll guess bunions.

My mother will shrug again, smart enough not to reveal the reason. She knew a brouhaha would ensue—something I didn't anticipate.

"Estelle is learning to drive," I will announce to Grandma B as I smugly lean against the silver bars that separated our line from the others. I didn't think anything of the announcement. I was proud of my grandma. I was proud that driving had been my idea. I was even proud that my idea had been the catalyst for the new Adidas. Yes, I was jealous. But no, I didn't blow my grandma's driving secret out of spite, which is what Rachel accused me of after word of Grandma Estelle's driving lessons surpassed talk of her new shoes within the line.

This happened thanks to Grandma B, who relayed the news to Aunt BoBo at a speed too quick for a movie camera to capture. The audience, however, will bear witness as word spreads to the senior waiting area, along with speculation that either Slip is losing his driver's license or my father is taking away the Cadillac as punishment for his beating up Big Sid. None of this will sit well with Slip, and so the audience will also see my father jump the holding chain and dart over to Slip to restrain him from attacking his fellow seniors.

Slip will jump on Estelle instead. "You had to go blabbin', didn't ya," he'll say as he meets up with us on our way to our table. His legs will move like lightning. So will his hands, as he opens and closes them to symbolize the blabbing. "A trip around a parking lot and a pair of sneakers and already you're a big shot. Maybe you want to give Gloria a lift to the hairdresser tomorrow?"

"Tomorrow's Christmas," Rachel will whisper to my mother. "The hairdresser is closed."

"You are embarrassing us," Estelle will say as she smiles and waves at acquaintances, doing her best to pretend that everyone at the surrounding tables isn't looking our way. "For a change," she'll mumble to herself, "there's a scene around the Melmans."

"If we just could make it to our table in one piece," my father will say as he brings up the rear. "I have some good news."

No one will be listening.

"Papa, you shouldn't blame Grandma," Marcy will blurt out. "She didn't tell, Davy did."

As I turn ashen, Slip will give me a friendly shove into the booth. "I find that hard to believe. Davy's my man." He'll slide in next to me.

The audience might expect my Grandma B to step up and take some blame at this point, but instead they'll see her conveniently drop to the back of the pack and busy herself with lighting up a cigarette, leaving me no choice but to break down.

"I didn't know the driving lessons were a secret," I'll cry as I slide further around the sticky seats of our booth. I'll repeat myself like seven times; repetitive talking was a ritual I used to ward off tears. In this instance, however, the routine didn't work, and just as the waitress, wearing a green elf cap with jingle bells dangling from the end, plunked down the trough of sour kraut and basket of bread in the middle of the table, I burst into tears.

I did not have a handle on what set them off, but my adult self can see that the catalyst was a concoction of things—the outing of my grandmother, the jealousy over the Adidas, the guilt over the jealousy, and the worry over Lucille Garlovsky's itch for an affair— all topped off by the fear that I had given legs to everything by suggesting the driving lessons in the first place.

"Don't you worry, Davy," my Grandma Estelle will say to me as she fishes a ball of Kleenex from her purse and hands it to me. "You didn't mean any harm." She'll pull me closer to her and kiss my head.

"Of course he didn't," my Grandma B will offer as she smiles at me to the best of her ability and flicks ashes into her ashtray. (She wasn't ill-intentioned, just depressed and lazy. Prozac would have done wonders for her.)

I'll keep crying.

My Grandma Estelle will keep talking. "You'll see. Another lesson or two and I'll be racing down A1A like Mario Andretti. We'll see who's laughing then." She'll laugh at the prospect of it.

"I'm glad you're finding this funny," Slip will rant. "Although

I suppose that if my wife doesn't mind everyone thinking her husband can't take care of her, get her where she needs to go, then I don't neither. What the hell do I care," he'll say as he shakes salt on a piece of bread and butter like a madman. "I hate everyone in that goddamn building."

"Except Lucille," Rachel will whisper to her own bread and butter. Luckily, Slip won't hear her because my father will be yelling at him for over-use of the salt, Estelle won't hear because she'll be busy comforting me, and Grandma B won't hear because she's deaf. Only Marcy, my mother, and I will catch the remark, and in reaction to it Marcy will whisper, "The hussy." I will start to cry harder and my mother, seemingly to no one, will say, "Put a cork in it."

"Thank you, Paula," my Grandma Estelle will respond, thinking that the comment has been directed at Slip. Estelle hated controversy as much as Slip thrived on it. They were like war and peace, like the oil and vinegar my mother drizzled over her dinner salad, and the yin and yang I'm billing Laurel and me to be.

In the movie, dinners will be delivered to the Melman table, and with them quiet. The tears over my mistake will be eased by my grandmother's handkerchief and her secret promise to get me some Adidas herself. Marcy will wonder aloud, "How does Santa Claus, if there even is a Santa Claus, deliver presents to an apartment building since there's only one chimney?"—and with that idiotic remark, the mood and conversation at the Melman table will transition back to normal.

For everyone but me. I still felt the undercurrent of tension that follows a family upset, and I, an alarmist by nature, a pro at extrapolating finality from every bump in the road, had no stomach for it. I assume the audience will gather this from the way the Davy character slumps against his grandma's side, his face pale, his chocolate shake untouched.

"If I may have your attention, please." My father will clank his spoon against a water glass. Then he'll pause and wait for us all, even Grandma B, to look at him. "I am happy to announce that I have it on good word that Slip will once again be allowed into the card room."

He won't say how the deal was worked out, or by whom. He'll

reveal no details, explaining that they aren't relevant. "But in the next day or so," he'll explain, "all should go back to normal."

That the reinstatement will be shrouded in mystery will not favor a return to normality. Instead of the unilateral outpouring of congratulations that my father is anticipating, based upon his own raised glass of Coke, conversation will splinter in six different directions. The audience will see Marcy applaud and cry, "Our first present from Santa." They'll see Grandma B ask my mother to clarify what my father just said. Rachel will ask the important question, "Did you have to do something illegal?" I will wipe my nose and say, "We can go back to our games, Papa." My Grandma Estelle, looking more concerned than happy, will whisper to my mother, "I hope my driving lessons will continue." My mother will rub Estelle's shoulder and tell her, "Of course they will. One thing's got nothing to do with the other." Then Estelle will offer up the rest of her navy bean soup to the table and my mother will ask my father, "So when can Slip go back?"

Then Slip: "I'm not going."

Followed by silence. Except for the sound of my mother, who has accepted the soup from Estelle, choking on it. "What do you mean? Why wouldn't you go?"

We will all be wondering the same thing, except for Rachel, who will tactfully say, "Because he was having so much fun at the pool today."

We'll put a camera under the table so the audience can see my mother kick Rachel in the shin. Rachel will grimace.

"It was fun, wasn't it?" Slip will say to Rachel, his icy eyes lighting up. He always perked up when he spoke to any of us, so his giddy reaction couldn't be called evidence of an affair, although that's what Rachel would contend. "But that ain't the reason I'm not going." He'll pause to tear up his chicken.

We'll wait in silence.

"I ain't going out of principle, Allen."

"Oh please," my mother will say, laughing. "When have you ever been motivated by principle?"

"Whether you realize it or not, Paula Pie, I'm a man of great principle and conviction." Slip will smile and wink at my mother.

"It's just that some of the methods he uses to defend his principles lack principle," Grandma Estelle will chime in. "Which," she'll add, "have led to his convictions." She, my mother, and my Grandma B will laugh at her joke.

"I don't know what kind of devil you made a deal with, but I don't do business with the devil," Slip will say, shoving his napkin into his shirt collar. "Take it from me, that can only come back to bite you in the ass."

"I don't think now is the time to start standing on ceremony," my dad will answer as he leans over the table to wind his fork around some of my spaghetti. "You like to play cards, now you can play."

"Seems like it's Allen here who has no principles." This will be Slip.

My father will drop his noodle-filled fork onto his plate and shake his head. "I can't afford principles, Dad. I've got you. I'm not leaving town without you safely back in that card room."

"But you've got no trouble heading back north with her racing around the streets of Miami. Not only don't you have principles, but you don't have brains, neither." Chicken juice will spray from the corners of Slip's mouth as he adds, "Let her drive all she wants. As long as she doesn't get near my Cadillac."

"Leave my driving out of this," Estelle will order. She'll pause to swallow her portion of the chicken and then say to Slip, as pleasant as if she were suggesting a Sunday drive, "How about if I mind my business and you mind yours?" She'll look at us all. "Truthfully, I don't care about Slip's car, I don't care whether Slip returns to the card room, and I don't care who the devil is, either." She'll dab the corners of her mouth and eyes with her napkin. "I don't care what happens, as long as I get to keep driving."

With these words, we won't just CUT from the scene, we'll SMASH CUT. We'll jolt the audience from the familiar Rascal House to the foreign bedroom of Gladys Greenberg—specifically, to the image of her, ideally in 3D, standing before her mirror, stuffed into a jungle print leotard and matching bunny ears and cackling like the Wicked Witch of the West. From this, the terms of the dirty deal my father and his patients struck will begin to sink in with the audience. They will slowly come to understand that in exchange for Slip's return to the card room, Gladys Greenberg has been given a spot in my grandma's chorus line. They will realize why the terms of the deal were kept secret and will either laugh at the sight of Gladys Greenberg bulging and kicking in the suit or grimace as they anticipate Estelle's reaction to the news that my father, her son, sold her interests out for Slip's. No words will be spoken, no music will play. We'll just watch and squirm and finally FADE, leaving my poor grandma in the dark.

As much as I hate the actual dark, I'm a fan of the figurative kind. I believe that ignorance is as blissful as it's billed to be. I'm the kind of guy who'd just rather not know. I was the kid who hid the envelope when the report card came in the mail. I am the grown-up who wore long sleeve shirts all last summer to cover a suspicious-looking growth on my arm. When my sister finally dragged me to a doctor, he confirmed what I'd suspected: it was skin cancer, or at least the beginnings of a carcinoma, obviously a result of my endless hours in the Miami sun. It was also, fortunately, curable since, thanks to Marcy, I caught it early.

I am also the man who didn't ask a single question throughout an entire week as Laurel deposited various acquisitions onto my kitchen counter. On Monday, she unloaded a bunch of to-go coffee cups she'd bought at Duane Reade. On Tuesday, she went to the GreenFlea Market on Columbus, where she "scored," as she said, some oversized brown and blue mugs. On Wednesday, she came over with coffee and bananas from Zabar's. Not until that Friday evening, as I sat on a stool exhausted from a grueling but miraculously successful week at work and finally took in the entire scene, did I realize that she'd converted my kitchen, a room which had never seen more than a single person and a bowl of cereal at a time, into a local hangout. Chuckerbucks, I was now calling it.

As I stared, Laurel stacked the cups and mugs next to the machine. Also on deck was a container of low-fat milk. "In case," Laurel had explained, "anyone wants a misto."

Whatever a misto was, the Krups Caffe Centro apparently made it.

I nodded as she set a bottle of cinnamon powder next to the cups, along with packets of Sugar in the Raw that she'd lifted from the Grey Dog Cafe. Also in the mix was Chloe, who was uncomfortable as me with her change of locale. She slumped at Laurel's feet.

This activity went down a few weeks after the machine first took root on my countertop, a few days after I missed the class on Transitions.

"Marcy is set to bring scones and jelly donuts," Laurel informed me as she worked. "Yummy."

"When?" I looked at my watch. "It's already nine thirty."

Laurel clarified that Marcy and the kids were coming over in the morning. "For the machine's big debut."

"Like a christening," I said for the sake of conversation.

"More like a coming out," Laurel replied as she organized supplies and pushed buttons to grind the coffee. The machine does that too, did I mention? It grinds.

"Who's coming out?" I asked. I walked over to the machine and studied it. "Is there something the machine wants to tell me?"

Laurel told me, above the grinding, that I didn't need to be so literal. She just liked the ring of coming out better than christening. "This is not meant to be a religious event. It's just a coffee maker. Let's not bring God into it."

"Well, first I would argue that it's more than just a coffee maker. And second," I added as I grabbed some milk from the fridge and returned to my stool, "I would say that at least the Mormon God is involved, since he doesn't believe in coffee and you bought a machine the size of Yankee Stadium. If anything, I'd call this a cry for help."

Laurel sighed and grabbed the machine's instruction manual. "Chuckerman, please. I don't understand your need to draw these sweeping conclusions from every little thing. The coffee maker is just a machine, and your family is just coming over to see it, as well as to celebrate your new client, whoever she is. God has nothing to do with this."

I said okay. But as I sat at my no-longer-recognizable countertop in my no-longer-recognizable kitchen, I felt certain that the coffee maker, the Chuckerbuck, wasn't just a machine, and the alteration of my kitchen, for better or worse, had something to do with God. How else could this have happened? To me, the developments at home were as incomprehensible as my new client—whose name I could finally announce, since the deal was signed—choosing to go with me instead of a big-name shop to brand her line of fragrance and body products.

We'd presented Omnipotence on Wednesday and gotten the word Thursday. It was a go. As I've mentioned, I'd been working on this deal for months. I'd pulled countless all-nighters along the way, including one the day before the pitch, which had caused me to miss Tuesday night's class—*Transitions, Getting Gracefully from A to B*, the syllabus called it. *And by golly* (as my Grandma Estelle would have said), *what a rotten class for me to miss,* I thought as I hopped off my stool and moved toward Laurel, because I had no idea how I'd gotten from A to B. Less than three months earlier I'd been a one-man shop, successful in my arena but by no means the go-to guy for A-Listers. Now here I was, about to hit the big time with a world-famous star while a Mormon and her cat redecorated my kitchen.

From David Melman, the Bachelor to Chuckerman, Manager of the Chuckerbuck machine and the Schnoz behind Bailey Pierce's— yes, that's right, Bailey Pierce—Omnipotence campaign. In the words of the great prophet Grandma Estelle, life is a crapshoot. She never believed that people had a hand in how one moment morphs into the next. So, I wondered as I stared around my kitchen, what kind of lesson on transitions had Laurel been teaching?

I told Laurel that okay, we could call the next day's gathering a coming out, because the more I studied the Chuckerbuck, the more I got the vibe that it was probably gay. "The name alone," I said.

Laurel laughed. She said she'd ask Marcy to weigh in on the machine's orientation in the morning when she came for the unveiling. "Let's call it an unveiling."

I asked her to halt her preparations for a minute so I could ask her out on a date. I explained that my new client, whom I could now reveal, as well as her stylist, her agent, Ezmerelda, and I were going to a celebratory dinner next Saturday night, and I wanted Laurel to join me. "I've never taken a date to a kick-off dinner," I said, casually leaning into the counter next to the machine and Laurel. "Well, that's not true. Once, right after Share finished recording her album, Estie accompanied me, but that was only because Share dueted with Nick Carter for 'I Got You Dave,' and Estie has a thing for Nick Carter. But Estie is my niece and you are"—I squeezed her butt—"not." I grabbed two Styrofoam cups from the stack. "Also, I've never worked or dined with a star as big as . . ." I began to do a drum roll on the counter with the cups. "You ready for it?"

She nodded yes as she began to bang the bottle of cinnamon against the side of the sink. Apparently, the bottle was clogged.

"It's big," I said, still drum-rolling.

She nodded again. "Let's have it."

"Bailey Pierce." I stopped drumming to allow her the appropriate time to react to the magnitude of the news.

She looked up at me from the clogged bottle of cinnamon, though she didn't stop banging it against the sink.

"Yes, you heard right. Bailey Pierce, Bailey Jane Pierce, Bailey— 'Baby Two More Times,' Best New Artist of 2000—Pierce."

"I know who Bailey Pierce is," she said. She stopped banging the bottle and began shaking it downward over the counter with the same crazy force Slip had used with the saltshaker, though she was looking at me.

"And you know who I am. So your attitude is a little laissez-faire for someone who was just invited out with both Bailey Pierce and David Melman."

The top of the bottle dropped off and cinnamon spilled all over the counter. Laurel swore at the pile. To me, she said, "I'm sorry." She put down the bottle and put her arms around me. Obviously, she was going to say yes, I'd love to go. A kiss would follow. In my head, I went as far as calculating whether the kitchen floor provided enough space to have sex, as the countertop, cluttered up with the coffee maker and now the cinnamon, was no longer an option. "That's incredible. I'm so excited for you, and I appreciate the invitation. I'm honored." She gave me a kiss. "But I can't go."

I moved out of our hug. "What do you mean, you can't go? This is the biggest night of my career. Not to mention, it's Bailey."

She didn't answer immediately. Instead, she began to mumble about how quickly time passes, how much she had going on between now and her move to LA. She fumbled for her messenger bag, which was on my kitchen table. She extricated her date book, flipped through the pages, confirmed with me that next Saturday night was August third, ran her finger down the page, and then nodded to herself. "I had a feeling." She clenched her teeth like one does before they drop bad news. "I'm going to be in the Hamptons."

I came over to study her schedule for myself, but she closed the book and jammed it back into her bag.

"Since when are you a Hamptons girl?" I asked.

"I'm not," she said, turning her attention back to the spilled cinnamon. She explained that the rabbi was going to be a guest lecturer at a yoga retreat. He'd be leading a special session on connecting to God through downward dog, and she had to attend since she'd recruited him.

I grabbed a paper towel, wet it, and told her to move out of the way. "Isn't that a lot of time to spend with the rabbi?" I said as I wiped up the mess. "You know, for someone who isn't really interested in converting." I was bothered, but too unenlightened to discern the exact cause of my bother. Was I upset that Laurel couldn't go with me on my big night, or was I jealous of the rabbi? I hadn't given much thought to him over the past weeks, opting for the dark instead, pretending that if I didn't hear or think about him, he didn't exist.

Clearly, however, he was alive and well. "Well, if you must know, I've been talking to the rabbi a lot lately. I'm toying with the idea of actually converting." Laurel rinsed her hands while she spoke. She told me that her connection to Judaism had recently intensified. "Did you know that Mormons believe they are descendants of the tribes of Israel, and that in some ways, Mormons are more closely related to Jews than to Christians? We study the Old Testament. The Star of David is a part of our symbol."

I shook my head. I had no idea. "So what's holding you back from converting?" I asked, holding my breath, the Vera Wang conversation and Rachel's marked words ringing in my head. Could this be where Laurel begins her transformation from cowgirl to New Yorker? I hoped not. As much as I wanted Laurel at the dinner, I was not ready for our Venn diagrams to begin to overlap. I was still telling myself that we had nothing in common. I still believed that having nothing in common was the key to our relationship's success.

"I'm not sure what I'm going to do. I'm in limbo, I guess, waiting for a sign to point me in the right direction." She smiled.

I held my breath. "A sign from who?"

"From the guy who usually gives them out, God."

Relieved to hear she was waiting for a sign from God and not me, I moved on—or, more accurately, *back*—to the rabbi. "So you think the sign might come in the Hamptons? Maybe while you're downward-dogging with the rabbi?"

"It's Amagansett, actually, but possibly. You never know." She reeled me toward her with my tie. "You can come with me."

"You already know I can't," I told her. I backed away and grabbed a bag of Doritos. Nothing beats a Dorito when you think the woman you're sleeping with just might also be sleeping with the clergy. "Not to mention," I added, "I hate the Hamptons."

She apologized again for missing the dinner. She seemed genuine; she said we'd celebrate another time. But I couldn't let it go. I was as troubled as I'd been that Christmas Eve at the Rascal House. Here, too, the catalyst was a concoction of things: jealousy over the rabbi, concern that Laurel was using me for my religion, embarrassment that Laurel had turned down my dinner invitation, disappointment that she didn't seem to care, and, at the crux of everything, the worry that I did. Even hours later, as I wrote my scene and Laurel slept peacefully, I stewed and blamed myself for taking her film writing class in the first place.

Before she went to bed, I'd pummeled her with a series of questions designed to subtly shed light on whether or not she was two-timing with the rabbi. "I imagine it's hard for the rabbi to do yoga with his long coat and big black hat," I'd suggested. If the guy looked like Moses, I figured, I had nothing to worry about. But Laurel said he was a jeans and T-shirt kind of guy. I asked if he wore a yarmulke. Laurel said, "Sometimes." I questioned further and she continued answering patiently, until I pieced together the following: the rabbi, whose name was Eric Lynch, had founded his own congregation, Mahot Adonai, four years earlier; not long after the establishment of Mahot Adonai—which apparently means Essence of God (and so is begging for its own fragrance, I told Laurel)—he enrolled in Laurel's class because he believed in the sanctuary as theater and services as performance art; his congregation now had over 150 members, and he had groupies; among those groupies was Susan's single daughter; through Susan, the couples club had found Laurel's writing class; through Laurel, the rabbi had discovered Marcy's yoga class; and now Laurel and ten others, including Susan's daughter and possibly Marcy, if she could get away from the bakery, were heading to the Hamptons. They were staying in a house that once belonged to Kris Kristofferson. "So we'll both be with musicians," Laurel said. "Spiritually, if not physically."

"You're all staying there? Even the guest lecturers? Everyone connecting to God together?" I winced as I spoke. Witnessing oneself come undone isn't easy.

She told me she didn't know. She also said that if she didn't know better, she would think I was starting to have feelings for her. She came over and gave me a kiss on the cheek. "And I know you wouldn't want to seem like you have feelings."

"I don't," I told her, hiding behind my glass of milk whatever emotions may have slipped out. "This is a fling," I said. "You should do what you want." I offered her the bag of Doritos and pulled myself together. She took a chip. I took a sip of milk. As Laurel commented on my repulsive combination of food and drink, I channeled what I could remember of my former detached, indifferent self and changed my line of questioning. "But I am curious. Why do you need a retreat to connect with God?"

She said she didn't need a retreat, per se, but she was better able to get in touch with herself and with God when she was on her yoga mat and surrounded by nature.

There was a pause while we chomped on Doritos and stared at one another.

I broke the silence. "You know, I connect with God right here in my kitchen."

"Is that so?" Laurel said, taking the bag from me.

"It is, and he's telling me that you should stay here the weekend of August third because if you don't, it will really piss off Bailey Pierce, and not even God wants to piss off Bailey. He's also whispering to me that you are obviously hungry since you are eating Doritos, which you don't like, and I should get up and make you something, since the way to a woman's heart is through her stomach."

For my own credibility, as well as for God's, I felt compelled to follow through with the command. So I pulled out of my junk drawer a Three Musketeers that I'd meant to give to Ryan months ago. "I'm going to make you a David Melman banana boat." I grabbed a banana, slit it open, stuffed the candy bar inside, wrapped the whole shebang in tinfoil, and stuffed it into the toaster oven.

"This is fascinating," Laurel said, smirking with amusement, as I set the knobs on my toaster to the appropriate settings. "What else is God telling you?"

"Not much. Is there something you'd like me to ask him?"

"Does he know whether or not my movie will get sold before I have to move?"

"He says it's iffy." I grabbed a fork in preparation to drag the bundle out of the oven. "He'd love to help, but he doesn't have much pull in Hollywood. If you really wanted to sell your movie, you'd go to dinner with Bailey Pierce. She's connected."

Laurel rolled her eyes. "I'd love to go with you, Chuckerman. But I can't."

For the sake of moving on with the evening and from further humiliating myself, I told her I understood. I pulled the tinfoil from the toaster and grabbed a couple of spoons.

We enjoyed the snack. But I didn't know where I stood with Laurel, and the uncertainty wasn't sitting well with me—which was probably why I was still awake at two in the morning. No girl since my lab partner in medical school had ever turned me down, and I'm pretty sure Annabelle Aston would have gone out with me if I'd told her that Bailey Pierce would also be at our table. So what was Laurel's deal?

I pushed my chair back, put my feet on my desk, and came up with several theories. The first—and to me the most likely—was that she was dating me and the rabbi simultaneously. Mormons do, after all, have a thing for polygamy. She probably liked us both, though, obviously, for different reasons. And because she'd been spending so much sack time with me, I figured, she was going to balance her relationships out by giving the man of God a getaway.

Also possible: Laurel was looking more for status than for love. Maybe Rachel was right, I thought now as I slumped back into my chair. Laurel was only in this to hook a Jewish husband—or possibly an entire Jewish family—so she could either convert or stay in New York. And she was test driving a couple of different models, no different than she'd done with the coffee pots she'd taken out of the boxes and examined on the floor of Macy's, to see which of us better suited her needs.

Whatever her driving force, I understood that she was in a sense just trying to save herself, no different than what my grandma had been doing with the driving lessons. And what was wrong with that? Hadn't the driving lessons been my idea?

I couldn't blame Laurel for covering her bases. However, that didn't mean I couldn't protect myself as well.

Despite what I'd told Laurel, I rarely connected with God in my kitchen or elsewhere. But I did talk to Slip. I looked now at his picture on my desk, a close-up of his face. It had been taken poolside, by Lucille of all people, a few years after the events in my movie took place. I studied his eyes, I heard his laugh. I considered how he would have handled my situation. He didn't answer; he never does. Ours are always one-sided conversations. Nonetheless, in the silence of the night, in the Bildungsroman that was my life, my next move came to me. I'd do as Slip would have done. I would prove to myself, to Laurel, to my sisters, and even to God, if he was interested, that David Melman was a man who owned his own road. Perhaps that was the reason I'd kept the Caddy all these years: to keep me in control of my destiny.

With my head leaned against the back of my chair, I closed my eyes and did a SMASH CUT in my mind to Monday morning, to my office in Midtown, where first I'd sit in a suit and tie and eat a bagel and have a Coke, and then I'd place a call to Share in Los Angeles. I'd ask her if she'd like to come with me to a dinner. I would take her, I'd tell her, to Cipriani Downtown, the trendiest of the trendy, for a feast with my new client. I'd tell her my new client was Bailey Pierce and that she and Bailey could chat, they could connect. If she was lucky, numbers could be exchanged and doors could be opened.

I felt guilty thinking about it. Talk about making a deal with the devil. Or maybe I was just looking out for myself, just like my father was way back when. I'm sure he felt bad about putting Slip's interests over Estelle's, but in the end, wasn't he really putting his interests over everyone's—finding a solution in the name of his own peace of mind and self-preservation? That, I reassured myself, was exactly what I was doing here. Besides, I didn't intend to sleep with Share, just to have some fun. I whispered this aloud, as if Laurel could hear me as she slept. I'd just take Share as my date. No one would get hurt. And if I didn't tell Marcy or Estie, no one would find out, either.

CHAPTER 12:

Spectacle Scenes and Lessons on Perspectives

The following week's class, class number seven of twelve, was entitled plain old *POV*. "Cryptic, don't you think?" I said to Laurel, pointing to the syllabus as we walked toward the classroom.

She walked faster than me, even though my arms were empty and her messenger bag was loaded to the hilt. Her bag reminded me of a clown car. New items continually emerged, like the shoes that currently formed the top of the pile. "You're joking, right?" she said, flipping her head over her shoulder toward me, several tile squares of floor behind her. "Point of View."

"Or Privately Owned Vehicle. Point of Value. Power Operated Vehicle," I offered. "Depending on your POV."

"Why would POV stand for Power Operated Vehicle in a film writing class?"

"All I'm saying is that it wouldn't have killed you to have spelled it out."

"What side of the bed did you wake up on?" she said as we entered the classroom. She dropped the bag onto the desk.

"You know perfectly well what side I was on," I whispered. I'd spent last night at her apartment, in her bed. It was the first time I'd stayed at her place since the purchase of the Chuckerbuck machine. I didn't like to spend the night in her walk-up due to the clutter, the cat, and the distance from my office. However, in an effort to compete with the rabbi, I'd decided to step up my efforts. Besides staying with her, I'd also agreed to go to a Barbra Streisand impersonator show the following Thursday night.

Some might call my behavior sucking up. Marcy called it being in love. After she set eyes on the Chuckerbuck, she said I was as whipped as the foam on the lattes Laurel had just made. I told her no, I wasn't in love, I just didn't like to lose. Even in a fling.

Who was I kidding? By staying at her place, I was also trying to assuage my guilt, since I had, as planned, gotten on the phone the previous morning and invited Share to my dinner. She could pick her hotel, I'd said, the tab was on me. She'd agreed before I'd finished asking.

Now Laurel rolled her eyes at me. "You know that's not what I meant." She began to line the shoes on the edge of the desk and told me to take a seat. "I will spell out POV for you now." And she did, in what I later told her was one of her best lectures. Probably because it involved props. Namely, a pair of high black heels that would have been perfect for her to wear to my dinner with Bailey, as well as her cowboy boots and a pair of dirty brown Birkenstocks, which, Laurel explained, came from the school's lost and found.

As I asked Don how much he wanted to bet that Judd would claim the shoes, Laurel began her talk.

"Every writer comes to the table with a unique take on the world based on her experiences and understanding of them," she said as she set out the shoes. "It's this interpretation that gives a story its meaning." She explained that the writer conveys his or her attitudes toward the human condition in many ways. One is by filtering her story through the eyes of a particular character. "Think of Nick Carraway in *The Great Gatsby*," she said. Then she formally presented her footwear.

"So you see, how your story presents itself to an audience will depend on who you pick to tell it." She paused to kick off her Keds, place them on the desk, and put on the high heels. She strutted back and forth a few times.

Don whistled.

"The woman who walks around in these is going to tell the same story differently than the woman who prefers these"—Laurel paused to lift the Keds from the desk—"who is going to tell the story differently from a person who wears cowboy boots." Here, she lifted a boot. "And all three of those ladies will tell it differently than the dude who wears these." She jammed the Keds under her chin so she could lift up the dirty sandals. She rotated slowly from one side of the room to the other, a human art installation. "As the writer, it's your choice."

As she set the shoes down, Laurel warned us to choose our POV character carefully. "Your audience will be walking in that character's shoes. Will they like his shoes? Will they relate to him? Will they want to take his ride?"

Like an idiot, I looked down at my shoes, my new moccasins— soft brown leather, totally dope. The rabbi probably walked around in some form of black comfort wear, or worse, Birkenstocks. *So as far as which of us offered the better ride from a footwear perspective, there was no contest*, I thought as Helene raised her hand and asked, "Is having your characters speak to the camera a good way to show point of view? We thought each character could speak directly to the camera as the ship goes down." She chuckled. "I was in foils in the salon at the time."

Susan, who had kept her old seat but had revamped her look—a little lipstick, a little blond—since last week's class, mumbled, "I got out of the group in the nick of time."

Candy, too, gave a snotty sigh, but Laurel told Helene, "I actually don't mind your idea." She pulled off one of the black heels and tapped it on Helene's desk. "But be careful."

She explained that the voice-over technique is like the Smash Cut, to be used sparingly. "It can be used to enrich a film, but not to tell the story. Movies," she said yet again, "are a visual medium."

She went on to say that many beginning film writers rely too much on voice-over to tell their stories.

"Your good buddy David is a prime example," she said. "He's got a great story but he tells it instead of shows it."

"What do you mean? I thought you liked my story," I said, sounding far more insecure than I'd intended.

She put the high heel back on her foot. "I didn't say I didn't like your story. My point is just that movies are told via action, gesture, image, and expression rather than words."

Candy threw in her two cents. "I would say that dialogue and camera position are more refined ways to convey point-of-view than voice-over."

Laurel agreed. "Never underestimate the intelligence of the audience. They will pick up a character's entire mindset from the smallest gesture."

The next thing I knew, the Mormon Rodeo was demonstrating her point using a real-life scene from her boyfriend's apartment in which her boyfriend (she shot no glance in my direction) made her a snack, a banana boat, out of the only food he had in his kitchen. "Not only because he realized I was hungry but because he realized he'd been giving me a hard time for not being able to go with him to a work event."

There was a delay, a pregnant pause, between the time she spoke and the moment I realized she was speaking about me, at which point I wanted to die or at least fling myself out of one of the windows, all of which were wide open due to the brutally warm weather. I imagined Laurel's story drifting down with the window-sill soot to everyone who stood on the corner of Broadway and 8th.

Clearly I was the banana boat maker, but I did not immediately identify as the boyfriend. Maybe she only used the term for simplicity's sake, as "one of the guys I'm sleeping with" was too clunky and might have detracted from her point—which, by the way, couldn't have been farther off the mark. I did not make her the banana boat because I felt bad. I made her the boat because I wanted *her* to feel bad. I might have raised my hand and offered my own point of view if I hadn't committed to keeping our relationship a secret.

On and on she went. "He was so sweet," she said. "You should have seen the way he scrounged around his kitchen, looking for any food he had." Her eyes communicated primarily with the women in the class, but the men looked equally as interested. "It was really just a mess of chocolate and banana, but he was so proud that he made me close my eyes to taste it." She sighed. "The cutest part of all, he pulled an extra fork from his back pocket, his own fork, so we could eat it together on the couch." At this point, Laurel pretended to pull something from her own back pocket to really bring me to life. "He told me that the way to a woman's heart is through her sweet tooth." She put her hands on her hips and shook her head, recalling the moment I'd long since forgotten.

The women in class oohed and aahed. The guys stared at Laurel, wishing they were the boyfriend, while I cringed, wishing I were not. For one thing, I didn't enjoy my private actions being subject to public analysis. Second, had I known I held the status of "the boyfriend," I wouldn't have gotten myself another date for Saturday night.

"How much really happened here? If you asked my boyfriend, he'd probably tell you, 'Nothing. I got some chocolate, melted it, and ate it.'" She used a fake male voice, a voice she's used to imitate me when I say something she thinks is boorish. "When you look at it that way, it was just an ordinary evening. But if you look at it my way, you see a magical, defining moment between two people." She walked up and down the rows of chairs as she spoke, playing with her necklace, making her way toward the back corner of the room—toward me. "A banana boat to some"—she knocked on my desk—"an expression of love to others." As she made her way back toward front and center, she added, "You know, the banana boat scene might find its way into one of my movies one day because it was so perfect."

Everyone murmured in agreement.

I rolled my eyes, although secretly, I couldn't help but think that Laurel had made me sound pretty good. One day, I'd simply made a solid snack; the next, I was a knight in shining armor. I felt proud. I sat up a little taller at my desk. I tried to not let the reality that the knight was slated to step out with another woman that Saturday ruin the moment.

Don whispered, "You're the boyfriend, ain't ya?"

"I'm actually not sure," I whispered back.

"I saw the way she knocked on your desk." He imitated the knock. "You're the guy." He announced to the rest of the couples club that I was the boyfriend.

Susan leaned toward me. "That's good, because you missed the boat on my daughter. She's dating a rabbi." She turned toward Helene and added, "They're going on some kind of outing this weekend. I couldn't be happier."

"Stop talking," Don told her. "No one's interested."

I didn't want to admit how interested I was.

Helene was interested, too. She told Susan, "Mazel tov," and asked the name of the rabbi's congregation.

Before Susan could open her mouth, Laurel, in her black high heels, took a few steps toward us and waved a hand in the air. "Enough," she said. "Let's move on."

Without another word, we did.

At least, most of us did. My mind remained stuck. Was I the boyfriend? What was the rabbi's status? Was the making of the banana boat really a sign of love? My conversation with Broc had taken place only weeks ago, yet my plan to take the road less traveled, a path that had seemed so clear and simple at the time, was already muddled. Not that Laurel and I shared any more common ground now than we did at the outset. The problem was that now I cared. I was not okay with caring. I hated caring. I had enough people to care about. History has made clear that caring only leads to concern and concern only leads to coronaries. Not to mention, how much could Laurel care about me given that she wasn't coming to my dinner and was possibly still sleeping with the rabbi?

As I took Laurel for egg rolls after class, my head was awash in worst-case scenarios, most of which involved me as an old man, a stone's throw from a cadaver, alone and broke after having been a faithful husband to a dysfunctional Jewish convert who over the years devolved into a hussy and finally upped and left when the fragrance business went bad.

Even after we arrived at the 3 Woos, I could only semi-participate in the conversation with Janet about whether her parents should expand their menu in order to expand their customer base. Given that we were, again, the only customers, I told Janet that menu expansion seemed like a decent idea. "So does a little re-branding."

Laurel said, "David's in marketing, he might be able to help."

Janet clapped her hands. "Can I pick your brain in exchange for free egg roll and a dish of our new offering, pad thai?"

"My brain is your brain," I told her, though I didn't mention that it was functioning at half-throttle since I was now wondering how I'd gotten involved with a woman who was also sleeping with a rabbi who was also, apparently, sleeping with Susan's daughter. Instead, I told Janet that she was welcome to come to my office any afternoon for a consult. "Maybe we could play with a logo," I told her. I added, as I entertained the possibility of Laurel, the rabbi, and Susan's daughter all sleeping together on the downward dog retreat, "I'll answer your questions free of charge."

"My parents are too proud to accept freebies, Chuckerman," Janet informed me. And so, while I considered sleeping with Share and maybe even Bailey on Saturday night to even the score against Laurel and the rabbi, we compromised. I gave Janet my business card and cash for the egg rolls, but I took a container of pad thai home with me, on the house.

I ate the pad thai four nights later, after my dinner with Bailey and Share. After I returned to my apartment around midnight, earlier than I'd expected. Hungrier than I'd expected. More anxious for Laurel's return than expected.

Once again, unable to sleep, I padded in my pajamas to my almost-empty fridge. I grabbed the pad thai. I took it to my window chair and took a load off while my mind processed the events of the evening. An evening that had singlehandedly shifted my POV on Share, banana boats, Laurel, and possibly my life.

I'd wait for Laurel to come home in the morning, I decided as I tore open the carton and dug in to the 3 Woos' new fare. We'd have a conversation, an honest one. We'd talk about where we stood with each other and how we felt. Although I'd never tell her about my night.

In the meantime, I'd eat and then I'd write another scene. *It's interesting*, I thought as I made my way through the noodles, *I never had trouble sleeping before I met Laurel. Was insomnia a side effect of the fling,* I wondered, *or of writing?*

———

THE POOL PARTY

CHRISTMAS MORNING. AFTER BREAKFAST. IN THE LIVING ROOM OF APARTMENT 1812

As the camera opens on the dining room area, Slip will come out of his bedroom dressed to kill. He always dressed smart, the narrator will explain. Slacks, a button-down, and a sweater seven days a week until the day he died. But on this day, he looked downright dapper. I remember the shorts because I'd never seen Slip in shorts before. None of us had. They were dotted with captain's wheels and ships' anchors. The shoes, too, were another item none of us knew he possessed. A WIDE SHOT will capture Slip, as well as the Melmans staring at him.

"Well, look at you, Slip," my mother will stop combing Marcy's hair to comment.

"See, Davy, you weren't the only one jealous of my shoes," Estelle will say.

"Dad, you want me to get you a pair of shoes like Ma's?" my father will ask.

"No thank you." As Slip straightens himself, he'll explain that his are boat shoes, not track shoes.

Estelle (also unrecognizable in her Adidas, jeans that she, too, pulled out of God-knows-where, and a Miami Beach T-shirt) will ask, "Are you going sailing?"

"Nope. My grandson and I are simply going to escort these two, beautiful young ladies to a pool party. It's not every day that I get such an honor." He'll wink at Rachel and Marcy and wave all three of us toward the door.

At this point Rachel will raise her brows, and mouth to Marcy and me, "Lucille Garlovsky." The movie audience may or may not be able to understand her, depending on their ability to read lips, but my mother did. In the movie, she'll slash her fingertips across her neck, and my sisters will cut it out immediately.

"Keep an eye on him, kids," my grandma will say. "Don't let him near Big Sid—or anyone else, for that matter. We don't need no more trouble around here."

My grandma was going driving. At breakfast she'd asked if she might come late to the pool party, explaining her excitement to take advantage of the empty Publix lot and her new shoes. Slip, with an uncharacteristic air of enthusiasm, had hit her on the back and said, "Go burn some rubber, baby."

Now Slip will order *us* to burn rubber. "Move it," he'll say. "Gonna blow the whole goddamn day, you guys are so slow. You're like old people."

My mother will walk with us to the elevator, but she'll head up to the 26th floor to help my Grandma B and Aunt BoBo make Christmas dinner. I guess I'll give her character a line like: "Time to make the Christmas meatballs with Grandma B," so the audience will understand. Every year, meatballs and a movie. This year we were slated to watch *Saturday Night Fever*.

The four of us will ride down to the sixth floor and make our way to the pool deck. Sounds of the season will precede us. The audience will hear holiday music and Eileen's voice blaring Christmas cheer over the loudspeaker: "Reminder, residents! Only one free hot dog per child and no guests on deck during the party." Then they'll see us push through the glass doors to the deck, which was wet with the rain that had fallen the night before, as it would on and off throughout Christmas day. Not enough to deter attendance but sufficient to keep eyes to the sky for lightning, low-flying gulls, and whatever else people came up with as predictors of life-threatening weather.

Looking back through an objective lens, the scene is one of contrasts. Contrasts between the dark clouds and the bright holiday lights, between the Santa statues and the puddles beneath them, of "Rudolf the Red-Nosed Reindeer" bellowing over the loudspeaker and thunder rumbling over the water, of adults huddled in the corner wrapped in towels and kids racing around the deck, back and forth from games to parents, delivering the tickets won in the games. Twenty tickets equaled a free hot dog—a prospect as thrilling to us as winning the Lotto.

For the second day in a row, the narrator will explain, we were alone with Slip, a change in our regular course of business—a change that we were beginning to enjoy. With Slip, as you can gather by now, you never knew what would happen.

Rachel, Marcy, and I will begin to throw our towels down in our usual spot.

"What are you doing?" We'll look up to see Slip, already past the corner mass of chairs and standing in the middle of the deck. "C'mon with me." He'll beckon with his finger and his head. We, like mice following the piper, will scoop up our stuff and scurry after him.

I remember the day clearly. Without hesitation, Slip pulled four lounge chairs from their poolside row and dragged them backwards until they rested against the long cinderblock wall of the pool deck—across from the crowds, the noise, the party. All of this while he puffed his cigar and we stared.

"Don't just stand there. Take a seat."

"Why are we sitting all of the way over here?" Marcy asked. Her head turned back in the direction whence we'd come, toward the swarm of yellow chairs, as if we'd just trekked the Continental Divide. We may as well have.

The camera will follow our gaze—a POV shot, as I just learned—so the audience will see the fanfare across the way. They'll see the party getting underway with Eileen racing about, Big Sid putting final touches on ring toss, Gladys Greenberg standing by his side.

"Are you here 'cause you don't want to be near Big Sid?" I'll suggest, channeling my own feelings and remembering my grandma's orders to stay away from him.

My grandfather will laugh. "You think I give a shit about him?"

"No," I'll say, laughing at my suggestion in such an exaggerated way that the audience will grasp that I'd already made a mental note to steer clear of ring toss.

"Then why?" Rachel will ask.

"Because it's good to mix it up a little," Slip will explain.

I privately disagreed, as I've never been one to stray from my comfort zone. Plus, I'd rather have been near Big Sid than the cinderblock wall. With its staggered cutouts, the wall petrified me. It seemed so flimsy, a sad excuse for a barrier between us and the deep, churning waters of the Intracoastal. Marcy, on the other hand, loved to stick her feet into the holes, climb up, and lean over to see the shadows of fish in the waves or the tops of cars in the parking garage below, which is what she did as Slip sat, Rachel complained, and I felt out of sorts.

I remember looking at the pool and laying eyes on White Lips, the man who swam laps day in and out, his body clad in a Speedo, his lips in zinc oxide. We never heard him speak. In fact, we weren't sure if he existed outside of the pool. We just knew that if we didn't bother him in the far lap lane, he wouldn't bother us. Another POV shot will follow White Lips through my eyes. Then I'll turn to Slip. "Why do we need to mix it up?"

"You gotta keep life interesting."

"By changing your seat?" Rachel, who is looking to mix it up with the boys from Long Island who are back in our regular area, will ask. To her, life was interesting as it was.

"Yes, my lady. By changing your seat." Slip will wink at Rachel. "Trust me. Sit back and relax." Slip will already be sitting back, relaxing, rolling his cigar in his fingers. "Have a little patience."

I admit, I was a step behind. Still fixated on White Lips, I mistakenly gathered that this lesson was about perspective, about seeing things differently depending upon how you looked at them. My teacher in school that year had made us change desks every two weeks for this purpose. I felt good about myself for thinking I already had Slip's lesson under my belt.

Slip's lesson wasn't about perspective, but for a moment, while we were busy having some patience, the three of us had a good time appreciating our new one. From where we sat, we could see the shuffleboard matches. We could hear the hum of boats and see the clouds as they passed over our heads instead of watching them roll in, anticipating what was to come. The difference was night and day, literally. Like looking at Amsterdam Avenue on my walk to the gym in the morning versus on my way home from work at night.

Suddenly, Slip elbowed Rachel. "See. What did I tell you?" He laughed and pointed with his cigar at three women and their grandkids heading in our direction. In the movie, the audience will see Lucille leading the pack.

"What's this all about?" she'll call to Slip. She'll smile and clutch her jump rope. I'll stare at her, just as I did the day before. But this time I'll notice that her lips are red and her cover-up is green.

"She looks like a Christmas tree," I'll whisper to Marcy.

"She means to," she'll whisper back, "'cause it's the Christmas party."

"Merry Christmas, girls," my grandfather will say to them.

"You too good for us already?" Lucille will respond. The other two ladies will laugh and give their grandkids, our friends, the okay to go play.

"Nothing of the sort, Mrs. Garlovsky," Slip will answer as he sifts through his wad of cash for bills small enough for Bozo buckets and offers them to me, Marcy, and friends.

"Then what are you doing all the way over here?"

"I like it all the way over here." He'll smile and puff and wink.

Whether or not he offered up further explanation I don't know, as I went off with my group to study White Lips from the new angle and play games. All I can tell you is that by the time we returned from our exploits, there'd been a migration. Like magnets, most of the folks normally crowded in the corner had moved to our area of the deck.

Folks seemed to be faring well in the new spot. Ida from 27 and Lil Sharp were smoking up a storm, and Rachel was in the thick of it with the Long Island crew. But at the center of attention, no longer seated, was my grandfather—who, we soon learned, had challenged Lucille to a jump rope contest.

Before we plunge into action, let me pause to explain that back in his day, as he'd say, Slip was an acrobat and a vaudeville dancer. We were all aware of his history and agility. The audience will be, too, from the newspaper clippings that will hang in Apartment 1812 showing him and my grandma winning dance contests, along with pictures of him in crazy contortions—on his head on the edge of a diving board, in a handstand in the sand with my grandma balancing on his feet. Slip was the one who taught Marcy to do flips off of the diving board, and thanks to him, we all knew how to Charleston from the age of four.

As Slip and Lucille take their positions, the narrator will explain that Slip's abilities were well known, so everyone was eager to watch the contest. And a contest it was. It was a show. Lucille in her heels going toe-to-toe with Slip in his boat shoes.

Laurel would call this a Spectacle Scene—though, in class, she stressed that the purpose of a such a scene (she used the piano scene in the movie *Big* as an example), is to both entertain and show a character change. That Christmas, nobody's character seemed to want to make a move. So we're stuck with entertainment.

When the contest starts, the audience will see me pull away from my friends and head to the front row of chairs. I wanted to get a good look but also make sure I could take action if Slip keeled over. I suppose I was still down on myself for having dashed out of the card room on the night of the brawl and had committed, although not consciously, to not letting myself chicken out again.

When I sit, Slip will hand me his cigar. I'll tell him to be careful. He'll say there's nothing to worry about. I'll smile, but I won't look convinced.

Lucille will go first. "Because the rope is mine," she'll say. "And because I'm used to calling the shots." She'll unwrap the rope and grasp the handles as she announces the first trick. "Three jumps, no double jumping."

"Piece of cake," Slip will reply when Lucille finishes. "What is this, kindergarten?" He'll take the rope, and he'll do it.

"Five jumps, no double jumping," she'll declare.

Next, five jumps followed by five high knees. These combinations did not challenge Lucille. I recognized the pattern from her everyday routine. So far, the steps were no big deal for Slip, either.

On and on the game went. With each round, Lucille upped the ante. She incorporated turns. First, half turns. Then a full. Right leg only. Then left.

"Look at the old man move," Lucille teased.

"You ain't seen nothing, Ms. Garlovsky," Slip shot back.

They were both in their element.

In the movie, everyone will cheer and count jumps. The women will root for Lucille. Slip will have the kids on his side. Paparazzi will converge. Phil Berg, the resident photographer who was commissioned to shoot the pool party, will snap pictures of Slip and Lucille with Big Sid and the pool party blurred into the distance, just like they faded further from my mind with each jump.

About halfway through, as a chance to catch his breath, Slip will ask, "Hey Garlovsky, what's in it for the winner?"

One of the kids will suggest a free hot dog.

"Does everything have to have a payout for you?" a woman will holler back. "Can't you do anything for the fun of it?"

"I could, but it's no fun. Always better to have something on the line. Am I right, Lucille?"

"Yes, sir," she'll say, giving a full-bodied laugh and adjusting the straps of her suit over her shoulders. Then she'll finish her combination, the toughest yet, with cross-throughs that require her to take off her heels. Her faction will applaud. Lucille will curtsy and hand the rope to Slip. "Let's see you do that for fun."

For the duration of the contest (in reality just a few minutes, but an eternity to me), I didn't breathe. As I've said, I worried that a walk to the elevator might do in my grandparents. To see Slip jumping and panting was more than I could bear. That wear and tear on one's heart was not necessarily a result of physical strain never crossed my mind.

As Slip completes his combination, resting his hands on his waist and circling Lucille to recover his breath, Lucille will make her declaration. "If Slip wins, he and three of his friends—if he has that many—will be allowed access to the Ladies' Card Room. If I win, there'll be a ladies canasta game in the Men's. How about it?"

The women will scream in amusement. The men will whistle. "We're rootin' for Lucille now," one of them will holler. "The Men's Card Room could use a little ass."

Most of the crowd will laugh, but a few women will tell him to shut his mouth with so many kids around. The kids, all lined up against the cinderblock wall, will laugh the hardest.

"C'mon Slip, throw the match," the same man will yell.

"Sorry boys," Slip will say, "I can't let a lady take me down."

If we perch the movie camera like a gull atop one of the silver light poles—a HIGH ANGLE shot, Laurel says—it will capture the scene. The crowds amid the clouds as they follow the commentary, the kids as they laugh and scream, and then, from nowhere, the biggest cloud of all: Big Sid. I didn't realize he was watching until he spoke.

"You people can't make a bet like that. Everyone knows women aren't allowed in the Men's Card Room," he'll heckle, his brazen voice bringing an instant halt to the fun. "I'm surprised at you, Lucille darlin', doing business with a shark. I thought you knew better than that."

This was the first I'd seen of Big Sid up close since the card room, and his presence frightened me. His nose, busted and bruised by my grandfather, upset me some. But the prospect of another fistfight brought on outright panic.

In the movie, I'll inch myself closer to Marcy. "Pray there's not another fight," I'll whisper. I worried that Slip was too tired from the jump roping to defend himself this time. I also couldn't stop my grandmother's request to keep Slip away from Big Sid from ringing in my head.

"Pray for rain," Marcy will answer. But the sky was beginning to clear.

While I pray, a shuffleboarder will tell Big Sid to go to hell. That won't work.

"I'm already in hell," he'll answer. "Melman, I hear my sister made you a pretty good offer yesterday. Why don't you take her up on it and go back to the card room where you belong. That way, I won't have to look at you out here."

"He means he won't have to look at Slip with Lucille," one of the ladies will say to the others.

"Talk about doing business with a shark," my grandfather will say. "Making a deal with your sister is the last thing I'd do." He'll chuckle in disbelief.

The women will nod in agreement. One of them will say, "He's got that right. Estelle would sooner die than let Gladys Greenberg onto her kick-line."

Those not already in the know about the terms of the deal my father and his patients had struck with Gladys Greenberg, including my sisters and me, will react to this remark with gasps of dismay and then chatter.

"Grandma's gonna flip out when she hears this," Marcy will say.

"She's gonna kill Dad," Rachel will say.

My eyes will follow Slip. "So that's the deal, is it?" he'll say. "They threw my wife under a goddamn bus?"

Another murmur will rip through the crowd, an en masse realization that Slip, too, was in the dark. The audience will see me inhale deep in preparation to hold my breath, something I've always done when life spirals and I'm not sure what to do about it. They will also watch as I fix my eyes on the ground and wrap my wrists under the plastic straps of the chair, a self-imposed restraint against my urge to get up and run.

Slip will spit on the pavement. "I ain't interested. My wife ain't interested. From now on, I'll hang out here on the pool deck with my new friend Lucille."

Big Sid will lunge forward into the crowd. "Talk about selling out your wife. Or maybe you're just too chickenshit to step back into the card room."

At this comment, the camera will lift from the pavement to Slip as I force myself to look in his direction. I was sure I'd see his fist clenched, his arm cocked back in that familiar position, his body barreling over the chairs to the back of the crowd.

Instead, Slip will say, "Seems to me like you're asking for a rematch." He'll swing the jump rope over his head as if he is about to lasso Big Sid, but his voice will be steady. His eyes will lack the steel they held that night in the card room. I'd hear him say later, after my father praised him for his restraint, that he'd had no choice. "I'd have loved to show my grandson how I could have roped in that bastard like a bull, if it hadn't been for all the ladies."

If it hadn't been for the *lady*, he should have said. Because before I even relinquished my breath or my grip on the chair, Lucille Garlovsky grabbed the rope out of Slip's hand and motioned for him to stop. And he did. With a single hand raise, the age-old signal to cease and desist, Lucille did what no one from my father to the Feds had done before. She worked a miracle.

Now will be a fine time for a close-up on Lucille and a slo-mo camera. Nothing conveys anticipation like slo-mo, and at this point, the crowd was full of it.

"Sid," Lucille will say, taking a few high-heeled steps towards him, her rope slung around her neck like a scarf. "You big baby, go mind your own business. There isn't anything less attractive than a jealous man."

The women will murmur in agreement. One of them will comment, "Except a jealous man with a broken nose."

From Big Sid, the audience will not hear another word. On command, as if under a spell, Big Sid, all six foot four of him, will turn and head back to ring toss.

At that, Slip will take the rope; I'll take a breath; Lucille will snap her fingers; and the contest will resume. *All the while*, the script will note, *White Lips will swim and White Christmas will blare from the loudspeaker.*

Here, we'll CUT from the scene.

Though we haven't reached the end of it. I've neither written the full scene nor told the full story. I didn't even learn the full story until a few years ago. Only then did I realize the all-too-human array of emotions and entanglements that were at work that day, which had more to do with Lucille's ability to thwart disaster than magic did. But that was what my ten-year-old self came up with—that Lucille Garlovsky, like the characters in the Harry Potter books I now read to Estie and Ryan, possessed some sort of supernatural ability.

Whether her powers emanated from her rope or the confidence that oozed from her, I didn't know. I didn't care. From then on, I approached her with awe and with caution, like any man with good sense would approach that kind of woman, the snake charmer kind, the kind that causes us men to act in ways that we ordinarily wouldn't—to put down the jump rope, to clog our counters with mammoth coffee makers, to spend Thursday evenings listening to Barbra Streisand impersonators, to feel like low-lifes for having another woman on our arm at dinner.

Not that I wished Laurel had been with me on Saturday night. In fact, I was glad she hadn't been, in much the same way I was glad Grandma Estelle had not been on the pool deck that day. The deck wasn't her scene, the dinner wasn't Laurel's.

My evening at Cipriani Downtown was a Spectacle Scene to end all Spectacle Scenes. This one even had a character change—although none for the better.

Share's transformation occurred the moment Bailey's bodyguards—Carlos and Toby, identical twins—pulled open the gold satin curtain on our back room and Bailey and company entered.

Not that her entrance wasn't a happening. It was. They don't call them pop stars for nothing. Even Ezmerelda let herself go for a moment: she allowed herself a small smile, raised her Manhattan and said, "Now this is what I call a dinner party."

As she spoke, Share rose from the chair next to mine and bumped Bailey's agent—a buxom woman named Camille—out of the way so she could sit next to Bailey. "A pleasure to make your acquaintance," she said in some sort of fake Southern accent. She held out her hand. "I'm Share."

With her genuine Southern drawl, Bailey said, "Relax honey. I know who you are." She gave Share a smile—her full megawatt. Her teeth were as white as Laurel's.

In the throes of recognition, Share apparently forgot she was from the South. She also forgot that she wasn't supposed to be from Long

Island anymore either, because in a New York accent heavier than Lucille Garlovsky's she said, "Holy crap. Wait 'til I tell my mother." Then she sidled herself as close as possible to the pop star. "What was it like singing while you were suspended right over a tiger?" A reference to her performance at the MTV Video Music Awards, Bailey explained to the table after telling Share that the tiger was a total rush.

"An interesting first choice of questions," I mumbled to Ezmerelda, "especially since I instructed Share to not ask any."

But Bailey seemed okay with it, so I decided I would be, too. Gradually, however, as Cosmopolitan number one turned to two and then three, Share started to get personal. "So, what was your scent of choice before David created Omnipotence?" She shifted her chair even closer to Bailey so that her leg, which was—along with her midsection—bare, pressed into Bailey's.

At this point, Carlos and Toby—I'm still not sure who was who— stepped in and simultaneously tapped each of Share's naked shoulders. They didn't say a word. They didn't have to, as they were armed and as broad across the chest as Bailey's agent, Camille, who had seated herself next to me, and who, on the opposite side of the clothing spectrum, wore an enormous piece of white fur around her own formidable shoulders. She was a modern-day Gladys Greenberg.

I'd met Camille before, so I was not completely surprised when she began her advances. I was, however, stunned by Share, who had ignored my warnings to not get personal with Bailey. She'd also clearly forgotten her roots, revealing not a trace of the once-modest Emily Kaplinsky.

I watched as she leaned toward Bailey as if she was going to whisper and then, oops, blurted out the question in her outdoor voice: "Are you and Jake really and totally over?"

Everyone at the table except Camille, who was busy sweating under the fur, signaled to Share to stop the personal line of questioning. But Share, showing her age and inability to hold alcohol, didn't listen. "I hope you guys get back together because you are like the ideal couple and your babies would make the cutest mini Mouseketeers." She laughed and put her hand on Bailey's shoulder.

Obviously, the combo of Share and Camille was God's way of

punishing me for having taken another woman out behind Laurel's back. I wondered how Carlos and Tony were going to reprimand Share for her inappropriate behavior. As the beef carpaccio came to the table, they returned to their spots on either side of her. I watched and readied myself. She looked at them and smiled. They raised their hefty bodyguard brows. She pretended to zip her lips with her fingers. They lowered the brows and went back to the bar.

"That's it?" I said. "A brow raise?" I turned to Ezmerelda. "Doesn't it seem like a second warning deserves something more?"

"Would you like us to shoot her?" Carlos or Toby asked from the bar. Bailey laughed.

Ezmerelda answered. "Maybe you could sock her. It's a pity to see those biceps go to waste."

Carlos and Toby did a few Popeye-style flexes while Ezmerelda and Camille applauded. Bailey continued to laugh. Truth be told, she didn't seem to be bothered by anyone's antics. She answered all of Share's questions in her charming Southern way. She was not dating anyone, she told Share. She was thrilled to be working with me on her new campaign. Here, Bailey shot me a wink. There's a small chance I winked back. I'm hoping I didn't but even if I did, no one except Camille would have seen it. They were all staring at Share, who squealed after Bailey said she would love to work with her one day. Bailey then smiled, the epitome of poise. She didn't even flinch when Share moved a hand to her thigh, and said, "Maybe we could duet!"

Bailey was either a real class act, I decided, or she was gay. Or maybe she was just used to this sort of thing. *Maybe*, I thought as Camille wrapped her fur thing around my neck, *she liked the insanity.*

Then they began to sing.

Share started by humming the chorus to "I've Got You, Dave," and Bailey continued it by taking the song from the top. "They say we're young and we don't know," she twanged. Share sang Nick Carter's part. Together, Bailey and Share carried out 10,000 "I've got you, Dave" choruses, getting louder with each one.

I got more annoyed with each one. "Can you please put an end to the madness?" I asked the bodyguards.

Bailey disagreed. "Relax and sing along, fellas," she told them. Because Bailey was boss, they did.

"I've seen it all now," Ezmerelda said.

"Not me," Camille said. She winked at me and rubbed her fur against my chin. "I can think of a little more that I'd like to see, Mr. Melman."

The idea of seeing any more of Camille than was already exposed was too much for me to handle. "I think I'll visit the men's room," I said, excusing myself from the table. As I left, the bodyguards, at Bailey's command, threw their arms around each other as they sang, and Share and Bailey laughed harder. I wasn't sure I would live through the dinner but assuming I did, I thought, I would love to tell Laurel about it. And she thought our banana boat scene was movie material. I laughed to myself. Imagine what a writer could do with this stuff.

After the eating and the singing died down, Bailey said to Share, "Should we call it a wrap in here and photo op?" As if Share might possibly turn her down.

Unable to contain her excitement or her alcohol, Share said, "Totally." And on that thoughtful note, we headed toward the front door and, apparently, the cameras.

As we made our way outside, the fur piece again made its way from Camille's shoulders to mine. "The reason I'm so hot is 'cause you are," she whispered.

I ignored both her comment and the fur around my neck and stared as Bailey and Share stood on the sidewalk in front of the restaurant's thick glass doors and embraced for the paparazzi. I considered the scene from Laurel's point of view and was thankful that she wasn't with me. Not that I liked the thought of her in the same house as the promiscuous rabbi, but she was better off in the Hamptons, possibly in the company of God, than here with me.

My moment was again interrupted by Camille. "Would you like to come home with me, honey? There's a lot we can do with my fur."

Share was going bar hopping with Bailey, Carlos, and Toby.

I returned Camille's stole (as Marcy has since told me it is called) to her neck. "No thanks, I'm good."

And I was. I rode home in my Town Car, happy to be alone. Not that long ago, I would not have been; I, like Share, would never have turned down the chance to bar hop with Bailey Pierce. As the car traveled up 10th and my eyes drifted over the billboards, the cabs, the cafés, I reconsidered my relationship with Laurel. Maybe this was no longer a fling, and maybe Laurel wasn't a snake charmer. *Maybe*, I thought as we passed 42nd and headed into Hell's Kitchen, *Marcy, of all people, was right, and I was just in love.*

CHAPTER 13:

Twists and Turns

D are I say that David Melman had a spring in his step the next morning as he went to meet Laurel, his love, his soon-to-be-serious girlfriend, at the West End Parking Garage? Typically, I'm more of a shuffler, way too preoccupied and self-conscious to spring. But on that Sunday, I have to admit, I had a little lift.

I'd last spoken to Laurel the day before. She'd called just as I was about to head out to pick up Share at the Plaza—what a waste of money that had turned out to be—and then head over to my dinner with Bailey. "Can we visit the Brooklyn Bridge when I get home from the retreat?" she'd asked. She said she'd gotten a sign from God through Simon & Garfunkel that had led her to conclude that the Brooklyn Bridge was symbolically a more appropriate bridge for an event depicting the loss of the American dream than the Verrazano.

"I'm not totally following," I told her.

"You don't need to, but let's just say that during a meditation session, the rabbi played an instrumental version of the entire *Bridge over Troubled Water* album. And it came to me, no one is more quintessentially American than Simon & Garfunkel. They are much more representative of New York than the BeeGees. Who sang on *Saturday Night Live* after 9/11? Paul Simon, not Andy Gibb."

"Andy Gibb is dead," I told her as I watched the hands on the clock above my desk tick away.

"You know what I mean, Chuckerman. It doesn't take a rocket scientist to put two and two together. If I want to stay in New York—and I do—I need my movie to sell. And if I want my movie to sell, I need to switch bridges. That's what God was trying to tell me."

Maybe I was too busy towel-drying my hair and envisioning my dinner with Bailey Pierce and Share to put two and two together. Or maybe Laurel had done a few too many downward dogs and wasn't even making sense. But she was adamant that if she was going to sell her movie so she could stay in New York, she needed to switch bridges. So I told her yes, I'd go with her to the Brooklyn Bridge when she returned.

She wanted to go as soon as possible because she was heading to LA on Tuesday to meet with her agent. They would be putting the final touches on *Mormons Don't Die*, as well as going to some fancy salon to get their hair relaxed. Due to the trip, Laurel had canceled our next class. Instead, she'd handed everyone a copy of an article she'd written for a *Screenwriting for Dummies* type of book. The article, "Twists, Turns and Revelations," was supposed to get us started on the plotting of our own twists and turns. "You are the writer," she'd told us. "You control the show. When you want to change your story's course, drop a bomb of information." We were told to read the article this week, and next week we'd finesse our technique.

I figured Laurel should finesse her driving before she left for Los Angeles, so I told her over the phone, "We can go to the bridge, but you are going to do the driving. As you know, the notion of a woman not being comfortable behind a wheel doesn't sit well with me. I drove to one bridge, you can drive to the other. Especially since you're going to spend next week in LA. No subways, no taxis." I paused. "And no me."

What I didn't tell her, because I didn't realize it myself until late that night as I was eating my pad thai (delicious, by the way), was that having Laurel drive the Caddy was the symbolically appropriate way to welcome her into the fold of my family. If she was going to become a permanent part of my life, what better way to inaugurate her than to have her drive my grandfather's car, the same way a girl introduces her boyfriend to her inner circle when she knows the relationship is getting serious? I'd never introduced anyone to the Cadillac before. Hence the spring in my step. Hence the shower after basketball, the clean shave, my lucky Cubs hat, and my moccasins.

When we met at the entrance to the garage, Laurel did not appear as excited as I was. Her eyes looked tense, though I didn't know what to make of the rest of her. She wore a cowboy hat. Two low ponytails dangled from beneath it. She also sported her cut-off shorts, the ones I loved, and a flannel shirt with the sleeves cut off at the shoulders. Her messenger bag, filled to the brim, was slung across her side.

"You'll be driving a car, not a horse," I said, although something about the cowgirl attire was hot. With my arms I motioned for her to come to me for her welcome-home hug.

"I was getting myself into the mindset," she said as I gave her a quick squeeze. "These are the clothes that come to mind when I think of driving."

"No wonder you don't like to drive," I joked as I grabbed her hand and her bag and escorted her toward the Caddy.

"My last boyfriend drove a Harley," she said.

"I know," I said, "you already told me that."

She smiled at me. "My father also drives a Harley."

"Of course he does." I smiled back. "Maybe in your movie, the father should drive a Harley over the side of the Brooklyn Bridge. Why don't you run that by your agent in LA? Talk about intense." I tossed her the keys.

"I know you are joking, Chuckerman, but you can see why I don't like driving. My associations with it are not the happiest."

"I could see it if I was asking you to drive a motorcycle," I said.

"Driving your Cadillac through the streets of New York is as frightening as driving a Harley through the back roads of Utah," she said.

I nodded in semi-understanding and for a moment considered aborting my mission altogether. Maybe my idea was a bad one. Hadn't Estelle's driving lessons resulted in disaster? But then, this was twenty-five years later. Hadn't I learned a thing or two since then? Hadn't I just won the business of Bailey Pierce? Wasn't I writing a Bildungsroman? I convinced myself to push aside Laurel's reservations and soldier on, still feeling fairly certain that when all was said and done, when the Cadillac was back (safely, I hoped) in its spot, Laurel would be mine.

Images of our initial encounter in her apartment floated to mind as I opened the driver's side door for her, and then came around and sat down in the passenger's seat. I dropped her bag onto the floor—a bag of Minis from Marcy's bakery and the *New York Post* spilled out—and then I oriented myself as Laurel did the same. She adjusted her seat, located her signals, and started the engine.

I started my conversation. I'd planned out my speech the previous night after writing my movie scene. I wasn't going to pull punches. However, I was going to allow myself to ease into the meat of my declaration with an introductory set-up line, which I went ahead with now.

"I have a proposition for you," I said. This statement was to be followed by an invitation to go home with me over Labor Day weekend, as well as a brief explanation about how my niece Julia, Rachel's oldest, was in a play, *The Rats of NIMH*, and I was taking Estie and Ryan home to Chicago to see it.

When I'd played it out in my mind, Laurel had reacted by taking her eyes off Broadway long enough to smile at me and say, "Are you serious, I'd love to!" At which point I'd proceeded straight to the "let's be exclusive" portion of our happily-ever-after ride to the Brooklyn Bridge, where we'd strolled hand in hand, boyfriend and girlfriend, over the pedestrian walkway of the East River with the tourists.

I had failed, however, to anticipate just how bad Laurel was behind the wheel. She could not even get the car from the parking garage onto 70th. For at least two minutes, she spilled the Cadillac forward out of the driveway and reversed back every time a car came into sight. Up and back we rocked, like she was getting us out of a snow bank. I was carsick before we left the garage.

Only after she finally maneuvered into the street did she address my remark. "A proposition? That sounds serious." She stared at the road as she spoke. She was making great use of her various mirrors. And her hands. They were wrapped like bandages around the wheel.

"Relax a little," I told her. "The beauty of this big yellow car is that everyone can see it. She's like the sun. She's a fortress." I gave the dash a few taps of endearment. Then I turned myself toward her and forced myself to fire away with my invitation.

She took her eyes off the road long enough to shoot me a sideways glance of confusion. "You want to take me home to meet your family?"

I nodded yes.

"Why?"

Already we were off script. I'd have to improvise. "What do you mean, why?"

"I thought this was a fling. You said the only thing you wanted to have in common with me was the coffee maker."

"Yes, I did say that. But"—I paused at the intersection of 61st and Broadway, my moment of truth, until a skinny girl with a green suitcase dashed across the street and I decided to proceed as well—"I've been thinking about your banana boat lecture. And I'm thinking you were right. I must love you."

Laurel clearly didn't see that coming, because she thrust her foot on the gas with the same force Rachel used to press the pedal during her piano playing days, and we darted into the intersection. A symphony of horns sounded, and she jammed on the brakes. The guy behind us, whose black BMW fender actually might have bumped ours, hollered that people like her had no business on the road. She leaned out the window and agreed with him. "I'd be much better off in a Bug," she shouted back.

She took a few deep, cleansing breaths, wiped her palms on her flannel shirt, and addressed the issue at hand. "Chuckerman, I haven't driven in fifteen years, I'm steering a sailboat, and this is when you decide to tell me you love me?"

"I didn't think you'd be so surprised," I said. "I mean, you said it yourself. You told the whole class your boyfriend must love you. 'A banana boat to some, an expression of love to others.' Those were your exact words."

"That's very sweet. I'm touched, I really am. But just so we're clear, I was trying to make a point to the class about point of view. I wasn't telling you how you feel. I'm a film writer, not a shrink."

"No, I know that," I backpedaled. I considered getting out of the car altogether, which wasn't an unrealistic option. Broadway was bumper to bumper. I'd suggested taking side streets to pick up the pace, but Laurel insisted on main drags, claiming it was safer. The more traffic, the slower she could go. I couldn't argue with this. We were rolling through Columbus Circle at two miles per hour. I could have easily opened the door and run, but I'd never abandon the Cadillac. So I kept on talking.

"I didn't mean that you told me I love you. I realized it myself. I got a sign from God last night. It wasn't as concrete as Simon & Garfunkel, I'm not sure what it was, maybe it was the pad thai, but let's just say I put two and two together, just like you did with the bridge. I realized that I was wrong. This wolf would like to try and change his spots."

Laurel rolled down the window and started to fan herself with her hand. As we rolled onto Central Park South, she shook her head and murmured, "It's a leopard, first of all. And second of all, I'd like to suggest that now isn't the best time for us to have this conversation. I was actually saving this talk for later, for after we survived this ride, but since you brought it up and because there is a chance we won't survive, I'll say it now. Could it be that your sign from God was a blow to the ego by Share? Maybe you are feeling like you might be losing your mojo after your sure thing blew you off for Bailey?"

I was sorry I hadn't abandoned ship back at Columbus Circle. It was as if Laurel knew I wasn't going to read her handout on twists and turns and wanted to make sure her most remedial student grasped the concept by giving him a live, in-real-time demonstration.

"What are you talking about?" I asked.

We passed my favorite building, 200 Central Park South, with its unending bands of balconies and floor-to-ceiling windows. If Grandma Estelle—a fan of big balconies if there ever was one—lived in Manhattan, this would be the building she'd call home.

"Don't play dumb," Laurel admonished, "You're terrible at it." Then she leaned over me and grabbed the *New York Post* that had rolled onto the floor. She tossed it on my lap. I ordered her to turn onto 5th and she ordered me to turn to Page Six.

"You were the talk of the bakery this morning," she informed me as I scanned the page. "Everyone, Marcy included, told me not to meet you today. I told Marcy that not only was I meeting you, I wasn't going to even mention it." She nodded toward the newspaper. "I told her we were just a short-term thing, no strings attached. But since you are now professing your love, I think we should clear the air." She took her hand off the wheel long enough to point to a picture of Bailey and Share coming out of Cipriani's. Share with her arm around Bailey. Bailey waving. If you held the paper to the window as I did, you could see me in the background with the fur around my neck. "Please explain," she said.

"Bailey Gets Her Fair Share," the caption read. The paragraph began by stating that after a business dinner celebrating the launch of her new fragrance campaign, Omnipotence, rumored to brand anything and everything Bailey, mega-star Pierce hit the town with semi-star Share. "Some might say Share, who's best (and most likely only) known for her song 'I've Got You, Dave' was a step down from the arm of Bailey's former beau, Jake Jones," it read. "But the twosome, clad in similar ACE bandage–style dresses, sky-high heels, and attitude, seemed to hit it off like white (trash, some might add) on rice. They dashed from dinner at Cipriani Downtown with David Melman, the mastermind behind Bailey's Omnipotence scent, as well as the personas of several pop stars, including Share, to Serafina on the Upper East Side. Melman has been linked romantically to Share, although by all accounts, on Saturday night, Share only had eyes for Bailey. Can you blame her?"

I put down the paper, horrified and honored all at the same time. "Well, at least they called me a mastermind," I said. I knew that my remark wasn't, as Rachel would say, materially relevant to the issue at hand. But in lieu of having any idea how to address the issue at hand in a dignified way, I decided to attempt a joke.

Sure enough, Laurel jumped all over it. "I'm glad that's your takeaway, Chuckerman." She stared at me and nodded. Slow nods, like she was trying to swallow a bad piece of steak. "I took away something else, besides the fact that you look terrible in fur."

"What's that?" I said. I was irritated at myself for not anticipating the celebrity coverage. Clearly I was the idiot here, because I've been in gossip magazines now and again for taking out up-and-comers, barely-knowns, and the reality that my evening with the world's biggest pop star would make headlines had never entered my consciousness until this moment. I'd been too mired in my own tiny state of affairs to consider the bigger and actual picture at hand. I could feel Slip looking down on me and laughing, the way he had when I'd made a rookie mistake at gin. I fiddled with the electric window control like I used to as a kid, jolting the window up and down.

"I think it's interesting that you took out Share last night, may have even slept with her if she hadn't dumped you for Bailey Pierce, but want to take me home to your family today."

Luckily, traffic was bumper-to-bumper down 5th from 35th to 23rd, because Laurel was no longer focused on the road. Her cutoffs had ridden up on her legs during the course of the ride, so she was busy unsticking her thighs from the leather seats. I was busy staring at the thighs, which had gotten nicely tanned in the Hamptons, and wondering what to say next.

"I'm actually glad you brought this up," I said after a moment's consideration. The article had called me a mastermind, so I figured it couldn't hurt to turn to what I obviously do best: spin. "I think this article is the greatest thing that ever happened to us. It's an opportunity to clear the air, which is just what you said we should do—and," I added, "was something I wanted to do before you came home to Chicago with me."

"I never said I would go home with you, but anyway, go ahead. I can't wait to hear this."

"If we are going to start off the relationship on the right foot, take it to the next level, we need to start off with a clean slate—air our dirty laundry," I said. I admitted I took Share to the dinner. I promised that I didn't sleep with her, and had not intended to. I also apologized for not telling her.

"Apology accepted."

"Fabulous," I said, gaining further confidence in my abilities as spin doctor. "Now it's your turn."

"For what?"

"To come clean. To admit to, you know, doing Yiddish on the side with the rabbi."

"What's wrong with Yiddish?"

"You know what I mean," I said. "Metaphorical Yiddish. Yiddish as in sleeping with the rabbi." I also told her something I'd later consider to be a bad idea: that her friend Claire from yoga had told me about the rabbi, Reb Irish Eyes, voted Hottest Rabbi in Lower Manhattan for three years running. In a showing of even poorer judgment, I added, "Marcy told me you were sleeping with him, and Susan said her daughter was sleeping with him too."

"Oh please," Laurel said. "Do you believe everything you hear? Consider your sources. There's no way Eric would sleep with Betsy, and besides, what does it matter?"

I paused the conversation long enough to get us back onto Broadway from 5th and to point out a bright orange sign indicating a hole in the road.

As Laurel jerked the wheel so we swerved around the hole but clipped the sign, I said, "I'd intended to lock things up on this ride, so it matters a lot." I was shocked that Laurel didn't understand why the two-timing mattered. Maybe she was right. Maybe a leopard can't change its spots; only she was the leopard, I thought, not me. She could dabble in Judaism all she wanted but she was a polygamist at heart. "You can take the girl out of Utah, but you can't take the Utah out of the girl," I mumbled.

"What's that supposed to mean?" she said. Her hat had now sunk over her eyes. I wasn't sure she could see. But apparently she could, because she pointed out that we were passing Union Square Park, the spot of our first date and now our first fight. "Ironic," she said. I agreed, and we sat in silence for a few blocks until Broadway and 11th, where the road opened up and so did I.

"My comment means nothing," I said as I pushed the hat up on her head. "But let's just say the rabbi matters to me because I'm bringing you home to meet my family and I thought before I did, it would be a good idea to—"

"To what? Clean me up? Package me right? Let's face it, Chuckerman. My life's up for grabs. I'm most likely moving to Los Angeles. No one is going to buy this movie no matter which bridge I use. You said it yourself, it's the feel-lousy movie of the year. So what's the point of taking me home to meet your family?" She looked at me as she answered her own question. "There is no point. I hate the Cadillac. I'm hardly going to fit in with the Melmans."

I hadn't considered how she'd go over with my family. She was already friends with Marcy, and Estie was one of her biggest fans. I assumed she'd fit in fine. I didn't think Laurel would care about fitting in with my family. I figured she'd feel happy to be brought into my family, happy to be able to stay in New York, and happy to be relieved of the pressure of having to sell her movie. But Laurel, it seemed, didn't want to be saved. She, unlike my Grandma Estelle, was familiar with Women's Lib. Because when I said, "I'm sure they'll love you," she said, "What they think of me is irrelevant. It's my life; I need to figure it out myself. Which is why what I do—or what you do, for that matter—shouldn't matter. That, to me, is the definition of a fling."

"So you are telling me that if I had slept with Share, you wouldn't care? What kind of woman doesn't care?"

"A woman like *me*, who can't afford to care. Your Grandma Estelle, too. She couldn't afford to care, either, that's why Slip's sleeping around wasn't a deal breaker for her." She said this slowly, as if she knew she was delivering a low blow.

I told her to leave my grandparents out of this. "Besides," I pointed out, "if this is a fling, there can be no deal breakers."

Bleaker to Houston to Prince went by before Laurel said, "Well if this wasn't a fling, this car would be a deal breaker. It takes up an entire city block. I've got news for you, Chuckerman, the reason we're not getting anywhere is not because there are so many other cars on the street, it's because this one is so big. It's a death trap, not a shrine."

She shook her head and the hat slipped over her eyes. She pushed it up. She told me she would drive to the bridge, but not home. She was never driving the Cadillac again. "Truthfully, I'd rather be saddled with a meth addict than this Cadillac."

"Fine by me," I told her, resorting to the tit-for-tat tactics I'd relied on growing up with my sisters. I told her that I would drive the Cadillac home and I'd continue to drive it until it would drive no more. "And a woman who won't drive this car is a deal breaker for me. So I guess it doesn't matter whether you end up in LA or not, because it doesn't seem like there's any way for us to end up together." I added that my offer to go home with me was off the table.

"Be realistic, Chuckerman, there never was any way we were ending up together," Laurel said.

I shrugged. Late last night, my plan for our future had seemed so straightforward. I didn't know where I'd gone wrong with my sign from God, but I sure had misread it. My only option now was to cut my losses. "So, I guess this is the end of the line for us. Just like for the father in your movie." I told her. "Everything ends at the Brooklyn Bridge. Maybe that's what Simon & Garfunkel were trying to tell you. Or," I mumbled, the spring now drained from my proverbial step, "maybe that's what they are telling me."

She said she didn't see why our relationship had to be over. "Nothing is that much different than it was before our drive."

I told her that depended on one's point of view.

We drove the last few blocks in silence, and my thoughts went ahead to Laurel's next lecture, the one she'd give on twists and turns. I wondered if I'd go to it. If not, I thought, I should probably ask her now what a writer does when he loses control of his script. Is there a special kind of bomb one can drop to get the day back on track? Of course, the bigger question was about the bomb that refused to drop. Laurel still hadn't said whether or not she was sleeping with the rabbi. I reminded her of this and she said, "If it didn't matter before, it really doesn't matter now."

The bridge's towers now loomed among the buildings. The sun blazed down on the water. Boats tooled around in it. Tourists mobbed the streets. Ironically, the ride itself had gone relatively well. We made it in one piece to the federal courthouse, where we parked and walked to Foley Square. There, I waited for Laurel while she walked the bridge. I listened to a tour guide, a lanky kid in a Fordham Law sweatshirt, lecturing a pack of visitors about John Roebling, the designer of the Brooklyn Bridge, whose foot got crushed between the pier and his ferry as he was taking final measurements for the project. He refused formal medical treatment, choosing his own "water remedy" instead and, the guide explained to his listeners, in a most unfortunate twist of fate, died before work on the bridge ever started.

⌁——

CHRISTMAS AT BOBO'S, PART I

CHRISTMAS DAY. POST POOL PARTY. TERRACE OF APARTMENT 1812

The camera will open on my mother squeezing gunk from an aloe plant leaf and rubbing it into my chest. Rachel, still in her suit, will lean against the metal railing and spy with binoculars on the people in the apartments across the way. My grandma will stand next to her, still in her driving clothes, the T-shirt and jeans. She'll fuss with her mass of white hair, disheveled not only from the wind but also from exasperation.

Word of Slip's jumping and betting with Lucille had reached Apartment 1812 before we'd returned to it, and his behavior hadn't gone over well with Estelle. My father, however, was actually happy with Slip's pool deck performance. When we first stepped into the kitchen, he congratulated Slip for not hitting Big Sid. My grandma rolled her eyes and said, "Forgive me for not feeling more gung-ho about Slip's restraint." Then she tsk-tsked her way to the terrace, where she started tsk-tsking to my mother.

"Maybe he should just accept that deal from Gladys Greenberg, whatever it is," my grandma will say in the movie. "Get him out of trouble."

At the mention of the deal, Rachel's ears will open. "So, Grandma, did your friends happen to mention anything about the deal?" she will ask without looking up from the binoculars.

"What about it, honey?"

Rachel will shrug, pretending to be coy. "I don't know. Like about, you know, what's involved."

My mother will kick Rachel in the leg but Estelle will not notice. Instead, she'll pat Rachel's back and say, "No, honey. Doesn't seem like anyone knows."

"Really?" Rachel will turn from the binoculars, surprised. My mother and I will show relief that my grandma is still in the dark. Not even the gossip mill, it seemed, wanted to touch this one. Probably since most of the mill had a hand in creating it.

"At this point, I'm just happy anyone's willing to deal with him at all," my grandma will continue. "He's apparently threatening trouble in both card rooms. On top of that, he was a terrible distraction at the pool party. Participation was way down." She'll shake her head in shame. "They're liable to throw us out of the building altogether."

"They can't do that," my mother will assure her as she grabs another leaf and rotates me around. "Really, Estelle, we are not talking about anything more than a couple of bruised egos."

"Oh no, more than that," my grandma will reply. "How about all those leftover hotdogs and popsicles? They won't keep 'til next year." Waste of any kind never sat well with Estelle. She'll shake her head in dismay, pop her hands on her hips, and declare, "I'm too disgusted to eat dinner."

Still rubbing in the aloe, my mother will shake her head in sympathetic agreement. "I know what you mean. I'm disgusted, too." From having overheard her conversation late last night with my father about his decision to give Gladys Greenberg a place in the kick-line, I knew she was referring to her own husband's actions, not Estelle's—but in this moment, she won't elaborate. "Men are fools, Estelle, what else can I say."

"You don't have to tell me," my grandma will answer as she stares into the Intracoastal and sighs. "If it wasn't for *Saturday*

Night Fever, I'd stay home altogether." With that, she'll leave the terrace and disappear into her bedroom.

"Not you," my mother will say to me, helping me pull the shirt over my head. "You're not a fool."

"I know," I'll say. "You said men are fools and I'm not a man."

Rachel will snicker.

With that, the camera will fade.

It will open again on a cleaned-up Estelle standing on a bigger, better balcony, Aunt BoBo's balcony, the much revered wrap-around terrace. As the audience takes in the change of scenery, the narrator will explain that on the sliding scale of status at Imperial Towers 100, a scale understood and appreciated by all residents, Aunt BoBo's apartment was the crème de la crème.

A two-bedroom convertible with a wrap-around terrace was to the residents what a penthouse on the Park is to me. Something to aspire to. Something to dream about. Owners evoked curiosity and inspired reverence. When you understand this hierarchy, you can understand why, despite life-threatening smoke issues, Aunt BoBo's was the only place for Christmas dinner to be served. The terrace was the first place Grandma Estelle would head. Only now do I see that in doing so, she was trying to escape, as she had much to escape from.

For starters, there was Slip.

Then, there was the stench. The smell of meatballs diluted somewhat the cigarette smell, as did the smell of Jean Nate, which all the grandmas wore. (And which, in my professional opinion, is underrated. If repackaged right, it could bring in a killing as a retrofume.) If we were to package the smell of Aunt BoBo's apartment—Eau D'Aunt Bo, we'd call it—we'd combine a note of Jean Nate, a few notes of sweet and sour meatballs, and a chord of Marlboro. Not appealing, but as I said, Christmas dinner never would have been served anywhere else.

I suppose Aunt BoBo's balcony also offered an escape from Aunt BoBo and the adults in the kitchen, who were, when we arrived, involved in a debate about whether they had enough meatballs for everyone now that BoBo had gone and extended a last-minute invitation to a couple of other guests. The camera, following the commotion, will pan from the balcony to the kitchen.

The audience will take in Aunt Bobo's apartment, as well as the chaos in it—the silhouettes of kids shooting paper airplanes over the balcony, hanging spoons from their noses, or coloring.

They'll hear my Grandma B admonish my Aunt BoBo, "You know we only cooked for twenty-two."

Eventually, they'll see everyone—Grandma B, Aunt BoBo, my mother, and Aunt BoBo's daughters—rotating around a pot, a silver trough, the kind they use in school cafeterias to feed the masses. They'll be eyeballing the quantity to see if they can "make do."

"Who'd you invite?" my mother will ask.

"You'll know 'em when you see 'em," Aunt BoBo will bark. "What difference does it make? They got nowhere to go for the holiday."

"As if this is even a holiday," my Grandma B will respond. "They got nowhere to go," she'll mimic Aunt BoBo and shake her head, mystified at the lack of logic.

By this time, I was among the crowd of kids balancing spoons on their noses. Like ours, the walls of Aunt BoBo's dining room were mirrored, and Marcy, our two cousins, and I were lined up in front of them seeing who could hang the spoons the longest. Because I had the biggest nose, I wrongly assumed I'd be a winner.

From where I sat, I could see the reflections of the commotion in the kitchen and of my father talking to my grandfather in these two pale blue bucket chairs that could swivel like a tilt-a-whirl if given the proper running start. I liked to think of them as the death seats, since BoBo's husband, Morry, had been sitting in one of them a few years earlier when he'd had a heart attack and died.

Through the mirrors, I watched my Grandma Estelle come in from the terrace and my father give his seat to her. Grandma Estelle must have noticed me staring in her direction, because she waved and told me to come see her as soon as the spoon dropped off my nose. "There's something I want to talk to you about," she said.

I saw my father, now sitting on the arm of my grandma's chair, give her a warning look and shake his head. The shake wasn't long enough to interrupt his conversation with my grandfather, but it was long enough to spike my curiosity. I dumped my spoon and headed for the death seats.

"How's my Davy Baby?" Estelle began all of her conversations with me this way. The question was rhetorical. "Listen to me," she continued, patting her lap so I'd sit on it, "I've been doing so much driving lately that it's a wonder my fingers aren't stuck to the steering wheel. And I'm not the greatest driver on the road, but I'm getting there. So how would you like it if tomorrow"—she paused to look up at my father, who didn't notice or pretended not to, and then continued, in a whisper—"how about if tomorrow you came with us for the driving lesson and I'll buy you shoes just like mine?" Her feet kicked up a little, as if clarification as to the aforementioned shoes was necessary. Estelle laughed and I punched my fists into the air. We both nodded our heads. The conspiracy was solidified.

"Pardon me," my father said. His arms were crossed in front of his chest, so I knew bad news was to follow. "I don't think I like what I think I just heard."

I'm sure I whined something along the lines of, "But Dad. . . ." However, I was stopped by my grandma's hand, which came to rest atop my head.

"Allen," she said. "This is my one and only grandson, and if I feel like buying him some fancy gyms, then fancy gyms it will be." In my ear, she whispered not to worry. "I'm old," she told me, "but I'm still his mother."

"I don't care about the shoes. You can buy him shoes for every day of the week."

At this point, the movie camera will have to home in on the various facial expressions around the room. On the face of the father, a look of concern. On that of Grandma Estelle, a look of confusion. On Slip's face, amusement and relief to, for once, not be a party to a conflict. On mine, total delight at the promise of Adidas. All of this facial gesturing will occur as the father continues with his lines.

"You know you have no business taking Davy in the car with you."

My grandma will shrug. "You let him get in the car with him." With her head, she'll motion in Slip's direction.

"Hey," Slip will say. "Leave me out of this." He'll wink at me and my sisters, who by now will have caught wind of the conversation and the hope of Adidas for all. They, along with everyone else (save Aunt BoBo and Grandma B, who will still be bickering in the kitchen), will now listen.

"He's had his license for fifty years at least," my father will say.

My grandma will fight back using her favorite, the rhyming put-down. "License schmiscence," she'll laugh and dab her eyes. "Whoever gave him a license either never rode in a car with him or needs to have his head examined."

"I've been driving longer than that," my grandfather will pipe in. "I've had a license for fifty years, but I was driving for ten good years before then."

"And I've been driving for three days now and we're equally as good." Estelle will laugh again. So will everyone else.

Aunt BoBo will enter the room carrying a bottle of Mogen David and offer wine. "What's so funny?" she'll ask.

No one will bother to fill her in, only to point out that Mogen David is a funny thing to serve on Christmas. Her mood will blacken even more. "You know what. Don't explain. I don't feel like laughing anyhow."

My mother will volunteer to bring Aunt BoBo up to speed, and while she does, my sisters will ask for Adidas, too, and Slip will suggest to my father that we all get into the car together. "Let Estelle show us what she's got." He'll chuckle and stir the ice cubes in his drink with his index finger.

The idea will get lots of verbal support from us kids.

"So we can all get killed?" my father will answer.

Slip's head will bob up and down. "At least we'll all go down together."

"Terrific." My father's head will shake from side to side, the shake of one who knows he is fighting a losing battle.

"So it was," the narrator will say, "that from the death seats the death ride was born."

"Behind my back," my mother will protest as soon as she realizes what has transpired.

But her time on the floor will be limited since, as the movie script will direct: *Just then the front door to Aunt BoBo's apartment swings wide open and a poinsettia appears. It is large and red, just like the lips of its bearer, Lucille Garlovsky, and the poncho of Gladys Greenberg, who is following behind.*

CHAPTER 14:

Sex and Subtext

C HRISTMAS DINNER AT AUNT BOBO'S, CONTINUED
"Merry Christmas." Lucille's arrival will be more conspicu-
ous than our own. She'll shove over the enormous homemade
challah that's sitting in the middle of the dining room table and set
the plant down instead. "Doesn't that look festive?" she'll exclaim.

As the centerpiece is discussed, I will digest a fully clothed
Lucille. The black satin scarf in her mass of black hair, the gold ear-
rings like hula hoops, the heels as high as the Empire State Building, the pants as tight as paint.

In the movie, as soon as Lucille and Gladys Greenberg make
their entrance, everyone will begin to speak. The audience will
hear chatter rather than conversations, because I don't think anyone held a genuine conversation. I remember my mother saying to
Grandma B, "Please tell me you didn't know they were the guests."

Grandma B will look up at her as if English is a foreign language and without a word, go into the kitchen. You can't count that
as a conversation.

Nor can you count my Grandma Estelle's comment to my
father and me, "I think Santa Claus forgot to use the chimney." She

was referring to Gladys Greenberg, who was clad in a white pant-suit beneath her red poncho and who spoke to no one in particular when she said, "There are so many children here. I didn't realize."

The camera will pan across the many non-conversations and come to rest on Slip, the only quiet one in the bunch. Moviegoers will have to decide for themselves what to make of his silence. Did his pause stem from his hatred of Gladys Greenberg or, as Laurel would claim, his love of Lucille Garlovsky?

The implication of a character's actions is called subtext, Laurel told us in the class on Point of View, the last class I attended. Subtext is what a character doesn't say or do, and these omissions can tell an audience as much about the character as what he actually says or does. "Real people usually don't say exactly what they are thinking," Laurel explained. "Sometimes, they say the opposite. Or they communicate with silence or body language, tone of voice, even sarcasm." Aside from too much backstory, lack of subtext is the number one sign of a novice script, she informed us. "Good writers," she said, "are good with subtext."

As an aside, let me say that Laurel must be a genius as far as writers go, because she let more than three weeks pass after our trip to the bridge without speaking a word to me. In that time, she came and went from Los Angeles. I came and went from Chicago. I played basketball. I worked. I counseled Janet of the 3 Woos on reimaging her restaurant. All the while, or at least most of the while, I thought about Laurel. I talked about her with Marcy, who advised me to "honor my heartbreak by laying low." She also apologized for contributing to my pain, since taking Laurel's class was her idea in the first place.

I only called Laurel once. I hung up after a single ring, but she would have known from Caller ID that I'd called. She made a couple of attempts, feeble ones, to inquire into my well-being. In yoga class, she asked Marcy how I was doing and if she knew whether I was going to come back to class. At the bakery, she asked Estie if I was still writing.

No class had been scheduled for the Tuesday after Labor Day. So the next one I might have gone to was the September 10th class, the second to last on the syllabus. I thought about going to it. I was cruising along with my movie and could have used the lecture on the Hallmarks of a Great Conflict. But I imagined walking into the classroom and having to face Candy, Judd, and the couples club. I imagined Candy and Judd rolling their eyes and laughing, subtext for, "You idiot, how did you blow it with our idol?" I imagined Don asking for his money back and Susan clucking her tongue and letting me know yet again that her daughter was no longer available since she was now dating a rabbi. I imagined myself screaming at her, "Your daughter and the teacher are sleeping with the same rabbi." And from there, my fight with Laurel would pick up just where it had left off. Who knew what Laurel would say next? Maybe she'd say nothing and instead just show Page Six to the class as a handout, for those who hadn't seen it already. So, I decided to stay away from any more classes of Drama for the First-Time Film Writer.

Unlike me, Slip, in my movie, will head straight for the drama. He'll stop swiveling. He'll take a swig of his drink and stare with a smile as the new arrivals enter the room and Aunt BoBo works her way to our end of it.

"Your lady friend is here," she'll say, chuckling, and give Slip's chair a shove, spinning Slip slightly toward us.

"You better go back to your meatballs, Barbara, 'cause you stink at matchmaking." Slip will poke Aunt BoBo on the shoulder. "I already got myself a wife." He'll wink at Estelle.

"By the skin of his teeth, he does," Estelle will reply as Grandma B joins the group.

"You're worked up over nothing," my grandfather will tell Estelle. "If Gladys causes any more trouble, I'll kick the shit out of her. Don't you worry."

"That's exactly what I'm worried about," Estelle will say. "A woman can only take so much."

"You women can take a lot more than us men," Slip will answer as he rises from his death seat. "I'm going to greet our guests." He'll wink and saunter away.

As he does, Aunt BoBo will explain to Estelle and my father how Gladys Greenberg and Lucille Garlovsky came to be at our dinner. According to BoBo, Gladys had asked her at the elevators that morning if she could come by at dinnertime because she had news from the Board that would interest the family. "I extended an invitation because I figured the news must be good. Who'd break bad news on a holiday, right?"

"For Christ's sake. It's not a holiday!" my Grandma B will holler.

Aunt BoBo will turn her back to my Grandma B and further explain. "Only *after* I invited Gladys to Christmas dinner did she tell me that she already had a date with Lucille Garlovsky. So what was I supposed to do? The last thing I'd ever want to do is cause trouble for Estelle. But I'd already extended the invitation. And if the news is good, it'll be worth—"

"It's okay, BoBo," my father will cut in. "No one's accusing you of anything. You're not causing any trouble for Estelle. Right, Ma?"

"If your name isn't Slip, you're not causing me any trouble."

BoBo will thank God and go to check her meatballs.

My father will sigh and look at Estelle.

Estelle will chuckle. "If only you guys had shoes like mine," she'll say, "I'd say we all make a run for it." She will dab her eyes with the Kleenex tucked up her sleeve.

I remember laughing with her in agreement, although my head was spinning as I tried to figure out the status of everyone and everything. I would have loved to have made a run for it or at least gone back to dangling spoons. But I couldn't shake the hunch that somehow the fates of both my grandparents and my Adidas were on the line.

If the director is any good, my audience will be as worked up as I was by this point. They might not maniacally bounce themselves up and down in their movie seats like I did in the open swivel chair, but at least they'll feel the Davy character's bewilderment and anxiety. What was the news that Gladys Greenberg had come to deliver, and how would it impact my acquisition of the shoes? And, more mysterious, why was someone as glorious as Lucille Garlovsky with someone as horrid as Gladys Greenberg? Subtext, I'm afraid, is often lost on a ten-year-old boy, and so even though I saw the sequence—Slip patting Lucille on the back and saying,

"You forgot to bring your rope," followed by Gladys giving the evil eye to Lucille and walking away while Lucille leaned a leather-clad leg against the wall and shot a hip out toward my grandfather—I didn't think anything of it. Had I been older, maybe I would have seen what Laurel did, and I would have understood what Lucille Garlovsky was all about. Or maybe I just chose not to see it.

I did not learn the truth for fifteen years. It arrived in my New York City mail slot one day ten years ago in an envelope addressed by my father. Inside was an obituary from the Miami Herald. It was circled in bold red. Lucille Faye Garlovsky, it read. She'd died at age seventy from lung cancer (probably contracted in Aunt BoBo's apartment, although it didn't make mention). The beloved sister of two, mother of one, wife of none.

I called my father as soon as I received it. "I thought she was seventy in 1977," I said. He said no, she was young, widowed early. I said I wondered what had happened to her in all the years since my Grandma Estelle died and we stopped going to Miami.

"Nothing," he said. "She never left Imperial Towers 100 and she slept around 'til the day she died. Always had boyfriends paying her way."

"So she *was* a hussy?"

"Of course," he said, laughing. "You know who her best boyfriend was, don't you?"

"Slip?"

"No," he said. "Big Sid."

I'd had no idea. Which was too bad, because that bit of information would have come in handy that season, during the Christmas dinner in particular. "Did she ever sleep with Slip?" I asked.

"Are you nuts?" my father replied. Then he qualified, "At least, I don't think he did—but who really knows?" He told me I could ask him myself, but I didn't have the nerve.

Rachel, however, the great inquisitor, did.

"What the hell do you think?" was Slip's response. He was probably the only person to ever resist cracking under her pressure.

The only tricks I ever saw Lucille pull were the ones she turned on the pool deck with Slip the afternoon of the pool party—none of which, by the way, had proved too much for him. Now that I think about it, I should probably go back and extend the Jump Rope Scene so it ends in the movie like it did in real life, with Slip's victory over Lucille. He told her he looked forward to seeing her in the Ladies' Card Room, and would see what he could do to get her into the Men's Card Room as a favor to the men. Cheering and hollering followed. And that was that. Except for Lucille saying, "You got a lot of stamina for an old man"—a comment that would, like so many do, take on more significance posthumously. At the time, we all ran off to swim and eat hot dogs. No one gave the matter another thought.

Except for Gladys Greenberg, who did nothing but stew on the situation. When the scene in BoBo's apartment picks up again, she will admit to Grandma B that she was flabbergasted about having been upstaged by Slip and Lucille. "I know like I know my name is Gladys that Slip's move to the far side of the deck was calculated," she'll mutter as my mother announces that dinner is ready. "Although I don't know whether he meant to piss off Sid or me. Either way, I've cooked up consequences."

Apparently, she had come to Christmas dinner to deliver them. Whether she'd intended to provoke World War III is another question, the answer to which we'll never know.

Dinner will start civilly enough, with folks gabbing and jockeying for seats around the dining room table. Slip will sit down next to Lucille, and Estelle will sit on Lucille's other side; my grandparents will be separated literally by the Hussy.

Interestingly, Estelle started right in talking to Lucille, although I didn't get to eavesdrop because the kids were shuttled into the kitchen. Except for Rachel. Because of the number of kids and because Rachel was the oldest, she was bumped up to the dining room table, a promotion she milked for all it was worth. The audience will see her, in her blue satin disco suit, studying the give-and-take between Lucille and Estelle and then reporting her observations to us kids. "Estelle doesn't seem to mind Lucille at all," she'll inform us. "She seems to like Lucille much more than she likes Aunt BoBo."

In hindsight, I can see why Estelle liked Lucille. As I mentioned before, my observation is that the world has two kinds of people—the goodie-two-shoes who live by the book and scowl at those who don't and the nogoodnickas, as Estelle liked to call them. Not the quintessential Bad Guys, but people who liked to bend the rules. People like her and Slip.

On their first date, Slip picked up Estelle in the company car. His business was bootlegging and his boss was a gangster. (If you watch the movie *Casino*, take note of the guy who gets blown away outside a restaurant. That guy was Slip's boss.) Under the wooden seat of Slip's boss's car was a stash of alcohol. The seat was covered with a flannel blanket. Except it was summer, 95 degrees and, as my grandma liked to say, the only air conditioning was Lake Michigan, which is where they were headed when a cop thought flannel in the summer looked suspicious and pulled them over.

My grandma, who knew what she was sitting on, crossed her pretty legs and smiled. "Why, Officer," she said, "my boyfriend's just taking me on a picnic." She was scared, and perhaps it was out of fear that she was able to drop a tear from her eye (or maybe this was the beginning of her watery eye issue). Nevertheless, the cop apologized and let them go. A few months later they were married. "A couple of nogoodnickas, we were," Estelle would say.

Well, Lucille the Hussy was cut from the same nogoodnicka cloth as Estelle the Gangster's Wife, so one can understand why they enjoyed each other's company—which is what they were doing, according to Rachel, when Gladys Greenberg, in her poncho the size of a parachute, said to Slip, "You better watch yourself."

In the movie, heads will turn toward Gladys Greenberg as she rises slowly like the steam off the meatballs, pressing her thick hands against the table to hoist herself to her feet. She will thank BoBo for graciously including her and Lucille in the family dinner while Lucille shrugs and whispers to my Grandma Estelle, "I thought we were just stopping in for a cocktail before heading to Jai Alai."

Finally, Gladys will begin. "As I presume you already know, the Board had agreed, thanks to Dr. Melman's patients, to allow

Slip back into the card room in exchange for, among other things, the promise of Slip's future good behavior."

"What do you mean, among other things?" From my spot in the kitchen, I could hear the panic in Grandma Estelle's voice, as if she could sense the jungle print leotard hanging in Gladys Greenberg's closet. I could hear my father tell my grandmother to relax and then Slip say, "I told you there would be strings attached." He didn't let on that he already knew what they were. Only BoBo was dumb enough to do that.

"Oh, there are strings," Aunt BoBo will say. "Heavy duty."

"How do you know?" Estelle will ask.

"Oh good God, Estelle, the whole building knows," BoBo will answer.

"Knows what?" Estelle will ask again.

"It doesn't matter," my father will say.

But BoBo, pumped with Mogen David, will not stop. "Wake up, sweetheart. In exchange for letting Slip back into the card room, Gladys is getting a spot in your kick-line."

"Says who?"

"Your son."

My father will scowl at her. "Does it ever dawn on you to keep your big mouth shut?"

Silence will fall over the dining room as everyone stares at Estelle, awaiting her reaction.

She'll stare at my father and slowly swallow her meatball. "You gave her a place in my chorus line?"

Still chewing, Gladys Greenberg will say, "I even have the costume."

"Shut up, Gladys." This line will go to one of my mother's cousins.

"I don't understand," Estelle will say in a whisper. "You sold me out? For him?" She'll toss her head toward Slip.

My father will nod his head in admission. "I'm sorry, Ma. I knew you wouldn't like it, but it's for your own good. If we can get Slip back into his routine, your life will go back to normal."

"Not with her in my kick-line, it won't." My grandma will point a finger towards the head of the table. "She's insufferable."

"And on top of that," my Grandma B will add, "she can't dance."

"Besides, who says I want it to go back to normal?" Estelle will say. "Now that I can drive, Slip's routine is of no concern to me."

Slip will interject: "Like hell you can drive."

Rachel will say: "She's showing us tomorrow."

Slip will answer her: "No she ain't."

Estelle will answer him: "You just wait and see."

Gladys Greenberg will interrupt the bickering by declaring that whether or not Estelle can drive doesn't matter. "The deal is off the table after what Slip pulled on the pool deck today."

"This is what you came to dinner to tell us?" my mother will ask.

"Are you talking about the jump roping?" Lucille will ask, her voice as slow and sultry as ever. "Since when is jump roping against the law?"

"When you are jumping rope with my brother, too," Gladys will answer, using finger quotes around the term jumping rope. Here is where that missing bit of information about Lucille and Big Sid being an item would have helped out us kids.

"Big Sid wasn't jumping rope," Rachel will say, using the same ball-buster tone and finger quotes around jumping rope that Gladys had. I remember that laughter at the innocence of her remark followed the meatball platter around the table.

Rachel and Marcy would spend days analyzing and repeating (with finger quotes) Gladys Greenberg's next words. "You can't just jump rope with every man you see." To my sisters' credit, they got as far as guessing that "jumping rope" was code for having an affair. But the nut was one they'd never fully crack because no one, not even Rachel, would accept that the dazzling Lucille would ever "jump rope" with the heinous Big Sid.

"How often does Big Sidney jump rope?" one of my mother's cousins, also using the finger quotes, will ask.

"Oh, for heaven's sake," my Grandma Estelle will exclaim.

Lucille will agree. "This is not what I had in mind when you said that we were just dropping by before Jai Alai."

"Gladys," my father will say, "if there's something you came here to say, why don't you go ahead and say it?"

"Fine." Gladys, now sitting, will have her white napkin tucked into her red poncho and the loose skin under her neck will shake as her mouth moves, making her look like a giant turkey. "When I asked BoBo to stop in on your dinner, I thought we'd be announcing the good news that Slip's sentence had been lifted. However, in light of this afternoon's fiasco at the pool party, the Board has changed its mind. Not only that, but we've decided that if Slip pulls any more shenanigans, the Melmans will be asked to leave the building. One more strike, you're out."

Because I was sitting in the kitchen, I didn't hear this remark or any of the discussion that followed firsthand. However, in the movie, cameras will be centered over the dining room table, a vast rectangular slab of wood that, with a combination of matching chairs and fold-ups, uncomfortably sat fourteen. So the audience will see and hear the whole scene, including someone—let's say my father, since he is a man of calm and reason—responding to Gladys Greenberg like this:

"I'm afraid I don't understand what you are talking about."

"She's saying that if Slip doesn't stop causing trouble, they are going to kick him and Estelle out of the building." This will be my Grandma B.

"Ma, you're screaming." This will be my mother.

Again, hers. "I'm just explaining."

Next, Aunt BoBo. "Out of Imperial Towers 100?"

"Out of *all* the Imperial Towers. Buildings One through Eight." This, of course, Gladys Greenberg.

Now, to mix it up, we'll give a line to Philip, Aunt BoBo's son—a do-gooder to a fault, but also a voice of sanity. "I think we understood what Gladys said. I think we are confused about how they can throw Slip and Estelle out of their apartment." The script will direct the actor who plays Philip to over-enunciate and, as he does, shake a meatball-tipped fork like a maraca.

Slip, his mouth full of meatball, will respond, "They can't do nothing."

Gladys Greenberg will answer, "Oh, they can do more than you think."

"They're like the mob," one of my mother's cousins will comment, and everybody but Gladys Greenberg will laugh.

Now the script will read: *Everybody talks at once.* People around the table will sputter comments like, "This is ridiculous" and, "I thought they owned their condo" and, "Who are *they,* anyway?" Mixed in with this substantive talk will be the banal, like, "Does anyone need more meatballs?" and "Are the kids doing okay?"

As it happened, I wasn't doing so great. I didn't like conflict, and I didn't like meatballs. I did enjoy sopping up the sauce, but I'd run out of bread. I went into the dining room for more just as Estelle got into the conversation.

"I don't understand why they're making such a fuss," she said. "Doesn't the Board have bigger fish to fry than Slip Melman?"

This observation turned out to be the catalyst for battle. Sides formed seamlessly—do-gooders v. nogoodnickas—which was, for the most part, the way people had seated themselves around the dining room table.

"Bigger fish, sweetheart?" Gladys Greenberg chuckled. She, as you might surmise, was on the opposite side of the table, next to Aunt BoBo and Grandma B. "Your husband uses the Men's Card Room as a boxing ring, he ruined the pool party, and he's threatening to send men into the Ladies' Card Room."

"You're talking about a senior citizen," one of BoBo's daughters said. "Let's not get carried away."

"Let's just hope he doesn't carry on in there with all of the ladies like he does with Lucille," Gladys Greenberg shot back.

"Excuse me?" Lucille looked up from her plate.

"Next year you should screen your Christmas guests more carefully, BoBo," my mother said during a nanosecond of stunned silence.

In the same nanosecond, the audience will see Slip lean toward Rachel's plate. "Can I have that?" he'll ask, stabbing her last meatball with his fork as Rachel nods.

BoBo will begin to defend herself, but Lucille will interrupt. She'll adjust her scarf, offer up an apology to the table, and say, "Rest assured the jump roping was all in good fun. And Gladys, your remarks are out of an inappropriate left field."

She'll push her chair back, and as she does she'll place her hand on Estelle's wrist. I found this gesture comforting—stabilizing, really—as I was worried that the news that Slip was carrying on with the ladies was going to cause Estelle to fall off her chair.

But Estelle didn't flinch. She seemed to accept Lucille's word that the flirting was all in good fun by taking Lucille's hand.

On camera, Slip will seem to rise out of nowhere. He won't scream, but he'll speak to Gladys with a bona fide force and an emphasis on the F words, like a gangster's last words before he pulls the trigger. "Who the fuck do you think you are, fatso?"

The script will order a beat.

And then, with the same fearlessness with which he punched Big Sid, he'll fire away.

"I just thought he was hungry," Rachel will exclaim as the meatball, a sweet and sour missile, rockets across the room. A slo-mo close-up will capture the meatball's rotation as it flies off Slip's fork and over the table, nicking the shoulder of Gladys Greenberg's poncho before detonating against the mirrored walls.

Reactions to the splattered meat (which in the movie we'll see initially in the reflection of the smeared mirror) will vary as much as the folks looking at it all.

I will stare.

Lucille will chuckle.

Gladys Greenberg will scream.

Grandma B will ask Gladys Greenberg if she's okay.

My mother will tell all the children who have been pulled into the dining room by the "fuck you fatso" remark to return to the kitchen, although none will.

My father will tell Aunt BoBo not to worry, he'll clean up the mess.

Philip the do-gooder will tell everyone to stay seated.

Aunt BoBo will go to get Windex and another bottle of Mogen David.

Finally, my Grandma Estelle will say in a voice new to me, "Sol Melman, that's enough with the nonsense. I've had it up to my ears. If you so much as step one of your childish feet into the Ladies' Card Room or start any other kind of trouble around here, you'll be moving out 'cause I'll be *throwing* you out." She'll throw her napkin onto her plate. "You can go live with Lucille for all I care."

The camera will zoom in on Estelle as she speaks and then pull back. The script will call for absolute silence. It will tell actors to put on their stunned faces. Except for Lucille, who will snicker and mutter, "No thank you, darling."

Of all of the stunned faces, mine was probably the most frozen. My grandma's tone, I imagined, was the one she'd used to admonish my father for his youthful transgressions—a tone she'd tucked away many years ago. She herself seemed shocked to hear it, as though she didn't know she still had the bite in her. From the way her hands shook and the color ran out of her face, she seemed to have summoned quite a bit of physical energy to bring it out.

Naturally, due to my ongoing concern that my grandparents' wells of physical energy were about to run dry, I worried that this was an outburst that Estelle could ill-afford. My father must have been on my wavelength because he filled a cup with Mogen David and gently pushed it in her direction.

"Just a little bit, Ma," he directed. "It'll settle your nerves."

When I told Laurel the story, way back during one of our walks to the Grey Dog Cafe, she told me that this whole scenario would have never occurred in her family because Mormons don't drink.

"Aren't your dinners dull?" I asked.

She said no. She said that growing up, she had a dormer full of brothers and sisters, enough to make dinners rowdy and too many for her parents to pay attention to. If she'd wanted, she could have taken a sip of anything without anyone noticing.

But she did admit that no one ever threw a meatball. Certainly none of the adults. The whole concept, not only that a grown man would throw a meatball but that the meal would continue on after the mess had been cleaned up—after Gladys Greenberg left and Slip apologized to Estelle and Aunt BoBo—was beyond Laurel's comprehension.

Nonetheless, that's the way it was. The kids returned to the kitchen. Conversation returned to murmurs. Plates were cleaned. Dessert was skipped because, in case you forgot, it was Christmas and everyone—nogoodnickas or not—was eager to see the movie. From there, we'll fade to black.

In her handout on twists and turns, which I begrudgingly read on my flight home from Chicago, Laurel talked up the use of the unexpected guest as a technique for creating a third-act twist. If well used, she wrote, the twist will be a moment of truth, revelation, and surprise for the main character as well as the audience. I like to think that the concept worked well in my movie with the introduction of Gladys Greenberg and Lucille Garlovsky. But I can tell you from experience that the ploy worked much better in real life when Laurel showed up as the unexpected guest three weeks later at our Yom Kippur dinner.

She arrived at Marcy's door on Monday, September 16 in much the same fashion that Gladys Greenberg and Lucille appeared at Aunt BoBo's door in my movie—just in time for dinner and with a challah in hand. Marcy plunked the challah down on the dining room table just as Lucille did with her poinsettia. I suppose we can draw further parallels between my movie and my life, between then and now. Gladys Greenberg and Laurel are both Antagonists, while Aunt BoBo and Marcy are both the Idiots. My role, however, in each scene is different. In 1977, I was the scared and sober ten-year-old. In present day, I was the scared and less sober thirty-five-year-old who, this time around, was on to subtext.

I'm not saying I interpreted all of Laurel's signs and silences correctly, but at least I knew they meant something. Her decision to show up at all, right into the lions' den of the Melman clan, when she'd been so uninterested in meeting them a month ago, had to mean something. Her choice of attire—a hideous, long grey skirt and a scarf she'd wrapped over her head, the same kind of bright colored *shmata* (to borrow a term from Laurel's Yiddish playbook) the women in Florida used to wear—had to mean something. Although even with this getup, she still had on the cowboy boots. I did not know what to make of that.

When we heard the knock on the door, my brothers-in-law, my father, and I were stuffed onto a couch eating mixed nuts and gearing up for Monday Night Football. The females were—as they usually are, as they certainly were that night at Aunt BoBo's—gathered in the kitchen. Only this time, they weren't analyzing meatballs. Aside from the soup my mother had made, the food came from Barney Greengrass. In lieu of cooking, Rachel was showing Marcy pictures of Julia in her play. Marcy was showing my mother designs for a new Knead Some Dough logo for her donut boxes. My mother was tending to her soup and singing along to her Jewish music.

Paula Melman has been playing the same record during the High Holidays for as long as I can remember. After all these years, I don't think anybody but her even registered that music was playing. However, to fully appreciate the evening, it should be noted that the dinner was backdropped by a woman named Debbie Friedman singing prayers about peace, love, and compassion.

Everyone in the family, regardless of activity, regardless of the concept of the Yom Kippur break fast meal, was also eating at the time of the knock on the door. Nuts, as I mentioned, for the men in the family room. The boys were stealing cookies from the dining room. My mother was stealing bits of this and that from the deli tray. Marcy's apartment is open access, a giant circle with half-walls separating the family room from the dining room, the dining room from the kitchen. Everyone could see everything. So when the knock came and Marcy answered, all eyes were on Laurel.

My first thought was that she'd made a mistake. She either had the wrong date or the wrong apartment. My second thought, after I took in her attire, was that she'd gone ahead and married the rabbi and was coming to break the news. Or, perhaps in her new capacity as the rabbi's wife, she was coming to bless our dinner. The truth didn't hit me until Marcy thanked her for the challah and said, "I'm so glad you were able to join us." With those words, all became clear.

"You invited her?" I blurted out. I was dumbfounded.

"That's such a kind way to welcome our guest," Marcy said. "And on Yom Kippur. Of all days to not be generous of spirit. Yes, I invited her. She's my friend and it's my apartment."

"Uncle David, it was actually my idea to invite her," Estie said. "She wanted to experience a traditional Yom Kippur. I hope you're not mad."

As Broc commented that ours was hardly a traditional Yom Kippur, I told Estie I wasn't mad at her. "I'm mad at your mother." Then, to her mother, I said, "How could you not tell me?"

Marcy smoothed out her apron. "I decided it would be better not to." She moved her hands to her hips. "In case you reacted like a fool and put up a fight."

"You're the fool," Rachel informed Marcy as she moved toward the fishbowl that was the foyer and said, "Let me guess, you are the Mormon film writing teacher." Rachel, in her perfectly tailored pantsuit, held a hand out to Laurel.

Laurel gave Rachel her hand and said, "I assumed you knew I was coming, so I didn't think I'd need an introduction, but I guess not." She laughed, a self-conscious kind of chuckle I hadn't heard before. I felt a little sorry for her, but I felt more sorry for me.

Until this point, I'd been having a great weekend. I'd taken my nephews, Ryan and Connor and Bradley, to the top of the Empire State Building. Rachel, Peter, Broc, Marcy, and I had gone to see *The Producers.* I'd gone with Estie, Julia, and Rachel on a carriage ride in Central Park. For the first time in weeks, I'd had a break from the sorry-ass array of issues currently making up the life and times of David Melman. The mastermind—the *Post* should have said—behind not only Omnipotence but his own impotence as well.

And now this.

"I have to be honest," my father said, "I didn't know who the hell you were when you walked in, but Rachel's introduction summed it all up."

My mother said Rachel's introduction was actually quite rude. "I'm sure she thinks of herself as more than a Mormon film writing teacher." She turned to Laurel. "Don't you?" Without waiting for Laurel's response, she threw her arm around her back and ushered her deeper into the apartment. "I'd never have known you were Mormon from looking at you," she added.

"So it was a good thing I included that detail in my intro," Rachel said. Now it was her turn for the awkward laugh. She opened her mouth wide but no sound came out.

Laurel apologized. "I didn't mean to blindside anyone."

Peter told her not to apologize. "The holiday needed some livening up."

"Don't worry about it," I added, heading into the kitchen, where Marcy had set up a makeshift bar on the counter behind the kids' table. Not the most logical place for alcohol but then again, as evidenced by the unexpected guest, Marcy has never been the most logical person.

I generally don't drink when I'm with my family. I like to have my wits about me when my sisters and mother are around. Nevertheless, I poured myself some vodka, straight up, and drained it down. Then I plunked the empty glass on the kids' table and said, "Laurel is welcome to stay. However, I'll be eating here." I pointed to the seat in front of me. "Estie, you can have my place in the dining room. You can sit right next to our guest if you want, since you like her so much."

So it was that Yom Kippur '02 unfolded in the same manner as Christmas '77, with tension in the air and David at the kids' table. This time, however, not only was I entitled to alcohol, I had unlimited access to it. All I needed to do to refill my glass was turn around in my chair, and I did so steadily.

Marcy's kitchen is separated from the dining room by a ledge with posts, like fancy prison bars, running from the top of the ledge to the ceiling. Because she had this Tibetan tapestry hanging on the dining room side of the posts and Estie's and Ryan's artwork on the sides that faced the kitchen, I couldn't see through the posts into the dining room—unless I leaned about six inches to the left, in which case I had an unobstructed view of Laurel sitting in between Marcy and Estie. My mother and father sat across from her. Their backs, fortunately, were to me. My brothers-in-law sat at the heads of the table and Julia, who'd protested when Estie got promoted to the dining room, was squished in between Marcy and Rachel. My four nephews, ranging in age from five to ten, were in the kitchen, behaving with the least amount of civilized behavior necessary to keep them out of trouble. No one was paying attention to me.

The reverse was not true. No siree, I was all ears at the Yom Kippur dinner.

The listening portion of the evening began right after the blessings over the bread and the wine, which Laurel was able to articulate like an Orthodox woman from the Old Country, with utter seriousness and a covered head. I choked on my wine when my mother commented, "That's very impressive, Laurel. I'd never know you weren't a Jew."

"Was that an insult or a compliment?" Rachel asked.

As she doled out bowls of soup, my mother said, "I meant it as a compliment."

My father reinforced the sentiment. "You're a Jew in my book, honey," he told her. "You know more Hebrew than I do."

At this point, I heard Marcy explain to the table, "Even though Laurel's not Jewish, she's a huge fan."

"It's true," Laurel offered. "Though I never met a Jew until I arrived here in Manhattan." Her voice was calm and composed—the opposite of how my voice felt, which was why I wasn't using it.

"Really?" my mother chimed in.

"There aren't many in the small towns of Utah. However, I will tell you that I was pleasantly surprised after spending some time here. It's the live-and-let-live credo that I really enjoy. It's the total antithesis of my upbringing. The Jews are a non-judgmental people, and I like that."

"I don't know what Jews you've been talking to," Rachel said. "I've never met a Jew who doesn't judge. That's what Jews do."

"Speak for yourself," my mother said. "I'm incredibly open-minded."

I was glad I'd had the sense to sit in the kitchen. I don't think I could have survived the strain in the dining room, even with the vodka racing around my veins. I didn't even want to lean the six inches to my left because I couldn't bear to watch. At the kiddie table, I felt removed. As if the dining room conversation were simply dialogue in a movie and my reactions, including my wince when Laurel offered that she knew some Yiddish, could not be seen.

I began to think that maybe Laurel's outfit, like her conversation, was for my mother's benefit. At first I could only hear bits and pieces of her dialogue with my mother, because of the rest of the family's chatter. Then they began speaking Yiddish to each other, and everyone else followed suit. Peter, a non-Jew, threw out "*Oy vey.*" Broc went for *kvetch.* Julia offered *schlimazel*, not intentionally referring to me, but Marcy and Rachel both looked in my direction and my nieces started to laugh. So did my mother and father. The tension, I could tell, was leaving the room. From the perspective of an inebriated outsider who still had feelings for the unexpected guest, the atmosphere was taking an irksome change for the better. Everyone was suddenly having fun, which was not how I'd imagined things going down. I'd figured Laurel's reception would be more akin to the reception Gladys Greenberg had received: she would be seen as the enemy and stoned—if not with a meatball, then at least figuratively.

I never thought that Rachel—the one who'd cautioned me against Laurel, who'd warned ages ago that I was on a slippery slope to Lucille Garlovsky, who'd encouraged me to make sure the coffee maker was the only thing we had in common—would make a special trip into the bar area and whisper to me as she poured this and that into a glass that she didn't even carry back to the table, "She's lovely, really. What a fabulous sport."

When I heard my mother ask, "Are you only taking conversion classes for research or are you actually planning to convert?" I leaned over in my chair towards the dining room and offered my two drunken cents: "From the way she's dressed, it seems like she's already converted."

Marcy started to retort in her friend's defense but Laurel stopped her. "Nice to hear from you, David, and it's nice to see you haven't lost your sense of humor over the past few weeks. But no, I have not converted." She looked at my mother and, as she played with the hair—newly straightened—hanging out the bottom of her *shmata*, added, "Though I would be happy to convert for the right man."

I assumed, from her emphasis on the word *right*, that I was the wrong man.

I leaned further forward in my chair, as if I'd benefit my cause by having other people hear what I was about to say. "That's good to hear because, as good as you look in the garb, I don't think conversion's the way to go." The folks around the table all turned to stare at me and I began to ramble about how another Holocaust is inevitable, judging from 9/11, which I experienced firsthand, although slightly sedated from the dentist's office in Midtown where I was undergoing an emergency root canal, and which in my mind was basically an insurgence against the Jews. "The next rounding up and offing of our people is just around the corner," I said. "So, if you married a Jew and had kids, it would make more sense, for the good of the children, if their mother played for the other team."

There was dead silence when I got done. Even Debbie Friedman had stopped singing.

"Well it's true," I said. "We all saw *Schindler's List*. History has a way of repeating itself."

"What if you don't have kids?" Estie asked.

"If you're not going to have kids, what's the point of getting married?" I said.

My mother turned around in her chair to glare in my direction. "Stop talking," she ordered. There was no question whose side she was on. I was the nogoodnicka in this scene. To Laurel, she said, "Sweetheart, if you like the religion, you should convert. And regardless, I think you are just lucky to have found a rabbi who is willing to let you sit in on classes."

"So basically, she's auditing Judaism," Rachel stated.

"Exactly," my mother said. "An audit of Judaism, what a lovely experience." She reached across the table and tapped Laurel's hand.

At this—the praising and the tapping—I forced history to repeat itself. More out of irritation with my family than with Laurel, I pulled myself into a standing position and ambled toward the dining room. "Yeah," I said, "I guess you could say that the rabbi is giving her a lot of bang for her buck." I didn't throw anything but I emphasized the B words the same as Slip had done with the Fs.

Estie asked, "What's that supposed to mean?"

Marcy told her, "Nothing."

If a platter of meatballs had been on the table, I'm quite sure my mother or my sisters would have pelted me. Instead, only remnants were left on the deli tray my mother picked at as she apologized to Laurel for whatever she'd done wrong as a mother.

My brothers-in-law started to laugh.

My nephews got up from the kiddie table and crowded around me.

Laurel said, "I think it's time for me to leave." She set her napkin on her plate and smiled gently at Marcy. Subtext, I knew, for "I told you so."

"Don't be ridiculous," my mother said. She asked Laurel to please stay and directed me to apologize to her.

I repeated her words: "Don't be ridiculous." I may have even thrown my hands in the air the way my mother had done.

My dad raised the bottle of wine. "Who wants another drink?"

"I don't think Uncle David needs one," Estie said. "He's swaying."

"Maybe he's the one who should leave," Marcy suggested.

I told Estie I was not swaying. "The boys are pushing into me." I put my arms around them and we did a round of high-fives. "We're the nogoodnickas," I told them.

My father said that he thought nogoodnicka was a word his mother used to use.

"It is," Laurel said. "It's in his movie."

"Yeah, it's in my movie," I said, now using the prison bars on either side of the entryway for support. "Which is actually pretty good. I'm almost done with it. Hey, maybe I'll move out to LA too," I said to Laurel, who was moving toward the coat closet where Marcy had put her shawl and messenger bag. "Me and you, we'll head out West. What do you say?"

"What do I say?" She spread the shawl over her shoulders. "Well, to your sister, I say thank you for having me. To your family, I say you are a lovely group of people and I apologize for ruining your dinner, I shouldn't have come here tonight, I thought it would go better, I thought David knew I was coming, I thought it would be a nice gesture on my part." She turned to me. "A way of saying I was sorry for shutting you down at the bridge and not calling. This is the day of atonement, after all." She finger quoted "atonement." "Unfortunately," she added, "being called out in front of your whole family for sleeping with the rabbi was not what I had in mind."

The audience—that's what my family had become—fell silent again. The line on Rachel's forehead grew deeper, more entrenched. The Mormon Rodeo had shocked the Botox right out of her system.

I heard Rachel whisper to Marcy, "She was cheating on David with a rabbi?"

Marcy nodded her head yes, quickly, her eyes never coming off of me and Laurel.

"That's bad," Rachel whispered again.

"He's really hot," Marcy said, as if that explained everything. Then she got up and headed toward the buffet. "If Laurel is going to leave early, and who can blame her, she'll have to take dessert with her." She looked at me as she spoke.

"Fabulous. You admit it," I said, still clinging to the pole. "Now we're finally getting somewhere. You've been sleeping with the rabbi. Or are you only apologizing because you found out your movie isn't going to sell? Are you here as Plan B, looking to become Mrs. David Melman so you don't have to move to LA?"

Laurel decided to defend her good name rather than address my questions. "I was in a relationship with the rabbi before David and I started sleeping together," she said to Rachel. "So technically, I was cheating on the rabbi with David, not the other way around—and not that I intended to share any of this with you. However, since I'll probably never see any of you again, I'll set the record straight." She slung the messenger bag over her shoulder. It added to her already special look.

"You were sleeping with a rabbi's girl?" my father asked me.

There was a chance I was going to pass out—vodka mixed with family sex talks are lethal. But I held firm. "Don't twist this around on me. I had no idea that you were mixin' it up with Rabbi Eric when you mauled me during *Schindler's List*. Or when you propositioned me in your apartment." I looked at Rachel. "Isn't adultery an intent crime?"

"Don't play dumb, David," Laurel said. "You knew perfectly well." Her voice, I noticed, had slipped into her teacher persona, her own defensive position. Non-emotional. Commanding. Persuasive. I didn't stand a chance. "Marcy told you I was sleeping with him."

Now everyone turned toward Marcy—except my mother, who was busy herding the boys into the family room. This conversation, apparently, was not meant for their ears.

I rotated my eyeballs toward Marcy. The rest of me was paralyzed. "You knew this? For a fact? You said it was just a rumor."

"I told you to stay away from her," she said.

"You told me she had issues to work out. You might have wanted to mention she was in a relationship with a rabbi of all people, a man of fucking God."

"I told you to stay away from her as a trick, and it worked. If I'd told you I wanted to set you guys up, you wouldn't have listened to me. So instead I told you to stay away from her, knowing that you'd do the opposite." She looked at me. "It's called reverse psychology."

"I actually think it sounds more like manipulation," Broc said.

"I'm sorry. I apologize to both of you," Marcy said. She put her hands in prayer position and looked to the ceiling. "May God forgive me for the sin I committed by not telling the truth to my brother about my girlfriend because I thought the two of them would make a great couple."

"Good call," Rachel said. "They're adorable."

While the attention was diverted to Marcy, I said to Laurel, "Regardless of how our relationship started, I would have thought you would have cut it off with the rabbi after the banana boat lecture. After you told the whole class that I loved you."

Laurel gave a frustrated, tired sigh. She stuffed the box of donuts from Marcy into her bag and pulled the shawl tighter around her shoulders, as if she was heading into the hinterlands instead of Union Square. "We've been through this, David. I was making a point to the class. I wasn't talking about us." She opened the door and, with a foot in the hallway, said, "And if you did love me, you could have been a stand-up guy and just said so yourself, instead of hiding your feelings behind my words."

With that, she was gone and all eyes were on me. Just the opposite of how the evening began. And just the opposite of how Christmas dinner 1977 ended, with folks cleaning up and moving on, forgiving and forgetting. The Day of Atonement '02 ended with a pall over it, with my head pounding and comments flying.

"How could he behave this way?" Marcy was saying to my mother. "Especially after he just got done atoning and promising to be a better person. What a way to kick off the new year. Mar the slates with a family feud."

"Well, if he loves her," my mother said. She was at the buffet now, assembling a platter of jelly donuts and mini meringues. Nothing interferes with the Melmans' dessert.

"Do you love her?" Rachel asked.

I moved my head up and down.

"How wonderful!" my mother said, her mouth filled with cookie.

"If you love her," Marcy said, "you're not only a drunk you're an idiot, too."

"Well if that's not the pot calling the kettle black," I slurred. "This whole situation, all my grief for the last month, is your fault. Isn't that swell." *And ironic*, I thought as I held onto the pole and the world swayed 'round. "She was the one who made me go to class in the first place," I said, now tattling to my father. "She said it would be good for me, that it would help me find myself. Well nice work, sis. Look at me now." I slumped down in the spot I was standing in between the kitchen and the dining room.

Suddenly, I sympathized with Share, who'd called the day after the dinner with Bailey Pierce to apologize for her horrible behavior. She'd been so overwhelmed by the presence of Bailey, her idol, so worried she wouldn't know what to say to her, so frightened that Bailey wouldn't give her the time of day, that she'd overdone it with the alcohol. I'd told Share not to worry, that the best of us abuse the booze every now and again, and I wouldn't hold it against her. Somehow I doubted that Laurel was going to be as forgiving. My family, for certain, was not.

CHAPTER 15

Dialogue

ᴍ

Proceedings were held in Marcy's family room after we finished our Yom Kippur dessert. The issue at hand was the status of my relationship with Laurel in the wake of the evening's events. Specifically, was it possible to restore it? Rachel, perched on the arm of the couch, presided. She hovered over my father, who sat on the cushion below her winding a napkin around his fingers, preparing to pull a tooth. Rachel's seven-year-old son, Connor, stood, mouth wide open, in front of my father. Connor was numbing his gum with an ice cube. Rachel's five-year-old son, Bradley, crowded in, waiting for the action to start.

My brothers-in-law sat together on the love seat watching the Eagles trounce the Redskins. My mother was in the kitchen with Julia and Estie, teaching them to play mah-jongg. I was sprawled on Marcy's carpet eating cookies, drinking coffee, and pretending to watch the game while I listened and sobered up. Conversation circled around me as if I didn't exist, which I didn't mind. I felt like I'd tuned into a call-in radio show and was getting solid cautionary tale advice based on some other pathetic soul's story.

"Here she was, looking to make up and move on. She gave him a chance and what does he do? He blows it. He waits until she leaves to announce that he loves her," Marcy said as she wrapped leftovers. A lot was being made of the fact that I'd said I loved her.

Rachel took a sip of tea and pulled Bradley on her lap to give my father more room to maneuver. "Yes, I agree. She had the decency—the balls, actually—to show up here dressed for some kind of Hebrew Halloween, and he had the nerve to shut her down. It was appalling. And she couldn't have been more clear about what she wanted."

I ran my hands through the brown and gold pile carpet and silently begged to differ. What Laurel wanted hadn't been clear to me. I waited, hoping Rachel would elaborate.

Marcy spoke instead: "He could've at least gone after her." I could tell she was genuinely upset because she was eating a meringue cookie. She never eats her own sweets. "A stupid move, especially now that we know he loves her."

My father told Connor to remove the ice; he was ready to go in for the tooth.

"'Y'all need to go easy on David," Broc said.

"Please," Rachel said as my father announced that Connor's tooth wasn't ready to come out. It was still attached to a piece of his gum and had to be further loosened. "Going easy on him his whole life is what's caused all his issues."

"What issues?" my mother hollered from the kitchen.

I propped my head up onto my hand, bolstered by the emergence of several allies. If anything, I was getting a solid feel for who my supporters were, which family members should be tapped to speak on my behalf, if and when I should go the way of the original Mort Chuckerman and die.

My mind must have still been under the influence of alcohol, because I was gripped by a sudden mesmerization with Mort Chuckerman. How profound and ironic that a cadaver, a dead body, had become a moniker, a term of endearment, for me. Talk about subtext. I might have shared this realization with Laurel had I not just chased her out the door.

"So what if David has issues," my mother was now saying. "We all have our issues."

As my father told my mother to speak for herself, I decided to speak for me.

"Any issues I may have come from being tortured by the two of you my whole life," I said, pointing at Rachel and at Marcy. "You're lucky I'm still alive."

"Clearly, he's still drunk," Marcy said. She looked to Rachel for support, but her head was too far into Connor's mouth, trying to see the piece of gum at issue, to notice.

"I would be, too," Peter said. "That was a pressure cooker situation. I don't know many guys who would have handled themselves any better."

Even my father had an opinion. "Let me just throw this idea out there: Has it dawned on any of you dummies that you are wasting your breath? Maybe Laurel doesn't love David." He looked at us, his forehead crinkled. "Maybe she left the meal early because she didn't give a damn, and this whole conversation here is for nothing."

There was a pause while everyone considered my father's perspective and my father instructed Connor to bite down on one of my cookies to help loosen up his tooth.

I handed Connor an oatmeal raisin and mourned the loss of my Chuckerman name while everyone else continued to analyze my life.

Rachel was all over my father's remark. "I disagree. She obviously loves him or at least cares about him a lot. Why else would she have shown up here?"

Surprisingly, Estie took her on. "Maybe because I invited her and she didn't want to say no to a kid. Or because she really just wanted to experience a traditional Yom Kippur dinner."

Broc repeated his sentiment that if one's goal is to experience anything traditional, she should not be wasting time with the Melman family.

"You can talk all you want about love, but the real question is, does he hear bells?"

There was a communal groan from the family room, including one from me, as we all knew my mother's position on bells.

"Call me old-fashioned, but if you ask me, no bells is a red flag. When that girl walked into the room this evening, Davy's heart needed to stop, the room should have lit up. He needed to hear bells. Even if she was dressed like my great-grandmother."

"Trust me, you are all wasting your time," my father said. "I'll bet that poor girl took one look at this family and headed back to Utah. If it makes you feel any better, Davy, I think we are all responsible for chasing her away."

At this, bickering began at a heightened register, with my mother yelling at my father for letting me off the hook, Rachel yelling at my mother for raising the bar too high with the bells, Marcy yelling at Ryan for not doing his reading homework, Connor whining at Rachel for not letting him have the cookie that might be the key to losing his tooth, and Broc yelling at everyone for drowning out the TV.

"Don't listen to her," Marcy whispered to me on her way to the kitchen. "Love is enough."

But was it? "Love matters a little but luck matters more," my grandma had told me that day on the pool deck. How could you make a decision about the rest of your life when luck was the linchpin between you and happily ever after? I looked at my father, who was again icing Connor's tooth.

Was it luck or bells or the fact that my father was out of the house for most of my parents' marriage that had made it so successful? On the other hand, Rachel and Peter spent almost all day every day together, and Rachel was the bossiest person I knew. Yet they seemed happy. So did Broc and Marcy, and Broc had never intended to marry Marcy at all. Had they just gotten lucky? Or were they all just acting? Maybe everyone was waiting for just the right moment to do as Laurel just did—as my Grandma Estelle longed to do—and head for the hills.

I didn't know and I didn't have time to ask, because at this point Rachel announced that she knew how to make the situation with Laurel right again.

My father, ready to try again with Conner's tooth, told her to give it up already. "That ship," he said, pausing long enough to take out the tooth, "has sailed." I was happy to have him on my side, though sad to hear that he thought I had no hope. I guess I wanted hope, which was why when Rachel said, "You need to track her down and beg for forgiveness," I propped myself up on my elbows and injected myself back into the conversation.

"What do you mean by beg?" I asked as Connor displayed the tooth to the rest of the family.

"You should have gone after her when she left," Marcy declared.

"He couldn't walk," Estie reminded her.

"Well, Laurel's class is tomorrow. He could go to that," Marcy said. Rachel's eyes lit up.

"I'm not going to show up to Laurel's class and beg," I said.

"Yes, you are," Marcy said.

Rachel told me that not only was I going to show up, I was going to dress up too. "I want you to look disheveled and distraught."

"The way you look now," Julia shouted in from the kitchen.

"Exactly," Rachel said. She tucked her hair behind her ears and leaned forward, her typical witness preparation position. "You're going to walk into class looking like you haven't slept. Then you're going to go straight up to her, look her in the eye, and say something simple, honest, and from the heart."

"Like, I'm sorry I'm a schmuck, but I love you," Marcy said. "Please take me back."

Rachel told her not quite. "Leave off the schmuck part, that speaks for itself. And leave off the please take me back. That, too, is implied by your actions. Basically, your job boils down to delivering one line, which I think you can handle. 'Laurel, I am so sorry. I regret my behavior, and I love you.'"

"He's trying to win back a girl, not apologize to his parents," Peter said. "It needs some dressing up."

My father agreed. He thought I should take Laurel's hands as I spoke. But Rachel felt that given the gravity of the evening's screw-up, less was more—"As long as his words are delivered with the proper level of sincerity." To ensure this, she asked me to repeat after her: "I'm so sorry. I regret my behavior, and I love you."

I told her I wasn't doing it. My nephews, on the other hand, were. Rachel should have seen that coming. They began to recite the line, pounding their thighs to the rhythm of the sentence. Then Broc joined in and bedlam broke out in the family room, with every Melman under fifteen, plus my brothers-in-law, chanting along. I didn't participate, but the sentence did stick in my brain so when I walked into class the next night as instructed—unshaven and in a dirty T-shirt—I was ready to deliver.

"What's with you?" the Mormon Rodeo said when she saw me. "You look like Judd." Gone was the Orthodox peasant girl. In her place seemed to be a younger version of Mrs. Martin, my first grade teacher, who believed in dunce caps and pulling loose teeth with a string and a door. Laurel wore a pale pink button-down and a khaki skirt to her knees, and her stick-straight hair was pulled off her face in a bun, tight like a ballerina. I'd never seen her look this way. She looked hot. She also looked intense.

I couldn't figure out if her hairdo or the debacle of the previous night accounted for her standoffishness. If she'd have looked this old-school on the first day of class, I'd never have had the nerve to talk to her. I didn't have the nerve now, either. Immediately, the lines rehearsed in Marcy's apartment went out the window. Instead of "Laurel, I'm really sorry about last night, I was an idiot and I love you," I mumbled, "Hey, how you doing?" And I took a seat.

"I think the better question is, how are you?" She stopped organizing her papers and looked at me. "I'm actually shocked, if not slightly disappointed, to see you are still alive."

I nodded in confirmation of my existence and tried to make sense of her nonchalance. Earlier that day, when I'd reviewed Rachel's game plan with Ezmerelda, she had speculated that I might not even be let back into the classroom.

But Laurel just continued to organize papers into bundles. *Maybe my father was right, she doesn't care*, I thought as I glanced around the room to avoid looking her. The television, the one she'd used to show *Schindler's List*, was in the corner. I asked her if we were seeing a clip today. She said no, she'd shown *The Godfather* during last week's class on Hallmarks of a Great Conflict. "Tonight's class," she said, "is about dialogue. No visuals. We're going to talk it out."

"Well, that works out well. There's some stuff I want to say to you."

"You don't say." She put down the stapler she was about to start using on the papers she'd been organizing. "I'm not sure I'm interested. However, I am curious. There is a difference, you know, between interest and curiosity. Interest is genuine. Curiosity is dangerous." She paused to ponder. "I shouldn't give in to curiosity. We all know it killed the cat. On the other hand, you look so pathetic." She threw up her hands in defeat. "Fine, I'll hear you out." She looked at me expectantly. So did the few others who had trickled into class.

I nodded toward the other folks. "Maybe after class."

"Whatever you want. In the meantime, why don't you make yourself useful," she said without looking up from her stapler.

"You mean, why don't you make yourself useful, *Chuckerman*," I said, trying to test the waters, figure out if I had any hope of a revival.

She didn't give me much. She rolled her eyes. "Whatever, David. Just get up and help pass these out."

I felt dizzy as I stood. Probably vertigo from the extremes of my day. That morning, I'd been sitting in a conference room, all oak and austerity, at the law firm that was handling the licensing of Omnipotence. Conversing. Negotiating. Making things happen. Now, I was distributing handouts and groveling.

The packets turned out to be excerpts from our own scenes that, Laurel explained, we were going to use for an exercise in dialogue. "Too many of your characters are talking to set up the plot or to just hear themselves talk. Rambling won't fly in film." Rambling a bit herself, she explained that when a character speaks, his words must have a purpose. "Conversations need to be brief and move the story forward. They need to teach us about a character, flip the balance of power between characters, or create tension. Good, old-fashioned dramatic tension."

She also told us that our characters should sound like real people. "How do you know if dialogue sounds real? You read it aloud. Hence," she said, pausing to hold up a packet, "our exercise."

For the first excerpt, Laurel tapped Rhonda and Carl, the guy who sits next to the window, to read.

"Run zigzag, Pharis, run zigzag. Gators can move, Pharis. So shake your ass." Carl spoke with none of the urgency that one generally associates with an alligator chase. Nonetheless, this was undoubtedly a scene from *Vile Bodies*. Judd beamed as though he was getting an Oscar nod.

Rhonda, in the role of Pharis, did a better job of getting into character, moaning and feigning tears as she read. "One more kiss, Caleb, one more kiss. If I die here in the reptile house, I want to go down heavy in your arms."

Carl: "You'll go down, babe, but in the arms of the beast. My arms and every other part of me will be long gone."

"I assume we are going from weakest pieces to strongest," I whispered to Don, who, along with the rest of the couples club, had given me a warm welcome-back reception at the start of class. Pats on the back from the men. Hugs from the women. They'd been worried about me.

Susan, her hair now even more blond, said, "If we are going from worst to best, then I'm sure mine is somewhere toward the back of the packet."

As Don groaned and Rhonda finished reading Judd's non-sense, I scanned the pages to see if any of the scenes Laurel had picked were mine. My guess was no, since I'd all but dropped out of the class. I didn't recognize any of the characters' names that lined the left-hand side of the papers. But, when I got to the last one, the words rang a bell.

Girl: Of course, I would be happy to convert for the right man. (Girl looks at Guy in a way that suggests he is the "right man.")

Guy: I don't think you should convert for any man, including me. If you get married and have kids, I think it would be better if your children weren't Jewish. (Guy polishes off a shot of vodka and pours another.)

Girl: Why?

Guy: In case there's another Holocaust, and there will be another Holocaust. It's inevitable judging from 9/11, which I experienced firsthand, though slightly sedated from the dentist's office in Midtown.

Girl: That's ridiculous.

Guy: Trust me, babe. History has a way of repeating itself.

Girl: What if we don't have kids?

Guy: Then why bother getting married?

I couldn't believe my eyes. I wanted to protest. Not only had the teacher paraphrased my conversation, the paraphrasing made me seem—if possible—like even more of a jerk than I actually had been. To protest, however, would be to acknowledge that I was the Guy. I decided to stay quiet and instead shoot an angry look to the front of the room.

Laurel ignored me until we got to the end of the packet. "Would you be willing to read this with me?" she said, strolling over to my desk and smiling to the extent that her super-tight hairdo would allow.

"Why don't you give me a moment to familiarize myself with the lines so I can—you know—get into the Guy's head."

She crossed her arms and smirked. "I don't think that's necessary, David. It's a class exercise. Just wing it."

So I did what the schoolmarm said and when we finished, Susan said, "That dialogue seemed decent to me." She asked Laurel if it was from one of her movies, noting that Laurel had mentioned taking conversion classes.

Laurel shook her head no. "But you are correct. It is an example of dialogue that works." She turned to me. Her eyes lit up. "Part of the authenticity comes from David, who did a fabulous acting job." She patted me on the shoulder. Then she turned her attention back to the class, asking, "What makes it work?"

Someone said it flowed. Other people thought the characters sounded honest and real.

"Duh," I mumbled. Laurel was still standing next to my desk. I mumbled some more. "Lucky for you I showed up today to read my lines."

"Not really," she whispered. "Marcy told me you'd be here." She winked and walked to the front of the room, where opinions over the passage were bounding back and forth.

"Personally, I think the Guy sounds like an ass," Candy said.

Another front-row girl agreed. "The Guy's lines are subtext for,

'I don't want to marry you but I'm too chicken to do the dirty work so I'm going to force you into breaking up with me'."

A less demoralized man might have gone off script and added, "What about the backstory, baby? What about the rabbi and the fling and your arrival as the unexpected guest?" Instead I spoke more generally and only to Don. "It seems like we're studying dialogue in a vacuum."

"You're the asshole, aren't you?" Don whispered.

I didn't even pretend innocence. I sighed, relieved to not be alone in this charade. "How'd you know?"

Don told me that I was a terrible actor, and that my face was stone white.

In the meantime, Carl at the window was arguing with Candy. "The girl seems desperate."

Laurel scrunched her brows. "I don't know about that."

"It's like she's forcing herself on him," he added. "Maybe he's not ready to think about getting married yet, and she's already talking a change of religions. That would freak me out."

"Yeah, I can see that," I piped in. "Like maybe he thought the relationship was just a fling."

Laurel rolled her eyes at me, shook her head at Carl, and then took control of the conversation. "Whatever your opinion, you can see how the dialogue moves the story along. The exchange reveals something about the characters and creates conflict, as demonstrated by our class discussion. It also leaves the girl with a choice about what to do next."

"She should jump ship," Rhonda offered.

"She should tell him he's an asshole," Candy added.

"Truthfully, I don't know why the Girl would want to be with the Guy anyway," Susan said. "He seems paranoid and depressed."

"And like he may have a drinking problem," Helene offered.

I felt like I was listening to Rachel and Marcy all over again.

At least I had Don. "If I thought another Holocaust was inevitable, I might have a drinking problem too," he offered.

Laurel didn't give me up. She worked the class with confidence.

"In movies, saying the wrong thing is usually better than saying the right thing. The wrong thing leads to conflict, conflict leads to pain and suffering, suffering spurs action." Laurel appeared to speak off the cuff but without skipping a beat, as if she gave this lecture every session. But I knew she didn't. Hadn't she said before, at our first meeting at the 3 Woos, that every session was different? That students and their characters dictated the course of the curriculum more so than the syllabus? I might have been on iffy personal terrain with the teacher, but I was as confident in my mind as she was with her words that no other class had gone quite like this. Because she wasn't lecturing the class, she was lecturing me.

She told us, when we wrote our next scenes, to have words come out of our characters' mouths that we'd never dare to say. "Make them ugly and uncomfortable," she instructed, "then sit back and see what kind of chaos ensues."

This assignment wouldn't be difficult for me to do with my movie. My next scene was *Saturday Night Fever*, and it oozed ugly and uncomfortable. My real life did, too. Though in my real life, chaos had ensued already.

SATURDAY NIGHT FEVER
   INT. OF THE SUNNY ISLES THEATER. 7:00 PM SHOWING JUST UNDERWAY

The scene will open into movie-theater darkness, as the narrator voices over. Large and once grand, like movie palaces used to be, the Sunny Isles Theater was, by 1977, just ten degrees above a rundown show. But expectations that night ran high for the folks who filled the worn red velvet seats. It was a sold out house, with the entire Melman family filling a row, balancing tubs of popcorn, boxes of candy, and Cokes on our laps, as neither the drink holder nor the concept of low-carb had yet been created.

That night, a few of Marcy's Junior Mints dropped onto my seat and mashed into my light-colored painter's pants when I sat down. So in my own movie, while Tony Manero, in his red satin shirt and black leather jacket, saunters down the sidewalk to "Stayin' Alive," the audience will see me yelling at Marcy for causing me to look like I'd had an accident.

My mother, sitting next to me, will whisper, "Shh, the stain will come out in the wash."

My father will lean over my mother. "Forget about the pants," he'll say, pointing to the movie screen.

My Grandma Estelle will lean over both my father and mother. "Don't worry, Davy, I'll get you some new pants at the mall tomorrow when we go to get the new shoes."

"Enough with the new shoes already," Slip, seated on Estelle's other side, will bark.

Finally, my father will tell us all to sit back and enjoy the show. "You are about to see some first-rate dancing," he'll say, as he's been saying for the past several days.

Ironically, he'd chosen the movie with my Grandma Estelle, a first-rate dancer herself, in mind. But, as I'm sure you know, the Electric Slide was not the Charleston and the Brothers Gibb were not the Gershwins. From the second John Travolta strutted onto the screen, I knew that the movie pick had been a mistake. With each pelvic thrust, I could feel the heat of my parents' faces intensify as they glared at me and Marcy.

If you've ever watched a show while someone is watching you in embarrassment and horror, you know that enjoying that show is pretty hard to do. Well, take it from me, enjoyment becomes downright impossible when you find your head suddenly covered in a sweater, which was what happened to me about twenty minutes in, around the time a nude dancer threw off her top. My mother removed and replaced the sweater throughout the film, as she saw fit.

"A prophylactic measure," I heard her say to my father. She also said that next time, she'd pick the movie.

I heard my father apologize but tell her not to worry. "If I have no idea what's going on, I doubt that they do."

I didn't say anything, but I understood enough to be happy that I was hidden beneath a sweater. As I've mentioned, I hated anything to do with even innocent interactions between the sexes, and I hated the movies. It strikes me only now that the only reason I sat through *Saturday Night Fever* was because I didn't have to watch it.

Marcy laughed at my covered head and I heard my mother say, "Not so fast, Little Miss, I'm only one more set of titties away from taking off my own shirt to cover your head too."

So you see now why my memory of the movie is spotty. Maybe then you'll also understand why I didn't notice my Grandma Estelle's knuckles clutching the sides of her seat. ("White and trembling" was the description I'd get later.) I didn't notice her gasping for breath, either. I didn't notice my mother handing her napkins to blot her forehead. I didn't notice my father instructing her to relax and breathe deep.

The audience, on the other hand, will be aware of both my ignorance and Estelle's symptoms, which will start during Disco Inferno. She'll stabilize for a while but relapse during the second dancing scene at 2001 Odyssey, so that by the time Tony leaves the club to bang Annette in the backseat of his car, my grandma can take no more.

From beneath the sweater and the blare of "You Should Be Dancing," I'll hear my father say to Slip, "Sit still. I'm going to get her out of here, get her some air."

"Perhaps she needs more than some air," my mother will say.

"He is a doctor," my Grandma Estelle will remind my mother. I remember being buoyed by the sound of her voice, although weak, as well the predictability of her statement.

"He's a dentist, Estelle," my mother will reply. "And you're not having trouble with your teeth."

"She'll be fine," Slip will mumble without moving his eyes off the screen.

The people behind us will wallop the back of my parents' seats and tell us to hush. I will push away my covering in time to see my grandfather turn around and tell the strangers to mind their own goddamn business, and my father stand and escort Estelle into the lobby. The aisle inclined, so the audience will see my father's hands press into Estelle's rounded shoulders as if to keep her from falling back.

"Good thing for her Adidas," I will say to Marcy.

"Let's go and make sure everything is okay," Marcy will whisper.

"We're going?" Rachel will lean toward me and, assuming that I am the reason for the departure, shoot me a look so dirty—snarled nose and scrunched brows—it penetrates the dark.

"No, *we* are not going," I will announce. I will push myself farther into my seat and pop a Milk Dud in my mouth to make clear my intent to stay.

"Fine, stay. But your grandmother may be about to die," Marcy will say as she shuffles down the aisle.

"Grandma will be okay," my mother will say. "Nobody has to leave." Then she'll mumble to herself, "Although we'd all be better off if we did."

I stayed. I watched as Tony's brother left home, as Tony's girl, Stephanie, moved to the city, as the two of them sat on a bench beneath the Verrazano-Narrows Bridge and talked about its construction. All the while, I imagined my grandmother lying on a bench in the lobby waiting for the paramedics. I listened for the sound of sirens. But any way you slice it, I didn't make a move. I regretted the decision as I made it and still do.

At the end of the movie, as I head out of the darkness of the theater, I will see the three of them lined up next to each other on a metal bench across from the door. My father will sit on one side of Estelle, Marcy on the other, where she will be rifling through my grandma's purse, chewing her Juicy Fruit, and slathering her peach polish on her nails. My mother will walk next to me, holding my hand, patting my head, hoping to undo the movie's damage with her affection. Rachel and Slip, the only Melmans to both see and enjoy the show, will walk ahead of us discussing the movie with the same enthusiasm displayed by Laurel's students when she shows a film in class.

"Now that was a movie," Slip will tell Rachel. He'll hit her on the back and do a few hip thrusts. "I could move like that in my day. Nobody was better than me, except maybe your grandma." He'll nod toward her on the bench.

As he does, the bench will come into tight focus, and the audience and I will catch the image of my father sitting next to my grandma. His arm will be around her and his hand will hold a red and white Coke cup that Grandma Estelle will sip from on occasion, as directed by my father. Intermittently, my father will swap the cup for a damp handkerchief that he puts against Estelle's forehead and, every so often, against his own.

"How Deep is Your Love" will play as we exit with—or, more accurately, as we are carried by—the tide of catatonic Jews eager to put this R-rated Christmas behind them.

"How is she?" Slip will ask my father when he reaches the bench. He'll pull a tub of popcorn from the inside of his windbreaker and set it next to my grandmother. "Hungry?"

"I'm just fine," Estelle will answer, but she won't look fine. Then she'll turn to me.

"That was some movie, Davy. Should we go see it again tomorrow?" She'll laugh. So will I. Who knows where I got the notion that a sense of humor was synonymous with sound health, but her joke gave me relief.

"I think we should take her to the hospital," my father said. "Have her heart checked."

"Now?" I asked. "Is the hospital open on Christmas?"

My mother told me that it was.

"But who knows what kinds of doctors they've got working," Slip said. "I say, if she hasn't keeled over by now . . ." He winked at my grandmother as he unwrapped a cigar.

"They've probably got all the Jews working," Rachel said. "This is a great time to go."

"Forget about it, Allen," my Grandma Estelle told my father. "It was indigestion."

"Indigestion from what?" Finally, the last of the moviegoers—my Grandma B and Aunt BoBo—will reach my Grandma Estelle. They will have watched the movie from the front row of the theater, per usual, so no one could block their view. It will seem that they, unencumbered by kids and unflustered by the foul language since they can't hear it, have taken to *Saturday Night Fever* like bees to honey—John Travolta being the source of attraction.

They'll point to Travolta in the poster above our heads, they'll refer to him as Johnny, and they'll talk about how well he wore his suit. "He didn't look nearly so handsome in *Welcome Back, Kotter*," my Grandma B will profess. She'll smile up at him as if he might ask her out.

"You watch *Welcome Back, Kotter*?" my mother will ask. I was thinking the same thing.

Marcy will interrupt. "Maybe the indigestion is from the meatballs?"

I'm sure others were thinking this as well, but it will be Marcy—never scared to get her hands dirty—who speculates aloud that the source of the sickness was BoBo's kitchen.

"Impossible," Aunt BoBo will assure us. "We've been making those meatballs for how many years now? No one's ever gotten sick."

"Maybe it's from the throwing of the meatballs rather than the consumption of them," my mother will suggest. "The scene at dinner was a bit unsettling."

"Unsettling? You don't know from unsettling," Slip will say. "Didn't none of you see what was going on at the dinner table in the movie?" Slip will demonstrate by slapping his cheeks back and forth a few times. "Throwing a meatball is minor league compared to what went on with those Italians." He'll give a few almost reverential shakes of his head. "You want indigestion, go to Brooklyn."

"It was the movie," Estelle will say. "That movie company ought to be ashamed of themselves. All you had to do to get a part in that film was swear like Slip and shake your hips." She'll shake her head back and forth. "And they have the nerve to call that dancing."

"They're calling it disco," Grandma B will explain as my father directs Estelle to sip water and stop talking. He doesn't want her to work herself up.

"Disco Shmisco." Estelle will stick out her tongue in disdain.

"Dancing's dancing," Slip will say as he again mimics some of John Travolta's moves. Whoever plays Slip will have to be smooth on his feet. He'll step his feet side to side. He'll throw in a spin, clap his hands, and ask Estelle how she's feeling.

She will sigh, tired and exasperated, and say she's as good as new.

"Good," Slip will say, nodding to the door. "Let's get the fuck out of here."

Aunt BoBo will shush him, waving her cigarette in my direction.

"Don't worry," I'll say. "We already know those words from the movie."

Then Rachel: "Go piss on it."

"Watch this, assholes," Marcy, in her yellow satin jacket, will yell as she sends her arm up and down across her body, the classic disco move.

"Fuck you," I'll say.

"Knock it off," my mother will say before reminding my father that next year *she* will choose the movie.

CHAPTER 16:

Words We'd Never Dare to Say

L aurel and I ended up having our conversation after class at the 3 Woos. The idea to talk there was Laurel's. First, she was hungry. Second, she thought I'd be interested to see what Janet had done with the place, and I was.

When Janet had come to my office a few weeks back, we'd made a list of possible changes ranked according to biggest return for least amount of buck. She should start, I'd told her, by replacing the bulbs in the 3 Woos' sign or else change the name to the 3 oos, which I actually didn't think was a terrible idea. It had a cachet. Janet agreed, but her parents did not. The name would remain.

The 3 Woos was lit like a Las Vegas casino and crowded like one, too, when Laurel and I walked in. Standing room only. They'd tripled the seating, going from three to nine stools, and changed the walls from pasty grey to dark red. Little white lights framed the windows. Chinese lanterns resembling red beach balls hung from the ceiling, and customers lined the counters. The clientele were kids from NYU, a market sector willing to stand or do almost anything for free food, which the 3 Woos now offered. I'd passed on the Melman secret for creating brand loyalty in the form of the Woo-You Special. Order two entrees off their new Pan-Asian menu, and get an order of egg rolls for free.

"Let's do that," Laurel said as we waited in line. "I'm starved."

"I'm nauseated," I told her.

She suggested the nausea was residual from the previous night, but I knew better. The nausea was anticipatory, brought on by the speech—if you could call it that—I was now going to have to deliver. I'd tried to spit it out on the walk to the 3 Woos. I figured I needed five seconds of floor time. Laurel could reply with "Regrettably, I'm not interested," in another five, and in a total of ten seconds, I could be on my merry way. Instead, Laurel kept hushing me up every time I opened my mouth, asking me to wait until she had the ability to focus. I didn't see, as I stood in line and got shoved back and forth like a tetherball, how the 3 Woos was the destination for focus. It was not unlike the Rascal House in its unruliness. People standing. Kids screaming. Janet hollering and ringing a bell every time an order was up.

"Just call out 'Chuckerman' when our order is ready," I told Janet when we reached the front of the line. "Don't ring the bell."

"For you, Chuckerman, I do anything."

I smiled, more pleased to hear my name again then with anything else. If things didn't work out with Laurel, I decided, I'd continue to come to the 3 Woos.

Janet told Laurel, "I give him free egg roll for life for everything he's done for us."

I smiled at Laurel hopefully. On the off chance that she was at least on the fence about forgiving me, perhaps the promise of never-ending egg rolls would tip the scales.

But all she said was, "That's a real feather in his cap. He did a nice thing."

"He's much better at the branding business than movie writing," Janet joked. "Don't quit the day job, Chuckerman."

"Actually, his movie isn't terrible," Laurel told her.

I was shocked by the praise.

"That is good to hear," Janet said. "If it ever makes it into theaters, let me know." In the meantime, she told me, her parents wanted to thank me personally for the help I'd given. "Too bad you're dressed so sloppy today."

We stuffed our tray in between two groups of kids, and as Laurel began to divide our egg roll order into our traditional one and a half each, I took a deep breath and readied myself to exhale my sentence.

"Don't," Laurel said without looking up from the sweet sauce container she was having sent down from one end of the counter to ours. I made a note to tell Janet to up the number of condiment stations.

"Don't what?" I stuck my hands in the pockets of my sweat-shirt, a demonstrative showing of my lack of intent to eat.

"Say anything." Now she was pouring sauce and dipping her roll. I waited until she finished and was free to look at me.

"How do you know what I'm about to say?"

Laurel's mouth was full of food. She spoke anyway. "Marcy told me."

I moved my hands from my pockets to across my chest. I shifted my weight from one foot to the other as, in my mind, I connected the dots.

"When she called to tell me you were coming to class, she told me what you planned to say." Laurel must have seen the image of me strangling Marcy in my head because she then tried to couch Marcy's behavior as altruistic. "She just wanted to get a feel for how I was going to react to make sure Rachel wasn't sending you into the lion's den."

"That's so great, looking out for me in that way," I said.

But Laurel didn't seem to notice my sarcasm. "You've got a really nice family."

I grumbled that they felt the same way about her, and added, "If that's all there is to say, I'm good to go." I thanked her for saving me the trouble of embarrassing myself with my speech, and added that it was just as well, the restaurant was too crowded for me.

"Stay," she said. "I'm not finished." She then asked the girls on the stools around us if they could scooch down a few inches, which they did.

I gripped the side of the freed-up counter space and said, "I think I have to get out of here, I'm feeling claustrophobic." I added for authenticity that the lanterns were dangling too close to my head. "They need to hang them higher."

"Then I'll leave with you," Laurel told me.

"That's not necessary," I said. "Finish your food."

"Fine," she said, finally bothering to wipe her face with a napkin. "But before you go, I have something to say." She took my hands in hers in just the same way that my father had suggested I take hers. "I'm so sorry. I regret my behavior, and I love you too," she said.

"You stole my line."

She kissed my forehead. "It was given to me."

The minutes after this were a blur, with the hugging and kissing that usually accompanies the receipt of unexpected good news.

Janet's parents seized the moment to parade out from the kitchen and, in their best and most likely only English, thank me for my services. Janet offered drinks on the house, which, in the wake of Yom Kippur, I declined. She also promised free egg roll for life to Laurel too. She raised a plastic glass, and the college kids followed suit. "A toast to the Chuckermans."

I toasted too. Chuckerman was back in business.

But then Laurel yanked her schoolteacher skirt, which had ridden up on her waist during the celebration, back into place, signaling with one swift gesture an end to the festivities. At least, an end to ours. The college kids kept going, so the rest of our conversation seemed to take place in a frat party. "David, I love you. I do," she hollered over the noise. "And I want to give our relationship a serious try, which is why I've quit the rabbi. I promise you, it's done." She brushed her hands together to reflect her doneness.

"Fantastic," I told her. I told her she wouldn't be sorry. Then I kissed her. The college kids whistled at us and I whispered to her, "I knew I had to be better in bed than he was. I imagine you must be somewhat inhibited when you are always so close to God."

She told me that was a point she'd never considered, and she, in turn, had something for me to consider.

I thought she was going to suggest moving in together. Or getting married. I tightened up. Yes, I'd set out to win her back, but

I hadn't prepared for any sort of permanency. *What a difference a day made*, I thought as she took a step closer, put her hands on my shoulders, and smiled.

She had egg roll in her teeth, a piece of sprout or something green, that on any other night I would have pointed out. But because I was on the verge of engagement, I kept quiet and let her do the talking.

"I think you should get rid of your car."

My stomach went sour. "What?" The older I get, the more I understand my Grandma Estelle's stomach troubles. "I thought we were putting the past behind us. Movin' up and on. Starting fresh. Clean slates. Hatchets buried."

"We are," she said. "Or, I'd like to, but I'm not sure how starting fresh is possible if you are going to bring along the Cadillac. I don't think I can take on that car."

Now I put a hand on her shoulder. "Say no more," I told her, not wholly understanding the situation but hoping that with a quick fix, full understanding would not be necessary. "I should never have made you drive to the bridge. You'll never have to drive it again."

"Thank you, but it's more than that." She pretended to brush crumbs from her blouse while she took another breath. "I've thought about this a lot. Your grandfather's car . . . I think it's holding you back. You might not have gained any insights about yourself by writing your movie, but I have, and David, that Cadillac is an anchor. It keeps you tied to the past, tied to your childhood, to your family. In movie lingo, your life is like one big, unedited scene. Your past, your present, your future are all rolled into one blob of time. Which is why I think that as long as you are hanging on to the Cadillac and everything it represents, you can't start a new act with me." She paused. "Or with anyone else, for that matter."

"I'm not hanging on to anything except the counter," I said as I renewed my grip on it. "Yes, I love my car, but I love you too. As much as I love the car." Hardly the most romantic line. It was a Hail Mary intended to save me from losing the Cadillac—or maybe from losing Laurel, I wasn't sure. The uncertainty only added to my panic.

"Exactly my point. I know this sounds silly, but I need you to love me more than the car."

"I get it," I told her. "That didn't come out quite right. You caught me off guard."

"Listen." She squeezed my hand. "It's great to know you love me and I love you too. But words are easy."

"Not for me." I crossed my arms and studied her. "Besides, I thought you loved my family. There was a time when I thought my family was the reason you were with me. You know, as a backup, in case you converted to Judaism and your family abandoned you. The Cadillac is part of the family."

"I do love your family. But I can't compete with them. You are an able, competent man. You were able to wrangle Bailey Pierce into your business. And yet when it comes to your personal life, you still play the role of the child. You can't make a move without everyone else weighing in. You need to separate."

"I don't ask them to weigh in. They just do."

At this point, Janet came around with pitchers, giving refills of the wine. Laurel held out her glass. So did all the other people in our area. Cups and bodies, including mine, collided in the struggle for a free top-off.

"I need to get out of here," I announced, and I headed to the trash with my uneaten egg roll.

Laurel followed, taking one last bite before she begrudgingly parted from her food. "My intention is not to punish you. I truly believe that getting rid of your car is for your own good, regardless of what happens between you and me."

"You know what I think? I think you're jealous of the Cadillac. I think my grandma was jealous of it, too."

"She wasn't jealous of the car, she was aggravated that she had no control over her life. Her life was Slip's, and Slip didn't always seem to treat her that well. Why should we carry the Cadillac, which to me symbolizes your grandmother's struggle, into our relationship?" she said as she followed me out the door.

"Because I disagree with you. To me, it represents"—I paused to take her bag for her and to think of what the car represented—"it represents my memories, and getting rid of it seems like a drastic measure. I don't think you can compare getting rid of the rabbi to getting rid of the Cadillac. Not unless the rabbi was left to you in your grandfather's will."

"You can compare them in terms of proving our commitment to our relationship. They were both holding us back."

"My car is more akin to your robe. And I would never ask you to get rid of your robe, however hideous it is." I zipped my sweatshirt.

Laurel said the analogy was not the same. "I separated from my family a long time ago. The robe is simply a token. Though if you wanted me to lose it, I would . . . And, I wouldn't ask if you didn't have your movie." She went on to explain that because I'd brought the car to life in my movie, I no longer needed to possess the actual car in order to own it. "I've seen enough characters brought to life in my bathrobe that its essence is with me, with or without the robe itself."

"How can you compare an entire car to a few pages of an amateur script? If they were actually going to make my movie and bring the Cadillac to life, *then* it might be a different story." I surmised that in that case, they could use the actual car in the film.

Laurel pulled a scarf from her messenger bag and mumbled, "I imagine they could." After the scarf was sufficiently wound around her neck, she told me that producing my script was irrelevant. "The writing is the important thing. It's the process of writing that brings people and things to life. That's the beauty of it. The more you write about an object, the more real it becomes. To write is to revive. To write is to immortalize."

I rolled my eyes and headed toward the street to catch a cab.

She followed me to the curb, where she pulled me toward her and set her hands on my shoulders, as if to steady me. Then she pushed my hair from my forehead and gave me a kiss. The college kids gave us a thumbs-up through the window of the 3 Woos. "Relax, Chuckerman," she said. "I do not expect you to go cold turkey or do it alone. I just think we owe it to ourselves to give us a fresh start." She said she would give me a little time to come to terms with the separation. She would help me through the process.

"How do you plan to do that?" To me, this question was rhetorical, unanswerable.

But for Laurel, the answer was concrete. She had a three-pronged approach to getting me comfortable with the idea of getting rid of my car, which she spelled out in baby steps, not unlike the manner in which Rachel had set forth her strategy for my grand apology.

As she spoke, I got the feeling that they—Marcy, Laurel and maybe even Rachel—were in cahoots, carefully scripting this entire series of events. Marcy and Laurel had been talking, hadn't they? In all likelihood, their conversation had not stopped with Marcy saying to Laurel, "Heads up, he'll be in your class tonight with a pre-planned apology." Women don't work that way. That was just the start, I decided as I waited for a cab and Laurel prepared to delineate the first prong. From there, I figured, Marcy probably asked Laurel what it would take for her to take me back. Perhaps a dollar amount was even offered. Melmans know how to stick out their necks for each other in times of need. We may not stick them in the right direction—as evidenced by Marcy's apparent agreement with Laurel on each of the three prongs—but our hearts are usually in the right place.

In exchange for me hearing her out, Laurel agreed to come home with me. I took her willingness as a sign that her three steps would be simple, possibly even involving sex. But then I heard about the yoga prong. Laurel wasn't giving in, she was buttering me up.

"I'm not much of a stretcher and bender," I said, hunching my torso toward the floor of the cab. My outstretched arms barely reached past the seat. "See?"

"Yoga isn't about flexibility. It's a nice side benefit, yes. But yoga is as much a mental thing as it is physical. It teaches you to stay calm and in the moment. It trains you to not react to all of the everyday thoughts and anxieties that float through your head."

"That sounds like being brain dead, which does not appeal to me," I told her as our cab darted down 14th.

"No, it means going with the flow. Trusting yourself. Learning to step outside your comfort zone. I'd still be a practicing Mormon if it weren't for yoga."

"I'm confused. I thought you were giving credit for your liberation to Judaism."

"Well, yes," she said as she rummaged through her bag for a piece of gum, which she eventually found and began to chew before she continued talking. "But I was only open to discovering Judaism because of yoga. Don't you see? We hang on to habits out of fear. When we realize that we'll be okay without them, we can let go. Yoga teaches us to let go."

"I'm not letting go of the Caddy because my grandfather asked me not to. I can do all the downward dogs in the world, and that won't change."

"He left it to you years ago. When you had no job, no money, and no idea what you were going to do. He gave you a set of wheels to help you along in life. And now, you're along. Well along. I actually think Slip would be horrified if he knew you went to meet Bailey Pierce for dinner in his old piece of junk."

"I took a limo, I didn't drive," I said. I also might have mentioned that she would have known I hadn't driven had she come with me, but I didn't want to open the door for more prongs to be added to her plan. "Besides, I think he would have been proud to see where his car ended up."

"I think he would have been proud to see where *you* ended up," she replied. "See? You can't separate yourself from the car."

She tried again to explain how yoga would do this. Something about anchoring the mind on bodily sensations to open the consciousness door. The first two prongs, finishing my movie and shopping for new a car, seemed like a walk in the park compared to the yoga.

"Sit with it for a week," she told me as I led her into my apartment.

I told her I would as I began to remove the scarf, the skirt, and every other piece of her outfit. Finally, she stopped talking about her prongs.

"I knew I was better in bed than the rabbi," I told her again.

"Let's see how you do on the yoga mat," she replied.

"Do we have sex in the yoga class?"

"It's actually a series of classes," she said. She'd already signed me up. Ten sessions. She'd negotiated a deal with Tatia, the owner of the studio. She paused to use her tongue to play with my ear, then added, "And I bought you your own mat."

She was naked on my bed. Her long, newly straightened hair covered my body. At this point, I would have agreed to one hundred sessions of yoga for this one round in the sack. Call me weak. Or stupid. Or male. I was back at the Rodeo. I couldn't say no. Still, the entire time we rocked and rolled, I couldn't shake the thought that yoga was the second class I'd been enrolled in on a complimentary basis in the name of self-reform. Was this a sign of personal failure? Or should I feel honored to have two women—one of whose breasts now stared me in the face—who cared about me enough to pull strings for my betterment?

I should add that I entertained this mental debate without a hitch in my performance in bed, which was a sign of mental strength if there ever was one. The ability to have first-class sex while simultaneously self-analyzing your strength of character seemed to me, if nothing else, a sure sign that I, of all people, did not need to waste my time with yoga. Not only could I be in the moment, I could be in two moments at once.

I didn't mention this to Laurel. Not then—I wasn't going to ruin a banner night. Instead, I'd do what she asked. I'd sit with it. I'd attend Laurel's next class. I'd attend a yoga class. I'd do whatever else Laurel wanted me to do. I'd go shopping for a car. I had no problem looking at cars. I'd write my movie, which I'd planned on doing anyway. And as luck would have it, I'd be writing about my Cadillac—which I'd be keeping. I mean, what's the point of giving something away and then writing about it to magically bring it back when you can just hang on to the thing in the first place?

〰——

THE MORNING AFTER *SATURDAY NIGHT FEVER*
CRACK OF DAWN. INT. SITTING ROOM OF APARTMENT 1812

"When I woke up the next morning, Grandma Estelle was gone," the narrator will say.

How's that kind of line to move your audience to the edge of their seats? Nonetheless, it's accurate. My eyes opened and I realized that no one had summoned us out of bed. When I ambled into the living room/dining room area, I saw my father and Slip both slumped in their chairs. My father's arms were crossed. His head hung. Slip spun an ashtray with his ring finger. They both looked up when I entered, but neither spoke. Instead, they stared for a moment and returned their heads to their original positions. The atmosphere felt like when brother Frankie quit the priesthood.

This was one scene in *Saturday Night Fever* that I'd been permitted to view, as it was relatively clean and familiar. The look of disappointment in a parent's eye was certainly nothing we'd never seen before.

Anyhow, back to my movie. When I get no verbal greeting in the dining room that morning, I'll creep back to our sleeping area.

"Something's really wrong," I will announce to my sisters, confused more than scared. You'd think I would have seen death written all over this scenario, but I pictured such a disaster to involve screaming, sirens, and wailing cries. I'd seen enough grandparents wheeled out of the Rascal House by paramedics to have a clear image of death in my mind, and this didn't fit the bill.

Marcy, however, was never as astute an observer as I. "Did Grandma have a heart attack?" she'll ask, throwing off her covers and scooting herself over to my pullout.

Rachel will lift her head from her pillow. "No, stupid. There are no paramedics." She'll look at me. "Where's Mom?"

I will shrug. "She's not in the bathroom." The bathroom was where Paula could be found every morning in Miami, taking a vacation from the vacation, as she liked to put it. She'd peel the towel from her hair. She'd smoke a cig. She'd put on mascara.

"There she is," Marcy will scream. Leaning over the back of my bed, she'll point out the window to the terrace.

Rachel and I will race to my bed and line ourselves up next to Marcy. We'll all stare out the window. The terrace, where the winds were a consistent gale force, was the last place my mother went, especially in the morning, with her towel just removed and her hair perfectly set in place. But on that day, the towel still sat on her head, which hung over the balcony. A cigarette dangled from her lips.

We'll knock on the window. My mother's enormous head will lift. She'll smile, stick her cigarette in the ashtray, and head toward the door. We'll cross into the living room in time to see the wind blow her inside and slam the door behind her.

"Well?" my father will ask. His arms will still be crossed. He will have hardly moved.

My mother will shake her head no.

"What's going on?" Rachel will ask. "Why were you looking over the balcony? Where's Grandma? Did someone fall?" Clearly, the Verrazano-Narrows Bridge scene had made an impact on the few who'd seen it.

Again, my mother's head will shake side to side. Her hands will go to her hips as she says, "There've been no accidents."

Slip will push his chair away from the table and mumble, "Not yet, anyway."

And now the news will break. My mother will blurt it out while my father is immersed in self-blame: "Your grandmother stole the car."

The actress who plays my mother will have to deliver this line seriously, in deference to the direness of the situation. My grandmother had, for all practical purposes, run away using a vehicle that she was neither licensed nor able to drive. However, the actor's face will have to reflect irony so the audience understands that my mother is fighting laughter. Her tongue will press hard into the space between her front teeth as she offers further detail. "She took your grandfather's Cadillac. We're not sure where she went. Her note didn't say."

At this point, the scene could go in two directions. We could continue on in Apartment 1812 with the chaos that broke out among us kids, pebbling questions at my parents like the press corps, the bickering that went on between my parents as to the course of action that should be pursued in the search and rescue of Estelle, and the pacing and head-shaking of Slip, who'd never been so silent, so shaken.

Or, we could leave the apartment and take the audience to the streets. We'll go to Collins Avenue, the southbound lanes, and slowly zoom in on the pale yellow Cadillac, the one going far beneath the speed limit with its tires clinging to the dividing lines like a security blanket, with its windows open and music (the '77 chart-topper "Baby Come Back") playing—but not loudly, because behind the wheel sat Estelle, and she needed to concentrate in order to stay on the road. Fortunately, at seven in the morning, the road was quiet and the skies were sunny. Estelle didn't have to deal with the distractions of other drivers or of Mother Nature. It was just her, the Caddy, and the open road.

Of course, we didn't know where Estelle was, which is why I think that cutting back and forth between the Cadillac and Apartment 1812 is the way to go. The audience—unlike the Melmans—will be able to see that Estelle is, at least for the moment, alive and well. In fact, she is better than well. She is like a geriatric Thelma or Louise, enjoying the fresh air and the freedom and looking forward to eating chopped herring at the Bagel Bar. Her first meal alone and in peace and quiet, she'll tell her waitress, that she can remember.

Also, cutting back and forth between scenes will allow the audience to experience both of them in real time. They will take two rides at once before the camera settles back into Apartment 1812 and onto the light blue piece of paper resting on the kitchen table.

My grandma wrote in script—sloppy but legible, and certainly identifiable. Without mistake, the note that will now come front and center is hers.

"Dear Family," it will read. "Going out for a time. Don't wait for me for breakfast and don't worry, I'm fine." Her initials, E.F.M., will be at the bottom, followed by, "P.S. Tell Davy that today's the day for shoes."

The kids will crowd around it, pushing each other for prime position, but nobody will dare to touch, as if to do so would taint the scene of the crime.

"Nowhere in that note did she mention taking the car," my father will holler in self-defense from his dining room chair.

As the family studies the piece of paper, the narrator will explain that the note was first discovered by my father when he came into the kitchen for an early-morning glass of water. My grandma's message didn't set off immediate alarm because it didn't mention going for a drive. So he'd finished his glass of water, used the washroom, and gotten dressed without a second thought.

"I assumed Estelle had gone to take a walk around the deck," my father will continue. "I was happy that she was feeling good."

"It's not like Estelle has ever left a note before when she's gone walking in the morning," my mother will say. "So why would you assume? Especially after her episode last night."

Now my father will yell. "Damn it, Paula, you are only making me feel worse. Until you have something useful to say, why don't you keep your mouth shut?" He'll speak with his back to my mother, but my sisters and I, lined up beneath the doorway in our Miami Beach pajamas, will see his angry face. My folks bickered all of the time, but they rarely fought—not because they were both pacifists but because my father was remarkably skilled at In One Ear, Out the Other, which is an ability like raising a single eyebrow: you either have it or you don't.

Anyway, on this morning of high anxiety, my father clearly wasn't himself. However, my mother still was hers. This made for some tense moments, which I, being the worrier I was, figured to mean the demise of my parents' marriage. Laurel says that had I been more accustomed to intramarital fighting, I might have been able to let it go in one ear and out the other. But I'm not so sure. As I said, it's something you either have or you don't.

Instead, I started to cry. The combination of a possible broken home and a lost grandma was too much to bear.

When this happens, my mother will lead me into the bathroom where, from atop the closed toilet seat, I will watch her apply makeup and listen to her explain that all people fight, even though they love each other, and all people make mistakes.

"When the going gets tough, the Melmans do not leave." She'll look at me through the mirror as I look at her reflection. Her cheeks will move in slow-motion circles as she rubs in her facial creams. "Well, maybe we leave temporarily," she'll add. "A trip to the bathroom, a ride in the car—just to clear our heads—but then we move on. We let water go under the bridge. Do you understand?" she'll ask me as she trades her mascara wand for a cigarette from an ashtray on my lap.

I'll nod into the mirror, although who knows whether or not I understood. One may argue that, given my aversion thus far to marriage, I understood all too well.

My mother will hand me Kleenex from the counter and tell me to blow my nose. "That said," she'll go on, shaking a finger at me, "and this is not to be repeated, your father's mistakes were bigger than mine. He should have figured out that Estelle took the car, and he never should have started with her driving in the first place."

For the sake of their marriage, I will offer an admission. The camera will show me gripping the sides of the toilet seat as I announce, "The driving lessons were my idea, not Dad's."

My mother will lift my chin with her mascara. "Look at me," she'll say. "I appreciate your desire to protect your father. It's a noble thing to do." She'll smile and tap me on the head with the mascara. For a moment I'll feel proud. After her next cigarette puff, however, she'll add, "But you can't save your father. His decision to teach Estelle to drive was plain old stupid. Let's just thank God that Slip tried to pull his car around early this morning."

Indeed, Slip—unable to find his keys—was the one who first realized my grandma had taken his car. I didn't see Slip make this discovery, but the moviegoers will. At the start of the scene, before they see me wake up, they'll see Slip, fully clothed and ready for another day of rabble-rousing, as he walks into the kitchen, rifles through drawers in search of his missing car key, stumbles upon the note on the kitchen table, puts two and two together, and storms down the hall to get my father out of the bathroom.

The same bathroom that my mother and I will now be leaving. She'll pull me up from the toilet and open the door, whispering as she does, "Let's just hope your grandmother isn't to Disney World by now."

Wherever Estelle was, by the time my mother and I emerged from the bathroom, a plan to retrieve her had been devised.

When we reappear, my father will announce, "Slip is going to hit the road in the rental car to cover possible destinations—the mall, the beach, the Marco Polo."

(The Rascal House had been ruled out already, as a phone call and an announcement over its PA system had concluded that Estelle Melman was not on the premises. No one even considered the Bagel Bar, probably because it was just our backup place, and because it was far—way farther than we figured Estelle would dare to venture. Also, no one knew she liked the Bagel Bar that much.)

My father will further explain that he and my mother will head to the lobby to see if anyone saw Estelle before she left and to ask Eileen for help. As building manager, Eileen had under her command a security guard whom she might be willing to deploy around the neighborhood. She was also the direct liaison to the police and paramedics. "Maybe," my father will say, "she'll be willing to send out a gratuitous word to keep an eye out for a brand-new yellow Caddy."

Yes indeed, the narrator will declare, divide and conquer was the name of the game on the morning Grandma Estelle went missing. The kids were assigned the task of staying in the apartment in case she returned. This job seemed easy enough. It was Slip's job that, in my mother's opinion, could prove difficult to do alone.

"Wouldn't it make more sense if I went with Slip to look while he drives?" She spoke extra nicely, these words being her first since coming out of the bathroom. I knew from her ultra saccharine tone (a tone that every woman, Laurel included, has in her arsenal) that she was going out of her way to demonstrate the water-under-the-bridge concept she'd explained to me in the bathroom.

"Wouldn't it be funny if Papa crashed into Grandma while he was looking for her?" Marcy offered.

I laughed and added, "Yeah, what if Papa smashed up his own Cadillac?"

My father, obviously feeling this scenario was more likely than funny, assigned Rachel to go with Slip. Marcy and I would stay behind. My mother would go with my father because Eileen, like everyone else, liked my mother. We were given two minutes to put on clothes, and then the parties dispersed. The hands on the oven clock read 7:26.

In the movie, we'll fade from the oven clock to the clock on the wall of the Bagel Bar. The audience will see the teacup clock come into focus with the spoon and fork hands, and it will become clear to them that while we've been strategizing, Estelle has arrived safely at her destination. As the camera expands, they will also see that she's ordered herself an onion bagel, chopped herring, a glass of orange juice, a cup of coffee, and the jelly donut my father never let her have.

The audience will see Estelle engage her waitress (Flora from the Philippines, she'll learn) in friendly small talk. They'll hear Estelle explain, "You know, I've been eyeing the jelly donuts for five years at least, and now I'm going to see if they were worth the wait."

"I'm sure you won't be disappointed," Flora will say. "I've gained ten pounds in my year here."

"Well, here goes," Estelle will announce. They'll see her fingers with the pale peach nail polish pick up the knife, turn the plate this way and that, analyzing the best place to sink it into the donut, and finally make a perfect cut. They'll see her offer half to Flora, who will shake her head no, smile, and walk away. They'll see Estelle pull the plate closer, open the Miami Herald to the crossword puzzle, take a pen from her purse, move her coffee closer, spread the jelly that squirted out from the initial cut back atop the donut, and bite. A small bite, so the red jelly doesn't mess up her white blouse. Then she'll sip, she'll chew, and she'll fill in the crossword, feeling the warmth of the morning sun through the window, hearing the hustle and bustle of the morning breakfast rush, savoring every minute and every morsel.

"It was a sugary little slice of heaven," she'll tell Flora when she stops by to check on her.

She'll sit there for thirty minutes (although it will seem to her more like thirty seconds), until the clock reads 7:55, before digging into her purse to pay the bill. She'll count out her dollars and cents several times, making sure to leave Flora a full twenty percent instead of the usual fifteen, as Flora has wrapped her bagel and herring to go so nicely.

And off Estelle Melman will go—purse and doggie bag in one hand, car keys in the other, holding her head, the script will set forth, like a woman who, despite her age, feels for the first time like an independent woman of the world.

As the glass door to the Bagel Bar slams behind her, the camera will fade from Estelle and open on the doors of the rental car slamming shut in the parking garage as Slip and Rachel emerge, having had no luck finding Estelle.

Slip will swear as he walks his straight-backed walk, with Rachel running to keep up with him, to the elevator.

"I'm sure by the time we get back upstairs, Grandma will be there," she'll holler in his wake.

Unfortunately, when they swing open the door to Apartment 1812, they'll find only Marcy and me amid all the white plastic Rascal House doggie bags (forty-six to be exact) that Estelle has stashed in the freezer. The bags will be lined up from one end of the apartment to the other, as if we're looking to head off a great flood.

"What the hell's going on in here?" Slip will bark.

This type of mess was not the sort that would normally have gotten Slip's goat, so I knew right away that they'd returned empty-handed.

"We were hungry," Marcy will answer.

I will laugh, because this was the truth, as silly as it sounded. We'd been searching for breakfast, opened the freezer for a roll, a bag fell out, and an idea to defrost the bread and have a bake sale at the pool was born. To this day, I stand behind the business concept; I'm certain that the novelty of it, combined with a captive pool deck market, would have offset need. (The same goods stocked most everyone's freezers.) We'd have turned a profit. We might even have covered the cost of the Adidas I was still hopeful I'd be getting that day.

"Your mother and father still ain't back?" Slip will ask, throwing the rental car keys across the kitchen counter.

"It sure doesn't look like it," Rachel will comment, staring at the mess.

Slip will order Marcy to open a bag of rolls. "One bag," he'll emphasize. "And toast enough stuff for the four of us." He'll start poking his head around the apartment. "So, no word from your grandma?"

Having been certain that Slip would return with Estelle in tow and having never seen him off-kilter, Marcy and I will shake our heads no without daring to look at him. Without a word, I will cram the bags back into the freezer, realizing as I reload that the bread sale, the counting of inventory specifically, was a fantastic distraction from the issue at hand. As bad as I am at letting things go in one ear and out the other, I am (and apparently always was) quite good at taking my eye off the ball.

For example, since Laurel set out her three-pronged plan, all I'd done was parse out each of her less-than-ideal traits and tendencies like bags of frozen bread: her messy apartment, her habit of chewing with her mouth open, her inability to drive, her desire for a Vera Wang dress. Rachel told me I was just distracting myself from the real issue of whether I loved her enough to trade in the Cadillac for her. "Don't worry," I told her. "I'm aware. I'm in full recognition of my nitpicking, and I'm doing it anyway."

"Don't worry," is what my grandfather will tell Marcy as she presses her face against the window of the toaster oven, waiting both for the bread to cool and for Estelle to come home. She'll shove a fifth bagel in the toaster for Estelle. "In case she walks in while we're eating," she'll explain, "it would be nice if we had one for her."

Even Rachel, who normally would have called Marcy's idea stupid, will nod in support of the extra bagel. We were all on guard, aware that we were alone with the man known as a loose cannon.

Slip will shake his head in frustration. "Move away from there," he'll tell Marcy as he pushes his way in front of the toaster oven. He'll order Rachel to get plates and silverware. He'll direct me to get peanut butter and jelly. "Have a seat. I'm going to tell you people something." He'll drop two handfuls of hot bread into the middle of the kitchen table, wait a few seconds for the bread and the kids to settle, and then say, "Are you ready?"

We'll nod our heads and stare. To the best of my ten-year-old recollection, we had never before heard a speech from Slip.

He'll begin with, "You may not realize this, but you guys are babies. You ain't seen nothing." If the movie director needs a visual, he can go with mounds of peanut butter piling on top of Slip's bagel as he spoke. Slip never bothered to slice. Instead, he tore his bagel into pieces. Condiments went on top, on a piece-by-piece basis.

"Me," he'll continue, "I was born before the Cadillac was even invented. And sure, I can't do fancy dives anymore like you people can, and sometimes it seems like I don't know my ass from my elbow, but lots of wild things have happened to me in all my years of living. Things way nuttier than an old lady taking the car without permission." He'll stop to hold up the jar of peanut butter, a last-call signal. When none of us budge, he'll screw the top back in place, shove it into the middle of the table, and motion with his finger for me to pass him the jelly, which he will scoop onto his next piece of bread.

He will go on to laundry-list the highlights of his life, which were actually a series of low notes in the Melman family history that, whether from Estelle or my father, we'd all heard about before. Big-ticket items like the Depression, World War II, colon cancer, and his favorite, a brief stint behind bars for bookmaking. "Some pretty nasty stuff," he'll say, "and yet here I am, enjoying a fine breakfast with my three grandchildren, not much the worse for the wear." He'll smile and lick his knife. "Want to know the secret to survival?"

We will all nod yes.

"Two words," he'll tell us. "Two itty-bitty words that, if you're smart, and I know you are, you'll stick someplace where you won't forget 'em."

We'll keep nodding.

"Two words," he'll announce, holding up two fingers. "Stay cool." He'll repeat the phrase about five times, then tell us that my mother and father don't know this secret, they're panickers. He'll make a spitting noise, as if to pooh-pooh panicking. "No sense in worrying. You got no control over how things are gonna play out in life so you gotta learn to fuck it all. Kick back and wait for the situation to come to you. *After* you're dealt the cards, that's when you react. Chasing all over Miami Beach looking for your grandma like a penny in the sand—that ain't reacting to the cards. It was a stupid goddamn idea." He'll pick up the lone bagel in the middle of the table. "Don't toast the bagel 'til Estelle comes home hungry. That's the moral of the story, the lesson for the day. You got it?"

We'll nod, whether we got it or not.

"Well what should we do with Grandma's bagel?" Marcy will ask.

"I don't give a shit," Slip will answer. He'll toss the extra bagel onto the counter behind us. "Class dismissed."

CHAPTER 17:

Moments of Truth

~~

Marcy thought Laurel's suggestion to get rid of the Cadillac was a reasonable one. From the speed of her response after I relayed my dilemma, I got a hunch that losing the car was her idea altogether.

"Trade the car for a family and then you can drive my minivan," she said. "Somebody ought to."

Whether the idea was hers or Laurel's, for certain a conspiracy was afoot.

The scheming did not, however, go all the way to the top. Rachel did not seem to be involved. "Love me, love my car," she said when I explained Laurel's ultimatum. "The car is who you are, David. She shouldn't try to change who you are."

But Laurel was attempting to do just that, as evidenced by the manhandling I underwent in the yoga class, Candlelight Meditation and Flow, which we attended the week after Laurel presented the three-pronged plan. From the fuss that was made by Laurel's friends, Marcy and Claire included, I concluded that everyone in the studio knew what was at stake with these classes. Tatia, the instructor, had saved two spots on the floor in front of her: one for

Laurel, another for me and my new mat, which Tatia took from me and unrolled. Though everyone else, I noticed, was doing their own unrolling. After that, she helped me into the cross-legged position that I was to assume for the fifteen-minute pre-yoga meditation.

"The lights will dim, music—a great chill-out mix—will play," Tatia explained. She was tall, lithe, and creamy. Brown skin. English accent. A one-time Broadway dancer or runway model, I speculated as she instructed me to close my eyes and shut down my mind. I did the first, but not the second. I also refused to take off my socks, as she suggested.

"You may slip," she whispered.

"He hates bare feet," Laurel volunteered.

I nailed the meditation, but from there we moved into the infamous downward dog position, which Tatia claimed was the ultimate relaxation pose. Since my association with it was the rabbi's guest lecture at the Hampton's retreat, even the name made me uptight.

Tatia came to my mat and guided me into the proper position. "Gaze at your feet," she said. I didn't know how looking at my feet was supposed to help me "let go," as Tatia was now whispering in my ear. She yanked my torso backwards and skyward. When I got the nerve to open my eyes, I saw behind me a roomful of women's rears high in the sky, along with one lone male's.

It was him, I decided, my torso still manually suspended by Tatia. This guy had to be him. The reams of blond hair falling over his head from beneath a yarmulke. The special non-stick socks covering his feet. Here was the rabbi, in the flesh, connecting to God through downward dog. He was tucked into the back corner by the door. He'd obviously slipped in late. Maybe during the silent meditation. Maybe, I thought, that was why they'd done the silent meditation: to allow the rabbi to sneak into class without me noticing. Maybe Tatia was also involved in the plan to separate me from my security blanket—if a security blanket was what the Caddy was to me, than that's what it was. *For once, I'll call a spade a spade*, I decided as Tatia pushed her hands in different directions on my back to "spread the vertebrae," she said. It felt so good, I might have moaned had I not been so preoccupied. Tatia couldn't tell the rabbi that he couldn't come to this class, I figured. And Laurel and Marcy knew that if I saw him already in the class when I arrived, I'd never agree to stay.

But Laurel and Marcy were wrong. They underestimated me. David Melman, grandson of Slip Melman, was not going to be shown up, even by a man of God. I began to repeat the mantra—Slip's, not Tatia's—to stay cool as I contorted my way through class. I forced myself to focus and to breathe, although the breathing was a distraction in and of itself. They tell you to tune out, but then they go ahead and stack the odds against you by having everyone breathe like they're on ventilators. The studio sounded like Apartment 1812 at night. Even without the rabbi, I couldn't concentrate. But I was determined to give it my all, to do yoga like yoga's never been done. I played varsity basketball in high school, I was no slouch on the athletic field, I could do this. I could wrench myself into the position Tatia was now in. The Warrior, she was calling it.

She appeared to be lunging forward and leaning backward at the same time, with her arms outstretched and her head rotated behind her. She actually resembled a warrior. Me, apparently, not so much.

"You look like you have epilepsy," Marcy murmured when my head turned around.

I pretended to ignore her while also pretending to gaze at a spot at the back of the room and not the rabbi.

Everyone else might have been flowing through the poses, but I was duking them out, one after another. Certain names held promise, like Tree and Chair. Words out of a first grade primer. How hard could they be? But names in yoga, I learned, are red herrings. The simpler the name, the more twisted the action. Bridge pose is downright dangerous.

By the end of the hour, I'd slipped a few discs, and my new mat was littered with sweat. By no means had this routine relaxed me. However, no one could say I hadn't given yoga the old college try.

Ironically, I had the rabbi to thank. Had I not spotted him, I would not have pushed like I had. My adrenaline was on overdrive.

"Duking It Out Through Downward Dog" would be the lecture I'd give at a yoga retreat, I decided as I dragged my mat to the wall along with the rest of the group, all of whom began throwing themselves up against it and into handstands. As Laurel flung herself upside down, Tatia came over and asked if I wanted her to help me into the pose.

"I'd love nothing more," I said from my splayed out, face-down position. I winked at Laurel as I crawled toward the wall, and she couldn't contain her surprise. She knew my feelings about being upside-down.

Generally speaking, I see no reason for my blood to flow any other way than in the direction God intended it to flow. I'm sure, had I stuck out medical school, I might now be in a professional position to discover a correlation between handstands and aneurisms. Instead, here I was, figuring out how to hold steady on my hands while the lovely Tatia tossed my ankles toward the cement wall.

"I thought you hated being upside-down," Laurel said. I couldn't see her, I was frightened to move my head, my entire being seemed to be so precariously balanced.

"I wasn't going to let the rabbi beat me at yoga," I answered, moving my mouth as little as possible.

"Who?" she said.

I motioned with my chin, the only part of my body that I could afford to move, toward the inverted rabbi, propped against the opposite wall. Upside-down, I had to be better looking than he was.

"For one thing," Laurel began, her cleavage bulging out of her top, "yoga is not a contest. You don't beat anyone." She paused to do a few deep, cleansing breaths. "For second, that's not the rabbi."

I landed with a thud that caused the music to skip and everyone to pivot their suspended heads in my direction. Tatia looked my way, said I'd done well for my first time, and asked if I'd like her to help me resume the pose. I told her no thank you. She suggested I take Child's Pose until the rest of the class was done.

"Child's Pose sounds appropriate," Marcy mumbled.

I told her to be quiet or I'd tip her over. Then, to Laurel: "That's not him?"

She shook her head, which was now the deep purple of a plum. "But he's wearing a yarmulke."

"He's a Jew, David. Obviously. But he's not the rabbi." Finally, she lowered herself to her knees. She formed her hands into fists, which I thought she might use to smack me; instead, she used them to demonstrate. "Where were you the day they taught Venn diagrams? Here is the circle of Jews who wear yarmulkes and here is Rabbi Eric. The two circles do not directly overlap."

Tatia was now unable to compete with the confusion in our area. Marcy, too, had come out of her handstand to ask what the fuss was about. Tatia directed everyone to come gently out of their inversions. We were going to do a few final poses to prepare for something called Shavasana, which sounded dangerous but turned out to be right up my alley. We all lay down on our mats. The teacher turned off the lights and told us to close our eyes.

"Like kindergarten," I whispered to Laurel, whose head was now right next to mine. She had put a towel over her eyes. She later explained it was to shut out the light, but I'm sure she was also trying to shut out me.

There I was. I had no towel. I had no desire to rest, either. If anything, I was all worked up, my mind racing as if it were late to be somewhere. A myriad of thoughts rushed around and—yes—even emotions. For starters, I realized, I was disappointed that the guy was not the rabbi. I'd gone all-out in my attempt to prove that I could keep up with him. I wouldn't have confronted him after class, I wouldn't have slugged him. My battle would have been fought on the mat. Only that battle, I now saw, was in my head. I was proving something to myself. What it was, I wasn't sure. I'd need another yoga class for that. And what this episode had to do with getting rid of the Cadillac? I couldn't tell you that, either.

This week's film class had been called Moving the Audience. During it, Laurel had explained to us that we should be reaching the point in our scripts at which the conflict and our audience's emotional investment are at a peak. "It's the point at which your protagonist confronts his enemy or faces his biggest fear. It's the moment of truth. The most exciting part of your story. The *pièce de resistance.* The climax," she hollered as if she were actually having one. "Call it what you will. Just move me, people," she commanded. "Move me to the edge of my seat."

A fair amount of chuckling and predictable joking went on due to the sexual innuendo. Don, for example, asked me if she was this feisty in the sack.

Judd snarled at Don as if his mind were not right next to ours in the gutter. My mind was gutter-bound from the minute I set eyes on her I Heart LA T-shirt, the same shirt she'd been wearing the first time I moved her to the edge of her seat.

To separate his intellectual self from us commoners, Judd raised his hand and ruined the mood. "Would you mind discussing the climax scene in terms of Aristotle and the classic three-act structure?" he asked. He was as obsessed with Aristotle as he was with Laurel. The evening I went with Laurel to the 3 Woos for the first time, he'd stayed after class to discuss Aristotle with her.

Laurel had told Judd then something similar to what she now told the whole class. "I don't believe in the three-act structure." She told us that every story has two basic parts: the act or event that causes the problem—the catalyst—and the act or event that resolves it. "In the middle," she told us, "there are forces that influence the outcome of the story. Antagonists. Obstacles. Crises. Let your characters follow their course instead of force-fitting scenes into a three-act structure." I'd had no idea what Laurel was talking about the first time around. I had a better idea now.

As I lay sprawled on my soggy mat, I realized that taking the yoga class was akin to force-fitting scenes, the same as searching for Estelle in Miami. Yes, I was exhausted from the yoga, I was even proud that I'd participated without incurring significant embarrassment, but I felt no more inclined to give up my car now than I had before. The correlation between the yoga class and the Cadillac seemed even more tenuous than the correlation between the film writing class and the Cadillac. Although I wouldn't admit this to Laurel. She'd obviously put energy into the yoga idea. Plus, she'd bought me the mat. For her benefit, I'd pretend I was on the fence, I decided in the silence of nap time, while I waited and hoped for something to happen that would make my next move clear. In other words, I'd try to stay cool and, as Slip advised, wait 'til the cards came to me.

———

THE CHASE SCENE
OUTSIDE. MORNING. NORTH MIAMI BEACH. HALLANDALE BEACH BOULEVARD TOWARDS 163RD STREET

I believe I left off with Slip's monologue—which, according to Laurel, I should try to break up, since monologues are hard to pull off on screen. So I think Slip will be seen on screen at times. But for the most part, the audience will simply hear him lecturing us while they see, for example, Grandma Estelle coming home, heading west down Miami Gardens Drive and then south down 163rd Street.

The audience will see the Caddy come to a crawl atop the 163rd Street bridge (every great movie needs a great bridge scene, I told Laurel), where Estelle will pray as she drives that the bridge doesn't lift, because she's not sure of the protocol.

She'd seen the bridge lift thousands of times from the pool deck. She'd traveled over it hundreds of times as a passenger. But she'd never paid attention to what type of warning signal drivers got when a lift was imminent. A horn? A red light? As the audience hears Slip talking to us about staying cool, they'll see Estelle turn off her music and roll down her window in case a horn gives the signal. The thought of sinking to death and dragging the Cadillac down with her gets her heart racing for the first time all day.

Luckily, the bridge stays down. The audience will see Estelle smile in relief as she rides over it, going even slower to glimpse Imperial Towers 100 from the other side, from the driver's seat, before she gently presses her Adidas to the accelerator.

Perhaps some tinkering will need to be done to the timing of Slip's speech, because ideally when he calls my parents panickers, we'll cut from Estelle glimpsing the exterior of Imperial Towers 100 to the building's lobby and the scene between my folks and Eileen.

I didn't witness this. But I feel confident that, drawing from the account my mother later gave us, I can take my audience there, to the enormous black desk that stood at the entryway to Imperial Towers 100. The desk was divided into two sections. Eileen used the first section as her outpost, which she rarely left because she could view all public areas 24/7 on the black-and-white television monitors below her desk. Thanks to them, she knew my parents were on their way down to the lobby long before the elevator doors opened.

Here's what I think the audience ought to see: my parents talking over the side of the high black desk with Eileen on the other side—except that, due to the great height of the desk (or perhaps the great shortness of Eileen), Eileen will not be visible to them, or to the audience. So they will see my parents seemingly talking to no one. But they'll know she's there because they'll hear her voice, loud and clear, telling my parents, "Yeah, I saw Estelle leave. She waved and headed to the garage. A few minutes later, Slip's car pulled out of the driveway and headed out."

"Did she say where she was going?" my mother will ask.

"Nope."

"You do realize that Estelle doesn't know how to drive."

"I do."

"Well, she hasn't returned."

"God bless her. Living with that hoodlum, I'm surprised this didn't happen sooner." There will be a pause while Eileen gives a raspy laugh. "May your mother live and be well."

At this point, the audience will see my father pull his wallet from his back pocket. A twenty will cross over the counter and Eileen's pudgy fingers will reach up to accept it. Then they'll hear her use her walkie-talkie to radio Franklin, the security guard, and order him to get in the security vehicle—a golf cart with a flashing yellow light atop it. "Do a sweep of 159th Street," Eileen will command him. "Go from Imperial Towers 100 to Imperial Towers 800 in search of a yellow Cadillac, Florida license plate SLIP 07."

So, in the movie, as Estelle's car makes its return trip down Collins toward 159th Street, the security vehicle will be setting out on it. Per Eileen, Franklin was to go twice around the palm-tree-lined street while my parents waited in the lobby, Slip sat in the apartment, and my sisters and I headed to the pool deck.

I hope the movie director will have the good sense to flip from locale to locale—from the Caddy to the guard to the lobby to the apartment to the pool—in order to build the requisite drama and suspense. Not like a grand assassination plot was about to be carried out. Nothing that rises to the level of action flick excitement. But then again, as Laurel likes to remind me, I am not writing an action movie. I am, apparently, writing about human relationships. Impossible, I tell Laurel. If anyone is unqualified to speak in any genre about the nature of human relationships, it is I, as I have only failed ones to my credit. In fear of the imminent addition of Laurel to my list of failures, I haven't yet told her about the car chase scene.

It'll be a slow-speed car chase—with music, of course. You might think this spot is prime for the big orchestral clashing of symbols, the subtle building of the strings, the ominous rumbling of the drums. But I'd suggest going with the song playing on Estelle's radio, "I Write the Songs." It was, she knew, by Barry Manilow, and had a melody she enjoyed.

After she clears the bridge, Estelle will dare to turn the radio a bit louder. Slowly, she will make the turn onto Collins, the home stretch, marked by the giant Coppertone Tan–Don't Burn sign, the one with the little girl with the naked tush who, she said every time we passed, reminded her of Marcy as a baby. And as she deliberately turns the steering wheel to pivot the car onto 159th Street, she'll allow herself to hum, an expression of victory.

Estelle will still be humming a minute later as my grandfather falls asleep on the couch, as my sisters and I stand at the end of the pool deck throwing bread to the birds, as my parents pester Eileen to radio Franklin for a status check, and as Franklin simultaneously radios to Eileen that he's hit the jackpot. Without waiting for her response, he'll hit the gas and take off in pursuit at maximum golf cart speed.

The Cadillac will be about two or three palm trees away from the building when Estelle first notices the flashing yellow light in her rearview mirror.

She was certain she wasn't doing anything wrong. The speed limit near the entrance to the building reduced to twenty miles per hour, but she was only going fifteen. Nonetheless, she was unlicensed and needed to get pulled over like she needed a hole in the head. So, as she reached the driveway, Estelle decided to take a page out of Slip's handbook.

"Okay," she'll say to herself. "Let's lose him." She'll switch off her radio and press her Adidas to the gas, and her speed will go up to twenty-five as her car turns into the parking garage of Imperial Towers 100 and begins to wind its way up the ramp to her space on the top floor of the structure, above which is the pool deck. The very section of the pool deck from which we're throwing bread.

And so, aside from Estelle, Marcy, Rachel and I will be the first to feel the impact of the Cadillac as it charges through the wall that separates the parking spot from the sky and, below it, the Intracoastal.

It was a "where were you?" moment. Right up there with the explosion of the Challenger and September 11. (For me, high school soccer practice and, as I've said, the dentist's office, respectively.) I'm sure anyone who was in Imperial Towers 100 on December 26, 1977 could tell you where they were when Estelle, in her rush, panic, and inexperience, brought her foot down on the accelerator instead of the brake as she maneuvered the Caddy into its space.

Most vacationers hadn't yet come down for the day, but walkers and shuffleboarders were on deck with us, and they felt the blow too. The reverberations brought all other activity to a halt. (If this is not a spot for the slow-mo camera, I don't know what is.)

The audience will feel the tremble and see everyone come running in our direction. Everyone except White Lips, who either didn't feel the impact under the water or, as we speculated, did not exist outside of it.

I remember one of the women, a walker, saying, "I think it's an earthquake."

To which her partner, a woman wearing a shower cap, replied, "You ninny, earthquakes don't strike Florida."

No one postulated a bomb, as certainly they would today. These days, terrorism would be everyone's first reaction.

By the time the crowd had assembled around the wall, Marcy, Rachel, and I already knew that neither Mother Nature nor faulty structural design (as one shuffleboarder speculated) had played a role in the crash. We knew because, unsupervised by adults, we'd plugged our shoes into the uppermost cutouts of the cinderblock wall and, with our bodies hanging over its edge, peered straight down the side of the parking garage. We knew because we could see all of the cars lined up in their slots, like the Matchbox cars in my carrying case—except for the Cadillac, whose big silver bumper and pale yellow hood were sticking out like a sore thumb.

We knew the crash, the crunch, the reverb had all been caused by one small woman: Estelle Melman.

The audience will hear Marcy scream, "Grandma!" over and over again.

They'll hear Rachel say, "Be quiet. You're embarrassing me."

As I whip myself down from the wall, fearing some sort of domino-effect collapse, they'll hear me ask, "What should we do?"

After a beat of silent communication, rare for Melman children, we did what we always did. We ran as fast as we could toward family—our parents and Grandma Estelle, now hovering over the Intracoastal in the Cadillac.

Details spun as the story spread, like a fire sweeping from the pool deck up the balconies, until in minutes, it seemed, almost everyone in the building believed that Slip had had a heart attack behind the wheel of his car, lost consciousness, and plowed straight into the Intracoastal. In some versions, he died from a heart attack. In others, he drowned. But in all, speculation existed as to who— the condo association or the Melman family—would be responsible for repairing the damage.

We'll have the cameras close in on the silver Cadillac emblem, ruined, dangling from its cord over the front bumper, before they slowly move toward the front windshield, through which my Grandma Estelle will become visible. At first, the audience will see only the top of her silver hair matted against her forehead. Her neck will bend toward her chest because, as they will see next, she will be quickly applying lipstick in the mirror of her little silver compact.

Whether she'd suffered whiplash or anything more severe, she didn't know. But she was going to look presentable when, whether by cop or by paramedic, she got dragged away.

Franklin the security guard arrived on the scene first, followed closely behind by my parents and Eileen, and then by the sirens.

The sound of sirens. Could it be that after ten years in New York, the city of perpetual sirens, I've become immune? Because I hear them now, and they are cacophonous, a disturbance, and, since September 11, jarring. But the whirring and blaring and honking no longer makes me pause at the prospect of personal calamity. The red lights are no longer an advertisement for imminent death.

I found out later that Eileen had called the emergency responders because Franklin had radioed to her that damage to the vehicle and the building had been sustained, with possible trauma to the driver, and protocol mandated that she do so. He was unsure of the severity of the injuries because, as he reported over his walkie-talkie, the victim refused to get out of the car until her son, my father, arrived.

In the movie, I think we'll see a cop knocking on the glass, yelling, "Yo, ma'am. Can you hear me? Please exit the vehicle if you are able."

For a moment Estelle will play deaf, busying herself with her compact. Then she'll crack the window and, without looking up, state, "I'm not going anywhere until I speak to my son. He's a doctor and I might be hurt."

By the time my sisters and I make it to the parking garage staircase, the sirens will be blasting. I remember thinking how much louder sirens sounded when they were coming for your family. My mind went to my Grandma Estelle. If the impact hadn't killed her, this noise would.

"Hurry up," Rachel will holler as we race up the concrete steps.

"I am hurrying," I'll answer.

"I was talking to Marcy," Rachel will scream. We'll dash across the lot toward our parking space as a squad car races up the ramp.

My greatest fear was coming to fruition. Death was coming to our door. Worse, so were the crowds. People began to hover from all angles. In the garage and above on the pool deck, hanging over the wall like they were watching a ship go down.

I noticed first a policemen doing crowd control, ordering anyone who was not heading to his or her car to leave the vicinity. Among the loiterers, I saw my Grandma B and Aunt BoBo. They'd heard from Gladys Greenberg, who'd been in the lobby when the call came in, that Estelle was involved in a car wreck.

I remember another cop talking to Franklin, who was taking full advantage of his fifteen minutes, cooperating with relish, giving his statement with grand gesture and minute detail.

My mother was speaking to a paramedic, who was taking notes on a clipboard.

My father was in the passenger seat of the Cadillac, talking to Estelle. In the movie, I'll run straight for the passenger's window and press my nose against the glass, like Marcy had pressed hers against the door of the toaster oven.

"Not right now, Davy," my father will shout through the window. He'll shoo me away with his hand, but not before my grandma looks up at me.

She'll wave with her fingers, lift her doggie bag from my father's lap, and mouth, "Are you hungry?"

Obviously, the gesture indicated that her injuries, if any, had not impacted her regular course of thought, and I was glad for that. But instead of the usual watering, real tears were coming from her eyes, and she didn't smile at me, as was her usual way. Her lips were smudged with her pink lipstick.

Eileen was hollering, "Where is Slip? Somebody go get Slip." Her face looked worried, not hostile. My Grandma B volunteered to get him—uncharacteristically altruistic of her, I thought, until I realized that she was being forced to leave the premises anyway.

Feeling dizzy, I turned my head the other way, but that direction was no better. Through the hole in the wall I could see the silver bumper hanging off the front of the car and pieces of cement floating where the breadcrumbs had been. The scene was chaos. Crowds and chaos.

I'm sure the movie crew will step up their game here in order to bring the audience into that disastrous morning of my ten-year-old, petrified self. Although the accident didn't happen to me, I'm the one who relives it. I'm the one who retells it. It's my story, so the camera should be on me.

After they capture the scene, the camera crew will have to bring focus to the young actor who plays Davy and subtly blur everything else into the background. From his twisted facial expressions and tottery physical gestures, the audience will be able to feel his heart knocking in terror against his frail ribcage, as a kid's heart is wont to do when he is scared to death of death, nauseated by destruction, and can't get it out of his head that the driving lessons were his idea.

They'll see him step, lily-livered, toward the broken wall, his hands running along both the hood of the Cadillac and the rental car next to it for support. Behind him the back door of the ambulance will open, and a stretcher will come clattering to the ground. At that—his glimpse of the stretcher rolling toward the Cadillac—the screen will cut to black, as cutting to black is, according to Laurel, the go-to film technique for when the point-of-view character passes out.

CHAPTER 18:

The Resolution

On Thursday night, four evenings after the yoga class, we were at Laurel's favorite piano bar on the Upper East Side for Show Tune Night, which was again being headlined by the Barbra Streisand impersonator.

"I've got good news," Laurel said as soon as our pitcher of beer arrived. "I sold my movie."

"Really?" I said, pausing mid-pour. "That's fantastic." And it was. Not only for Laurel, who could now afford to stay in New York, but for me, who might now get away with keeping my car. For some reason, I assumed that Laurel's Cadillac ultimatum only kicked in if Laurel ended up staying in New York because of her relationship with me. If she sold her movie, and therefore remained here independent of me, logic dictated that I'd remain an independent agent too. I finished pouring our beers and raised my glass to toast the news. "Who bought it?" I screamed over the singing.

"Well, it's a little more complicated than that," she shouted back, leaving my toast hanging. "I was going to tell you later, but . . . David, they not only optioned the script, they green-lighted it. They want to make it into a movie."

"Shows you how much I know about movie writing," I said. "You couldn't have paid me to make your movie." Again, I raised my glass for a toast. "I bet they're paying you a boatload. Maybe you can get a new apartment."

Her glass didn't lift. "Well," she said, picking through our basket of popcorn—a stalling tactic, I see now, "I'm going to have to get a new apartment."

"I'm going to help you find one," I said. My glass, the glass of an idiot, was still raised.

"You're welcome to, David. If you're willing to go to Los Angeles."

I felt my mouth open on its own. Slowly, I moved my beer to my lips to make the gape less obvious.

"That's the thing: They want my script but they also want me to adapt a few others. They want me to move to LA." As I took a drink, she said, "I have another week to decide."

She timed her bombshell really well, Laurel did, so that she finished as the song—"Happy Days Are Here Again"—crescendoed. The piano was going gangbusters. The crowd was belting out the chorus.

"Do you think I should take the deal?" she hollered. "Or do you think I should stay?"

I set my glass down, taking the time to center it perfectly on my black-and-red cardboard coaster. Hadn't I known it was going to eventually come down to this? I was so busy wondering about what to do about the Cadillac, I hadn't considered what to do about Laurel. From the get-go, from the first time I'd set foot in Drama for the First-Time Film Writer, I'd been headed toward this day. But the road to this moment, the moment of truth, had not been a straight shot, and it had been muddled by so many smaller issues that I hadn't expected it to actually happen. I knew perfectly well what Laurel wanted me to say: "Stay, Laurel, stay here, forget the offer. We'll get married." *Go ahead*, I told myself. *Say it.* But I couldn't. "Do you want the job?" I asked instead.

A long pause followed my question, during which the room applauded and Laurel and I sat in silence. Then, as the impersonator moved on to "People," Laurel said, "Do you want me to want the job?"

I answered her truthfully, with an "I don't know." Except, I didn't say this—I shrugged it. It was the ambivalent shrug of a guy who felt he was asking his girl to chose between his life and her own—not, as Laurel claimed moments later as we stood on the side-walk outside the bar and she screamed at me, the shrug of a guy with commitment problems, or of a guy who wasn't sure he was in love.

"Your sister warned me not to get involved with you," she said. "I should have listened. You are thirty-five and never married. Right there, a red flag. A flag I should have paid attention to." She quieted down as a few people passed. She shook her head and whis-pered to herself, "When will I learn?"

Then, after a beat, she switched gears and started to rant. "We've been dating for five months. You're thirty-five years old. You took me back. You said you love me. You went to my yoga class, which I thought proved you love me, because why else would a guy as closed-minded and inflexible as you go to yoga. And if you love me," she hollered, while I put my hands on her shoulders to try to calm her down, "you should want me to stay." She pushed away my arms. I'd never seen this side of her—the angry, explosive side.

"You seem so good," she went on, staring up at me, stomping the cowboy boots at the beginning of each sentence like a human exclamation point. "Your family seems so normal. Well, not nor-mal, but you know, close. You are successful and sweet; you take such good care of your niece and nephew. Why are you so scared to have your own family? What happened to you as a child?"

I stared at her. She was crying. Her hair was messed. She looked pretty. She was pretty. She was smart. She was successful. She was sexy. She wasn't *funny* funny. But she thought I was. What was wrong with me?

"I don't know," I told her. I stared at the ground. As I lined up the tips of my Nikes with the crack on the sidewalk, I said, "I don't want to screw it up. Melmans don't leave, they don't get divorced. They make it work, they stick it out. It seems to me that if you are going to take that kind of leap of faith, you'd better be damn sure going in."

"Wake up, David. If you are waiting to be damn sure before

you get married, you'll be waiting a long time—too long for me." With that, she headed into the street to hail a cab.

I did not follow her, but I did call out, "That's the same thing my sister said when she told me to take your class. That I needed to wake up and smell the coffee. You can't say I didn't try. My script is almost done and lord knows my apartment reeks of coffee."

"One thing has nothing to do with the other." She flagged down a taxi and pulled her hood over her head. "You can write movies about your car and your childhood all day long and you still won't know for certain whether I'm the one for you."

———

In the days following our street fight, as I finished my movie and thought about Laurel's words, I tried to answer the question myself. My movie-writing experience had shed no light on whether I was ready to move on and get married, or what made a marriage work, or whether Laurel was the one for me. If I said yes and told her to stay and asked her to get married, where would we be in forty years? Getting by like my grandparents, simply due the grace of God and a well-structured routine? I had no idea.

What I did take away was that my movie was about Estelle as much as it was about Slip. Even though the car belonged to Slip, the story belonged to Estelle. The title of my movie, if I started over, would not be *Slip Gets a Caddy* but *Estelle Finds Her Way*. Yes, the Caddy symbolized my grandfather, but what it honored was Estelle and her longing for a little Women's Lib. Laurel had that, and I wasn't sure I had it in me to ask her to waste it. Yes, if our marriage didn't work, we could always get a divorce, but Laurel would not get back this opportunity in Los Angeles.

If I could talk to Estelle now, or if I could go back to that day we walked on the pool deck, I knew just what I'd ask her. If she'd had the chance to move to Los Angeles and make it big as a dancer, would she still have chosen bootlegging with Slip? And if she'd gone to LA, would she have still craved, some forty years down the road, the joyride and the donut?

I didn't know what she would have answered but I could hear what she'd say to Laurel: "Love matters a little, honey, but luck matters more. So whether you get married or not, I think you should secure your own driver's license right away."

———

THE SCENE AT THE SCENE
PARKING GARAGE. BACKSEAT OF MELMANS' RENTAL CAR
"This is not what I meant when I told you to stay cool."

I was lying in the backseat of the rental car when I heard Slip's voice. The paramedics had laid me across the long leather seat after I'd dropped. Marcy, who'd been standing next to me, came to my rescue (or, as she claimed, saved my life) by screaming, as she will in the movie, "Davy died! Or maybe he fainted. Someone please help."

Luckily, the scene was heavy on paramedics waiting around for my grandma to emerge. If you are going to faint, I recommend this scenario. Instantaneously, apparently, I was whisked into the arms of a rescue worker. I also backhandedly became somewhat of a hero because due to my loss of consciousness, Grandma Estelle became willing to exit the Cadillac.

When I came to, I was lying with a damp rag on my forehead and Marcy was kneeling next to me watching the activity out of the back window.

"You're alive!" she exclaimed. She smiled and clapped as my eyes opened. "Stay still," she ordered, and then gave me a blow-by-blow account of what I'd missed—the taping off of the area, the arrival of the tow truck, and the silencing of the sirens, which I somehow hadn't noticed until she mentioned it.

"Uh-oh," she said next. "Slip's here."

Several minutes after this, he stuck his head in our door and made his remark to me about staying cool. To Marcy he said, "What did I tell you? Doesn't look like we needed to go toasting your grandmother any bagels."

"How do you know she's not hungry?" Marcy asked.

"Cause it seems that while we were combing the streets, she

went and took herself out to breakfast. A big, fancy spread at the Bagel Bar." He shook his shoulders up and down as he spoke, in rhythm with his words. A physical show of fancy. Then he leaned back and pulled his cigar from the roof of the car, where he'd stuck it before poking his head into the rental.

"Sit up," he told me.

I did.

Slip pulled the towel from my forehead. I remember how neat he looked. His pale blue sweater, his white slacks, his boat shoes. Perhaps he'd been planning for another day on the deck. His thin body rested against the doorframe of the rental car. He looked around, his face devoid of expression.

Then he motioned with his finger for us to get out of the car. "Breathe the fresh air," he said as he puffed his cigar. "Take a look around."

So I looked again, as the audience will as well. They will see, as I did, much order restored. They will see Eileen and my father speaking to a cop, all of them motioning in the direction of the car and the missing wall so that dialogue will not be necessary for the understanding of their conversation.

They will see Grandma Estelle sitting on a gurney surrounded by a paramedic, who will be taking her blood pressure; Rachel, who will be holding her hand; and my mother, who will be talking to her in between bites of leftover bagel, which she will be dipping into the container of chopped herring. Again, no dialogue will be needed.

In the middle, between the cops and the gurney, will be the tow truck.

"What's it doing?" Marcy will ask.

Slip will explain that the tow truck driver is waiting for the folks who own the cars parked behind ours to move them so the tow truck can get in at the right angle to do its business with his car.

At this point, the camera will, as we did, scrutinize the Caddy. The back half will still sparkle with its new and splendid glory—a stark and sickening contrast to the front half.

For a second, there was silence.

Then, there was Marcy. "Are you mad?" she asked Slip without turning her head from the window. I thought she was brave to ask this question, because I was sure I already knew the answer.

Slip scrunched up his eyes and pulled the cigar from his mouth, which turned up at the ends in a slow-motion smile. His wrinkles—thousands, it seemed—pulled tight across his skin. Behind his silver-framed glasses, his eyes began to shimmer.

"At who?" He smiled real big.

"Grandma," Marcy answered. Her tone said, "duh."

"Your grandma certainly did a number this time, didn't she?" Slip looked down at us.

We nodded in agreement. Marcy laughed. Relief was in her voice, as if she already understood what Slip would say next.

"I ain't mad." Slip shook his head. "What the hell do I got to be mad at?" He chomped on the cigar for a moment before he went on. "If I got a bone to pick with anyone, it's with the crew over there." He pointed in the direction of my father, Eileen, and Franklin. "If they'd had the sense not to go scaring the crap out of my wife, we'd be looking at a whole different scenario now, wouldn't we?" As he spoke, he began to wander in the direction of the damage.

I watched his hand slip slowly along the hood of the car. It moved, as he did, toward the hole in the wall. There, at the spot where the car met the wall, my grandfather stopped and for a while he stood looking out to the water, his face invisible to me, his thoughts impossible to know.

The sight of Slip and his banged-up Cadillac was almost as traumatic as the sight of Grandma Estelle, who was now seated in the back of the ambulance. She rested upright, covered in a heavy grey blanket. Her Adidas dangled from beneath it and her purse headed in the direction of Grandma B, who stood at the open doors, her arms outstretched.

"I assure you, Estelle, you'll be better off without it," she said, taking the purse into her hands. "One less thing you have to worry about getting stolen." She also assured her that she'd be by the hospital each day with books and decent food, and that she'd watch after Slip, who by now was with us at the back of the ambulance.

As Grandma B talked, I stood behind her and stared. As I

stared, Slip kneed me in the rear end. I didn't see it coming, and I don't know if anyone else saw him, but the audience will. I've never admitted this to anyone—that a force other than my own emotions, instincts, or courage pushed me toward the ambulance doors.

I took a breath before I let myself look inside at the tubes and machines—the separators, as I saw them, between life and death. The paramedic who was tending to my grandma smiled at me, and then my grandma did too. "It doesn't look like I did so good with the lessons, Davy," she said.

"The driving was probably a bad idea in the first place," I told her.

"Don't be silly," she assured me. "Driving was a great idea. I would have been just fine had no one come following after me." She rolled her eyes in my father's direction.

"Stop talking," my father told my grandma. "Save your energy."

"I won't be gone long," my grandma assured me. "Keep an eye on you-know-who for me." She winked and nodded toward Slip.

I nodded and tried to not cry. "Can I be the one to keep your purse?" This gesture surprised me as much as Slip's kick in my butt.

"Davy, that's the best idea I've heard in a long time. There's no one I'd rather have guarding my belongings," Estelle answered, motioning for Grandma B to hand over the goods to me. I took the bag, and as I did Estelle called to me, "Come close."

Leery as I was about entering an ambulance, I climbed up and sat alongside her.

"Davy," she whispered, "if you look inside—not inside my wallet but in the lining of my bag—you'll find some money hidden away for a rainy day. Or another Depression. Find the money and tell your father to take you for Adidas on my behalf."

I smiled at her. "Okay."

"Don't forget."

I promised her I wouldn't forget and I never did, although I never spent her money. Oh, I dug around in the purse to see where the cash was hidden alright, and I gathered up the loose quarters and dimes and put them in her change purse where they belonged, but that was all.

After I returned to the ground, Marcy and Rachel came up to me, wanting to know what the secret was, but I didn't tell them. To this day, I've only told Estie and Ryan—and now, of course, my audience.

As Grandma B told me to move away from the ambulance, Estelle touched her hand to her pink lips and then threw a kiss to me like she was tossing a baseball. She laughed and said, "Catch!"

I pulled an arm out from under her purse and blew one back to her. I think that was the first kiss I'd ever blown.

Then the doors to the ambulance closed and my father stepped closer. "Don't worry," he said. "She's just going in for observation. We're just making sure everything's okay."

ᵦ————

Everything was okay. Estelle stayed in the hospital for three days, longer than we'd expected but less time than the Cadillac spent at the mechanic's. In fact, we left Florida before the Cadillac returned to the garage. Not until the following season would I see it again, and when I did, there would be no sign that the car was any worse for the wear, although Slip swore that its emblem tipped slightly to the right and the transmission was never quite the same.

The same could be said of Estelle, who'd been diagnosed with a heart condition that would have to be watched but was not supposed to interfere with her regular activities or lifespan. Though she'd have to cancel this year's New Year's Eve vaudeville review.

Slip's card room privileges were restored—perhaps not the day of the crash but during that trip, because I remember sitting next to him during the annual New Year's Eve poker game. I didn't play. Poker confused me, and since it was New Year's, the stakes were too high for my twenty-five-cent blood. But I was happy simply sitting next to my grandfather again and watching him do his thing.

"Make sure he doesn't lay a hand on anyone," my grandmother had directed me early in the evening. Specifically, I was charged with making sure he didn't go so far as to even look at Big Sid.

To the best of the collective recollection of my family, Slip's card room expulsion was never formally lifted. He just returned. As if the damage to his Cadillac had been punishment enough. As if God were acting in the best interest of Estelle. Or, most likely, as if the attention of Eileen, Gladys Greenberg, and the Condo Association (not to be confused with God) had moved on to a subsequent and more heinous wrong-doing in Imperial Towers 100—in the form of damage to the building itself by a resident who'd been unlicensed to drive.

As for the end of the movie, I'm not sure. Endings, it seems, are not my forte. I suppose we'll put the camera on Davy in his New Year's Eve best, sitting next to Slip in the card room. We'll see him stand up to leave, and his grandfather ruffle his hair as he goes. We'll follow him into the Ladies' Card Room, where we'll see all the women wearing Happy New Year's hats as they study their cards. Among them will be Estelle, who will look up, see Davy, and beam. She'll offer him a seat next to hers, which he will decline with a shake of his head. She'll offer him her New Year's hat, which he also will decline with a laugh. We'll see him give Estelle a hug and we'll hear Lucille Garlovsky, at the next table, say, "Trust me, Estelle, he's gonna be a real heartbreaker one day," as he walks out the door.

As he heads down the long hallway, the screaming from the game room will charge through the air, almost suffocating "Stayin' Alive," which is also blasting in there.

His thin body will strut to the elevator, feeling pretty good. He'll get on an open car, and we'll watch the doors shut behind him. Perhaps we'll see, as the car carries him on his way, the numbers above the elevator door light up one by one, starting with two and gradually closing in, blurring, so that as we get to nine and then ten, one number seems to blend into the next, until nothing is really clear at all.

CHAPTER 19:

The End

Laurel and I didn't talk for four days after our fight. They were four uncomfortable days for me, primarily because I'm not the kind of person who stops talking during a conflict. I am the other kind. As you well know by now, around-the-clock discourse is what I'm used to.

Not so much with Laurel. In fact, just the opposite. Her family was big on the silent treatment, something she despised yet is remarkably deft at replicating, as she proved when she hailed a cab last Thursday night and never looked back.

That's not entirely true. She stuck her head above the door of the cab just before she lowered herself into it and said to me, "You know where I stand. The ball is in your court."

I stood on the sidewalk, my hands in my pockets of my jeans, and wondered what to do with the ball as I watched her cab pull away and disappear into the mix and mayhem.

If my real life were a movie—and believe me, at this point it feels like it could be—we'd watch the door of Laurel's cab close and then the door of my grandfather's Cadillac open days later, as Laurel gets inside. How's that for a smooth transition? Laurel would be proud of it if she knew about it. At least something she taught me sank in, right? The importance of smooth transitions and the use of meaningful objects to link one scene to another. So in this scene, the link will be doors. As one door closes, another door opens. That's what they say, and also what I imagined I'd tell Laurel, something along those lines, when she shut the door of the Cadillac behind her and sat down next to me in the passenger seat.

I'd called her that morning, Monday morning, unable to bear the silence, not sure about what to do with the gargantuan coffee maker that glared at me like Laurel's angry girlfriend every time I entered my kitchen. I told Marcy I could donate it to her bakery but Marcy, who is actually one of Laurel's girlfriends, told me she didn't want to aid and abet a crime, and that the coffee maker was collateral damage, full of bad karma, that she didn't need in her shop. Business was tough enough. But she did agree to deliver the final scenes of my movie to Laurel at the bakery on Sunday morning.

If I told you I'd kept my dilemma to myself between the time Laurel left in the cab and arrived in my Cadillac, I'd be lying. I told my sisters, who in turn told my mother, who left me a phone message saying that one can't give or take advice when it comes to matters of the heart. I'd have to figure this one out on my own. But, she asked, did I hear bells?

"Hi," I said when Laurel sat down in the passenger seat on Monday afternoon. Her hair was in a ponytail. Her cowboy boots were on, her messenger bag was over her shoulder. Everything as usual. She hadn't gone out of her way to do herself up, to win me over with her good looks or femme-fatale ways—antics I'd been expecting based on my previous breakup experiences and which I was, honestly, disappointed not to see, as the absence of drama seemed to make my decision all the more difficult.

She smelled ever so slightly of cigarettes, which I assumed she'd turned to during the stress of the past few days, just as I'd turned to work, basketball, and Doritos. We all have our vices. The odor of hers fit in with the cigar stench of the Cadillac. I was about to tell her so after she said hello—the association of smells seemed like a perfect segue into what I intended to say—but no hello was forthcoming.

"So you think I should go to LA?" She picked up where our last conversation had left off, as though no time had passed. This tendency to hang on to, tuck away, and then retrieve every last word you've ever spoken is another mesmerizing ability of women. "Is that what you're saying—or not saying—with all this silence?"

I hadn't anticipated our conversation starting on this type of pull-no-punches note; everything I'd rehearsed went out the window. "Hey," I said, "you were the one who drove away. And I don't know about you, but I've been talking plenty over the past couple of days, so I don't know who you're calling 'silent.'"

"Well, you weren't talking to me. That, to me, is silent." She leaned over to her messenger bag, which she'd set on the floor, and flipped open the lid. "Here you go." She lifted a small blue binder, my manuscript binder, out of the bag and dropped it onto my lap. "I don't imagine you'll be coming back to class—there's only one left anyway. I gave you my comments. Your script actually turned out pretty good, much better than the Mort Chuckerman idea." She spoke fast, her face had none of its usual expression. I got the feeling that her lines were rehearsed as well. "Although," she added after a beat, "I'm not sure I like the end."

"What do you mean?" I asked. "It ended the way it ended."

"It ended up in the air and wishy-washy, if you ask me. What did the main character learn, how did he change or grow? He didn't! He just rode up in the elevator, as lost as ever, and here he is now, twenty-five years later, just the same. That does not make for any sort of compelling drama." As she spoke, her voice got louder and her arms began to talk too.

"Well," I said, flipping through the pages of my script—which, sure enough, were marked up but good. Red, like blood, spewed all over. No wonder Laurel was relatively composed. She'd taken her anger out on my script.

"Well what?"

"Well, would your impression of my character change if I got rid of the Cadillac?"

"What do you mean? I don't understand." Her shoulders came down slightly. Her hand went toward the charm on her necklace.

I could see a softening. Ever so slight. Or perhaps her change was a figment of my imagination, my mind playing tricks, making me believe that my setup line had won her over and I was now about to say the perfect thing.

I stuffed the binder back into her bag, pulled the key to Slip's car out of the ignition, and hung it in front of her. "Here you go. It's all yours."

Her hand went from her necklace to her forehead. Her other hand joined it. She rocked her head in both hands while she made some sort of noise—laughter or sobs, I couldn't tell. Now would have been the right moment to turn on the radio to fill the awkward silence, except the keys, along with my words, were dangling midair.

Finally, she lifted her head and her hand moved to the key, which she took but continued to let hang in the air. When I saw her smirk, I knew she'd been laughing.

"Did I hear correctly? You are giving me your grandfather's car?"

I ignored her sarcasm—I had no choice at this point—and smiled at her. "Bingo."

I found my finger running over the top of the dash. I'd thought carefully about giving the car to Laurel, but I hadn't thought at all about how I'd react once the giving was done.

Clearly, I hadn't thought about how she'd react either.

She didn't smile back at me. Instead, she turned up the side of her mouth and nose, the way Estie sometimes looks at Marcy, and asked, "Why?"

My palms started to sweat. I went to crank the window but that wouldn't work, either, without the keys.

"Oh for God's sake," Laurel said, sticking the keys in the ignition and leaning over me to press my window button. "Take a couple of deep breaths and then please explain."

"It's not that complicated," I said. "I know you don't think I should keep the car, and I know you'll need a car."

"I don't drive."

"If you're going to live in LA, you'll have to. You can pack your things—this trunk can even hold your coffee maker—and be on your way."

I'd intended to be generous and supportive, to do with my car for her as Slip had done for me. But as soon as I heard my words, I knew, just as Rachel had warned, that my idea was lousy.

"You've got to be kidding me," Laurel whispered. "So not only do you not want me to stay in New York, you basically want me to get out of town as quickly as possible, in any way possible, no matter how unsafe." She kicked the underside of the dash with her boot, then she called herself an idiot and me an asshole, which is what Rachel had also called me when I'd told her my plan.

And an ass I must be, because I honestly believed that Laurel would see the gesture as I'd meant it—as a gesture of love. Like a banana boat. "That's what Rachel said you'd say."

"You told your family?"

I nodded, staring at the steering wheel, not her. I couldn't face her at this point. This was not a proud moment for me.

"What a shock," she said. "But hey," she went on, practically spitting, "you didn't listen to their advice. Now that is a shock."

"They really like you."

"Clearly more than you do."

I set my hands on the steering wheel and pushed the middle of it in frustration. The horn went off. Laurel jumped. So did I. I honked again. And again. The honking felt good.

Laurel stuck her hand over the horn. "What are you doing?"

"I'm frustrated," I said. "'Honk if you're frustrated' would make a great bumper sticker."

"That's why people honk in the first place," she said. "You don't need a bumper sticker for that." That's one of the things I love about Laurel, she's willing to tangent at any time. Although her willingness in this moment, given the heated nature of the main topic, was brief.

"Why are you frustrated?" she demanded. "'Cause your plan didn't work like a charm? Cause I'm not pulling out of the garage as we speak?"

"Because you don't understand," I told her. "Giving my car, my heirloom, to you is one of the hardest things I've ever done. Watching you go is *the* hardest thing I'd ever done. So when you combine the difficulty of getting rid of my car with the difficultly of losing my girlfriend, you can see my frustration." I honked a couple more times to symbolize the emotion.

"I think that's the most honest thing you've said in the entire past five months," Laurel said. She fiddled with the knobs on the radio, flipped through a few stations, and then turned it off. "So why are you doing it?"

I shrugged.

She pushed my shoulders down. "Speak."

"Because you need wheels. You are going places," I said. "And it's not my place to stop you. I'd rather give you the car now than have you steal it from me one day."

"When you have a really fancy one," Laurel joked.

"You know. You read the script."

"So it's a preemptive strike?"

"I guess so." I shrugged again.

We sat in silence for a few minutes, then Laurel opened the door, walked to the front of the car, and sat down on the hood. I followed her.

The air was cold, typical of October. The river looked rough and uninviting. The wind off the water seemed loud. I raised my voice above it to say, "The crest of the Cadillac family."

Laurel looked at me, confused and silent.

I put my hand on hers, which was toying with the emblem on the hood of the car—boinging it back and forth, twisting it, like we used to do as kids. Laurel, of course, was twisting with anger and upset rather than amusement and curiosity.

"That's what the emblem is," I explained. "The coat of arms of the family of Le Sieur Antoine De La Mothe Cadillac, the man who founded the city of Detroit."

"I know," she said. "I read the script." She spoke toward the water; then she looked away, but I saw her wipe away a tear that had pooled in the corner of her eye. She got to it before it fell, so I wouldn't see. But I did. Don't forget, I had a grandmother who had a side job wiping her watery eyes. Tears were something I was tuned into.

What struck me at that moment was not how bad I felt—though, believe me, I felt terrible. Show me a guy who doesn't feel bad when he makes a girl cry and I'll show you a schmuck. What struck me at that moment was that I found myself wondering what Laurel would look like when she got old. I reimagine women all the time, but never with age. I pictured bags under her eyes, hanging like they'd hung from Estelle's. I tried to picture extra skin dangling from her chin, the color gone from her hair, but I couldn't. On the day when Slip took Estelle for their first ride, I'm sure that Slip didn't imagine it, either. Estelle looked beautiful and Slip simply liked having her by his side. He probably didn't think about what would be, what was to come, the end of the line.

I picked up Laurel's hand, the one fiddling with the emblem. "It's fragile," I said, nodding at the emblem so she wouldn't get excited and think I was referring to something deeper, like our relationship or my psyche. "Ever since it broke the first time."

"Right," Laurel said, taking her hand away from mine. "You know what I think? I'm going to tell you what I think and then I'm going to go. I'm going to go by foot. You can keep the car. I hope you two are very happy together." She gave the hood of the car a pat. "But I will tell you"—finally, she turned to look at me—"that I think it's ironic that a guy who keeps a car as his mascot is too scared to make a move. It's ironic and sad. And, for your information, I don't think Slip would have let Estelle drive to LA by herself. He wouldn't have tossed the keys at her and told her to go it alone. He would have stepped up."

I put my hand on her knee. I nodded. I understood, and I also felt guilty that she'd been sucked so deep into my issues by my movie. On the other hand, nobody had ever known me so well. "I think," I said, "Slip would have done whatever the hell he wanted, and I don't think I'm necessarily like him."

Laurel put a hand on my knee. "I disagree on both counts." She moved both of her hands into her jacket pockets and turned back toward the river. She whipped her head to shake away the strands of hair the wind was blowing across her face.

The first time I took Laurel out in the car, after we went to the

Verrazano Bridge, we'd sat in the park together, and as she talked, I'd stared at the freckles on her legs, wanting to touch them and to make her laugh. "I'd go down with the ship," I remember I told her, referring to the car, the Cadillac, in the event of disaster. And it seemed that now, I was.

Laurel slid off the front of the car. "And I've got news for you. I'm nothing like your grandmother, either. True, I don't drive, and yes, I am willing to put up with all of your nonsense, but I have a career, I have a life."

"I'm sorry," I said, unsure of whether I felt more sorry for me or for her. Somehow, endings are never as depressing for the party moving on, which is what Laurel began to do.

She took a few steps backwards. "I am too, Chuckerman. I hope you will be happy." With nothing more, she turned and walked toward the stairs.

I watched her go, like the guys in the movies always do.

When she disappeared through the door, I got back inside the Cadillac. Laurel had left the keys on the passenger seat. I grabbed them. I didn't know where I was headed, but I needed to go somewhere to escape, to clear my head. Ironically, the reason I'd taken Laurel's class in the first place had been to do exactly that. *Look where that got me*, I thought as I slid the key into the ignition.

I didn't debate whether I'd done the right thing. It was as if I hadn't had a hand in the matter. People are who they are. It is what it is. You can't make a tiger or a leopard change its spots. You've just got to play the hand you're dealt.

I turned on the radio to see what kind of song I could find to match my mood and as I played with the buttons, I saw her purse.

Laurel's ugly brown messenger bag was resting on the floor of the passenger seat. I reached down to it and pulled out my movie binder, which I opened on my lap. In the back, she had attached a critique. I scanned down the page for my grade like a kid who cared what my teacher gave me, as if it was going toward my grade point average.

She'd given me a B. A fat capital B, written in royal blue marker. Her review said essentially the same thing she'd told me: something about failure of the characters to evolve and too much reliance on the narrator in telling the story. "Please know," she'd written, "that your grade has nothing to do with the ending of our personal relationship." I realized that she'd known before she met me here what the outcome was going to be.

With effort, I lifted the entire bag onto the seat next to me and poked though it. Sugar-free Bubbalicious, lip gloss, tampons, highlighters, sunglasses, seashells, a cigarette lighter, a paperback dictionary, and, on the bottom, a bunch of loose change.

I scooped up the coins, slowly sorted them into piles in my hand, and dumped them into the side pocket of Laurel's wallet, where they should have been in the first place. Then I turned the key, because suddenly I knew where I was going.

Not that I heard bells. I don't believe in bells. I wasn't sure whether the kick came from Slip's spirit, alive and well in his car, or from Estelle, sending me signs via the scattered coins, or simply from my own self, but what did it matter? I warmed the engine and slowly backed the Caddy out of its space. Laurel would soon miss— if she didn't already—the absence of the weight on her shoulder, and she'd be back. I pulled the car up to the door of the staircase and waited with the motor running.

The garage exit faced west. If she was willing, I would tell her, I could leave right now. I would drive her to Los Angeles.

I would drive her wherever she wanted to go.

Acknowledgments

I started writing this book when my kids were five years old, and now they're licensed to drive. Its chapters were written, rewritten, and then rewritten some more. Without the encouragement, guidance, wisdom and workshops of the wise and funny Steve and Sharon Fiffer, I could not have seen this thing through. Therefore, I am forever grateful to the Wesley Writers Workshop. Thank you, too, to my fellow "Wednesdays" for the years of listening, sharing, and support, especially to Joyce, Barb, Diane, and Bill who've been with me since the beginning.

For turning my manuscript into a book and for getting my book into the hands of people beyond my parents, I'd like to thank Brooke Warner, Cait Levin, and the team at She Writes Press, and Crystal Patriarche and her BookSparks team, especially Ashley Alfirevic, for their creativity, leadership, and dedication to women writers.

Finally, my family. I'll start with my husband, Kenny, who deserves thanks more than anyone else for his neverending patience, faith in me, and every imaginable kind of support. Thank you, too, to my daughters, Lilly and Gracie, for being my two most favorite people. Next are those who came first, the Arensons. To Arthur, Merle, and Joey, thank you for providing me with decades of love and laughs—as well as with much of the material for this book.

A few special shout outs to Randi Olin and Lauren Apfel at *Motherwell Magazine*, for their loyal support of my work; Nan Doyal for graciously sharing her publishing knowledge with me; Jen Unter of The Unter Agency for her generous advice and assistance; Julie Kaplan of Julie Kaplan Photography, for making me look so much better in my author photo than I do in real life; Randee Newman, for her willingness to read the earliest, unedited draft; all my girlfriends, for always sharing and liking and listening; and to my mother, for her dedicated and complimentary promotion of my work, her honest opinion, and among other things, the Adidas.

About the Author

F rancie Arenson Dickman has been using her family as the source of writing material her whole life. Her personal essays have appeared in publications such as *The Chicago Tribune, Huffington Post, Today Parents, Motherwell Magazine*, and *Brain, Child Magazine*, among others. She lives in the same suburb of Chicago in which she grew up, with her husband, twin daughters, and dog, Pickles. She received her BA from the University of Michigan and her JD from The George Washington University School of Law.

Author photo © Julie Kaplan Photography

Selected Titles from She Writes Press

She Writes Press is an independent publishing company founded to serve women writers everywhere. Visit us at www.shewritespress.com.

A Tight Grip: A Novel about Golf, Love Affairs, and Women of a Certain Age by Kay Rae Chomic. $16.95, 978-1-938314-76-6. As forty-six-year-old golfer Jane "Par" Parker prepares for her next tournament, she experiences a chain of events that force her to reevaluate her life.

Arboria Park by Kate Tyler Wall. $16.95, 978-1631521676. Stacy Halloran's life has always been centered around her beloved neighborhood, a 1950s-era housing development called Arboria Park—so when a massive highway project threaten the Park in the 2000s, she steps up to the task of trying to save it.

Tzippy the Thief by Pat Rohner. $16.95, 978-1-63152-153-9. Tzippy has lived her life as a selfish, materialistic woman and mother. Now that she is turning eighty, there is not an infinite amount of time left—and she wonders if she'll be able to repair the damage she's done to her family before it's too late.

Warming Up by Mary Hutchings Reed. $16.95, 978-1-938314-05-6. Unemployed and depressed former musical actress Cecilia Morrison decides to start therapy, hoping it will get her out of her slump—but ultimately it's a teen who cons her out of sixty bucks, not her analyst, who changes her life.

Start With the Backbeat by Garinè B. Isassi. $16.95, 978-1-63152-041-9. When post-punk rocker Jill Dodge finally gets the promotion she's been waiting for in the spring of 1989, she finds herself in the middle of a race to find a gritty urban rapper for her New York record label.

Wishful Thinking by Kamy Wicoff. $16.95, 978-1-63152-976-4. A divorced mother of two gets an app on her phone that lets her be in more than one place at the same time, and quickly goes from zero to hero in her personal and professional life—but at what cost?